The Little
Cottage in
Lantern
Square

Helen Rolfe writes contemporary women's fiction and enjoys weaving stories about family, friendship, secrets, and community. Characters often face challenges and must fight to overcome them, but above all, Helen's stories always have a happy ending.

You can visit Helen at:
www.helenjrolfe.com
f @helenjrolfewriter
𝕏 @HjRolfe
◉ helen_j_rolfe

Also by Helen Rolfe

The Little Café at the End of the Pier
The Little Village Library

The Little Cottage in Lantern Square

Helen Rolfe

ORION

An Orion Paperback

First published as ebook novellas in Great Britain in 2019
by Orion Fiction
This paperback edition published in 2020 by Orion Fiction,
an imprint of The Orion Publishing Group Ltd
Carmelite House, 50 Victoria Embankment,
London EC4Y 0DZ

An Hachette UK company

1 3 5 7 9 10 8 6 4 2

A CIP catalogue record for this book is
available from the British Library.

ISBN (Mass Market Paperback) 978 1 4091 9140 7
ISBN (eBook) 978 1 4091 9141 4

Typeset by Input Data Services Ltd, Somerset

Printed and bound in Great Britain by Clays Ltd, Elcograf S.p.A.

MIX
Paper from
responsible sources
FSC® C104740

www.orionbooks.co.uk

*For Mum and Dad who sent the best care packages
when I lived on the other side of the world . . .
chocolate, knitted garments for my children,
photographs, and most important of all . . . marmite!*

Prologue

'We're here!' Hannah announced to Smokey and Bandit as she pulled up outside Lantern Cottage. There was no reply – of course – from her two feline friends, who'd resisted getting into the cat baskets a few hours ago but had since accepted their imprisonment and settled down to sleep in the footwells of the back seats. The next two weeks were going to be fun, keeping them inside the cottage so they'd get used to their new territory. Smokey and Bandit hated being confined anywhere. Rain, hail, or shine, they liked to be free and explore. Hannah got that. She'd waited a long while to feel like her old self and it had taken way more than two weeks.

She climbed out of the car and stretched after the long drive from Whitby, fanning her T-shirt to circulate some air. She must look like a crazy woman, smiling so broadly standing here on her own, but she couldn't help it – because here she was at last, in Lantern Square, the heart of the cosy Cotswold village of Butterbury, in front of her new home. Named on a weathered sweet-chestnut plaque next to a soft-green ledged-oak front door that showed its age, Lantern Cottage was the home she'd saved diligently for. Buying her own place had been a long time coming and, with everything in her life being so spectacularly thrown up in the air, it was as though it had all come down to the ground again, settled, and marked a fresh start.

Beautiful spring blossom from the trees in the square carried a subtle scent her way as Hannah turned and waved at the sound of a loud toot-toot. She'd managed to fit plenty into her tiny car along with the cats, but her dad had followed her in a van filled with the rest of her belongings, and here he was pulling up behind her. She checked her bumper, but she couldn't move any closer to the car in front unless she wanted to touch park. She spoke to her dad through his open window because four doors down the charmingly named Honey Cottage had a driveway and the van was so long that it well and truly blocked access. 'Let me go and have a word with one of my new neighbours. I'm sure they won't mind us being here to unload.' Hannah had already seen a curtain twitch when she'd used hand signals to guide her dad, who was out of his comfort zone in this van, being used to his modest Golf that shunted him and Hannah's mum from A to B.

'Right you are.' *Crunch*. Bless him, he drove an automatic car and the van had gears which he wasn't used to, though he'd announced it was going to be fun reverting to a manual.

Hannah knocked on the door of Honey Cottage, noting its plaque was in much better repair than hers. Well-tended window boxes, filled with purple and white blooms that looked as though they'd escaped the April storms that had battered every other inch of the country a few short days ago, flourished in front of pristine glass.

The door opened a crack.

'Hello, I'm Hannah, and I'm moving into Lantern Cottage today.' She beamed a smile at the occupant when the door opened some more. 'I wonder if you'd mind us parking here while we—'

Hannah didn't get any further before the woman said, 'You're blocking my drive.' She looked older than Hannah's dad, perhaps mid-seventies, with beady brown eyes flecked with glimmers of gold. She was keeping the door ajar just enough that she could engage in conversation, and closed enough that she could slam it quickly if she didn't like who was on the other side.

'I know and I'm very sorry. There doesn't seem to be anywhere close enough to park other than here and we have furniture to unload.'

'That's not my problem, young lady.'

'It'll only be for an hour. I'd really appreciate it.'

'Fine, one hour. Then I'm calling the police if you don't move.' And with that she shut the door.

Hannah stood on the path of Honey Cottage and took a deep breath. The estate agent listing hadn't remarked on a crotchety old woman four doors away and she hoped not all of the residents were as unwelcoming.

'Good to go?' Her dad had already opened up the rear doors.

She chose not to elaborate about her awkward neighbour in case her dad worried. 'I should've taken up weight training before I insisted I didn't need to pay removal men to do this,' she joked as she climbed into the truck after him to take one end of the tabletop.

'Don't make me laugh or I'll be too weak to lift,' he said, smiling, and with a surge of necessary energy, they got going. Hannah would let the miserable neighbour stew inside her cottage. Nothing was going to ruin moving-in day for her if she could help it.

It took over an hour and another knock on the same woman's door to make sure she didn't follow through and call the police before Hannah and her dad were done with the unloading. Hannah's arms were probably stronger than some, but this was one job she'd readily admit needed a couple of big strong men.

'I hope your neighbours make you welcome.' The worry lines on her dad's forehead deepened as he set down the last of the boxes by the door to the kitchen.

'It'll take time to settle in, but I'll get there.'

'It's different from London, that's for sure.' He held up his hands in defence. 'I'm not criticising.'

'Mum is, though.'

'She worries, that's all, but doesn't always show it in the same way as I do.'

'Mum doesn't seem to understand this is what I need.' She didn't understand that Hannah didn't need her boyfriend Luke any more either, or that she'd chosen to change career. Big changes didn't come along in her mother's life and in some ways she was treating Hannah's recent decisions as a personal slight. All Hannah wanted was for her mum to see things the way she did, or if she really couldn't, then maybe keep her opinions to herself. Surely that wasn't asking too much? 'Are you sure you won't stay for a cup of tea?'

'And upset Mrs Busybody four doors down?' More curtain twitching had given the game away. 'And you know I'm more of a coffee person – at least, when your mother isn't looking. I'll grab one at the services, might even sit and read the paper for a bit before I take the van back.'

'It's a long drive up to Whitby.'

'I'm not past it yet, love. I'll be grand. And your mum gave me enough sandwiches to cater for a town picnic. I've still got those to keep me going.'

'At least have a cold drink. I know this box has glasses in.' She wasn't going to take no for an answer and produced a glass from between sheets of newspaper, gave it a wash and filled it at the tap. From the speed at which he glugged it back she knew she'd made the right choice.

He set his empty glass down by the sink, narrowly avoiding tripping over Bandit, who, happily released from the cat carrier, had been weaving in and out of their ankles. 'You cats are going to like it here,' he said to him.

'These two are going to hate being shut inside, more like.' She watched Smokey go off on the prowl, most likely upstairs.

'Only two weeks, guys. Two weeks to settle in to your new home.' He hugged Hannah tight. 'I'd better leave you to unpack and organise yourself.'

They'd got everything in and, aside from the big items put in their proper places – the bed upstairs, the table which Hannah had struggled with even though the legs had been taken off for transport and her dad had taken most of the weight, the sofa and armchair in the sitting room – there were boxes cluttering every available bit of floorspace. Hannah had never been one for pristine living quarters, but even she couldn't wait to get it sorted.

'Do you need anything before I go?'

'I'm fine, Dad. Stop worrying.'

'It's in the job description.' And with a characteristic wink he scooped Bandit up and gave him a cuddle. He put him down to exchange him for Smokey but couldn't see him. 'Where's the other one gone?'

It was then Hannah felt a cool breeze lick around her bare arms. 'Keep hold of Bandit!' she yelled, running down the hall towards the sunlight blasting through the door she'd been forewarned could be temperamental and down the path, just in time to see and hear a sleek black car come to a screeching halt outside.

Smokey shot past her, back into the cottage he'd been so desperate to escape, and Hannah was confronted by the driver of the car as her dad shut the front door to stop the same thing happening again.

'I almost swerved and crashed!' the man yelled from behind dark sunglasses.

'I'm so sorry.' She shielded her eyes to get a better look at him. The fresh air mingled with a woody aftershave from the man in tailored suit trousers, a crisp white shirt and a tie obediently unflappable in the spring breeze.

'I should think so too. Bloody irresponsible.'

'There's no need for foul language,' she said, although she found it hard to reprimand someone as attractive as he was. First impressions counted and, right now, his height and broad chest that suggested superior upper-body strength she could've used about an hour ago as she and her dad wrestled the bed posts and frame up the narrow staircase, made her nerves flutter away in her body despite his rudeness.

His mouth set in a firm line, he climbed back into the fancy car and pulled away with another screech of tyres.

'Maniac!' Hannah yelled after him. Arrogant, un-welcoming tosser, she wanted to add. But she wouldn't, not out loud. She wanted to at least attempt to make a good impression on day one of living in Lantern Square.

But moving day troubles weren't over yet, because the same woman from earlier was right behind her. 'Only been here an hour or so, and you're already upsetting the locals.'

'It's not my intention, I assure you. Who was that anyway?' Her interest wasn't only platonic, judging by the way the butterflies in her tummy did a giddy dance. Despite his rudeness, the man had been good to look at. She supposed nobody had ever taught him anything as basic as manners.

'That was Joe; he's the local GP.'

The butterflies disappeared entirely. 'You don't mean Joe Altringham?'

'Dr Joe Altringham, yes. Do you know him?'

'In a manner of speaking.' Today wasn't the first time she'd had cause to dislike the man. After she'd bought her cottage she'd lined up an on-air interview with the local radio station to talk about her new business and generate more custom but at the last minute Joe Altringham had come along and they'd pushed her aside, just like that. She wondered what he was like with patients, given his apparent disregard for anyone else other than himself, both on the road and off.

She reiterated the sorry tale to her new neighbour, thinking it might help their relationship, but she got no sympathy, so instead of talking about the local GP she tried to make peace with this woman in a different way. 'We don't seem to have got off to a very good start. As I said before, I'm Hannah.' She held out her hand.

'Mrs Ledbetter.' The woman took her hand with an air of suspicion. 'Is it just you moving in?' She eyed

7

Hannah's little car parked outside. 'Just the one car?'

'Don't worry, the van is a one-off. Moving-in day and my dad's helping out.'

'You had an awful lot of boxes for one person.'

So she really had been taking it all in from behind those curtains, not just watching and waiting for parking time to be up. 'I run my business from home, so I have a lot of things delivered in bulk.'

'Business? What sort of business?' Mrs Ledbetter eyed Hannah suspiciously, as though expecting her to announce she ran a brothel or an illegal gambling den.

'It's a care-package business – I deliver gifts to people as a pick-me-up, something to make their day a little brighter.' The business had started as a seed of an idea a long time ago, and Hannah would always be glad that something wonderful had come out of such a painful personal experience.

Mrs Ledbetter seemed unimpressed. 'I hope you're not going to have delivery vans dropping off or picking up at all hours of the night.'

'Strictly a daytime business, I assure you.' She was rescued from further questioning when a voice behind her called out to greet her neighbour.

'You're glowing this fine day, Mrs Ledbetter.' A man in his early thirties bumbled across the street from the square. He had mud all down the front of his overalls, a spade in one hand, a cap in the other as he let the air get to the riot of auburn curls on his head.

Hannah almost gawped as Mrs Ledbetter reversed her demeanour completely. It was like seeing a totally different woman. 'Good morning, Rhys,' she said warmly. 'How are you?'

'Grand.' His smile was as wide as his deep-set eyes. 'And who's this?'

Hannah thought it best she take the lead. 'I'm Hannah, I just moved in to Lantern Cottage.'

'Well, congratulations and welcome to Butterbury,' he said, beaming. 'I won't shake your hand, I'm filthy. I'm Rhys, gardener extraordinaire, employed to look after the gardens in the square.' He pointed across the street to the wrought-iron railings that ran all the way around Butterbury's famous Lantern Square. 'The flower beds are looking really great, even though I do say so myself.'

He certainly was chatty. At last, someone friendly. 'Do you live here too?'

'I wish I did. I live in the next village. Any gardening you need, give me the nod. And if you need evidence of my talents, you could check out the flower beds here in the square. Tulips, bluebells, lilacs – all my handiwork.' He put his cap back on and tipped the peak. 'Actually, I'd better get on soon or the council will put me on a warning for slacking off. Got to oil the wooden benches, Mrs Ledbetter, so no sitting down on your way through there for a few days. We want them looking pristine for the summer fair in August.'

'I wouldn't dream of it.' Was that a smile she managed? 'And I'd better get on too. Lots to do.' She made sure she was the first to walk away.

'Don't worry.' Rhys leaned a little closer. 'Her bark really is worse than her bite.'

'I'll take your word for it.' Hannah grinned. 'What's the summer fair?'

He briefed her on what it entailed: the community

coming together with stalls, food, even dancing. 'I think you're going to like living in Lantern Cottage.'

'I think you might be right. The cottage needs a little bit of attention, though.'

'The front looks tired, but settle in first, there's no rush. And don't let Mrs Ledbetter's cottage put you off. The rest of the residents only aspire to have the fastidiousness of that woman.'

Hannah managed a giggle. 'Is she always so disapproving?'

'Not when you get to know her.'

Hannah reached for a tall, dark-stemmed weed by the gate and began to pull. 'Better start attending to the weeds out here before I give her anything else to complain about.'

'Whatever are you doing, woman?' He stepped forward to rescue the plant. 'It may not look like much at the moment, but any day now this will have bright crimson flowers.'

'So not a weed, then.'

'Definitely not a weed.'

'I'm not exactly green-fingered.'

'Tell you what, I'll pop over when I've finished doing the benches, give you a quote for a spruce up of the front and back, plus maintenance should you want it. No pressure. But if you're interested, it could stop you killing off any more innocent plants.'

She agreed and when Rhys went on his way she returned inside to rescue her dad from cat patrol so he could go home.

She was buoyed by meeting the friendly face of the local gardener, the sunshine gracing the square on her first day here and the promise of new beginnings behind the weathered front door of Lantern Cottage. The only thing that made her frown again was when the sleek black car honked its horn as her dad began to pull away from the kerb, then roared on past, its owner not in the least bit cautious of other vehicles, a man crossing the road up ahead, or the possibility of cats darting out from surprising directions.

Lantern Square was picturesque, a pretty perfect place to start again. But Hannah guessed you couldn't have everything. It seemed the locals might well take a bit of getting used to.

Four months later . . .

I

Hannah's first few months in Lantern Cottage had flown by in a whirlwind of unpacking, working, meeting the locals and starting to make friends as she went about her daily routine, exploring the village to get her bearings.

The day after she arrived she'd seen an advert in the post office window asking for volunteer companions at Butterbury Lodge, the care home at the top of the hill that led out of the village, and so Hannah had decided it was the perfect way to immerse herself in the community. Mostly it was friendship that was required, or reading books to residents, playing card or board games, and through her regular visits she was slowly getting to know more and more people. The square was beginning to hold the promise that it could be her forever home, a notion she'd thought unattainable not so long ago.

Despite her best efforts, Hannah hadn't managed to entirely avoid Mrs Ledbetter's disapproval since she arrived, whether it was complaints about her cleaning her car and the water trickling towards her neighbour's garden path, Hannah and her new friend, Lily, chatting outside Lantern Cottage after the pub one night, or the many other complaints the woman had listed. And today, Mrs Ledbetter's opinion looked set to take another nosedive.

'I promise it won't happen again,' she told Mrs Ledbetter as with a bit of manoeuvring she scooped Smokey from her neighbours' arms. Hannah had soon come to realise that the local busybody liked to have her nose in other people's business whenever she could, and for some reason her disloyal cat had taken to the woman.

'The last car to go past almost squashed him beneath its tyres!' Mrs Ledbetter continued her lecture, looking Hannah up and down, unimpressed with her tatty dungarees and old T-shirt underneath. 'You really should keep a better eye on him.'

'I will. And sorry, again.'

Mrs Ledbetter readjusted the handbag looped over one arm. 'I do hope you'll wear something a little smarter to the summer fair today.' She primped the back of her salt-and-pepper hair in case holding Hannah's cat might have in some way ruined her pillar-of-the-community image. 'It's an important event on the social calendar.'

'I've heard it is, and yes, I'll blend in well, just like everyone else.' At least she hoped so. She wondered whether she'd stick out like a sore thumb, being new to the summer fair, and Mrs Ledbetter's observations weren't helping matters.

Mrs Ledbetter didn't miss the opportunity to wave at the local doctor, who chose that moment to roar past in his sleek, sporty black car. He had a real habit of doing that.

Hannah cuddled her cat close, but in the interests of fitting in, gave a reluctant wave to Joe, a man she found to be arrogant and quite frankly, right up his own arse. She wouldn't mind betting he'd glimpsed her standing at her front gate in her scruffy clothes with a piece of wool hanging from her bobbed brunette hair – Smokey had just alerted her to the problem by retrieving it with a swipe of his paw – and decided she lowered the tone of the neighbourhood. However, Butterbury was full of characters with a jumble of personalities, and ever since she'd moved to the little village Hannah had felt as though she'd soon fit in. More so, in her opinion, than the village GP who wore well-cut suits as though it was a uniform for that car of his. She wasn't sure she'd ever seen him in casual clothes. Maybe he didn't own any.

'You youngsters don't value your possessions, that's the problem.'

'I can't be with my cats twenty-four hours a day,' Hannah retorted, bristling, although she told herself that she should know by now to just let it go. Ever since she'd moved in to her cottage she'd been fighting a losing battle, trying to be chummy with this particular neighbour. Everyone else seemed to be welcoming enough, but not this local. Instead of continuing to argue back, Hannah put a smile on her face and said, 'Looks like the summer fair has brought plenty of visitors to Lantern Square.'

'Hmm . . . I'll be glad when they all go home. Your cats probably will be too. Less chance of getting run over.'

She'd walked right into that one. 'He's safe now. Anyway, I'd better get back to work. Maybe I'll see you at the fair later.' She couldn't help being friendly! Hostility wasn't something she'd come looking for in Butterbury. She'd had enough of that to last her a lifetime.

When Mrs Ledbetter harrumphed, Hannah gave up and went back inside her cottage. She could still hear the woman mumbling something or other even when she'd shut the door behind her.

'You need to stop getting me into trouble,' she told Smokey, who promptly leapt from her arms and trotted in the direction of the dining room. Mrs Ledbetter was forever finding fault with something. Last week she'd even taken umbrage to Hannah's music – soft to any ear, even if you were sitting right up next to the speaker – which had apparently drifted four doors down from Hannah's cottage while she had her windows open to grab a bit of fresh air on a warm summer's evening.

'And don't even think of going anywhere near the table,' she called, as she followed Smokey into the room at the back of the cottage with its double doors that opened out onto her little garden. Her latest packages were waiting for her trademark finishing touches that had built up the brand for her care package business, Tied Up with String.

Hannah had launched the business twelve months before from her old bedroom in her parents' house. Not ideal, but it had been a start, and now Hannah's home at Lantern Cottage doubled as her business space. She also designed her own greeting cards, selling them via her website or, more recently, to Castle Cards, a boutique stationery shop on the outskirts of Tetbury. Thanks to her involvement with Castle Cards she'd had write-ups in both the local and national press – and she'd even had a mention in Mrs Ledbetter's personal 'village voice'. As much as she disliked gossip, Hannah had to admit that Mrs Ledbetter's description of 'a strange girl who sent mysterious boxes to strangers' had been perfect advertising, piquing local interest only weeks after she moved to the area, and even got her business a double-page spread in the local newspaper when a journalist heard about Tied Up with String and wanted to do a feature. Her nosy neighbour had made the business sound more illicit than it was, but Hannah had been able to make the publicity work to her advantage. Tied Up with String had started slow, but soon transitioned from a business that was just about coping, to one that was almost overwhelmed with requests. And her neighbour's interference, which had led to the extra exposure, was probably the only reason Hannah had never lost her temper with Mrs Ledbetter – or told her, quite simply, to bog off!

Hannah got back to fulfilling her orders, which she'd been in the middle of doing when Mrs Ledbetter's thump on the door had made her jump. She made up a flat-packed piece of cardboard into a postal box and wrestled its sides until they slotted together. When Bandit decided to get in on the action by leaping up on to the table, she shooed him away and he protested by leaving the room entirely for the front room, no doubt to curl up in the shaft of sunlight that came in through the latticed windows there. His brother had already taken custody of the big carver chair in the corner of this room and the remaining chairs were taken up with all manner of paraphernalia, and all alternate shelf spaces were full to the brim. As well as a long sideboard along one wall stacked high with clear boxes containing inventory, all clearly labelled with stickers to save rifling through each one every time, there was a large cupboard in a corner of the room which was filled with smaller items for her business – plentiful supplies of clear adhesive tape, rolls and rolls of traditional brown packaging paper and the balls of string that went so well with it, bubble wrap rolls, tissue paper reams and poly-styrene chips that could be used to cushion and protect items in transit.

If she worked hard now, she'd soon be able to head over to Lantern Square where the summer fair was well under-way. She'd seen the excitement mounting when she passed by on her way home this morning from buying some of the regular and most popular supplies for care packages – tea in all manner of flavours, from Earl Grey to pepper-mint and chai, novelty chocolates plain, milk and white, various scented candles, soaps in different shapes and sizes, and more of the blush champagne ivory confetti to add a finishing touch should the customer prefer it to the ice-blue alternative she had in the cupboard. When she'd stood talking to Mrs Ledbetter out front she'd glanced over at the square where children were playing in the sunshine that looked set to stay all day. A kite was tan-gled in the huge oak tree that dominated one end of the square, a toddler was wailing after dropping his ice-cream in the gutter, and the cake stall already had a queue snak-ing all the way out of the square's gates and into the road, getting in the way of anyone who tried to pass through Butterbury on such a busy day. Somehow, though, Joe had managed it in his posh car. He was one of those men people seemed to just get out of the way for – although quite why, she had no idea.

It was late August and soon many kids would be off to university for the first time or returning to their stud-ies, a few tackling the separation from home with bravery, others revelling in their newfound independence. Hannah had already put together a few dozen care packages and sent them on their way, but the order she was working on now had come in later than the rest and she really wanted to catch the last post. She picked up the printed email and reread the list she'd agreed with her customer, lining up the items: three small pots of single-serve instant porridge – all banana and strawberry flavour – a reusable takeaway coffee cup and a collection of individual coffee sachets, a packet of disposable razors, shaving foam, a small first aid kit which Hannah hoped wasn't related to the previous few items, plus a jar of Marmite, a portable phone charger with spare cable, and a couple of pairs of extra-warm socks. She wrapped everything individually in blue tissue paper – she'd hate to have lost concentration and picked up the roll of pink paper, only for this male student to be teased by his new friends as he unwrapped the package – before placing everything carefully in the brown box.

When she'd started Tied Up with String she'd imagined, as the song from *The Sound of Music* went, brown paper packages, tied up with string, heading out to customers far and wide. But her research had soon proven this notion to be completely impractical. Unlike in the past, where a cutesy package could have been wrapped exactly the way she'd intended, both domestic and international postal services had to contend with faster sorting and delivery services, introducing the hazards of conveyor belts for string or loose wrapping to get caught in, and sorting machines that would jam if she didn't make up her parcels properly. Reputation in business was everything, and so Hannah wrapped each parcel the way she intended, but each went into another box filled with biodegradable chips for protection in transit, ensuring recipients didn't miss out on the enchanting, olde worlde feel with the brown paper and tied, distressed string when the care package arrived at their door.

This particular parcel she was working on was not to have any confetti added to it, not even the ice-blue kind, an omission the recipient would likely appreciate as much as the blue tissue paper rather than the pink. And with every item safely tucked inside, she retrieved the traditional brown paper from the cupboard, cut it to size and neatly wrapped the box, folding any cut edges, securing them with clear tape and finally tying the whole thing with brown string, ending in a neat bow ready to be tugged open. She set the brown paper package inside a white box, sealed the whole item, and copied the delivery address from the email onto a label and stuck it onto the package. She added her company stamp, a gift-shaped outline with crescent writing saying Tied Up with String over the top of the illustration, and she was done. Another parcel ready to go out into the big wide world and put a smile on someone's face.

She left the package on the large wooden table – the only item of furniture she'd brought with her from the townhouse she'd shared with her ex, Luke. It had at least appeased him when she had the removal men take it away. He'd never liked that table. They'd bought it on a whim, more on her impulse than his. It had barely fitted inside their kitchen – something that generated a loud 'I told you so' from her other half – and in the entire thirteen months they'd lived together, furnishing a rented home, making plans for their future, they'd never really used it apart from the Christmas before they split up when she invited her family to stay with them, something that hadn't gone down well at all. Whereas she got on with her in-laws famously, he'd struck up a rapport with her mum but never really clicked with her dad.

She glimpsed the tiny dent in the edge of the pine. The wood was softer than it looked, and the removal men had knocked it as they tried to get it on the truck. Looking at the mark now reminded Hannah of how hurt Luke had been the day she'd told him their relationship was over. She ran her hand across the wood of the table, which looked so much more at home in Lantern Cottage than it ever had in the city, its patina in keeping with a home that was itself a little quirky and lived-in. Not entirely perfect – but perfect for her. Lantern Cottage had been rewired the year before Hannah bought it, and apart from the boiler going on the blink and needing replacement within three weeks of moving in, the only other signs of age were the ones that gave the place its character – the exposed stone area in the hallway with several segments discoloured from years of being the main thoroughfare, the knotty beams in the ceilings above, the small stained-glass window in the downstairs toilet which was no bigger than a coat cupboard and only for the most petite of guests. Coming to Lantern Square had marked a new beginning in a different part of the country where nobody was around to question her decisions or bring her down, and already Hannah was starting to feel happy again.

She checked her watch. She had just enough time to change so she'd look at least semi-respectable for the fair so she ran upstairs to put on some fresh clothes. She'd been so overwhelmed with orders recently that as well as dropping the ball on housework, she'd also neglected her laundry. She rooted through her drawers and her wardrobe twice in case she'd missed something the first time.

But no luck. The only items still on their hangers were either too wintry for this beautifully hot day or more akin to what you'd wear if you were decorating your house. That was another benefit of working from home. She wore her scruffs whenever she liked – just like now. She even wore pyjamas some days, or simply threw on leggings and her treasured Robbie Williams T-shirt, complete with a hole from gradual wear and tear that was only safe from exposure if she popped a cardigan or coat on to go outside. But there was no way she was turning up to the Lantern Square summer fair in what she had on now or anything threadbare, torn or unwashed.

She shut the doors to the freestanding wardrobe that slotted in neatly beneath the ceiling beam and slumped down onto the bed. All she could think about was Mrs Ledbetter and her claim that this was an important event on the social calendar for Lantern Square. Hannah didn't want to make a bad impression; she was fitting in well so far, and she wanted to keep things running smoothly, to become even more a part of the community. Over the last few weeks she'd heard the fair being discussed in passing, and it sounded as though it wasn't like any of the village fairs she'd been to before. According to Dawn, who ran the Lantern Bakery along with her husband Troy, people made a real effort, particularly for the dancing and evening entertainment, which gave the event a certain air of sophistication.

Bandit had climbed the stairs and jumped up onto the bed next to her, stretching out languorously as Hannah tickled the top of his head and down his nose, making him purr and dribble. 'What am I going to wear, eh, Bandit?' He nudged her hand when she stopped fussing and she resumed stroking but not for long. She had to get a move on if she wanted to make it to the post office in time.

With Hannah preoccupied, Bandit decided she wasn't paying him nearly enough attention and skulked back downstairs, leaving her to sift through her laundry basket beside the wardrobe to see whether anything was salvageable. But when she caught her little toe on one of the wardrobe's feet her eye was drawn to a sealed dress box pushed underneath, gathering a thick layer of dust. Her mum had stored it for a long time – it hadn't been something Hannah had been comfortable taking with her when she moved in with Luke – but she'd brought it here with her to Lantern Cottage when she'd moved in, mainly because her parents' place wasn't much bigger than here and, now she was in her thirties, it was high time she stopped storing her excess baggage with them. At least in the physical sense, anyway. But this box hadn't been opened in a very long time. Not since that terrible day.

Hannah could hardly believe it herself when she saw an opportunity. But it was either be brave and wear the dress and fit in with everyone else who'd made an effort, or not go to the fair at all. And she so wanted to go – she wanted to put on something nice and be reminded that, even after everything that had happened, she was allowed to be happy.

She was particularly looking forward to the grand finale of the fair, which had been so vividly described to her by Cate, one of the friendlier locals who had once run after Hannah to return the credit card she'd dropped leaving the post office in a hurry, and now always stopped for a chat. According to Cate, once the sun went down, lanterns on top of the gateposts would glow against the darkening sky and residents would dance the night away to a live band that would carry on until midnight. Cate had told her that it wasn't a dance where you needed to have a date or feel silly without one either. Cate had been on her own the year before last and danced with a whole cast of characters, including Terry Granger, who ran the local sweetshop and had secret talents doing the waltz, and some of the workers Rhys knew from the farms dotted down the long lane extending out of the village past Hannah's cottage. Dancing was a free-for-all, with everyone whirling around right up until the music stopped, when shoes were kicked off, people hobbled home, and everyone yearned for their beds. And, right now, Hannah longed to be a part of all that.

Determined, Hannah lifted the box and sat back on the bed with it on her lap, brushing the dust from the top and letting the grey fluff fall to the floor for her to pick up later. She tugged at the ribbon that still secured the box together and, holding her breath as if jumping off a high ledge into water, she tore off the lid. Her fingers tentatively touched the beautiful material.

She took off her clothes, dumping them on the bed, lifted out the vintage polka-dot, navy-blue dress and slipped it on before she could change her mind. She was surprised to find herself smiling as she wiggled up the side zip, glad it still fitted over her curves. She flipped her head over so she could tie the bow of the halterneck and smoothed out the full skirt. In the bottom of her wardrobe she found her gold ballet flats that went so well with everything, and slipped them on to complete her outfit. Deep breath in, deep breath out. She'd done it; and now she was ready to join in with the people in the village who had been going to this event for years.

With the parcel in her arms, she stepped nervously out of the cottage and into the sunshine, wondering what she'd say if anyone asked the perfectly normal question, 'where did you get that dress?' She tugged the door firmly and double-checked it was closed. It was unbelievably temperamental, as she'd found the hard way when Smokey nearly got crushed under the wheels of Joe's car on moving-in day, and again last month when she'd come home to find the door wide open. She'd stood at the gate, too scared to go in for fear that a burglar would still be inside. Unluckily for her, Joe was driving past at the time, and had pulled up and wound down his window. She'd been obliged to explain what was going on and, even worse, forced to let him save the day by inspecting her house for intruders and concluding that she hadn't shut the door properly. And she'd had to *thank* him, of course, which didn't come easy when they hadn't exchanged a single nice word since her arrival in Butterbury.

She'd only just shut the front gate to her cottage when Lily, who worked at the Butterbury Arms, called out to her. Rhys had knocked on the door of Lantern Cottage exactly a week after Hannah's arrival to tell her that she'd had plenty of time to settle in, and now it was time to go to the local pub. He'd introduced her to Lily that night, and Hannah had been in there a couple of times on her own when she'd had a quiet evening and craved a bit of company. She'd passed the evenings chatting across the bar with the bubbly pub worker who had a diamond nose stud and striking two-tone ombre wavy hair, deep brown at the roots through to a natural blonde at the ends.

'Hey, Hannah!' Lily adjusted the potted sunflowers she was carrying as she headed towards her parents' home on the opposite side of the square. 'Quicker to go round than cut through,' she laughed. 'Gorgeous dress!'

Hannah might have known she wouldn't escape the inevitable comments when most days she hung out in completely different clothes. 'Thank you,' she said and managed to smile.

'Go get some flowers for the cottage before Rhys sells out,' Lily encouraged. 'These sunflowers are mum's favourite. I'll see you later. I'll be back for the dancing.'

'Give your mum my best wishes,' Hannah called over.

Lily's mum had recently undergone heart surgery and was now recuperating at home. The day she'd been taken away in an ambulance all the residents of the square had rallied round, and Lily had come to stay with Hannah at the cottage while her dad, Tony, sat at her mum's bedside. Hannah had immediately occupied Lily by getting her to help put together a care package for when Liz came out of hospital: two books by her favourite author, a selection of herbal teas, a wheat pack scented with lavender, her favourite cookies from Dawn and Troy at the Lantern Bakery and a special sleep balm to rub on her temples. Both having recently turned thirty-three, Hannah and Lily had plenty in common, and it was nice to be forging a good friendship – especially since Hannah's falling out with her former best friend, Georgia. They'd gone into business together and Hannah had found out the hard way that not everyone had the same moral standards as she did.

Hannah set off in the direction of the post office at the far end of the high street. Lantern Cottage was at the opposite end of the village, where the road beyond twisted and meandered towards farming fields, some dotted with cows, others with sheep, many with crops. And all of them emitting unfortunate smells at regular intervals during the day, but it was all part and parcel of life here in Butterbury and slowly she'd got so used to it that it felt more normal than the traffic fumes and the noises of a big town or city.

'Good afternoon, Mrs Addington,' Hannah called across the street, her voice managing to carry over the brass band playing from a raised stage inside the square. The golden coating of the instruments gleamed in the sunshine and reflected the light through the trees as the sounds of trumpets, tubas and a trombone filled the air.

'Be sure not to miss the fair,' Mrs Addington smiled. 'It gets better every year.' She was someone Hannah always called by her full name, never Judith. Maybe one day she'd feel more comfortable and do so, but the retired judge commanded a certain respect – perhaps because she lived in the grandest thatched cottage in the village, or because of her eyes that glittered with wisdom, and missed nothing. And she never stood for Mrs Ledbetter's nonsense either. Lily had told Hannah that when Mrs Addington's son had come out and moved in with another man, even kissing him in daylight near the local pub, Mrs Ledbetter had set the local gossip mill turning by telling whoever she could – but Mrs Addington had quickly put a stop to it. Hannah could tell that this woman would've left nobody in any doubt as to who presided over the courtroom when she was a judge.

Mrs Addington held up a jar of something and after a trio of kids had run on past with their ice-creams precariously hovering on wafer cones, said, 'It's local honey, meant to be wonderful.'

'Just got to get to the post office and I'll be over,' Hannah assured her.

'Make sure you try the honey.'

'I will.'

Hannah walked on. She'd wanted to be at the fair earlier today, perhaps even to help out Rhys on the flower stall, but her business had to come first. She adjusted the parcel in her arms, not wanting to get all sticky and sweaty even though the sun had other ideas. Malcolm Styles, the local teacher she'd met when Rhys introduced them beneath the cloudy skies of early May, raised a hand to wave across at Hannah as he emerged from the square, his thick-rimmed spectacles in place as usual but with his cords and button-down shirt replaced with shorts and an airy white polo shirt. Hannah smiled her hello, not daring to loosen her grip on the package.

His wife, Miriam, caught him up and waved enthusiastically. 'Gorgeous dress, Hannah!' Miriam, who had once been a teacher, too, now ran the haberdashery right at the far end of the high street and was a wonderful seamstress, so beautiful clothes were never going to fly under her radar. Today she had on a floaty blue and white sundress, cinched at the waist with a thin, shiny red belt.

'Thank you, Miriam.' Hannah swallowed hard, glad that the quaver in her voice was disguised by the brass band cranking it up a notch. She'd once been told that this dress was made for her, that it skimmed over her curves beautifully, and the day she'd heard those words she'd twirled until the skirt flared up, almost revealing too much. But since that day she'd put it back in the container it had come in – it had arrived as a gift in a posh box with its own silky white ribbon – and the painful memories it evoked meant she hadn't worn the dress until now.

She checked her watch for the time and quickened her step. With the long summer days and daylight that lasted until way beyond nine o'clock, it was easy to forget the time, and it was already ten minutes to five. But when she arrived at the post office Hannah found it relatively empty thanks to the fair, and with swift service from Marianne Temple, who'd worked there for nineteen years – about as long as she kept you talking some days – Hannah was in and out quickly. And when Hannah saw Mr Temple sitting on a chair in the corner, waiting for his wife to close up, she realised they were as eager as everyone else to get to the summer fair. Perhaps Marianne had called a moratorium on conversations so she'd be able to get away quicker today. She hadn't even passed comment on Hannah's unusually smart appearance when normally she'd have one or two things to say about anything out of the ordinary.

Smiling to herself, Hannah left the post office, a spring in her step, a confidence that came from either the sunshine or her outfit, her black velvety bag over her shoulder. Another parcel done. Another person who would receive a little gift of kindness to lift their day and brighten their world. Another cog turning in the wheels of the business she'd loved starting and making a go of.

She turned the corner, ready to cross over to the square to join in the fun, and *bam*, she bumped straight into someone whose coffee cup sloshed right onto the neckline of her dress, splashing all over the polka-dot fabric.

She looked up to see Joe, coffee all over his hand, a look

of horror on his face. He pulled tissues from his pocket and waved them at her.

'I'm so sorry. Hey, at least it's iced coffee!' She could tell he was trying to console her, but his sense of humour, or charm, or whatever it was he was trying to convey, didn't work. Especially not today.

Hannah turned and fled and didn't stop running until she reached Lantern Cottage. She never should've worn the dress. Plain and simple.

Because bad things happened when she did.

2

The front door of Lantern Cottage not only took a lot of effort to ensure it was shut properly, it also took a good shove to open it.

Hannah leaned on the door once she was eventually inside and shut out the rest of the world, mortified to have run off like that. She should have kept her cool and brushed it off – now she'd be dreading all the questions about whether she was all right when she eventually went back to Lantern Square. People looking at her, wondering why she'd overreacted to a little spill. Because she didn't want to miss out on the fair altogether. It was a long time until next summer and she knew she'd regret it, especially now she'd been brave enough to put on the dress in the first place.

Bandit trotted towards her and weaved through her ankles the second she took off her shoes and put them to one side. The stone floor, cool beneath her feet despite the warmth of the cottage, was a welcome respite and she scooped the cat up in her arms. 'It's just a dress,' she whispered into his fur as she went through to the kitchen with him. 'No spill or cat hair or snags from your claws can really make any difference.' Nothing could make up for what she'd once had and lost. But still she set him down gently when it was time and only after she'd checked he hadn't put his claws into the material. Bandit liked his cuddles but not for too long. He liked a fuss, but do it too much and he'd give you a little nip to say 'enough now'.

You heard about people throwing themselves into their jobs to avoid their problems and it had worked well for Hannah. Burying herself in Tied Up with String meant she had little time to concede that other areas of her life might need some attention. She'd made a mess of so many things, but this was at least something she was doing right. Tears still streaming down her face, she picked up some debris from the floor. She dangled a piece of leftover brown string in front of Smokey's nose for him to play with, although the way he opened one eye and gave her a disdainful look suggested he thought she should probably get a life.

And so, despite what had just happened, she did the one thing she knew how to do: she worked. She had a request from Canada for a package to arrive in time for a one-hundredth birthday celebration, another care package to be made up and sent to a tween in Wales who had a major gymnastics competition coming up. That package required a bit more thought and, as well as pamper products, Hannah had found a mug online with the silhouette of a gymnast doing a backwards bend. She'd ordered a phone case with motivational words and also wanted to buy some trendy hair ties which had been the mother's suggestion.

She pinched the top of her nose, feeling a bit of a headache coming on and threatening her focus. She needed a drink. It was way too hot for the usual cup of tea so instead she took out the filter bottle from the fridge which contained the apple and elderflower infusion she'd made up that morning. She poured a generous glass, added ice cubes and gulped back half of it, leaning against the bench top for support. She'd always been a coffee drinker back in London, but when she got going with care packages and her research had revealed plenty of people favoured the multitude of teas on the market nowadays, she'd tried a few and was soon hooked.

She topped up the cats' water, trying to ignore the few stray hairs on the top of her dress next to the decidedly brown tinge spreading across a good number of the white polka dots. She'd take some more iced tea outside and enjoy it in her compact little garden – get some perspective. Thanks to Rhys's input her outdoor space was a haven filled with colour for the summer months: bold red crocosmias showing off, flamboyant purple dahlias demanding attention, and delicate creamy white peonies that caught the eye over in their patch in the far corner beyond the modest square of lawn.

A knock at the front door interrupted her plan to go outside and, although she was tempted to ignore it, she couldn't avoid people forever. Wallowing in self-pity was something she knew how to do far too well, and despite being home now, with every minute that passed she was desperate to pluck up the courage to get back out to the village event that would show her the sense of community she'd craved for a long while since leaving London behind. She left her iced tea on the kitchen benchtop and went to see who it was, not forgetting to check her reflection in the hallway mirror beforehand. She ran her fingers beneath each eye to wipe away the streaks of telltale mascara, along with the tears she thought she'd been done with shedding a long time ago.

She pulled open the door to find Miriam on the other side. Had this woman seen her bolt from the post office to the cottage? And how many others had been witness to it, she wondered? 'What can I do for you, Miriam?' She adopted an upbeat tone, a pretend-nothing-has-happened voice.

'May I come in?' Pale blonde curls shone beneath the sunshine.

'Of course.' The only time Miriam had ever been inside Lantern Cottage was a few weeks ago when she'd come to Hannah to order a care package for her elderly mother, who'd sadly passed away soon after. 'I was about to take an iced tea into the garden – like to join me?' Ever since she'd come to Butterbury, people had gone out of their way to make Hannah feel welcome, so she was always looking to repay the favour whenever she could. Rhys had given her an excellent rate for gardening services, Mrs Addington had brought round a chicken casserole on moving-in day so she didn't have to worry about dinner, Dawn from the bakery had welcomed her to the village with some scones and a parcel containing clotted cream and jam that they'd devoured in the kitchen before it was all systems go again, and even Mrs Ledbetter managed a courteous nod hello now and then when she wasn't complaining.

'Now that sounds lovely.' Miriam followed Hannah down the tiny hallway and into the kitchen.

Hannah took the filter bottle from the fridge and made up a second glass before topping up her own. 'This one has a lovely flavour, hints of liquorice and layers of vanilla apparently,' she said, and smiled.

Out in the garden Miriam sat opposite Hannah at the bistro-style table set. It was gleaming white given she hadn't had it all that long and she'd retrieved the pale blue cushions for the chairs from the tiny lock-up shed this morning, anticipating the fine weather.

'This cottage has always had a lovely garden and I'm glad you've kept it so.' Miriam admired the flowers, the riot of colours. 'Plenty of young folk wouldn't have the time or inclination.'

'I'd better fess up, then.'

'Fess up?' Miriam rolled her eyes. 'That's how I know you're a different generation to me. The flowers almost had me fooled.'

'I'm not a particularly good gardener. See those dahlias?' She pointed to the gorgeous purple flowers showing off as they swung in the light breeze.

'Beautiful, and not easy to maintain. What's the secret?'

'You should ask *who's* the secret?' Hannah sipped her iced tea. 'Rhys. He's become a good friend and he insists on coming over at least every fortnight to make sure I've not killed them. Said it would break his heart if I did.' She glanced down at her dress, noticing that the marks were setting fast, and wondered whether she should've changed before inviting Miriam in. But she had nothing else to wear, and anyway, it was dry clean only and most likely ruined, so sitting here, letting the summer sunshine fix the stains in place, probably wouldn't make much difference.

'Rhys is a lovely man. I thought for a while that you and he were an item – I clearly hadn't been investigative enough to realise he was doing your garden.' Miriam let out a laugh. 'That could be a euphemism if we let our minds go there.'

Hannah grinned. 'We're just friends. Good friends.'

'Do you know I once taught him at school?'

'He never mentioned it.'

'Probably because most people already know. Don't worry, you'll soon feel such a part of this place that you can't imagine being anywhere else.'

Hannah loved learning snippets of residents' pasts; it gave her an insight into the new friendships she was starting to build. 'Was he always into plants?'

Miriam reached out to admire the lavender, one of the few things in this garden that had an independence and did well enough on its own. 'He was one of the more disruptive members of my class.'

'I can't imagine that.'

'Well, believe me, he was a challenge. He could never concentrate, his gaze was always directed out of the window. At first I thought he was merely misbehaving – he'd flick paint on his peers when it was time for art lesson; he'd hum to random tunes in maths class; whenever he had to queue up he'd find some way of playing up, whether it was doing a headstand in the middle of the hall or pulling a girl's hair. But he wasn't naughty, he was just different. I taught him a couple of years later when they shuffled the teachers around and, oh my, what a change. He just needed to find his groove, and science, anything messy and experimental, that was it.'

'Sounds just like him now.'

'I taught Joe too.'

'Joe?'

Miriam looked her in the eye. 'Yes, Joe, who spilt the drink on you, the clumsy fool.' No need to wonder whether she'd seen the entire turn of events, then. 'Now

Joe was *always* academic, had good grades from the beginning. He was well-mannered and he did his homework to a standard others could only dream about. My only concern with Joe was whether he really had a friendship group. He seemed to be something of a loner – but again, I saw him a long time later, and he'd developed into a fine young man. He was at university by then and excelling as he always had.'

Hannah wondered what had ignited this trip down memory lane – what was Miriam trying to say? Yes, Joe had done well for himself, but it didn't mean he was all good. And the spill outside the post office hadn't earned him any extra brownie points. 'I find him a little arrogant at times.' She wanted to be honest, but polite. 'And he drives that car too fast, doesn't give a toss about the safety of anyone else.'

'He does drive too fast. He always seems in such a rush, out on patient visits and other matters.'

Hannah wondered what the other matters were, but it was still no excuse. He'd beeped her last week too when she'd had to pull across the driveway to the doctor's surgery to let someone past. Talk about impatient. And she could probably go on a lot longer about his apparent self-importance, how he'd smiled at her in the street the other day in a way that hinted he was laughing at her rather than trying to be friendly. Perhaps she was being paranoid, but just because everyone else, including the women she'd noticed coming and going from his house, bowed down to the local doctor, it didn't mean she had to.

Hannah explained the near miss with her cat on her first day in Butterbury. 'He was very rude to me.'

'That's not like Joe. Have you tried to talk to him since?'

'Not really.' She watched a bumblebee wiggle its bum before diving for pollen in a nearby flower.

'You know, it's easy for me to forget that both boys, Rhys and Joe, have grown up. As a teacher I found I'd get attached, as if they were an extension of my family. Probably because the village is so small, everybody knows one another. Now Rhys . . . well, I can still see that disruptive streak, the part of his personality that beckons him outside with a need to get dirty and up to mischief, foraging in the ground. With Joe, I occasionally still see the unguarded side he showed at school, before he qualified as a doctor, before he became the local GP. I saw it with him today after he bumped into you and you fled.' She sighed. 'Sometimes it's easy to think we know people when they could be hiding all manner of things.'

Was Miriam warning her to be a bit nicer? The words suggested she might be but her tone and smile hinted she was only trying to help. 'I probably did overreact.' Hannah tilted her face to the sun before finishing the rest of her iced tea.

'I have a daughter around your age, and I got pretty good at reading the signals over the years. When she overreacted to anything, there was always something going on beneath.'

'It wasn't just about the spill on my dress . . .' Hannah's fingers inadvertently touched part of the material.

'I'm sure it wasn't. And that's why I came here. You're still fairly new to Butterbury, you've made friends, but when I saw you dash past as I came from Lantern Square, I knew there had to be more to it. Malcolm tells me not to pry, not to involve myself too personally, but I got used to it in my years in teaching and I can't behave any other way.' She let her comment settle. 'Would you like to talk about it?'

Hannah hadn't talked about 'it' in years and she almost refused the opportunity now, but something about Miriam was so approachable that instead she looked at Miriam's empty glass and asked, 'Can I get you another iced tea?'

'That would be lovely. And take that dress off, let me see if I can't get rid of the marks.'

'It's dry clean only.'

Miriam winked. 'You're forgetting, I know my fabrics.'

Miriam hugged Hannah as she left to return home to take the dog out for a walk and get back to the fair in time for the dance.

Miriam had raided Hannah's cupboards at Lantern Cottage and found a variety of ingredients, including white vinegar, dishwashing liquid and baking soda. Whatever potion she'd concocted, it had worked like magic on the dress, which didn't seem to have suffered from the lack of respect given to the care symbols on its label.

And now it was time to head over to Lantern Square and join in the summer fun. Hannah went back up to her bedroom and, seeing the dress hanging up on the front of her wardrobe door, she felt a sense of calm that hadn't been there earlier. Perhaps, in a way, the coffee spill had been a good thing. Now that she'd confided in Miriam she felt less of a freak for reacting the way she did and, as she stepped into the garment once more, this time teaming it with strappy gold heels for the dance, she felt much like any other normal thirty-three-year-old old about to go to a party. It had been crazy to think a dress was a bad omen. It was a bundle of material and had no more control over the world than she did.

As she walked towards the square, the sun was still beaming in the sky as though it had no intention of fading away and a smile spread across Hannah's face. A black galvanised iron fence ran around the square's perimeter, interlaced with foliage that must have sprung up over the years, ivy weaving through its bars at random. Bunting in all colours of the rainbow looped from tree to tree, or post to post, like party streamers. A lovely Indian Bean tree stood at one end of the square, gracing the air with its white flowers, and beneath were chairs and tables forming a mini oasis in which people stood or sat sipping drinks, enjoyed an ice-cream or a hot dog from the old-fashioned street cart that had been wheeled in through the gates.

'Penny for them.' It was Cate, guiding a pushchair through the smaller gate at the side of the square and following the path through the centre that Hannah had just joined herself. It was hard to hear her talk with the brass band playing so fervently, but as they brought a lively rendition of 'Nobody Does It Better' to its conclusion, Cate strolled alongside Hannah.

'Sorry, I was miles away.'

Cate adjusted her daughter's sunhat, but Heidi had other ideas and promptly pushed it off to the side again. 'Work busy?' Cate tried one more time with the hat but it was clearly a losing battle.

Hannah was relieved Cate hadn't witnessed her dramatic flight from the post office earlier. At least she didn't have to face a barrage of questions just yet from the girl with fiery red hair who'd welcomed her to the square and made this fair sound as special as it really was. 'Very busy, but I love it. And this is wonderful.'

'I told you it would be. And don't you think the band are brilliant?'

'Who hired them?'

'No idea. Probably the same person who organised the chocolate treats hidden in the square for Easter. But who-ever it is, I'm glad they seem to love Butterbury as much as we all do. Rumour has it that it was the WI.'

'The Women's Institute?'

'I'm doubtful myself, I'm pretty sure they wouldn't have the funds.' She tried, to no avail, to put the hat on Heidi's head again.

'How's motherhood treating you these days?' Hannah looked at the little girl, sleepy from the sunshine, cud-dling her teddy bear.

'Exhausting, hard, rewarding – and a blessing.' She finished with a contented smile that gave away how happy she was, despite the challenges. 'Heidi seems to have finished teething for now, so we'll have a breather and all get a bit more sleep until the next round.'

Hannah stepped aside as a young boy ran after his sister with a water pistol, soaking her red curls and making her giggle in delight.

'It'll be doubly hard soon.' Cate patted her tummy. 'Baby number two is on the way.'

'That's amazing! Congratulations. You told me how hard you tried to have Heidi.' Cate and Hannah had stood outside the bakery one day soon after Hannah's ar-rival in Butterbury and, chatting over oatmeal and raisin cookies fresh from the oven, Cate had told her all about the rounds of IVF treatments, the hopelessness thinking it would never happen, the joy when she eventually realised she was pregnant. She'd heard the whole story a second time from Mrs Ledbetter, when Hannah turned up at Cate's home to deliver a care package ordered by her husband. He'd wanted the package to be a kind of pick-me-up after he'd worked away for a fortnight during which she'd been struck down with a bout of stomach flu and still had to take care of a little one. To give Mrs Ledbetter her due, she'd also been neighbourly that day after she heard Cate wasn't well, and when Hannah bumped into her she was delivering a beautiful flower arrangement. As formidable as the woman's presence could be, her heart *was* in the right place – and she also had wonderful taste in flowers.

'This happened on round two of IVF,' Cate explained, 'so I'm grateful it happened quickly. It's not an easy road.'

'I'm sure it isn't. When are you due?'

'End of January.'

As they chatted on about how the pregnancy was going, speculating about how Heidi would likely cope with a younger sibling, Hannah nodded her approval to Rhys at the flower stall. He'd donned a money belt for his role today and was busy making two pensioners chuckle with his tales. He was good at talking the talk, getting up to devilry when he could. Miriam's description of him as a little boy suddenly seemed so fitting.

They came to the stall run by Dawn and Troy. 'Cookies!' Hannah smiled at the delights. 'I wondered what you guys would do this year. Cate told me about the speciality breads last summer and everything that happens at Christmas.' Apparently, at the previous summer fair the bakery had displayed everything from Marmite loaf to pumpernickel rolls on their stall, then at Christmas they'd offered a whole range of novelty cakes so clever they had to be seen to be believed. One design had had a chimney on top with an upside-down Santa Claus diving into it, only his legs and black boots still visible.

Troy rubbed his hands together in glee, recognising Hannah as another customer who lacked the necessary willpower to resist. 'Can we tempt you with anything?' He had on the usual dusty baker's apron, his wide-brimmed hat stopping the sun from getting to his freckly skin.

Heidi's attention had been piqued and she was pointing at the offerings, straining to escape the confines of the pushchair. Troy's speciality, brown butter oat cookies, were front and centre, with chocolate cookies positioned next to them. They appeared to be quite plain, but Hannah knew from experience that when you bit into one of the melt-in-the-mouth surprises, gooey chocolate oozed around your taste buds, making you surrender all hope of stopping at just one. There was a toffee crunch variety, soft on the inside and firm on the outside, shapes of all sorts including shoes, handbags, sunhats and flip-flops with brightly coloured icing, and ginger cookies with their tips dipped in milk chocolate.

'My treat,' Hannah declared as Cate scooped a wriggling Heidi out of the pushchair and into her arms. 'What can I get this little treasure?' She ran a finger across Heidi's cheek making the child giggle and turn to shyly snuggle into her mummy's neck.

'I think we'll take two of the lantern cookies, how does that sound?' Cate asked Heidi. 'They're decorated with green,' she elaborated to Hannah, 'and my girl likes anything green.'

'Even vegetables?'

'Broccoli is her absolute favourite.'

Dawn grinned as she joined the conversation after taking cash payment while her husband put the cookies into bags. 'Don't tell me, in a cheese sauce?' She too had on a dusty baker's apron – Hannah rarely saw her without it – protecting her pale blue shorts and white T-shirt, her soft, dove-grey hair held at the nape of her neck with a chunky clip.

'It's true,' Cate admitted. 'Doused in cheese sauce she'll eat plenty, but without it we don't stand a chance.'

Hannah chose a toffee crunch for herself and they walked over to the edge of the square. Hannah's feet were coping surprisingly well in her heels, but she knew that if she danced too much later, she'd most likely have at least one blister to show for her efforts.

Cate bought them both a cold juice from the stand near the horse chestnut tree and they admired the set-up. 'I think it gets better every year.' She passed Heidi her sippy cup of water from the basket below the pushchair.

'Won't be long before Heidi is into the face painting,' Hannah observed, looking at two little girls painted as bunny rabbits: white, pink and black paint outlining a button nose, whiskers, and the characteristic buck teeth. The girls were giggling happily, holding hands as they hopped through the fair. Once upon a time she'd been close enough to her friend Georgia to warrant doing something so special together. But those days were long gone.

Hannah and Georgia had met when they were seven years old. They'd both found themselves in a new area, starting at a primary school where the building and the people were complete strangers. They'd bonded that day and a strong friendship had taken root. They'd played elastics in the playground in the earlier years, ridden their bikes to school when they grew older, were each other's confidant when they hit the teenage years and boys held as much fascination as anything else. Their friendship lasted until the end of secondary school, was resurrected when they ended up working for the same firm in London, and had then spectacularly fallen apart and they'd gone their separate ways after what happened. Friendships rarely survived that kind of mess.

'She'll love it, I'm sure. And the art station over there.' Cate pointed to the area with kids milling about, using huge leaves to paint and impress on paper hanging from bulldog clips against easels, others using pieces of potato – or at least it looked like potato printing from this distance.

'Did you make the raspberry jam for Hilda's stall?'

'I'm sure you already know it's my mum's thing, don't you? I help, but it's all down to her expertise.'

Hannah smiled. 'All I've heard is that it's legendary.'

'I'll tell her – she always likes to hear praise.'

Cate's family lived on one of the farms just outside Butterbury, off the road that snaked way past Hannah's cottage, away from the village high street, up the hill and was bordered by rolling green fields dotted with mature trees, wildlife and cattle. Part of Cate's family's land was dedicated to fruits and vegetables and last month Hannah had gone there to pick cherries, while last week it had been plums. She'd even managed to make a plum crumble for when her mum visited a few days ago. Home cooking always reassured Annette Simmons that her daughter was doing just fine and it stopped her focusing on how untidy Lantern Cottage was with Hannah living there and running a business that came with a great deal of paraphernalia. Baking something herself also prevented the inevitable nagging if Hannah dared to serve up something shop-bought. When she was living with Luke, Hannah had tried to cover her tracks by picking up a blackberry and apple pie from the nearest bakery the first time her parents came to visit. She'd warmed it in her own dish rather than a tell-tale supermarket aluminium container but her mum had realised what she'd done and launched into a lecture about how she'd had two children and a husband and never a day had gone by when she didn't serve up fresh food.

Hannah swore she'd only made so much fuss because Luke was there and his mum was renowned for her afternoon teas. Nothing shop-bought there, and Hannah's mum had always had a thing about keeping up with the Joneses. Or in that case, Luke's family, the Youngs. 'You never know what they'll put in it,' she'd told Luke that day, although she'd eaten two servings of the pie. Hannah had exchanged a smile with her dad who let most of his wife's fuss go over his head and later on he'd whispered that at least the fuss about the cooking detracted from the less than perfectly tidy home; the dust in the lounge was thick enough to write your own name in, he'd told her conspiratorially.

Hannah and Cate had a nosey around at the other stalls. They flicked through the selection of books on the stall manned by Freya and Nicholas, both home from university for the summer and doing their bit. They ate hot dogs as they sat and chatted with more of the locals, and when young children and tired parents began to filter out of Lantern Square and the crowd evolved, Hannah said goodbye to Cate and offered her help to Rhys who was gathering up what was left on the flower stall.

'Lily told me to buy some sunflowers,' she said, and smiled.

'All gone, sorry. You snooze, you lose.' He was buzzing, high on the scent of the blooms and the success of the day.

'I wasn't snoozing.'

'So what were you doing?'

She grinned. 'Do you want my help or not?'

'Yes, please. Did you water your poor, neglected garden?' Rhys, his tall sleek physique tanned from all those hours outside and the auburn of his hair catching the evening light as the sun began its journey down, indicated that she should follow his lead, taking the remaining flowers in their wraps and slotting them into the buckets, ready to transport.

'I did it this morning before I started work.'

'That's because you know that your mind is too busy once you get going on those packages.'

She slotted in the small cluster of white lilies next to the chrysanthemums. 'Where to now?'

'Now we empty the remaining buckets and stack them all up.' He eyed her footwear, entertained. 'Can't believe you're in a dress and heels. Your dahlias stand no chance of long-term survival if this is your approach to gardening.'

'My dahlias will be just fine, thank you. And I'm assuming you're not going to require me to do anything too taxing.'

'I'm winding you up.' He winked. 'You look lovely tonight, by the way.'

'Why thank you. I thought I'd make the effort.' She

emptied a bucket into the nearby bed tended by Rhys on days when Lantern Square wasn't quite so filled.

'You didn't have any clean clothes, did you?'

'How did you know?'

'Because you never wear dresses. You're strictly jeans, dungarees and shorts. Sometimes it's hard to remember you're a girl.'

She picked up another bucket and angled it back ready to swoosh the water all over him.

'Don't you dare or you'll be dancing alone later.'

She let him off the hook and turned to slosh it into another section of the flower bed which was protected by low-lying green wire fencing, curled over at the top to look pretty, but as she threw the water it was as though everything happened in slow motion. Because as well as soaking the flower bed, she also managed to get the person standing right in front of it.

With a steady voice, but without his usual arrogant smile, Joe looked down at his drenched jeans, and straight up at Hannah. 'Well, I guess that makes us even.'

3

A couple of hours later the sky had turned dark and was pin-pricked with stars. Twinkly lights around trees and looped through railings in the square, as well as the golden glow from the lanterns on gateposts, gave Lantern Square a whole new atmosphere.

The remaining produce had been cleared from stalls and taken back to homes or retail premises, tables had been moved to the outer edges of the square or as far as they could without encroaching on the flower beds that dipped and curved, and a livelier band had taken over. Men in waistcoats played instruments and moved about the makeshift stage freely, having just as much fun as the guests. Hannah was reliably informed that the enormous instrument carried by one was a sousaphone – which looked challenging to carry, let alone play – and the residents and visitors of Butterbury soaked up the musical delights from the ensemble that also included a saxophonist, another member on a trumpet, a man rhythmically tapping a drum fixed in front of him and a trombone player who pumped music into the early evening air with each movement of the instrument's slide.

The hot-dog stand was still in full operation, as was

a doughnut cart that Hannah hadn't even noticed when the square had been so crowded earlier. It was only as the sweet, fried smell had snaked her way that she'd noticed Annie and Ellen's venture. The two sisters had moved into the square just after Hannah herself and planned, long-term, to open up a bistro. Looked like they were getting in some culinary experience while they could.

Hannah took the opportunity to say hello as they served the last customer standing waiting, at least until more people caught a waft of the sweet, warm morsels and came to check them out.

'Hey, Hannah.' Annie grinned away. She looked a lot like her sister. Both had the same butterscotch gold hair and trusting, heart-shaped faces, except Annie didn't have Ellen's olive skin and needed to be extra careful in the sun. 'Heard you've been throwing liquids at Dr Joe.'

Word certainly travelled fast. 'It was an accident.'

Ellen wiped her brow with the back of her arm, her skin tanned nut-brown and shown off in a vest top beneath the lights strung in the branches of the tree behind. 'You know he's single, right?'

'I like the cart, girls.' Hannah deflected their focus away from her or Joe.

'It's fab, isn't it?' Ellen beamed. 'We painted it ourselves.' Navy blue and nautical, it was certainly original.

'What gave you the idea?'

'Our bistro is a long way off, and we're both stuck in our city jobs for the moment' – Annie gave a bowl of batter one last mix and poured it into the giant aluminium mixing bowl at the end of the stretched-out doughnut machine – 'but this gets us started with food. It's all good practice, and take it from me, they're yummy.'

'She's going to have to take up boot camp if she eats any more,' Ellen put in after she'd handed the customer their doughnuts. 'Don't worry,' she said, grinning at Hannah, 'Annie can't hear me; the machine's too loud! Can I interest you in one?'

'I'll take two, please,' Joe's voice came from behind as Hannah watched the pushed-out rings of dough drop into the sizzling fat before progressing along their journey on the machine that would turn them from pale gloopy mixture to delicious, sugar-crusted treats.

'Coming right up.' Ellen waited for more doughnuts to flop into the tray beside the machine. She took them as they arrived and dipped them straight into a tray of granulated sugar. But Hannah knew she also had one eye on her and Joe to see where this encounter was heading. Maybe she was looking around to make sure no liquids were in sight.

Hannah faced the inevitable and turned towards him. 'I apologise for soaking you earlier. It really was an accident.'

He seemed dubious about her apology but finally went with it and, instead of the unreadable expression, he gave in to a smile. 'It's OK. The jeans dried quickly anyway and it was kind of nice cooling down.' So he did own clothes besides those expensive suits. She hadn't noticed earlier when he'd literally run into her with his iced coffee. 'I probably should've worn shorts today.'

'Then you'd be cold tonight,' put in Ellen. 'The temperature has dropped a bit. Although dancing will warm you up.' Hannah did her best to ignore the none-too-subtle wink from Ellen that came her way.

If he hadn't gone home to get changed, then where had he disappeared to? He'd certainly not been around at the fair unless he'd hidden from her for fear he'd get another soaking. She'd been worried she'd really offended him, and even though she wasn't his biggest fan, she didn't want any animosity. 'Well, I am very sorry,' she said again as Ellen passed him the bag of doughnuts.

'I am too, and the stains came out – that's a relief.' He was looking at the top of her dress and she wasn't entirely comfortable under the scrutiny. 'I'm sorry I upset you. Peace offering?' He passed her one of the doughnuts from the bag.

She didn't know what to say and they did smell good so she went with a 'thank you', and as he tucked into his she stood next to him by the doughnut cart, relieved that Annie and Ellen had somewhere else to channel their energies when a group of teens came over to investigate what was on offer.

Joe and Hannah moved to the side and between mouthfuls he came right out with it and said, 'You don't like me much do you?'

'I hardly know you.'

'But I'm right, aren't I?'

The band had taken the tempo up another notch and Hannah was glad of the noise surrounding them as she shovelled more doughnut into her mouth so answering him was impossible.

'How are the doughnuts, kids?' It was Charles Bray, the elderly gentleman who lived in Butterbury's tiniest cottage, appropriately called The Little House, as proudly proclaimed by the slate plaque positioned by the buttercup-yellow front door. Lantern Cottage was small, with a lounge, kitchen and dining room downstairs, and two bedrooms and a bathroom on the upper floor, which felt even cosier given its slanted roof and the wooden beams that gave the house such character, in common with most of the other residences surrounding the square. But Mr Bray's home, where he and his late wife had raised two sons, was a miniature version of her own – she'd seen it once when he insisted she come in for a cup of tea after she helped him in the street when he dropped a bag of groceries that went everywhere. His home had a kitchen and lounge downstairs, a spiral staircase from the centre of the lounge up to one bedroom and minute bathroom, and a courtyard out the back to finish the home. Wherever they'd put two boys was anyone's guess.

Hannah swallowed the last piece of doughnut, glad of the reprieve from her supremely uncomfortable conversation with Joe. 'They're good. Would you like me to get you one?'

'Maybe later.' Charles stood back as though the prescription for his glasses hadn't been quite enough to notice her until he was up this close. 'Now, don't you look beautiful tonight.'

'Mr Bray, you're making me blush.' And he really was.

But the grey-haired man who only just surpassed her own height of five foot four seemed nervous. 'Me and my Geraldine were regulars at Lantern Square dances back in the day. We'd go all the way to Tetbury too, show off our routines. And please, call me Charles. I told you before, remember? Over a cup of tea.'

'That's right,' she smiled. 'You did.'

Joe had balled his napkin into the nearby bin. 'Charles and Geraldine were the talk of the village,' he explained to Hannah. 'They won competitions with their dancing talents.'

'I still have the framed certificates on my wall,' said Charles. 'In the sixties we mastered the waltz and by the seventies we were experts at the foxtrot. My Geraldine stole the show.' His eyes glistened at the memory. 'How you women manage to do all those moves in beautiful, elegant shoes I'll never know.'

'Give me flat shoes for dancing any day,' Joe agreed, both men glancing at Hannah's shoes and making her self-conscious with her legs on display.

'You dance?' The question to Joe was out before Hannah could stop it. She was still flummoxed that Joe had remembered personal details about anyone else. He always seemed so wrapped up in his own world.

The corners of his mouth twitched at her failure to hide her surprise. 'Not like Charles, but I can move.' When she laughed he added, 'Hey, don't assume all men are uncoordinated or uninterested.'

Charles looked down at Hannah's feet. 'Your shoes are made for dancing, that's what my Geraldine would've said. She had rows and rows of shoes, all colours, and in our tiny cottage, I was forever tripping over them. And she had enormous feet too. Yours look very delicate in comparison.'

Hannah and Joe exchanged an amused glance before Kenny, who worked shifts at the post office, took the mic. Usually softly spoken and hiding behind a curtain of dark hair, his voice managed to reach all four corners of Lantern Square as he declared the start of the summer night's dance by ushering ladies and gentlemen to the floor.

'Would you mind?' Charles asked Joe who seemed to understand the question perfectly.

'Go ahead, she's all yours.'

Charles held out an arm to Hannah and the penny dropped. 'Are you dancing?'

'Are you asking?'

'I am.'

'Then I'm dancing!' She grinned. She was sure her parents had first got together following a similar banter at the local dance and no matter how much she clashed with her mum these days, it reminded her that, once upon a time, Annette Simmons had been an easy-going girl at a dance with a boy she'd gone on to fall in love with. She hadn't always been quite so judgemental.

Hannah's dress swished around her legs as they made their way onto the dance floor. The first tune had them moving their feet faster than Hannah had done in a long time and Charles proved he was no typical old-age pensioner when he'd got a rhythm and enthusiasm behind him.

Up next was 'The Way You Look Tonight'. Charles took her hand and she followed his small steps as he twirled her beneath his arm, led her backwards, to the side, forwards again and even leaned her backwards making the whole of Lantern Square spin dizzily around her.

The song finished and Charles did a small bow that Hannah returned with a curtsey. 'Is that what they do?' she whispered to him.

'At class, we always finished that way,' he confided. 'Now, if you'll excuse me, I'm going to have one of those doughnuts, a sit down, and then later we'll dance again. My old legs haven't seen that kind of action since last Christmas.'

'You go rest up, I'll need you in top form later.' The

heady scent of nearby roses almost made her giddy as she came down from her dancer's high. She watched him go with a smile; he was just as friendly as some of the other elderly folk she'd got to know during her time volunteering at Butterbury Lodge, the elegant retirement home situated amongst the green pastures that led out of Butterbury beyond the post office.

When she turned to leave the dance floor herself, she bumped into a rather solid chest.

'We keep colliding.' Joe's deep, mellifluous tone took her by surprise. But not as much as the gesture when he held out a hand.

'You asking me to dance?'

'I am. Though you and Charles looked like professionals out there; I can't promise you the same with my two left feet.'

She wasn't sure she wanted to be that up close and personal with Doctor Joe but she'd heard it wasn't the done thing to say no to such a request at the Lantern Square dance. It had sounded lovely at the time, but now, in a situation where she'd rather do a runner, she almost wished it wasn't so frowned upon to turn someone down. She considered faking a blister, or sore ankles from wearing inappropriate footwear, but he was already leading her to find their own space in the sea of people out to mark the end of another wonderful summer.

The band began to play 'Fly Me to the Moon' and Hannah had a sudden reminder of piano lessons when she was seven and she'd attempted to play the tune herself. Thankfully, these guys had a much better version prepared.

'So,' he whispered against her hair as they moved closer

just like everyone else, 'Mrs Ledbetter was in the surgery this morning and she told me I upset you.'

Hannah looked up at him rather than eye level – hers only reached his collarbones. 'You've already apologised for the coffee incident, so are we talking about when you almost ran my cat over? Or when you tooted at my dad who was trying to drive a van he isn't used to? Or do you mean when you stole the radio slot?'

He smiled that irresistible smile that left her nervous. 'The third one.'

'That was an underhand move.'

She swore he tightened the arm around her waist as his other held her hand in the air, in case she tried to run away. 'I'm very sorry. It was out of order.'

With his arms around her she had no choice but to endure the conversation. 'I'd lined up the slot to advertise my business.' Mrs Ledbetter's magnificent need to spread gossip had probably been far more beneficial ever since, but that was hardly the point.

'Gift packages, right?'

'*Care* packages.'

'What's the difference?' He copied the dancers next to them and twirled Hannah beneath his extended arm until they came back together and she was pressed, once again, against him.

'They're sent to show someone you're thinking about them, that you care, to lift up their day. I suppose it's the same as sending a gift but the word *care* makes it feel different, at least to me.' He smelt warm, fresh, familiar almost. And this close to the skin on his tanned neck, the wide chest beneath his shirt, the strong line of his jaw, she felt discombobulated.

The song came to an end but Joe didn't let go when the band launched into a slower number which meant dancing even more closely. She was trapped, their bodies against each other.

'I made them promise to line up another slot for you,' he went on, 'and they did.'

'You could've taken an alternative slot yourself,' she batted back. She was now due to have some radio coverage this autumn, a time many people turned their minds to preparations for Christmas. It was probably ideal for her business so long as he didn't swoop in and try to take it again.

'It wouldn't have worked for me. I really needed that one.' His jaw tensed the more argumentative they became.

She could've throttled him. He had no idea what it was like, running your own business, worrying whether a quiet period would send you under – or worse, scurrying back home to your parents only for your mum to say 'I told you so'. 'Why did *you* need it so badly?' She hadn't listened to his segment, she'd been too incensed with him going to the radio host who'd known him for years and begging for the rescheduling. She guessed, as a doctor, he'd have mini projects on the go all the time and wanted patients to see him as a pillar of the community. Whereas when he did things like that, she saw him more as the pillock of the village.

'It's a long story. And besides, yours was for business.'

'And yours wasn't? You weren't trying to get people to come in to the surgery and talk to you? Drum up business to keep you here in Butterbury?' She'd heard the local doctor's surgery was tiny and had whittled down from two doctors to just one, him. It wouldn't surprise her if he was given his marching orders soon and everyone would have to trek to the next town and see one of the doctors there. Luckily Hannah had only needed to see a doctor once since she'd arrived and she'd managed to do that when a locum took Joe's place after he swanned off on a week's holiday.

He seemed amused by her accusation. 'I'm busy enough, far too busy – I don't need any more people coming to see me.' When she floated the idea that the surgery might close he said, 'I'm hoping it doesn't. Overheads are low, and I think it's important to Butterbury. I'll be doing everything I can to keep it here.'

The song came to an end and so did her line of questioning. Funny, the more they'd talked, the more she'd forgotten her body was almost moulded against his as they moved in time with the music. They shifted away from the crowd and Hannah perched on the edge of a table.

'Your feet sore?' Joe wanted to know.

'They are a bit. I'm used to spending most days with bare feet or in socks.'

'Let me get some drinks. Something cold?'

'Lemonade, please, if they have it.' So he wasn't completely arrogant. He could be nice if he put his mind to it.

'I'll be right back.'

She watched as a curly-headed lad handed a girl about his age a doughnut – she recognised him as one of the teenagers who caught the school bus from Lantern Square. From the way his eyes kept darting to the girl's face, she wondered whether it was their first date. Young love. It was so very simple, they had none of the hang-ups or baggage grown-ups did. Goodness knows, Hannah had her fair share.

She was toying with the skirts of her dress, reminded of past love, when Joe returned and handed her a lemonade.

'Thank you.' She sipped the cold drink, a blissful relief in her ankles as well as the soles of her feet as her legs dangled from the table. She waited for Joe to sit beside her. 'I wanted the radio slot to drum up business and yes, it was about profit, but my business is a service.' She couldn't let the matter go, not without standing up for what she believed in.

'Still a luxury.'

'A luxury, yes, but also a bit like you helping people; I can let someone know they're being thought about. Take the care package I sent last month as an example. It went to a twenty-four-year-old man who just had an operation to remove a lump from a very – very sensitive place. His younger sister emailed me because she had no idea what to get him so I asked his hobbies, favourite foods, a bit about him. His older brother had some suggestions.' She began to laugh. 'The package had a sweet side but a naughty one too. He wanted to include condoms in there and chocolate body paint for when his brother finally got better and managed to get a girlfriend.'

'I hope he saw the funny side.'

'He did. His sister called me the day after he'd received it and said it had made him laugh so hard, and he hadn't done that in days.'

'I get it, you cheer people up.'

But she hadn't finished yet. 'Or take the woman I sent a package to only last week. She's expecting baby number three but is on bed rest in a hospital thirty-five miles away from home. Her husband works full-time and has the other kids to look after, so most days she's on her own all day. After a few emails back and forth I put together a package with one of her favourite albums on a CD, drawings the kids had done that the husband sent me, some luxury bath products to make her feel special, a pretty journal for her to write in along with a fancy pen, a couple of novels her husband knew she'd like. And I imagined her opening it up, there in a hospital where her only visitors during the day might be the nurse checking her vitals.' He was smiling now. 'Don't laugh – it's a proper business, a service.'

'I'm not laughing at all, it sounds wonderful.' He was looking at her so intensely she had to look away. 'My slot with the station was about loneliness and the importance of reaching out if you need help. Maybe if I'd realised what it was you did and not been so cynical about it all being for profit, we could've teamed up that night and done the radio show together.'

She hadn't been expecting him to say anything like that. 'R-right . . . yes,' she stuttered.

Before they could talk more they were both dragged into the crowd by a couple of locals as the music livened up again. It seemed Kenny had requested this tune, his Irish roots playing out as 'Irish Rover' began.

Smiles filled Lantern Square and Joe and Hannah were dragged into one of the circles of people which formed, everyone holding hands and dancing round and round in one direction, then the other. Hannah could see Charles in the group next to them, just about managing to keep up. Kenny had everyone following his lead as people paired off, crossed arms and kept the dance going. The crowd was in its element, faces highlighted by lanterns perched on the posts at each of the three entrances to the square, others dotted at various points along the railings of the perimeter. Dancers swapped groups, and back again; Hannah danced with so many people, some of whom she knew, some she didn't. Her feet ached in her gold shoes, but she felt alive. Her dress twirled as she did, and it was only as the song came to a close and she collapsed down onto a bench next to Lily, who'd come to join them, that she saw Joe again.

But he wasn't dancing this time. This time he had his arm around a brunette Hannah had never seen before and they were leaving Lantern Square together.

No doubt about it, he was working on his Lothario reputation. And to think, she'd almost begun to like him.

4

Butterbury was a close-knit village and the next day, well after nine o'clock, it was time to do what had apparently become known as The Big Clean-Up.

Hannah heaved the full bin liner around the outside edges of the square. Bins had overflowed last night and residents had far too much respect to leave it for the council to clear or put up with the mess for any longer than was necessary. She picked up napkins, paper cups, kids' paintings that hadn't quite made it home, and half a discarded doughnut which had miraculously survived any early dog walkers this morning.

'This reminds me of the clean-up after the Easter egg hunt,' confided Pamela from Number Six, securing the top of her own bin bag when the pair of them confirmed they were done. Plenty of other people milled about the square, taking part in the same operation. 'At least there's no puke this time.' Her narrow shoulders shook with amusement beneath an old Guns N' Roses T-shirt.

Hannah laughed. What fun it must have been. Although thinking about all that chocolate didn't do much for her growling stomach. She'd only had a cup of tea this morning, keen to be part of the Big Clean-Up before the heavens opened. Today's sky was a stark contrast to yesterday's when powerful summer rays had filtered through any fluffy clouds that cruised by. Now bruised clouds made their way overhead, Butterbury seemingly their next stop to unleash a downpour.

'We never found out who organised the egg hunt,' said Pamela, 'and I doubt we ever will. But the kids in the square had a grand time. Little Heidi found over a hundred eggs, all hidden in flower beds, behind trees; it was far more exciting than the Easter egg hunts I organised at home when my own kids were little. Our garden is a tiny concrete square, not many hiding places there.'

'We never did it growing up,' Hannah admitted. She felt hot already and took her cardigan off to tie around her waist. The sun might have run off to hide but the humidity lingered, a by-product of the summer days she loved but wasn't always sorry to see the back of.

'Everything's more commercialised now. It's a shame in some ways.'

Hannah picked up Pamela's bag along with her own and took them over to the pile with the rest ready for the council to collect tomorrow morning. It wasn't a great look but it was far better all in one place than strewn about their beautiful square. In the short time she'd been here, Hannah had fast started to think of this place as her home, and she took pride in it looking as good as it did.

'How's your Mr G?'

Hannah accepted the offer of antibacterial handwash from the tube Pamela proffered and rubbed it into her hands. She smiled at the reference to Mr G, a man she'd got to know well ever since she'd been volunteering at Butterbury Lodge. The first day Hannah walked in to the care home it had been chaos. A few residents were laughing hard, staff were flapping around and there was a man standing on a coffee table. Hannah had expected a quiet environment – nothing more than gentle chatter, and certainly not such raucous laughter that had more than one resident look as though they were on the verge of wetting themselves. The man responsible for the madness was Mr G, who'd been swiping away any request for him to get down from the table. When he finally did as he was told, he explained that a spider had run behind the painting on the wall and if he didn't get it then it might land on someone quite unexpectedly and cause a heart attack and sudden death from the shock. Hannah had begun to giggle at his antics, Mr G had winked at her across the room, and their friendship had blossomed even more when he asked if she was any good at playing cards.

'He's wonderful. He's had family visiting him from Lincoln but I'm off to see him later this afternoon.'

'Take him some doughnuts. Annie and Ellen have decided to put the cart to good use again today, seeing as they're not back at work until Tuesday. And between you and me, I did hear whispers that they may operate the cart on a more regular basis. Not particularly good for the waistline.' Pamela patted a rounded stomach beneath her shift dress. Her babies were teenagers now, and last week when Hannah had bumped into her in the bakery she'd lamented her love of pastries, saying it was high time she admitted to herself and everyone else that it wasn't baby weight she was carrying but bakery weight. Pamela was vocal in that way, one of the reasons her bubbly character fitted so well in Lantern Square.

'I'd better watch it too or I'll put on all the weight I lost when I was in senior school.' Hannah had been plump all through school but managed to find a happy medium and embrace her curvy figure as she approached late teens and early adulthood.

Pamela waved to her mum who lived in the cottage two doors down from Hannah's. She was crossing the square, stepladder in hand.

Hannah frowned. 'Is your mum OK doing that?'

'Don't you let her hear you say anything to suggest she's getting old.'

'I didn't mean it that way.'

'But she'll take it that way, I assure you. She's becoming more and more stubborn as she gets older – she's never ever wrong, for instance, but I wouldn't have it any differently.'

'Living so close together, you mean.'

'Exactly. She helped a lot raising Angus and Ryan after my husband died. Dad did too, until he got sick.'

'I'm sorry, I've totally brought the mood down, haven't I?'

'Not at all, it's life,' Pamela sighed.

Rhys appeared with another ladder balancing lengthways on his shoulder. 'Taking the bunting down,' he explained. 'Could use some help!'

'On my way.' Hannah followed Rhys into the square where Pamela's mum called over that she'd start at one end if they could start at the other. And between them – Rhys unhooking it and untying the knots, Hannah gathering it up in her arms beneath him and steadying the ladder in the more perilous sections, especially when it involved low-lying rockeries and flower beds he didn't want to ruin – the bunting was down in no time.

By mid-morning Butterbury was almost back to normal and it was time for Hannah to head home for a shower and get on with her own working day before she went to Butterbury Lodge. She enjoyed her time there, especially with Mr G. They talked about anything and everything: travelling, the sailing he did in his youth, books, movies, sometimes politics – although he usually lost her when the subject went that way. She often smuggled out the newspaper crosswords from the communal room, even though they weren't supposed to, and she read out clues that he could solve almost faster than she could recite the words. A retired schoolmaster, he was a clever man, his brain showing no signs whatsoever of taking a rest. Sometimes she wondered if their rapport stemmed from how much Mr G reminded her of her own grandad, whom she'd been so close to until he passed away.

Hannah was just leaving the square, shaking off thoughts of people suddenly leaving your life – thoughts that could only lead her into the doldrums – when the pillar-box-red door to Joe's house opened and out he came. As usual, he'd favoured a suit, a stark contrast to her dungarees, a tie-dyed T-shirt beneath and a pair of Converse on her feet. She waved across, determined to keep it civil, to be friendly no matter what she really thought of him, and as the drizzle began she prepared to make a run for it in the direction of her own house. But she hadn't missed the brunette from yesterday, still there the morning after, wrestling with a bottle green umbrella as they took the step down from his porch and headed for the sleek black car parked out front.

Sometimes it took a while to get to know a person and to find out their story, but with Joe . . . well, it seemed pretty clear. She ran all the way home despite her feet still being on the delicate side after last night's dancing, took off her shoes and appreciated the flagstone floor that cooled the second summer dared to take a breath.

She scooped up Smokey after he squeezed through the cat flap and into the kitchen. 'Hey, you. I neglected you last night, out until all hours, I was.' He purred against her, his eyes closing as he enjoyed the fuss. 'We'll curl up later when I've finished work and seen Mr G.' She set him down and he ran straight to the little bowl of dry cat food on the plastic mat near the back door.

In the dining room it was time to get to work. She fired up her laptop, paid an invoice and updated her accounts spreadsheet, then caught up with emails. There were a couple of thank-you messages from customers, which always made her day, and she asked permission to quote from one to add to a promotion picture on some advertising.

Hannah's work ethic had been drummed into her by her parents a long time ago. But the problem with working from Lantern Cottage was that Hannah's homemaking skills inevitably suffered – something her mum berated her for. Rather than tidying and cleaning, Hannah's spare minutes were filled with rifling through supplies to ensure she had everything she needed, heading off to retail outlets to collect or search for appropriate items, responding to customer queries, sorting through orders, sourcing new and original items, reordering stock, or dreaming up new designs to include in the packages for customers and making mock-up examples of greeting cards.

She had another three orders to fill today as well as an order of gift cards to make for Castle Cards. The gift card market hadn't been intentional, but Hannah had added them to her website, at first merely for the inclusion in care packages she put together. But then, when business was relatively slow at the start, she'd realised it could be another way to top up her income and so she'd sold them as a standalone item in packs of ten. Orders had gradually gained momentum, especially around Valentine's Day, Easter and Christmas, and then, last September, she'd been approached by the owner of a stationery store to supply a Christmas range after one of their staff recommended her work following a personal order they'd placed. They sold like hot cakes and she'd done a second batch and a third. This year they wanted a lot more, and she was determined not to leave the cards until the last minute.

She began with the care packages. The first was for a teenager who'd broken his leg and needed some TLC. Hannah had liaised with his dad and put together a package list that included a smartphone cleaner she'd had to order online, an iTunes voucher (no doubt to load the said smartphone), the latest Stephen King book and some novelty shortbread. Creating bespoke packages was something Hannah had done right from the start, and she loved how personal it allowed her to be, but when she had orders close together it was a challenge. She also had plenty of standard packages for customers to choose from: the corporate package with stylish stationery and champagne; male or female birthday packages with a few bands for different age groups; the pamper package or foodie gifts. Really, those categories were just to spark thought, so she had another page on her website of all products currently in stock for the customer to select from. She had everything from various tea flavours, coffee varieties and posh hot chocolate, to cufflinks, pretty costume jewellery, wax candles and socks. At this stage she didn't want to restrict choice to just what she kept in stock, but maybe in time, if Tied Up with String continued to grow, she'd have to streamline some of her processes or else she'd be forever running around like a crazy woman to make these packages.

Hannah moved on to a package for a couple moving into a new home. She included a scented candle, a white distressed wooden sign she'd picked out from her favourite gift supplier that said 'It's Good to be Home' in curly writing, a keyring set that she kept stock of because care packages were often requested for new homes and this one was delightful, each keyring one half of a silver house that fitted together perfectly when next to each other. Two parts of a whole, like a couple very much in love.

She sighed. It felt like a lifetime since she'd had someone that special in her life. She added in some luxury bubble bath and hand soap to the package, a bottle of French red wine and tossed in a good handful of the blush champagne ivory confetti to finish the package off. And once she put together the last one, she took her special trolley out from the cupboard in the dining room. When she'd first bought it her mum had laughed, because apparently her nanna had had more or less the same one. They were designed largely for people with mobility issues, but Hannah had quickly pointed out that the wire frame and the raspberry-checked sturdy casing would be perfect for trips to the post office. She couldn't carry more than one or two parcels at a time, and so a trolley saved time as well as her back muscles. Her mum had always worried too much about what other people might think. Hannah bet that if one of the trendy high street shops her mum bought her linens and posh crockery in started selling them, she'd see it differently.

With the parcels carefully loaded inside, she made a dash to the post office beneath a big pink umbrella before coming home to a bowl of soup and more of the gift cards. By now the rain was belting down, hammering the poor roof and windows of Lantern Cottage. She put on her Kate Melua album to keep her company, and lost herself in creativity. How she'd ever worked for a big conglomerate, scrutinising accounts, let alone thought about making her own future in an accounting business, she'd never know. And to put all that trust in someone else back then had been a big call. And a stupid one, as it turned out.

Now she was her own boss. And the only person who could screw it all up was her.

She took out the flat, recycled cards, and piled them in front of her along with white card, scissors, glue, self-adhesive foam sheets, and a set of pens designed to add bold colours to wood, porcelain, glass and paper. She'd always loved crafting and Luke had forever been complaining at the little piles of coloured paper, the trails of glitter or off-cuts from greeting cards she'd made being strewn around the townhouse. Usually she left a mess because she'd got so absorbed in what she was doing, and at least here, in her own place, she had nobody to tell her off but herself.

With five hundred cards to do, she planned on having a hundred of each design. Some would have snowmen, others a Father Christmas; a Christmas pudding was another favourite, then a stocking, and lastly she'd do some with a gift-wrapped present. First up was the Christmas pudding design, which would have Merry Christmas written at the top in an arched shape. She used a pencil to get the sizing of the writing correct, outlined the design, added colour, put shapes onto foam mounts, and when she finished each one she set it aside to dry at the end of the table out of the way.

As the time crept round to four o'clock, she finished up for the day, praised the cats for their lack of involvement and not jumping onto the table while she was working. They knew their place was at chair or floor level in that room and she *always* shut its door whenever she left the house.

Now the rain had abated and brought a freshness to wipe out the humidity, Hannah made her way along the street towards Lantern Square and called out to Charles who had paused by the railings surrounding the square. 'How are your feet after last night?'

'Feeling it,' he called from across the street. He was using his walking stick today, she noticed, and took a seat at the bench on the pavement just outside the square.

She scooted across the road. 'You look exhausted.'

'In my day I could've danced all night, out-partied the lot of you.'

She squinted against the dazzling sun, caught out by the change of weather. She would've brought her sunglasses if she'd realised the day would brighten up so much. 'You know, you probably still could – and don't worry, my feet are still a bit sore too. I didn't get off that lightly.'

'You had the fancy shoes, that's why. And the beautiful

dress. What have you got there?' He gestured to the bag at her side. 'A gift for Mr G?'

'Hardly. It's my dress, ready for the dry cleaner.' It didn't have any stains on it, thanks to Miriam's tender loving care, but she'd honour the label's request and get it seen to professionally.

'Cleaning it for next time?'

'Maybe.' You never knew, did you? If someone had told her she'd wear that dress and more importantly, feel comfortable in it after all this time, she'd never have believed them. 'It was a privilege to partner you at the dance last night.'

'Likewise,' he beamed. 'And how was Dr Joe?'

'We could just call him Joe, you know.' Although when she felt at her most peeved with him, the addition of his title sounded better as she walked around her cottage cursing him.

'Dr Joe stops me confusing him from Jo, my granddaughter.'

'Well yes, I suppose it does.'

'You looked good together.'

'Hardly.'

'He's not a bad dancer. You know, in my professional opinion.'

'You watched us?'

'I may have hung around for a time. I sat down at the edge of the square, thinking how much my Geraldine loved the summer fair. She adored this village, never missed a community event.'

'I wish I could've met her.'

'She was bossy, too. I wasn't always a regular at the village events; I was a bit of a misery when we were younger but she soon knocked that out of me. And now I can see why she bothered. Without you all, I'd be stuck looking at the four walls of my house.'

'Well, I'm glad you're sociable too,' she said, smiling.

'I heard you were throwing water at Doctor Joe after he spilt coffee on you.'

'Sociable *and* blunt, I see.' But she found it endearing rather than offensive.

'He was always a bit clumsy, that man.'

'Well, I think it's all fine now. We're friends.'

'I saw him with a young lady earlier on. Was she dancing last night?'

Hannah felt her cheeks redden. 'She came towards the end, I think.'

'And . . .?'

'And nothing, Charles,' she finished good-humouredly. 'I know nothing; all I know is that I have to go.' She held the bag aloft. 'I need to get this to the dry cleaner and then I'm off to see Mr G.'

'Give him my regards.'

'You should come with me, he'd like to see you.' Mr G and Charles had once played tennis matches together at the local club, he had told her. Mr G was never one to hold back on details and Hannah felt as if she'd got to know as much about the village through him as she had by meeting residents and actually living in Lantern Square.

'Another time.' He had his hand firmly on his walking stick, and she wondered whether last night's dancing had been even more taxing than he was letting on. Hannah made a mental note to keep an eye on him.

'I'll see you soon then.' She gave him a wave goodbye.

She dropped her dress in at the dry cleaners run by newly-weds Billy and Stella. They'd dated on and off since high school and then finally realised in their early thirties that there wasn't anyone else for either of them and taken the plunge. She'd seen them dancing together in Lantern Square as she moved around in Joe's arms and wondered if she'd ever again find what they had. She'd found it once and lost it.

Perhaps she'd had her turn, and that was it.

She walked on up the hill away from Butterbury's centre and Lantern Square itself, the sun warming her back but a fresh breeze keeping her cool. When she reached the brow of the hill she took the stone steps up to the big white house with its enormous windows, went through the whitewashed wooden front gate and followed the path. There was a car park accessed from another direction, but this was the pedestrian way and the most picturesque. As she often did, she turned and looked down the hill, the way she'd come. Lantern Square was just visible in the distance below and the rest of Butterbury looked like a model village, going about its business as usual, the odd car moving along the street, tiny figures hustling and bustling about.

Inside Butterbury Lodge the reception area was warm and bright, the large bay windows ensuring it was never in the dark. It was always lovely – and clean, too, an air of house-proud care everywhere you looked, from the small vases dotted on the tabletops and the reception desk to the modern paintings on the wall. Even her mother would appreciate these standards. And Hannah definitely approved of the place. Rather than coming here to live out the rest of their days in a clinical, depressing building with no personality, residents had another home in Butterbury Lodge, one that was welcoming and friendly.

'So, when's the film night going to be?' Not even a hello from Josephine, a resident with a cane who had told Hannah her mind was much more agile than her legs these days. She'd clearly decided to cut any small talk and get straight to the point the second she'd spotted Hannah by the front desk.

'Hello, Josephine, how are you?'

'Still alive. So when's it going to be?'

'Have you all talked and decided what you'd like to see?'

'There's some agreement . . . and a lot of disagreement.'

'No surprises there. How about you give me a few suggestions and I'll get organised?' She wanted to arrange for a huge screen to be brought up here and put in the main lounge because she wanted it to be a proper event that residents could look forward to and that they'd be talking about long after the film finished.

'Right you are.' Satisfied for now, Josephine added, 'Thank you for the chocolate chip cookies last week,' before she went on her way. Hannah had begun to bring cookies up to the lodge, surprising residents with different flavours and when Dawn and Troy cottoned on to what she was doing they'd been only too happy to donate cookies that were left over at the end of the day and still fresh. It seemed the entire community was behind Butterbury Lodge in one way or another, and Hannah loved the feeling of inclusion.

She whispered a hello to Frankie who was manning reception. Tumbling ebony curls were piled up high on her head, revealing porcelain skin that looked as if it had never battled a spot in its entire twenty-six years. Her bright red lips moved animatedly as Frankie chatted away on the phone and simultaneously tapped on the visitor's book to remind Hannah she should sign in. Luckily for Hannah, Frankie was on a telephone call that sounded in-depth, or she would've been kept chatting for ages when she really needed to get on.

Another member of staff, Maggie, a couple of decades older than Frankie, her ash blonde pixie cut as sharp as she was, led Hannah towards where she'd find Mr G, but in the corridor, Hannah stopped when she thought she saw someone she knew. A woman she'd once known very well, in fact. Her breath caught in her throat; her mouth went dry.

'You OK?' Maggie asked.

Hannah had only got a glimpse and already the woman had gone, taken the stairs to the next floor. She shook away the feeling. 'Of course.'

'Hannah!' Bernard, Butterbury Lodge's longest standing resident shuffled past on his way back to his room. 'Wonderful to see you.'

'Looking good, Bernard. How's the arm?' He'd hurt it last week lifting a table he should have asked someone else to move.

'Weak. Maybe I should take up yoga.'

'I'll have a word with Frankie.'

He leaned closer. 'She's too noisy for yoga.'

Hannah giggled and followed Maggie into the gener-ous lounge. This room didn't have a view of the hill or Butterbury, but did look out over magnificent landscaped gardens filled with summer blooms and colours to look at and to potter around alone or with a friend or visiting family. There was a pond too and through the open windows Hannah could hear the trickle of the water coming from the bronze effect fairy holding a delicate flower at her centre.

'Mr G, you have a visitor,' said Maggie. On her first visit he'd admitted to Hannah that his surname was Gettenberg, but he'd said it sounded like a slice of dodgy coloured cake and so preferred to go by the name of Mr G – and somehow that fitted him more than the original.

Mr G was sitting in his favourite maroon armchair at the side of the room. 'Hannah!' His eyesight was still good; he'd always tell her it was one thing that was taking a bit longer than the rest of him to fail, but he still loved to be read to, explaining that his eyes tired easily and his hands found holding a book difficult.

Hannah made her way over to where he was, greeting a few of the other residents on the way. She'd come to know some very well and she touched her hands onto Grace's who was sitting next to a young female visitor. Ninety-one-year-old visually impaired Grace loved to be read to as well, favouring anything by Jane Austen – as long as it was *Pride and Prejudice*. 'I'll see you again soon, Grace,' she told her, 'and we'll see what Elizabeth is getting up to.'

Ever the gentleman, Mr G moved to get up out of his chair, as he always did when Hannah arrived. And as *she* always did, Hannah reached his side before he could do so. 'Save your legs, sit down.' She leaned in and kissed him on the cheek. She'd never delved into his exact health issues and he'd told her he was just old, but not so old he wanted to sit here in a chair alone every day. She'd left it at that. And since she'd first volunteered here when she arrived in Butterbury they'd become firm friends, looking forward to each other's company. Coming here as a volunteer had helped Hannah settle in to the village as much as it helped these residents who craved a variety of company.

'I hear you were the belle of the ball last night,' Mr G told her, pale blue eyes dancing with mirth.

She laughed. 'Word certainly travels fast!'

'Grace told me because her niece told her, and *she* heard it from Charles Bray when she bumped into him this morning. He's one of the most sociable men I know – not that I know many these days. At your age you get invites to weddings and christenings: me, I get death notices!' He leaned closer and confided, 'Do you know, there's a much bigger ratio of women in here compared to men.'

'You sound like you're complaining.' She set down her bag and perched on the maroon ottoman.

'Some of them are all right, I suppose.' The corners of his mouth tugged upwards, suggesting he was pretty happy with the situation. No doubt he thrived on being one of the few men, and there were some lovely women in here, all around his age of eighty-eight years. She knew how old he was because he'd celebrated his birthday three weeks before and she'd sent him a care package from Tied Up with String. She'd sent it in the post rather than bring it herself, even though she was in there later that day to see him. She knew how exciting it was to get anything in the post these days, and he could have fun opening all the little gifts before he had to share the moment with anyone.

'So, what's news?' she asked.

'Never mind me. Same place, same faces,' he said and gestured around him. 'I want to hear about the dance. Come on, humour an old man.'

'You should've come along to the fair. Frankie said if she had some help she'd drive down and you could have had a wheelchair if you needed it.'

'Nonsense, I can get around just fine.'

'Then let's try to arrange for some of you lot to come down to the New Year dance in December.'

'Do you think we'd be allowed?'

Hannah patted his hand. 'Leave it up to me, I'll have a word. You guys go on shopping outings and last month you went to a stately home, so why not a local visit to Lantern Square? It's down the hill, the closest venue ever.'

'You have a point. You're on. And we won't take no for an answer.' Their hands met for a high five.

Hannah found a pack of playing cards on the mantelpiece. In the winter months there would be what she was sure would be an impressive fire burning in the grate below and this room would be at its cosiest – and when the snow fell outside the windows, it would be at its most beautiful. 'What's it to be, Mr G?' She dragged one of the nearby tables over from the stack of three and put it between them both. 'Gin rummy? Cribbage? Whist?'

He thought about it. 'Go Fish.'

'Seriously?'

'I played cribbage with Larry this morning and he can't stand to lose. We had to keep going until he won. And he's rubbish.'

'Come on, then.' She dealt out seven cards each and placed those remaining face down on the table. 'You go first.'

With a bit of effort he managed to fan out the cards in his hands the way Hannah had done. 'Got any . . . threes?'

She smirked. 'Go fish.' He took a card from the pack and she asked, 'Got any tens?'

He reluctantly gave up two of them and she let out a triumphant cheer. 'I'm in it to win it, Mr G.'

They continued that way with Hannah winning four games, Mr G three, and when they'd finished Hannah poured out the peppermint tea from the pot Frankie had brought them while they were mid-battle. She'd added a few digestives on a side plate too.

Mr G finished his biscuit, smiling as he did so. 'Simple pleasures,' he said, picking up his cup of tea with a not-so-steady hand, so a little slopped into the saucer beneath. 'Now, I need to hear all about this dance.'

'There'll be a band, I'm sure. It'll be cold, given it's late December, but apparently there were so many outdoor heaters last year, Cate told me that some complained of being too warm.'

'A lot of people just like to complain. But I didn't mean that dance, I was talking about the one you've just been to.'

'Oh, that one.' Her immediate thoughts went to Joe and she wondered if Mr G would pick up on something.

'I heard Charles got to dance with you.'

'He really is talented and he hasn't lost his rhythm.'

'And did you dance with anyone else?'

He hadn't missed a thing. 'The look on your face tells me you already know the answer to that.'

He shrugged as she tidied up the stray cards, stacked them on top of the rest and wound the elastic band around the pack.

'It's not right, you know,' he said after she'd returned the cards to their rightful place.

'What isn't?'

'You being in that cottage on your own.'

'I'm an independent woman, Mr G. And Lantern Cottage is the perfect size for one. Don't you worry about me.'

'Joe would make a fine husband.'

She laughed hard now. 'I love the way you don't hold back with voicing your opinion.'

'When you get to my age you're well aware that time could run out at any moment.'

'So dramatic.' She shook her head. 'But you don't need to try to marry me off. I'll bet your daughter wouldn't let you do that to her if she was single.'

'You're quite right. I'll stop now, if you'll take me outside for a walk around the gardens.'

'I'd love to.'

He held her arm the entire time, a little unsteady on his feet, asking her to slow the pace a few times. They talked about the flowers showing off their glorious colours and watched a frog leap from the pond to the undergrowth, sheltering at the side to avoid anyone's gaze. When they were finished Hannah read to her companion before it was time to head back towards home.

She'd only just stepped outside the front of Butterbury Lodge when a familiar voice told her that her earlier hunch at the foot of the stairs hadn't been wrong at all.

Hannah felt heat rise in her cheeks because she hadn't seen Luke's mum since she ended her relationship with her son.

'I thought it was you.' Linda Young followed her out of the front door and shut it behind them. She smiled and extended a hand, and when Hannah met the gesture

Linda wrapped her other hand over the top. 'It's so wonderful to see you after all this time.'

A sense of relief hit Hannah so unexpectedly she barely knew what to say. 'H-how are you?' she managed.

'Good, thank you.'

Linda looked as elegant as ever. She'd always dressed well: trousers, never jeans; a blouse, never a T-shirt. Her almost-white curls bounced as they always had done, and her lips bore the same coral lipstick. Luke had vowed never to return to the boring Cotswolds once he'd sampled London, but Hannah had never been able to understand how he didn't want to spend more time at his parents' gorgeous sprawling property in the neighbouring village to Butterbury, with its enormous grounds, orangery, tennis court, and the most magnificent treehouse that afforded views of Lantern Square in the distance. Hannah and Luke had often taken picnics up to the treehouse, which had once been his teenage hangout, a way of getting away from the adults. Maplebrooke Manor was a haven away from the chaos, but Luke somehow didn't see it that way.

'It's been too long,' said Linda when Hannah still couldn't think of anything to say. 'Are you enjoying Butterbury?'

Luke must've told her she'd moved here; she hadn't kept it a secret. 'It's a beautiful part of the country.'

'Life looks like it's treating you well.'

'And I should say the same for you, you look wonderful, as always.' It had been almost a year since she'd seen Linda – eleven months, to be exact, a few days before she'd ended her relationship with Luke. Hannah hadn't seen a single member of his family after the break-up and even now she had no idea what their reaction would be to her when it had been her decision that hurt Luke so badly. She and Linda had once been so close, Luke had even joked it was as though Hannah was her offspring rather than him. 'How are you?'

'So-so. Rupert's mother came here last month.'

From what she remembered, Luke's gran had been a tiny version of his dad, very softly spoken and kind, and well into her nineties. 'I'm surprised I haven't seen her – I've been volunteering here for a while.' Then again, some residents came and went without her ever being introduced. Not everyone wanted an extra visitor; some people had plenty of family to keep them going or else would rather keep themselves to themselves.

'Unfortunately she wasn't here for very long – less than a fortnight – before she died.'

'Oh, I'm so sorry.'

Linda gave her a gentle smile. 'Thank you. But she lived a good life.'

Hannah had heard from Mr G that a woman had died soon after becoming a resident here. Bernard, who liked a bit of a joke often at his own expense, had overheard them talking and described the woman as holding the record for the fastest check-in and check-out time at Butterbury Lodge. It must have been Luke's gran. And to think, she'd never realised. She assumed Luke hadn't been here to see her, or maybe he'd intended to but she died before he could. 'Well, she came to the best place, Linda. You couldn't have chosen better.'

'Do you think so?' Linda, hand against her chest, confided, 'You hear such terrible things about old people's homes.'

This one included, apparently, but not since new management had taken over a few years ago. Since then, staff were carefully selected, and hygiene and cleanliness were top priorities. And according to Mr G, who'd been here in the bad old days, the food was now a veritable cordon bleu quality in comparison. 'I know so. It's well run and residents are properly looked after.' A waft of Linda's familiar Chanel scent carried on the air as they talked and Hannah had a momentary pang of sadness when it evoked memories of sitting chatting with her in the garden or as she prepared afternoon tea in the kitchen.

'Rupert is taking it well, although we didn't expect to settle her so quickly and then have to pack up all her things. That's why I'm here now. We've been so busy making funeral arrangements that neither of us had time to come. The staff are wonderful, though, and they've been very courteous.'

'They're a nice bunch of people.'

'Nice and chatty,' Linda agreed. That was probably down to Frankie. 'Who are you visiting?'

As they made the most of the shade afforded by the nearby willow tree, Hannah explained how she often came to read to residents or keep people company. 'Some don't have too many visitors, if any at all.'

'You were always very kind. I wish you'd stayed in touch.'

Hannah's gaze lingered on the trumpet-like flowers of the honeysuckle next to the footpath, its sweet, heady scent being enjoyed by a white butterfly fluttering between the pale orange blooms before moving to the hedgerow behind. 'I didn't feel it was my place. I thought it might be easier all round if I stayed away.' She waited for Linda to ask what happened, why things with Luke had ended, but she didn't. 'When's the funeral?'

'Tomorrow.'

'I hope it all goes well.'

'Thank you. And do pop by and see us some time. We're so close by now, it would be a shame not to.' She took Hannah's hands in hers again. 'Rupert and I would love to see you, I could make us afternoon tea.'

'You do make the best afternoon teas . . .' Hannah had made the mistake of extolling the virtues of Linda's afternoon teas to her mother and it hadn't gone down well at all. There'd been a lot of mumbling about having enough money that you had the time to perfect your cooking to such a high standard. Hannah had simply let her mum's rant continue and shared a conspiratorial eye-roll with her dad before finishing the rest of the dishes and settling down to drink coffee and eat scones in the lounge, over plates of course. Heaven forbid a crumb ever touched the furniture. Hannah felt sorry for her dad; it was almost as though the second he moved her mum would have the Dustbuster out to suck all the bounce back into a sofa cushion as though nobody's bum had dared to grace it at all.

Linda still had a hold of Hannah's hands. 'Well, the offer stands, always.'

They said their goodbyes and Linda headed off to the car park while Hannah set off down the hill towards home. Hannah had fallen in love with Butterbury after visiting the village once when she'd been staying with Luke and his parents. One visit had led to several and she'd longed to live in the area when she became tired of London. And she was glad she'd bumped into Linda today. She'd been avoiding walking past the manor ever since she moved to the area because she had no idea what to say if she ran into the woman she'd laughingly called mother-in-law for a time. But she supposed she needn't have worried. She'd never once had cause to be irritated by Luke's parents; they were a family she would've loved to have been a part of. But staying with Luke just because she felt she should, and to avoid hurting him, would never have been the right thing to do.

Realisation began to dawn as she walked down the hill, because if it was Luke's grandma's funeral tomorrow, it meant that even if Luke hadn't made it to the area for a visit to see family so far, there was no way he wouldn't do so now.

And not only had she not seen Linda since the break-up, she hadn't seen Luke since he'd yelled at her to get out and leave him the hell alone.

5

Hannah picked up her dry cleaning on Tuesday morning, but instead of boxing up her polka-dot dress once again, she slipped it onto a hanger and slotted it at one end of her wardrobe. She looked at it for a while until Bandit jumped up on the bed behind her and demanded she make as much fuss of him as she was making – as he saw it – of a collection of meaningless material.

Smokey and Bandit had come to Hannah when a close friend moved overseas and didn't want to subject them to being stuck in the hold of a plane for more than fifteen hours. And they'd been part of Hannah's life long before Luke, too. He'd never appreciated them; it was something he and her mum vehemently agreed on. Cats left hair on your clothes, they were likely to claw furniture and they were always in the way. Luke had endlessly bemoaned the fact that he had to regularly use a clothes brush on his suit jackets and Hannah could've sworn both Smokey and Bandit purposely targeted his clothes rather than hers as a kind of revenge tactic for the man who didn't really want them around. They frequently leapt up onto the computer desk too, often when he was working. And after the time Smokey was left inside too long with the cat flat locked and left a big welcome poo on the door-mat, Hannah could safely say that Luke wasn't a cat lover. But as soon as Luke was out of the picture, Smokey and Bandit had been more of a comfort to Hannah than ever. It was nice to have the company.

'You're a big softie,' she whispered to Bandit now as he stretched out as long as he possibly could, his front paws kneading her tartan-print duvet cover while she made a fuss of him before he contentedly curled himself into a ball by her pillow.

She looked once more at the dress in the wardrobe and then, leaving Bandit to it, she took the dress box down-stairs. She barely hesitated as she ripped it into pieces and pushed it into the recycling bin beside the shed. She could probably have used it for something else, but given how far she'd come with its contents, she didn't want to have it hanging around. It had been doing that for long enough.

In the dining room she got her working day off to a start by putting a care package together for Charles. He'd been so kind at the fair and she'd really enjoyed their dance, so she thought it might be a kind gesture to thank him for making her feel so welcome. She put in a pair of cush-ioned socks in case his feet still hurt from the dancing, a book of large-print crosswords she'd found at the post office yesterday, and a jar of local honey she'd picked up at the summer fair on Mrs Addington's recommendation, but not yet opened. She knew it was too sweet for her, but she'd purchased it as a support for the local farm who made it, and when she remembered Charles had told her that good quality honey was the key to his good health and ability to keep on going, she included it as part of the package. This way it wouldn't be going to waste.

After Charles's care package she answered customer queries that came via her website, uploaded a review to her blog, added photographs to her Facebook page and carried on with the batches of Christmas cards for the stationery shop. She put together another care package, this time for a soon-to-be teacher, wishing them luck on their first day of term, but as she worked her thoughts drifted again to Linda's invitation to afternoon tea. Creativity was something she and Hannah had in common, although Linda's was delivered through the art of cooking: Linda's afternoon teas really were something to behold. Maybe once things settled – or, more importantly, once she knew Luke would be safely tucked away back in London – she'd take her up on the offer. He'd been so angry the day she ended things that she wasn't sure he'd be too nice to her if he saw her again. It was the first time he'd raised his voice like that and she'd been shocked, assuming he'd seen the end coming too. But perhaps he hadn't. Maybe he'd been content to keep plodding along as they were. Then again, he didn't really know enough about her to realise that she'd started the relationship when she was vulnerable and looking for a safe harbour, and he deserved more than that. They both did.

She took out a brown box and into it put the mug she'd used her special pens on yesterday to illustrate a pencil, ruler, an apple for the teacher and a jumble of words to adorn the china: supportive, wise, bookworm, multitasking, kind, and a cluster of other appellations. It was the recipient's first teaching job and her fiancé had organised the package to wish her luck in her new position. The first item Hannah had suggested had been the mug. She could remember her primary school teacher always had a special vessel for her morning tea, with one of those captions that told her to keep calm and carry on teaching.

Luke had never been particularly enthusiastic about this care package business idea, thinking it frivolous, a pipe dream, not like accounting or an office job with a reliable salary, a pension, and perks to sustain the lifestyle they both enjoyed. He'd said she'd be wasting her business brain, but she'd batted back that she was doing something boldly entrepreneurial, questioning why he doubted her. That was a while before they ended things, but that moment really showed Hannah how different their aspirations were. He'd carried on with his rant after she told him her business plan for Tied Up with String, telling her she'd have to kiss goodbye to the stability she'd built, the outings to lavish restaurants, weekend escapes in Europe, nice cars. She hadn't pointed out that most of those things were what he had chosen, not her. She'd merely been swept along without thinking about it too much.

With the mug all wrapped up, Hannah added in a luxury hand cream to the package, a personalised coaster, some exquisite chocolates decorated with gold leaf, and a leather-bound notebook.

When the doorbell chimed a couple of hours later, Hannah made sure neither cat was in the dining room to jump on the table and ruin those cards she had laid out, and went to answer it.

'Joe!' She hadn't expected the handsome doctor to be on the other side and she almost wished she'd had a chance to check her appearance before opening the door.

'I appreciate it's unusual for customers to turn up on your doorstep, but I was passing, so . . .'

It was definitely unusual, and despite her frustrations with him she wasn't sorry he'd taken the opportunity. 'What can I do for you?'

'I need a gift – well, a care package.'

'For yourself?' He seemed unusually unsure of himself, the complete opposite to the first time they'd met on the street when he gave her a piece of his mind, or when they'd danced so intimately at the fair.

'For a friend of mine. Would you rather I sent the order via email?' He shook his head as though annoyed with himself for turning up. 'Sorry to have disturbed you, I'll send it from my phone.'

'Don't be silly, you're here now. Come in. Cup of tea? Coffee? Cold drink?' Words tripped off her tongue in an attempt to disguise any discomfort. And for a fleeting moment her mum's voice came into her head. Now this man she would approve of with his sharp suits and fancy car.

'I'm fine, thank you. I was out walking, clearing my head, but I'm due back in the surgery in half an hour.'

'Right you are.' She changed tack and instead of going into the kitchen, led him to the dining room. Before the Lantern Square fair, all she'd been able to see him as was the man who'd bitten her head off the day she moved in, the impatient driver who'd tooted his horn at her dad, and the arrogant individual who had snatched the radio station slot away from her. Now, she couldn't help but associate him with heady summer nights, music and laughter.

She pulled out the stool at the far end of the table for him, the opposite end to her cards lined up and ready to be boxed once she was completely sure they were ready.

She never liked to put them in too early for fear of crushing the design and the more they were handled, the more she panicked that she would dislodge something and ruin all her hard work.

She pulled her own stool up at a right angle to him and grabbed the notepad and pen from the centre of the table, flipped away from the current scribbles and onto a fresh page. 'It's probably easiest to take the recipient's details first.'

'Right.'

This was going to be hard work if he couldn't give her the basics without hand-holding. 'Name?'

'Vanessa.' When he rubbed a hand against the side of his face she heard the scratchy sound of the same stubble that had grazed her cheek when they'd danced and he'd dipped his head as he tried to talk to her above the noise of the music. 'Vanessa Sullivan.'

'Address.'

He reeled off an address in Tetbury.

'And is the care package for a special occasion? A birthday perhaps? New job?' Judging by the way it was so difficult to get him to part with information, prompts were entirely necessary.

'Just because . . .'

'Right.' She wrote Just Because on the paper and underlined it. This was why email was easier: she didn't have to face the person and ask; usually, when the order was placed and discussion ensued, the other person was far more forthcoming when hiding behind a computer screen.

'I'm not being too helpful, am I?'

'It might be easier to look at the website and email me

through some details,' she suggested. 'I need to know a bit about Vanessa to make sure I design the right package for her. I can include a personalised gift message if it helps, or you can stay anonymous, it all depends what you prefer.'

'I'll email you then.' And he stood up to go.

'I'm sorry, I hope I haven't offended you.'

He swished a hand in front of him. Despite being dressed in his usual attire – smart trousers, shirt and tie – he looked much more ruffled than usual. 'No, not at all. I'll be normal and email. Turning up at your house probably wasn't a good idea.'

As Hannah led him to the door she remembered what Miriam had said – how he'd always been awkward when it came to social situations at school and it took him a while to find his groove. Perhaps it was the same with someone he didn't know that well, although while they'd danced he seemed to be the more confident one of them, and how he coped as a GP made her mind boggle. She couldn't help wondering about Vanessa, too, and whether she was the girl who'd been at the dance with him. But it wasn't any of her business. Her only concern should be putting together the care package for the best possible outcome for recipient and customer.

When they reached the front door she took a business card from the pile on top of the ornate key box and handed it to him. 'My email address is on there, let me know the details. And take a look at the gifts on my website, it might spark some ideas if you're more comfortable making suggestions. I have some items in stock but I can look for others or make items too.'

He stepped out into the sunshine but turned back again. 'Thank you for the dance at the fair.'

Flummoxed that he'd even broached the subject, she smiled awkwardly. 'I had fun. And my dress went to the dry cleaners and came back just fine, so . . .'

'So I'm off the hook?'

'It was an accident and I overreacted.' He was about to say something else but Hannah's gaze had already drifted off across his shoulder, past the little gate, over the pavement and the street to the other side, so she wouldn't have heard another word.

Because the only person she could see now was Luke. Here in Butterbury. In front of Lantern Cottage.

And there was no hiding now.

6

Unlike Joe, Luke did accept the offer of a drink. Hannah's hand shook as she filled the kettle to make a cup of tea for each of them. 'Earl Grey with a dash of milk,' he'd recited in answer to her question, although she could remember his preference anyway – he'd had enough cups of tea with her for it to be ingrained in her mind.

In the corner of her eye she saw him roll up the sleeves of the tailored shirt he was wearing. Luke had always been a smart dresser, even when he wasn't at work, wearing designer jeans and a T-shirt with a brand name at the very least. She wondered if he was looking at her now, confused as she moved around in slouchy clothes, the way she dressed more often than not these days. When they'd lived together he'd often bought her expensive clothes when they were out and about and she'd grown used to wearing them, but it was almost as though the second she left him and the corporate world behind, it called for a complete overhaul of her wardrobe to dress down rather than up.

'I'm sorry about your gran.' She poured boiling water over the top of the teabag in one cup and then in the other. As sad as she'd been to hear about her death, on this occasion it did make it easier to know what to say to him.

'Thanks. She'd only just moved up to Butterbury Lodge and Mum said she was happy there. We were set to celebrate her birthday next month.' So, he'd have been coming to the village anyway. 'You always loved it here, I remember.'

The look they shared made her shift uncomfortably as she took the milk from the fridge. He knew her well. And the last time she'd seen him he'd yelled at her in anger, frustration, and perhaps sadness that their relationship was ending through no choice of his.

Hannah had fallen in love with the Cotswolds and the first time she'd seen Lantern Square it had made quite an impression. One night when they were staying at Maplebrooke Manor, she and Luke had climbed up to his treehouse with its veranda just wide enough to fit them both, and she'd seen clusters of lights in the distance. It had been the coldest day of the year, with snow threatening to fall over the next week, but the lights of Lantern Square had made the darkened skies glow, and when he'd described the village to her she'd insisted they go and see it the following day. They'd driven there, but while she was in awe of the tiny shop fronts, the welcoming square, the quintessential thatched roofs of some homes and the chocolate-box charm of the countryside, he'd been anxious to make an early start back to London. Hannah had never forgotten the place, and when her former business had been scuppered by her supposed friend and they'd called it quits, and Hannah had ended things with Luke, she knew it was only a matter of time before she made Lantern Square her home.

When Hannah told her parents where she intended to move to, her dad had been worried about the proximity to Luke's family. 'I know you love the Cotswolds, but it's so close to the Youngs,' he said one morning over waffles and golden syrup. Her mum had been fussing around, wiping the table for sticky bits, glancing at the floor to ensure no crumbs made their way down there.

'They're not the Mafia, Dad.' Hannah had demolished the waffle so quickly he hadn't had time to make her the second but pushed it into the toaster before her mum could put the packet and accompaniments away. Hannah bet her mum couldn't wait for her to move out of home, again, and take all her messy arts and crafts stuff with her, not to mention the cats she didn't have a nice word to say about that got under her feet.

'I'm worried Luke took the break-up badly,' her dad went on.

'He was upset, but he's hardly likely to be looking for revenge. You like Luke, remember?'

Her dad nodded and she was reminded that the statement hadn't been strictly true. Her mum had always loved him, but her dad seemed reserved and she knew it stemmed from his own background. Luke came from money; he seemed to carry an air of privilege with him that didn't always come over well, especially not with her dad who'd worked so hard to provide a home and put food on the table for his family. Luke and Hannah had grown up in very different circumstances. Luke's family had enjoyed space to roam around the house itself as well as in the gardens. Hannah had spent her childhood in the house her parents still lived in; a narrow, terraced house in Whitby with a cute cottage garden, its interior immaculate if a little squashed. Her mum became more and more house-proud as the years went on and her attitude shifted up a notch. When Hannah and her brother, Brendan, were little their mum had been relaxed, almost happy-go-lucky, but as they got into their teens and started at a local grammar school it was as though she felt she had to compete. She and her husband had both spent their childhoods in council houses, on rundown estates where the local comprehensive school struggled to attract kids who wanted a better future. Hannah thought her parents should be proud that they'd both worked hard and managed to buy their own place, but instead, when Hannah had brought a friend home from school, a friend whose parents had a holiday home in the south of France, her mum had told her not to mention they'd once lived on a council estate. Hannah had laughed and her mum had given her that stern look, the one she usually reserved for when one of them had done something very naughty, like the time Brendan had grabbed one of her mum's blouses from the linen basket, mistaking its colour for a tea towel, and used it to mop up a coffee spill on the kitchen floor. Hannah often wondered how her dad could be so down to earth and her mum so highly strung – and, if she was honest, a bit of a snob.

Hannah had smiled at her dad and thanked him for the second waffle. Dale Simmons was far more content now he'd retired from the public sector. He was a financially secure family man with a good pension and had even taken his wife on a cruise to the Norwegian Fjords. They'd both always longed to go but had never been able to afford to holiday outside of the UK in more than twenty years. Hannah had been allowed to tell anyone she liked about that one.

'He's an OK lad,' her dad had said that day as she finished her waffle. 'Just not for you.'

Now, Hannah handed Luke the mug of tea and leaned against the kitchen bench in Lantern Cottage. It seemed too personal to go through to the lounge and the soft sofas she liked to curl up on in the evening. It seemed too welcoming to take him out to the bistro table set in the garden where she often whiled away a lazy afternoon or evening. And if they got too comfortable she'd only think about how Luke had once given her a much-needed sense of security and safety, and she'd forget the reasons why she'd ended their relationship in the first place.

'How did the funeral go?'

'It went as smoothly as it possibly could. Gran was cremated, so we're going to scatter her ashes on the Suffolk coast, her favourite place.'

'That sounds nice.' She remembered his family had a holiday house there. They'd stayed in it once. 'It's beautiful up that way.'

'Do you remember the storm in Woodbridge?' It seemed he remembered their holidays too.

She smiled, cradling her mug of tea between her hands. 'I'll never forget it.'

'You were so frightened you asked to go home.'

'Only because I heard those roof tiles coming off.'

'We were better off staying in than we were venturing out.'

From memory, they'd had a very good time staying inside and when his gaze held hers, Hannah set down her mug. 'Luke, why did you come? Here, to the cottage I mean.' Since she'd collected the last of her things when he wasn't around and they'd altered the lease on the flat so that it was in his name only, neither of them had exchanged so much as a text.

He followed suit and put down his own mug – although knowing how he couldn't bear his tea anything other than piping hot, he'd probably end up leaving the rest. 'Mum said she'd seen you, and I thought it was about time.'

She shook her head, cringing at how distraught he'd been when she last saw him. 'You were so angry with me.'

'I'd just been dumped, that's why.'

'You told me you never wanted to see me again, you called me a few names, if I remember rightly.'

'I'm sorry, Hannah. You didn't deserve me to say those things. I reacted badly, but I came here today to clear the air, if you'll let me.'

Luke's parents were lovely and their only fault, that Hannah could see, was that they rarely told their son 'no'. He'd grown up thinking that if he ever wanted something, there'd be a way to get it. It was an attitude that served him well in his job as a management analyst, where he often had to give advice and recommendations and prove that his way would be the best way. He took no crap in the boardroom, was never afraid to speak his mind, and he had a way of persuading people round to his point of view. It was probably why, when they first got together and she was so vulnerable, they'd hit it off immediately. She'd needed someone to lead the way and he'd certainly done that.

They'd only come close to a heated argument once in their time together, which, Hannah had begun to realise over time, was because she usually went along with what he wanted. At least, she had until she'd left her job and begun a new venture that didn't involve him. He'd once confided in her about his plans for his parents' home here in the Cotswolds. They'd been to a company function, she, on his arm, impressing the bosses, and they'd both had a lot of champagne. He told Hannah that instead of keeping Maplebrooke Manor as a home, he wanted to turn it into a business when he finally inherited the place. He figured that in years to come his work in London would be done, that hungry twenty-somethings battling their way into the profession would be too much for him, but he still wanted to be a businessman. He planned to open a luxury spa and his parents had the perfect land in the ideal location. Hannah had told him it was ludicrous, that it would spoil the landscape and he probably wouldn't get permission from the necessary councils. He'd told her it was decades off yet anyway and asked why she was so bloody unsupportive for something he dreamed about. It was the first time he'd slept on the sofa in the flat, nowhere near her. His mum had had a similar reaction to Hannah's a couple of months later when he began talking about it, thinking she was out of earshot. That time, Hannah had kept her mouth firmly shut.

'It was some time ago now,' she told him as he lifted his mug to his lips. She wasn't surprised to see him change his mind and set it down again when he felt how tepid it was. 'You seem happy now, is work going well?' He'd come to make peace and the least she could do was let him.

'It is.' He tipped the rest of his tea down the sink. 'And how's your business going?'

Pleased he was even interested, especially when Smokey came trotting into the kitchen and wound his way around Luke's ankles, she said, 'It's going really well – care packages and greeting cards have taken over my entire dining room.'

'I'll confess, I knew you were doing greeting cards. I

saw your design and signature in the stationery shop on the outskirts of Tetbury.'

For some reason his revelation really lifted her spirits. He could see the success she was making of Tied Up with String, the business he'd doubted. 'Castle Cards were the first to take my designs, just a small order at first, but more have followed and I'm hoping it continues.'

'Good for you, it's great you're doing so well.'

She glowed with the praise. 'Thanks.'

'And this cottage,' he said, looking up at the beams running the length of the kitchen ceiling. 'It's a lovely home.'

'You know, I find it hard to believe sometimes that I once thought I could make a go of an accountancy business. It . . . well, it wasn't me.'

'It wasn't your friend, either. Not when push came to shove.' Luke had never got on with her best friend Georgia, even less so when Georgia had stuffed things up for them. 'You did well to get out.'

'I appreciated your support back then, with Georgia, I mean.' Hannah hated confrontation, had thought the accountancy business would be a pleasant arena to be in. But it had turned out to be as fierce and competitive as any other industry, particularly when her partner wasn't exactly on her side.

'I was happy to help.'

She moved to the sink to rinse the mugs, trying to hide her confusion. She hadn't expected Luke to be kind and understanding. She had been so sure of her decision to end their relationship at the time, but now she was reminded of how supportive he'd been during the time they were together, and a little part of her questioned whether she'd made a huge mistake. Her mum certainly thought so; she'd told her enough times that it wasn't too late to sort all this out.

When she said nothing, he changed the subject. 'Mum mentioned asking you to afternoon tea.'

Hannah smiled, despite herself. 'Her afternoon teas *are* legendary.' She'd never forgotten her first one, the delicate sandwich selection, chocolate eclairs filled with melt-in-the-mouth cream.

'Will you come?'

She'd hurt him badly and never really forgiven herself. What was the harm in having afternoon tea and friendly conversation with people she knew so well?

'Hannah? At least say you'll think about it. Perhaps not when I'm around this time, but another time, soon. I feel we ended things so suddenly. I know you were upset, your career was up in the air. But I want the chance to at least be friends with you, even if it's never going to be anything more.'

Could it ever be more than a friendship? Not seeing him for months had convinced her she'd made the right decision but when he was here now, right in front of her in the cosy kitchen of Lantern Cottage, her feelings were all over the place.

'I promise I'll think about it,' she said at last. It was the least she could do when he was trying to make peace after all this time. Because not only had he been her boyfriend, she'd once agreed to marry this man. He'd been her fiancé, she'd worn a ring on her finger, making her decision to leave him all the more brutal.

But how could she have possibly gone ahead and married him, when she knew she'd always be in love with someone else?

7

As Hannah drove along, following the winding road from Butterbury towards the next village along in the Cotswolds, she took in the breathtaking views of the surrounding countryside. The nearby fields were still bursting with a mixture of verdant greens, while hues of mustard yellow hinted that seasons were about to change from the tail end of summer to the beauty of autumn. Cool air filtered in through the windows and she almost forgot to be nervous about her visit to Maplebrooke Manor until she indicated to turn off the road and into the driveway.

Ever since he turned up at Lantern Cottage, Luke had continued to pester her about the offer of afternoon tea with him and his family – and Hannah had continued to wriggle out of the invitation. Whenever the request had come her way via text message, she'd always found another excuse. But yesterday she'd bumped into Luke and his dad outside the pub, and when he invited her to his parents' home yet again, this time she'd found herself saying yes.

Maplebrooke Manor's grand proportions continued all the way down the impressive driveway. Flanked by mature oak trees whose leaves had already started to turn golden and crisp, and floated down nonchalantly in the light

September breeze, Hannah drove ever closer to the house she'd once known so well. While she was still sitting in her run-around, fun-size purple Fiat 500 which spent most of its days sitting idle outside her home at Lantern Cottage, unless she needed to see a supplier or shop for specific care package items, she felt safe. Safe from having to confront her feelings head-on when she saw Luke again. She'd hesitated about coming here, not because she didn't feel welcome or because she wanted to avoid his mum, Linda, who'd been perfectly civil when they'd bumped into each other in the summer, but because she wasn't sure Luke's feelings were one hundred per cent platonic. And she couldn't say with absolute certainty that hers were either.

The gravel crunched beneath her tyres as she turned in front of the house and parked up beside Luke's familiar BMW, although on closer inspection she realised there were subtle differences and he must've upgraded since they were together. The last one had white leather seats, this one had cream; the previous model had a walnut dashboard, this one had leather and the dials looked more sophisticated. He must be doing well and Hannah found herself feeling pleased for him, glad he hadn't fallen apart after she left.

Hannah had fallen in love with this house and its grounds the first time she ever came here. She and her one-time best friend Georgia had been out in London to celebrate the launch of their new joint venture, being plied with cocktails by Georgia's friend Jason, when he'd invited them both to his mate's party in the Cotswolds, telling them the more the merrier. Up for adventure, Georgia and Hannah had come along to this amazing manor in the country with a live band, stunning grounds and more people than Hannah had thought possible for one family to ever know. Hannah had soon found a treehouse hidden in the garden, and was looking for the best way to climb up when she'd heard a voice behind her, declaring that only 'very special people' were allowed up there. She'd turned to find a man leaning against a tree, ash-grey eyes dancing with mischief. Luke had grabbed her attention at once with his quick wit and captivating good looks, and Hannah had felt a stirring of hope that she might find happiness again. For the first time in a long while, she had fun, and it was beneath that treehouse that they'd shared their first kiss.

Now, unsure of what the visit would bring, she crunched across the driveway peppered with acorns that had dropped from the mighty oaks nearby. She pressed the button on the ornate brass doorbell and it gave a melodic chime – the kind of sound that let you know you were about to step into a home so grand and vast that it would be easy to get lost within its walls. During her visits to Maplebrooke Hannah had got lost on the way to the bathroom more times than she cared to remember, and on her first stay had opened the door to the study, covered in only a bath towel, to find a bewildered Rupert, Luke's dad, looking at her in confusion. That was the first time they'd met and it certainly broke the ice, with all of them seeing the very funny side.

Linda greeted Hannah moments after the melody at the front door came to its conclusion. 'Hannah, welcome.' She hugged her guest and invited her inside. 'I'm so glad you came, we're due a proper catch-up.'

'Thank you for inviting me.'

'I hope you didn't just come for the food.' It was Rupert,

folder of papers in hand, heading down the L-shaped staircase from the partially galleried landing above. He greeted Hannah with as much enthusiasm as his wife. 'I'm sorry I can't hang around, off to make a house call. Birthing a horse,' he announced.

Rupert was in his early seventies now. A veterinary surgeon renowned in these parts and appreciated by farmers dotted along the outskirts of Butterbury and beyond, he would've more than earned his retirement, but it seemed there was no stopping him. Even if he hadn't had a medical emergency Hannah suspected he would've grabbed a couple of petite sandwiches from the afternoon tea, had a cuppa and then darted out on some errand or another.

'Next time,' she said without really thinking.

'I'll hold you to that,' said Rupert before he disappeared out the door. 'It's lovely to see you back again.'

She didn't have much time to panic that Luke's family might think this was the first visit of many, that she and Luke might be picking up where they left off, because Luke appeared with a beaming smile.

'Hannah. Good to see you.' He came from the corridor to the left, which if she remembered rightly, led to the kitchen and then into the orangery. She'd always thought it so grand when she first visited and had asked in a hushed voice why that particular room wasn't called a conservatory. Her parents had one of those and Hannah had never been sure of the difference. Rupert had overheard the debate and shared some of the history of the manor house, told her how years ago having an orangery was a sign of prestige, how once upon a time it was used to house citrus trees in the winter months. Greenhouses had taken over some of the job these days, but the room would always bear its original name. He was as passionate about this home as he was about all things veterinarian and following the orangery education he'd taken Hannah around the rest of the manor pointing out features that were hundreds of years old, and newer additions that had been sympathetically chosen to fit in.

Linda lead Hannah and Luke through to the drawing room where in the winter a roaring fire would be going and bathing the library shelves in a soft glow. But today, the mild temperatures didn't call for it and Hannah sank comfortably down onto the cream sofa.

'This place is still as wonderful as I remember,' she told Luke when Linda went off to make tea for each of them.

'Home sweet home.' He sat down next to her. 'And it's wonderful to have some time out.'

Her gaze flicked to his because Luke buzzed on the constant vibe London provided, he'd never once sought solace in the country. 'You must be feeling your age.'

'Cheeky.' He nudged her arm and then lay his own across the back of the sofa. 'Can't believe I'm thirty-three. I still think of myself as a kid when I'm here. Mum fusses around as though I've no idea how to do anything for myself.'

'She likes looking after you, I suspect.'

'I think she likes to stay busy. Dad still works plenty of hours, she has this place to manage and she volunteers with the Women's Institute.'

Hannah had once thought Luke got his conscientious streak from Rupert, but perhaps a little of it came from Linda too. When they were together, Luke had always been restless, he'd wanted a piece of everything. If he wasn't at work he was booking a fancy restaurant, if they weren't eating out he'd be enjoying wine, simultaneously researching what variety to purchase next even though they had barely any room at the flat to store it. And when he wasn't doing either of those things he was travelling for work or going to the gym. Some people joined a gym, paid an annual membership and used it once, twice or never at all. But not Luke: he was regimented, and made it at least four times a week whether it be very early morning, noon, or before he turned in at night.

Linda brought in the afternoon tea and caught the end of their conversation before recounting the times in Luke's childhood when he'd barely been able to sit still. 'He was terrible on a long car journey, always fidgeting, always asking questions including the inevitable When are we going to get there?'

Hannah smiled and laughed through the ensuing anecdotes, safe in the bosom of this family that at one time she'd never thought she would leave. Linda asked after her parents, they talked about her settling in to Butterbury and both Luke and Linda wanted to know all about Tied Up with String: how it worked, and her involvement with Castle Cards, a well-known retailer in Tetbury.

'It sounds as though you've built up a lot of trust, a good reputation,' said Luke. 'I'm really impressed.'

'Thank you. It's taken time but I'm getting there.'

'I'm intrigued.' Linda smiled, holding her delicate teacup in one hand, the fancy saucer in her other. Only the finest porcelain for this house, not like the mismatching mug collection at Lantern Cottage where any guests were guaranteed to get different pieces of crockery. It was something else her mum bemoaned every time she visited, which thankfully wasn't all that often. 'What gave you the idea to start the business?'

Hannah froze, stumbling over her response. She couldn't tell either of them the truth about the beginning of Tied Up with String – she'd never told anyone. 'Oh, I read an article about care packages somewhere and then the idea spiralled. I did some initial research, followed by more in-depth studies of the consumer market, and used my savings to get started. I had enough for a deposit on my cottage, I found a temporary accounts job so I could secure a mortgage while I built up the business.'

'You went back to accounting?' Luke didn't bother to hide his surprise.

'It was very short-lived, while I was living back with my parents. I also worked the night shift at a supermarket stacking shelves.'

'Sounds exhausting,' said Linda.

'It was, but it was worth it. The business picked up, I got the mortgage, and then I could move down this way.'

'Tied Up with String is an adorable name for your business,' Linda smiled. 'And Castle Cards are one of the most exclusive stationery stores around. I always buy my cards there.'

'I was stunned when they approached me, but I'm hoping the orders continue.'

'I'm sure they will,' Luke put in. Hannah was amazed by his interest, making her wonder why he'd never been this supportive before. Perhaps he had changed. He'd always been kind, loving and there for her in so many ways, but he'd never backed her creative side especially when it came to the possibility of doing it as a job.

'And to think, you could still be in accountancy,' said

Linda. 'Life's too short to do something you don't enjoy. I'm enjoying more time in the gardens here and less paper-work for Rupert as he prepares to retire.'

'Your home and gardens are wonderful, as they always were,' said Hannah, looking at the rolling lawn outside the window.

'Thank you, we love it.' She looked around the room as though committing this part of their home to memory. 'This will be Luke's one day when we're gone, and the garden will be his to manage. Maybe he'll have children running around,' she teased.

Unlikely. Luke wasn't what you'd call the paternal type. Irritating cats were just the tip of the iceberg for him, unless he'd mellowed since they split up. 'Not if he turns this place into—'

'Mum, enough talk about me and my future,' Luke interrupted, 'you know I'd rather not think of you and Dad popping your clogs just yet.' He didn't meet Hannah's gaze but she felt sure of what he'd do if she mentioned the spa word again. Hannah had been about to make a joke about the suggestion he made years ago of turning Maplebrooke Manor into some kind of luxury spa hotel, but probably a good job he'd stopped her, because the last time his mum had overheard their conversation along those lines, her exact words had been Over My Dead Body. And Hannah hadn't exactly been impressed. This home was magnificent; why he wouldn't want to enjoy a future here was incomprehensible to her as well as to Linda.

They chatted some more, avoiding conversations about the future of the house, and Hannah stayed far longer than she'd intended. Linda's afternoon tea didn't disappoint either. They ate roast beef with horseradish sandwiches, free-range egg and watercress brioche, freshly baked scones with clotted cream and the homemade blackberry jam Hannah remembered so well. Linda had sent jars their way with every season: blackberry jam in autumn, plum in the winter, and raspberry, strawberry or elderflower jams in the warmer months. Upon the delicate china tiered plates, there was also a good selection of sweet bites including Linda's renowned blackberry, lemon and frangipane tart as well as marbled coffee cake, and by the time Hannah set down her silver fork on the edge of the same duck-egg blue china that matched her teacup filled with a second cup of Darjeeling tea, she thought she'd never eat again.

Linda kept both Hannah and Luke talking for another hour before she left them to it when it was time for her to go and join the other ladies in the local WI and carry on with their plans for a Murder Mystery Evening. Apparently last year's event had been a sell-out and they were hoping for the same to happen this time round.

It was such a gorgeous afternoon that the gardens surrounding the manor house couldn't be ignored and Hannah accepted Luke's suggestion to walk outside and work off some of the sumptuous feast they'd just eaten.

'I thought it was afternoon tea, not a four-course meal,' Hannah joked as she looked at the vast green space she wouldn't have a hope of staying on top of if it belonged to her. Despite the turn in season from summer to autumn right around the corner, the garden was still awash with colour.

'You know Mum, she likes to spoil people.'

Linda had always looked after her guests and in some ways coming here had felt like a hotel break. The peace, the quiet, the space. 'How does she manage this garden so well?'

'She has a gardening team, although she still does a lot of it herself. Never understood where she got the patience.' Luke pulled his sunglasses down as they followed the pavers beneath the wisteria arch on the side of the courtyard area.

'That's right,' she grinned, 'you're not into gardening.'

'That's why we were a good match,' he winked.

The familiarity jolted her for a moment. It was a reminder of the intimacy they'd once shared and she'd walked away from. She tried to keep her mind on their friendship rather than anything else. 'I think we did well in London with the space we had. I grew some herbs, a chilli plant.'

'True,' he conceded.

They passed the bed of apricot roses that followed the curve around the outside of the manor house. Beyond those was a potting shed, a bigger outhouse which Hannah knew contained plenty of machinery for the gardens – a ride-on lawnmower to tackle the acres they had here, a hedge trimmer, a leaf blower, rakes and forks and all manner of paraphernalia for bigger jobs as well as small.

'I have a little garden now, but I need my local gardener to help out,' she admitted. 'I wish I was a bit more knowledgeable about it all really.'

'Mum could always give you some tips.'

'I'm sure she knows plenty.' Part of her would love that, the other part of her was jumping up and down waving a red flag warning her not to get too involved with Luke again. And that included his family. 'With Rhys's help – he's the gardener – my aim is to keep the space looking as good as it did when I first moved in. The garden was one of the wow factors for me. It's compact, but suits my needs.'

'So this place would be too big for you?'

'It's too big for most people.' She ignored any attempt from Luke to make this more personal than it needed to be as they continued walking towards the treehouse.

'A kids' paradise,' Hannah surmised as they wound their way through the copse of trees surrounding the wooden structure. Well-kept flower beds led the way with clusters of vibrant pinks and purples and creams. Soon this place would be filled with crunchy leaves and the path to the treehouse impossible to take silently as the rustling gave away any approaching visitor.

'It sure was.'

Hannah picked up a leaf that floated past her shoulder, not yet crisp enough to break when you squeezed it in your palm. She twirled its stem between her fingers. 'Luke, why did you stop me mentioning the spa idea to your mum just now?'

'You're really asking?'

'I remember how upset she was when she heard you mention it the first time, but it was just a pie in the sky idea, wasn't it?'

'Of course it was. But I didn't want to upset her all over again.'

'Knowing your mum, she'd laugh it off.'

'Didn't want to take the risk,' he smiled. 'She's been exhausted working for Dad and running this place, she deserves a bit of peace and quiet.'

'She certainly does.' Hannah looked at the wooden structure nestled in amongst the limbs of one of the biggest oak trees in the garden. 'I don't think this has changed at all.'

'It was built to last.' His almost-black hair caught shafts of sunlight through the branches above. 'Mum organises plenty of charity lunches via the WI and kids come and play in the treehouse. In fact, I think Maplebrooke Manor is almost better known for its treehouse hidden in the woods than for its grandeur.'

'Woods?'

'I know they're not, strictly speaking, but that's what these gardens have come to be known as.'

'Is your mum heavily involved with the WI then?'

'Very involved. I don't know what she'd have done without them. She had a serious road accident last year.'

'I never knew.'

'We haven't been in touch.' His soft smile that reminded her of when they'd first got together came her way, the same smile that had drawn her in and made her feel safe. 'She was out of action for a while and it nearly drove her crazy. She was frightened to get behind the wheel for a long time.'

Hannah felt bad she hadn't known about the accident, she wished she could've helped in some way. What was it they often said? You didn't just marry the person, you marry the family. She'd ended things with Luke before they'd committed to each other through marriage, but their long-term relationship had still brought his family very close.

'Mum has always been too busy with this place and supporting my dad's business to do much for herself but she'd begun to dabble in involving herself with the community via the WI when she was recovering and not able to get out and about or work in the garden. The work she did at the computer, researching, organising events and coordinating activities – well, it kept her mind busy and was a good distraction.'

'She seems really well now.'

'She is. It's good to see. And these gardens have kept her going as well as the charity lunches she holds here. I can't see her stopping those for a long while yet, although I've heard her say to Dad a few times that this place is far too big for the two of them to be rattling around in.'

Hannah was having trouble adjusting to this new version of the man she'd only ever known as work-hungry, a little self-absorbed at times. He seemed to have changed and she wondered whether her leaving had made him step back and assess what he really wanted out of life. She enjoyed the way this version of Luke rambled on about the majesty of the gardens, his mum's love of this home, how it was so wonderful others could appreciate all her hard work when she opened it up for events.

'Do you think retirement is on the cards for your dad?' She reached out to feel the vibrant pink, conical flower petals of the nearby snapdragon. She knew the name of this one because Rhys had planted some in one of the beds near Lantern Square.

'It should be.' Luke leaned up against one of the posts of the treehouse.

'I can't believe he's off birthing a horse today.'

'I can.'

'Does he ever take it easy, sit in a chair, relax?'

'Not often. But today he's helping to birth a horse rather than doing it all himself. He's in the process of handing over the business or at least taking a step back.'

'He and your mum deserve some time to take it easy.'

'Not sure how mum will cope having him under her feet all day.' He looked up at the treehouse entrance. 'Wonder how many spiders have taken up residence.' A look of naughtiness crossed his face. 'Want to see?'

'We can't go up there!'

'Why?'

'It might not be safe.'

'I told you, Mum has charity events and kids come up here all the time. She wouldn't let them do that if it wasn't safe. And Dad built this with castle-like foundations, made to withstand anything. It's survived snowstorms, bolts of lightning—'

'I tell you what. You go check for spiders and when I know the coast is clear I'll come up.' She hadn't intended any of this. But all of a sudden she was reminded of the reasons why she'd once fallen for him, and she allowed herself to get caught up in the moment.

Luke deftly climbed up one of the rear posts of the treehouse using the footholds his father had put there for the purpose. He put his arms out when he reached the top. 'Wasn't sure I could still scramble up here quite so quickly,' he called down, before making his way around the narrow veranda to the door and the space in front where he slowly let down the rope ladder. He'd told her once that part of the adventure when he was young was to use the rope ladder during the day and then pull it back up again like a drawbridge at night so that nobody around could reach him or trespass. Of course, it wouldn't have taken much for anyone else to find the same footholds he'd used, but the adventure had had him captivated.

'Come on up,' he coaxed from the top.

'Do the spider check first,' she reminded him, shielding the top of her face to stop the shaft of sunlight coming through the trees preventing her from seeing anything.

He disappeared inside and called, 'Coast clear,' not long after.

Hannah put her foot on the bottom rung, then her other on the next, gripping the wooden sides as she heard Luke laughing.

'Come on, you used to be up here before I was.' They'd often raced, her on the ladder, him using the footholds.

'I'm out of practice.' It was wobblier than she remembered, higher off the ground too. But when she was almost there he offered her a hand to steady her up the last rung and onto the safety of the platform. She ducked to go inside the bigger-than-expected space. 'Wow, it's still really cosy. Bit warm though.'

'Hasn't been aired in a while.' He opened the window the other side.

There wasn't much up here. A small bookshelf held a few Roald Dahl classics – *Charlie and the Chocolate Factory*, *The Twits* – as well as a mishmash of other genres and titles. There was a small desk where a pot of crayons had been knocked over and Hannah stacked them up again as Luke took the cushions from the miniature couch outside and banged them to rid them of dust.

'Bean bags should be safe,' he said when he came inside again.

'They weren't in here last time.' She sat on the black beanbag chair decorated with silver stars and Luke slumped down onto the black one decorated with sky-blue crescent moon shapes.

'Mum put them up here for the kids.'

'It's so peaceful.'

'I did a lot of school work inside these four walls,' he recalled, looking around him, drinking it all in.

'I remember you saying. Must've been lovely. You can't even hear the road much from here. I battled my brother's stereo system and the sounds of my mum hoovering every morning as I tried to do my studies.'

'How is your brother?'

'He's good. I miss him but he's busy hiking in Scotland with his girlfriend and when he called last night he was talking about interrailing through Europe next.'

'He sounds as though he's really caught the travel bug.'

'I doubt he'll be around at Christmas this year,' she grinned. 'He's contemplating trying snowboarding.'

'Good for him. And I'm glad you're settled again now, you know, after leaving London.' The reminder that they had a deeper history than a handful of memories was all too easy to ignore making small talk about everything else.

'I really am. And how is London?'

'Did I mention I'm in line for another promotion?'

'That's wonderful.' And she really meant it. He'd always worked very hard to get where he was.

'Sometimes I wonder . . .' His voice trailed off as he looked beyond the window, 'I wonder what it's all about. Coming here reminds me there's another world outside the rat race.'

In some ways she felt she'd got to know more about Luke today than she had in the whole time they were together. Maybe it was the country air, drawing things out of him that were suppressed in the city. 'It's a different kind of life. Sometimes I worry that the care package orders will dry up, but I've got greeting cards and I hand-make items too so there are always different avenues. I do get in a bit of a panic in the quiet times, but I try to remind myself there are peaks as well as troughs.'

'You've got a good business head on your shoulders.'

'I do my best.'

When the sky began to darken Hannah realised how long she'd been here at Maplebrooke Manor, her earlier apprehension dissolving as she'd relaxed with Luke and his family. 'I should really be going.'

'You don't have to.'

'I'd better. I have more work to do or I'll never finish the orders I have to fulfil, and Smokey and Bandit will need a top-up of water,' she rambled. She'd already seen to it before she left the house, but the more they sat here, the more familiar it began to feel and she wasn't entirely comfortable.

Luke led the way and climbed down the ladder before holding it steady for Hannah as she tentatively took each rung slowly. It was far easier than on the way up, with someone literally watching her back.

She stepped onto solid ground, breathed a sigh of relief and turned. Luke was still standing close enough that she could feel his chest beneath his Abercrombie and Fitch T-shirt.

'Remember our first kiss?' He didn't move away as the breeze lifted her hair from her face.

Hannah gulped. How could she forget? She'd fallen for him quickly that day, right here in this very spot.

And under his spell, exactly as she'd been at his party that day, their lips met again.

8

Hannah hung up the phone with a smile on her face. She'd stopped work at the dining table in Lantern Cottage to take a call from Linda, and they'd had the kind of lovely chat you have when the woman who'd always felt like an extension of family calls to say thank you. Hannah hadn't seen Luke since the day at Maplebrooke Manor and the unexpected kiss, and she'd ignored the text messages he'd sent over the last few weeks as her thoughts continued to swing like a giant pendulum of confusion. But she'd been grasping at how to thank his mum for the beautiful afternoon tea put on in her honour, and so yesterday she'd posted Linda a care package filled with bergamot and field-mint hand cream, the novelty milk chocolates Hannah remembered as her favourite, a pair of beautiful gardening gloves with a rose design, and a mini bee-house in pastel green.

Bandit gave up trying to catch the skittering leaves beyond the glass door as they lifted with the wind into the air and teased him behind the divide. 'Be thankful you're a cat,' she told him when he hopped up onto the carver chair next to where she was re-reading the email she'd just received from Joe. 'Life for you is far simpler.'

Luke occupied her thoughts, especially since the kiss – but so did Joe. He'd been terrible at communicating what he wanted in the care package he'd ordered after the summer fair, and it wasn't until now, in late September, that she'd actually received any detailed email correspondence from him.

It had taken her a long while to stop thinking about their dance: what it felt like to hold her body so close to his, swaying in time to the music beneath the stars and the heady temperatures that had, for once, engulfed England and given them a proper summer. She wondered if he'd felt something too and that was why he hadn't been in touch about the care package. Perhaps it was all too awkward for him, although he seemed to have plenty of female company at his own house in Lantern Square. Hannah had seen enough comings and goings over the last couple of months to realise there were no dry spells in Doctor Joe's healthy love life. Then again, when she had Luke lurking in the background, who was she to talk?

Hannah did her best to turn her mind back to business. She ran through the list to check she had everything lined up and ready to assemble into the care package for Joe. This was to go to a woman called Vanessa who liked anything lavender, enjoyed reading, preferred white chocolate to any other variety, didn't drink coffee but adored tea. Hannah wondered if Vanessa was the brunette she'd seen him with the night of the dance, or the redhead a week or so later, or even the blonde from last week? Whoever it was, she hoped she'd be delighted with the package, Hannah thought, as she added cranberry and white-chocolate fudge, an eye mask, a salt scrub and a scented candle, before securing the brown box and tying it up with string. She put it inside its extra protective box, addressed it and left it by the front door ready for her trip to the post office later.

Keeping so busy with her business was Hannah's only route to sanity right now, the only way to avoid obsessing with her appalling track record when it came to men, or rather relationships. 'Maybe I'll be a cat lady all my life, Bandit,' she told the feline who showed no interest other than momentarily opening one eye before deciding there wasn't much to see.

Hannah was almost there with her order for Castle Cards which was due to be with them by early October. Three hundred and seventy-five down, one hundred and twenty-five to go. She made a start on another batch of five with one design and the message 'Merry Christmas' across the top in an arc, then moved to another batch of five with an alternative design and the message 'Season's Greetings'. But she messed up two of them by smudging the writing on one, and accidentally cutting off Santa's boots on another. Her mind was wandering and when the post dropped onto the doormat it was all the distraction she needed.

She narrowly missed tripping over Smokey in the hallway as he went on the prowl to investigate too, and she crouched down to pick up the bundle of letters before taking them into the kitchen to open while she boiled the kettle for a cup of tea.

A couple of pieces of post went straight into the recycling bin. Honestly, with the push to recycle and save the environment, people sure got away with sending out a lot of meaningless rubbish. She'd had leaflets for assisted living, another for a men-only gym, and more for a parenting seminar. Surely part of marketing was to know your audience. She opened up her gas bill which was thankfully meagre in comparison to the last one, and when she set it aside she came to the last piece of post, a handwritten envelope bearing the postmark for Cambridge.

The kettle had boiled but the cup stood idle, awaiting a teabag. Hannah's fingers hovered near the seal of the envelope but knowing exactly who it was from she couldn't quite manage to open it. Because every time she got one of these letters, it set her back that little bit further. Just when she felt in a good place in her life, despite the confusion over her kiss with Luke, not to mention her undeniable attraction to Joe, these letters threatened to undo her.

She put the letter with the others she'd got but never opened on the high shelf in the hallway. She knew she couldn't ignore them forever, but right now, she didn't feel ready.

'Why is life so complicated?' she asked Smokey when she returned to the kitchen. She gave him a little tap when he jumped onto the benchtop the second he thought she wasn't looking. He rarely did any more and she swore he did it just to keep her on her toes. She dropped a teabag into the mug, tried to forget about Luke, Joe, and the letters, and went through to the dining room, leaving her cup on the coaster on the shelf within easy reach.

She made up a second sample of another card design that she intended to make and then sell on her website. Castle Cards had only approved those she'd already discussed with them, but she liked to keep them interested and she'd include this one with the Christmas order and perhaps she'd get the go-ahead to make some for next year.

For the time being she'd sell the design as an 'exclusive' on her website. Customers liked 'exclusives', especially if they thought this was the only chance to snap them up. This design had a white backing, and at the front after she had drawn the circle using a compass, she used a craft knife to cut out the centre ready to make the main part of a snow globe. Then, using a combination of sequins, pieces of material and felt cut-outs, she fashioned snowflakes falling, settling on the tops of pine trees and fixed it to the cut-out from the opposite side so it looked like a snow globe. She drew the outline and coloured in the base of the globe before using a chunky charcoal pencil to write the words 'Season's Greetings' at the bottom.

After completing the sample it was back to the big order for Castle Cards and time soon marched on as she lost herself in the task. Thank goodness for the alarm she'd set on her phone as a reminder she was due up at Butterbury Lodge. She set the last card she'd worked on to one side, gave Smokey a fuss – and Bandit when he demanded as much attention – shooed them out of the room and shut the dining room door before going upstairs to get changed.

She'd somehow managed to get glue on these dungarees and on her sleeve and when she caught sight of her reflection she had a little chuckle. Her mum would have a fit if she could see the long-sleeved grey top she had on beneath her dungarees. She'd worn it the other day for a very long arts and crafts session and even a strong laundry detergent hadn't got rid of the signs of creativity, the tell-tale streaks of paint across the front, and more on the cuffs. Hannah's mum had always been one to keep up appearances and never hid her disapproval either, especially when it came to some of Hannah's choices, including abandoning a career in accounting for the frivolous care package business she had now, and finishing her relationship with Luke. Hannah was sure the latter caused even more discomfort than the former.

Hannah pulled out some fresh clothes from the wardrobe and as she shut the door she caught sight of the polka-dot dress again, the special dress she'd worn to the summer fair when she danced up close to Joe, now squashed beside a purple velvet hoodie and a Christmas jumper. She took out the small album she kept at the bottom of her wardrobe beneath a shoe box containing the gold heels she'd also worn to the dance. She didn't pull the album out very often, but thinking of those letters sitting on the shelf downstairs, waiting to be opened, she really needed to do this today.

Her first love, Liam, smiled out at her from the opening page. His blond hair, cropped neat and very short, had always suited him. He'd never been one to fuss over his appearance but the second his hair got too long he'd be down to the hairdresser. When he came home she'd always loved to rub her hand up the back of his just-cut hair and feel how fuzzy it felt beneath her palm. She smiled at the memory and her fingers lightly touched the glossy image. Liam had always hated having his photograph taken so of course she'd done it all the more, to wind him up, but she was glad she had. The scenes in the photos were her memories now, and she didn't really need to look at any more pictures, because he was always there in her mind, sometimes in her dreams. Liam was the reason she'd gone to pieces and why she'd been looking for something or someone when she'd got together with Luke. She'd only gone to the party in the Cotswolds, the place they met, because everyone from her best friend Georgia to her mum and even her brother had constantly reminded her she should get out and live her life.

Liam had never left her head or her heart, even though he'd left her, and maybe that was part of her problem, the reason why she never felt settled with anyone else.

Tears sprung to her eyes. Funny how together she could feel one minute, and the next, a bit like when Joe spilled his coffee on the dress, she could fall apart so spectacularly.

When her phone rang she snapped out of her daydream and answered it to Frankie, calling from Butterbury Lodge. 'Grace wondered if you were reading again tonight. She says she's eager to know what happens in the book, even though she's read it a few times before,' Frankie informed her.

Hannah made sure her voice sounded bright, that she didn't give anything away. Frankie's call was a reminder that she wasn't quite the mess she sometimes felt she was. She had her life together at least enough to carry on each day.

'Grace really wants some company, and she likes you,' Frankie went on. 'I think she's ready for some more Mr Darcy.'

'Aren't we all?' Grace's favourite book was *Pride and Prejudice* and Hannah suspected she knew the book so well that she could recite it verbatim if asked. What Grace really wanted was companionship and friendship. 'Tell her of course I'm coming. I'll be there in thirty minutes.' She'd only been planning on meeting up with Mr G tonight for a few games of cards, then reading to Ernest, who was partially sighted. Ernest loved audio books and had told her he liked to discuss the stories after he'd finished them, but explained to Hannah that he'd sound like a right nutter talking to himself.

She pushed the album back in the wardrobe, changed into a fresh pair of jeans and a white linen shirt, grabbed her bag and car keys and headed off up to Butterbury Lodge, ready to spend the evening talking books. Anything to get her mind back on track.

'Best movie I've seen in years,' said Josephine the moment Hannah stepped in to Butterbury Lodge. Josephine was on her way back to her room but didn't miss a chance to share her opinion on anything and this time it was the movie night Hannah had been responsible for. 'I wonder what would happen if we did a Butterbury Lodge calendar,' she winked and went on her way.

Last month Hannah had organised the first movie night here and it had been a hit. They'd hired a big screen that covered almost the entire wall of the lounge and necessitated the moving around of a lot of furniture, much to the residents' delight, and along with popcorn and cups of tea, *The Calendar Girls* had had everyone talking long after the final credits rolled. She wasn't sure what they'd do for the next film night, but everyone had been so kind and thanked Hannah time and time again for her efforts. It had made her feel a real part of the lodge, even more of a part of Butterbury.

She found Mr G in his usual spot beside the bay window in the lounge. 'Got here before anyone else. A big thunderstorm is moving in and it'll be wonderful to watch. You be careful outside when it's time for you to go home. So many leaves have fallen, it'll make the footpaths slippery.'

'I'll be careful, don't worry.' Hannah joined Mr G, equipped with the pack of cards she'd grabbed before anyone else did. They were often a double act when it came to bagging things first, or taking possession of the crossword before someone else tried.

Hannah shuffled the cards. 'Three games, then I'll read to Ernest, then Grace, then perhaps one last game before I go home.'

'You're too good to me.'

'Nonsense, I enjoy coming here.'

'Well we're all fed and watered, so we're all yours.'

'Good to hear. What was on tonight's menu?'

'Roast beef and Yorkshire pudding.'

'I shouldn't have asked! I haven't eaten yet and now you're making me hungry.'

'You youngsters don't prioritise. You need a good dinner in you every day. How else will you get to live to my age and look as good as me?' he winked.

'I've got something ready to go at home, don't worry.' It wasn't a lie. She had plenty of tins of baked beans in the cupboard. A couple of slices of toast and a good grating of cheese and she'd be on her way.

They played gin rummy three times and she won each game, assuring Mr G she'd be back after she'd performed her reading duties. She found Grace in her room and took a seat in the wing-backed chair by the window as she read *Pride and Prejudice* from the last place they'd left the story. She found Ernest shuffling along the corridor to meet her in the lounge, disappointed at finding no fire lit, again. 'It's too hot,' Maggie told him, to which he rolled his eyes and said that was a lousy excuse, with the rain pelting down outside.

Back with Mr G once more, they moved on to a game of Scrabble and from their position near the window watched the storm clouds roll in. Rain lashed against the glass, the sky had turned a sinister shade of purple and lightning zig-zagged across it as though someone had scrawled using a white-tipped pen.

He looked down at the board and happily moved his letters into place. 'I do believe that's used the triple word score. Cyclone!'

'Let's hope we don't get one of those.'

At the end of the game, which he won, and which had attracted the attention of plenty of the other residents including a cursory glance from Butterbury Lodge's newest addition, Flo Carnegie, Mr G accepted the offer of tea and biscuits from Maggie as she did the rounds.

Hannah leaned closer so she wouldn't be heard. 'Do you think I should ask that lady to join us?'

'Flo? I wouldn't. She only communicates in grunts as far as I know.'

'Mr G, where's your compassion?'

He patted his heart. 'Right in here, but I'm telling you, she's not interested in getting to know any of us. I've seen her sort before. Come in here, wishing they were somewhere else.'

'Then it's up to you to change her thinking.'

'Are you telling me off, Miss Hannah?'

'I might be.' When they looked over again and caught Flo's gaze, the woman quickly looked away. 'Has she had many visitors?'

'I don't think anyone has been to see her since she came here.'

Hannah found it hard to stop looking at the woman who sat alone in the solitary chair looking out of a side window across the fields. Hair longer than it needed to be was wound into a tight bun at the nape of her neck, her build so slight that she seemed like a tiny bird too scared to leave the nest, and she gripped hold of the front of her baby-pink cardigan tightly as if it was protecting her from the rest of the world.

'Maybe she'll talk to people after she's been here a while,' Hannah suggested. 'Everyone needs friends.'

'That they do. But we can't force her.'

'No, I don't suppose we can.'

He finished tipping the Scrabble tiles back into the bag, Hannah picking up the stray few he didn't quite manage to get in. 'But for you, Miss Hannah, I'm going to keep trying to talk to her.'

'You're a good sort, Mr G.'

He looked over again at Flo. 'She's made me realise how lucky I am to have family come to see me and to have a friend like you. Although I think you should spend more time with people your age rather than us geriatrics.'

'You let me be the judge of that.' People of Mr G's age were far easier to get along with half the time. They told it how it was, as though their advancing age brought down the barriers the rest of society tiptoed around. There was a sense of honesty and Hannah liked the level of trust she felt the moment she stepped into the walls of Butterbury Lodge. And they shouldn't give up on Flo. Everyone deserved happiness and friendship.

*

By the time early October came around, the heavy rain of the week before had passed and bright autumnal colours had begun to make more of an appearance, with the leaves on most of the trees in Lantern Square turning yellow and gold, others red and beginning to fall. At Lantern Cottage Hannah had been able to light the log burner for the first time, but rather than allowing her to relax it had simply served as a reminder of how much work she had to do between now and the end of the year. She'd finished and sent off her completed order to Castle Cards and they'd quickly come back to request fifty of her new design; she'd had plenty of requests for care package orders for students who were battling their way through the first term of the academic year, and she'd assembled parcels with everything from jars of Marmite and packets of Munchies to iPhone chargers and pocket tissues for the upcoming cold and flu season. She'd fulfilled international requests for two customers, one whose daughter had emigrated to Canada and another who was working in the UK and wanted to send his parents a gift of quintessentially English products – clotted-cream fudge, a cotton tea towel bearing the Union Jack and red double-decker buses, and a voucher for two to enjoy afternoon tea at Claridge's – to whet their appetite for a visit next spring.

Hannah loaded up her trolley with the three latest care packages ready to go on their way, pulled on her favourite chunky-knit cardigan that came down to mid-thigh, and set off for the post office. She waved to Lily who looked as though she was heading for a shift at the pub, she called her hellos to Declan from Number Twenty-two, who was out walking his labradoodle Roxy and as she passed by

Lantern Square she looked up at just the right – or was it wrong? – time to see Joe coming out of his front door laughing along with another woman, a new one she hadn't seen before. Hannah smiled at them both, shook her head and went on her way, surprised that local busybody Mrs Ledbetter hadn't cottoned on to the shenanigans.

'You look happy.' Ellen held the post office door open for her and her trolley. Ellen and her sister Annie planned to open their own bistro one day but for now they were testing out their target market, the residents of Butterbury, by positioning a tempting cart in the square on a regular basis. They'd had the most divine doughnuts at the summer fair and Hannah's tummy grumbled at the thought of them now. 'Care to tell me your secret?'

'Just a lovely day, that's all.' And she'd ignored those letters sitting on her shelf, again. She wondered whether she'd ever be ready to open them.

'It's dry.' Ellen put her thumbs up. 'I love the cold but I don't do damp.'

'Me neither,' laughed Hannah, joining the queue and looking over to where Mrs Addington and Dawn were inside having a good old gossip.

'I've enrolled in your Christmas wreath-making workshop in early December,' Dawn told Mrs Addington as she stuck stamps on the letters laid out on the table beside the service area.

'It's not *my* workshop,' Mrs Addington assured her without rancour. 'But I did volunteer my home. I thought it would get me in the Christmas spirit.'

Hannah had a couple more people in front of her in the queue and smiled over at the two ladies as they chatted, doing her best not to eavesdrop.

'Last year must've been awful with your Bobby passing away so suddenly,' Dawn sympathised.

'Well this year I'm determined to be a lot more cheerful. Bobby was always a big lover of Christmas, so this year I thought I'd start by letting the WI use my place.'

'Well it's very generous of you.' Hannah could feel Dawn's eyes on her. 'Hannah . . . fancy making a Christmas wreath this year?' She tutted the second the words were out of her mouth. 'What am I saying? You're already a dab hand in arts and crafts, not hopeless like the rest of us.'

'I could always come along and help out.' She wanted to absorb herself in the community because the more she did, the more she felt at home. Slowly but surely she was finding her place here.

'Would you really?' Mrs Addington seemed surprised but delighted. 'It would be a great help. I might be supplying the use of my home but I have no creative skills whatsoever.'

'Makes two of us,' Dawn laughed, her soft grey hair held back at the nape of her neck with a clip that picked up the shine from the lights inside.

'Let me know if you need a good supplier for materials,' Hannah offered. 'I can get pretty good discounts.'

'Thank you, but it's all in hand. All financed by the WI so we're lucky.'

After she'd sent the parcels on their way, Hannah headed back to Lantern Cottage and found Mrs Ledbetter fussing over Bandit who was prowling the length of the low wall at the front of the cottage. She only hoped Mrs Ledbetter hadn't found him playing in the road again, or she'd have to face another lecture.

'Hello,' Hannah smiled. If she wasn't mistaken, the old

lady had been talking to Bandit in a very pleasant voice. Maybe he'd been behaving himself after all.

Mrs Ledbetter snatched her hand away and sniffed, barely able to acknowledge Hannah's greeting in return. Hannah was tempted to call after her, 'Have a nice day', but she'd settle for peace rather than a telling-off as Mrs Ledbetter went down her own garden path towards her front door. The woman reminded Hannah of Flo up at Butterbury Lodge, keeping herself to herself, everyone else at arm's length. And if she wasn't mistaken, the sniff had been because of a bit of a cold and Mrs Ledbetter didn't look her usual perky self.

Hannah made up her mind there and then to be the bigger person when it came to the woman who poked her nose in and liked to tell her off whenever she got the opportunity. She'd take Mrs Ledbetter a care package, a pick-me-up to show she wasn't completely alone. It was a long time since Hannah had seen anyone visiting her home and now, the thought saddened her more than anything else.

Hannah pushed her keys into the lock of her front door but the cooler weather had already started to tamper with it and it took a good shove to open it this time. She'd only just stepped inside onto the mat when the breeze from the push caused one of the letters she'd put onto the shelf to float down to her feet, taunting her to open it. But with both Luke and Joe doing the rounds in her head, she couldn't cope with anything else and pushed the letter back on the shelf, this time wedged with the rest of them beneath the telephone directory that was gathering dust.

She was about to shut the front door behind her when a voice she recognised only too well stopped her.

It couldn't be, could it?

She turned slowly to face a person she never thought would dare to show her face again. Not after everything she'd done.

'Hello, Hannah.'

Hannah was pretty sure her jaw had hit the floor, but she had to pull herself together. She'd go ten rounds with Mrs Ledbetter rather than face her current visitor. 'What the hell are you doing here?'

'That's not a very nice hello.'

'What do you expect?' She only kept the anger out of her voice because this was her village now, a place where she could start over and leave everything else behind.

Standing at Hannah's garden gate, her blonde hair in the same high ponytail, her healthy glow only marred by the look of shame she'd brought with her, was Georgia. Her one-time friend had a real nerve coming to Lantern Cottage.

Georgia stepped towards her. 'I've come to apologise.'

Hannah knew she should say something, even if it was an unsavoury expression that meant go away and don't ever come back. 'I've moved on,' was what she managed.

'May I come in?' Georgia ventured, ignoring the negative vibes, the undercurrent in Hannah's words. She had guts, no doubt about it.

'I don't think that's a good idea.' She churned over what Georgia had done to her. 'I'd like you to leave.'

'Please, Hannah, I need to apologise to you. Give me a chance.'

Hannah was about to shut the door on her former friend and the history they'd shared, all the way from primary school to starting their own business, but when Mrs

Ledbetter came outside again and hovered near her garden gate watering some of the hardier flowers in her window boxes that had survived autumn so far, clearly eavesdropping on the conversation, she decided she had no choice but to bring her personal business inside. 'I suppose you'd better come in.'

What was she really doing here? Because by Hannah's reckoning, there was no friendship left to salvage. They'd gone their separate ways and there was no turning back.

If the letters sitting on the shelf above her now had brought confusion to Hannah's world, then this brought utter chaos.

9

Hannah's heart thumped inside her chest as she shut the door to Lantern Cottage. She and Georgia had a lot of history together: lots of it good, but lots of it very bad indeed.

Hannah and Georgia had started their business, G.H. Bookkeeping, together. Having both worked for top London firms in the City, they knew their stuff when it came to year-end accounts, income and expenditure reports, and company tax returns. Initially they took extra courses on self-assessment and making tax digital and brought those skills into their business. At the start all the signs pointed to the venture being a huge success, with a healthy client list.

But Georgia's lack of business acumen hadn't taken too long to show. Hannah had no idea what her friend had been like in the workplace before, whether this was her slacking off, or her behaviour was down to her being confused and not fully grasping how different having your own business was to working for someone else, but soon after things were looking so promising, Georgia managed to lose a couple of big clients. With the first, she'd failed to respond to several urgent correspondences meaning the client took their business elsewhere, and with the second she'd had a fling with the account holder which ended so badly that the business had been taken away from G.H. Bookkeeping regardless of the satisfactory service they'd received. It was as though Georgia had this huge ambition to succeed but couldn't quite fathom the effort required to achieve her goals.

Hannah did everything she could to make the business work. She enrolled both herself and Georgia on further courses to hone their skills, she signed them up to seminars addressing latest trends in the industry and she made a point of subtly checking Georgia's work to ensure she was staying on top of things and to correct any errors that perhaps were part of her friend's learning curve. She followed up Georgia's clients as well as her own, which meant her workload was ridiculous. One day after Hannah had been to see the doctor with a multitude of symptoms her GP had told her they were most likely to be stress related, and Hannah realised she couldn't keep going on the same way. She'd sat down with Georgia and thought the conversation would be on the mature side. They'd known one another for years, been the best of friends as little girls, she'd thought surely Georgia would see what was wrong and they'd work through it. But right from the start Georgia had been defensive, accusing Hannah of wanting to push her out and take the business and profits all for herself. Hannah heard from more than one client that some rumours were flying around about G.H. Bookkeeping and some creative accounting on Hannah's part, and Hannah was left in no doubt as to who had started those rumours. Clients got wind of the waves within the company, some let it be known they didn't want to be involved with anything that wasn't totally legitimate, and others had made their excuses before drifting off to more reputable bookkeeping firms.

In order to start G.H. Bookkeeping Hannah and Georgia had both used their personal savings, and from a financial side they were doing well, but after the rumours and lost business Hannah took a closer look at the expenses, and it wasn't difficult to see that some things really didn't add up. There was an expense for a weekend away at a country spa in Northumberland supposedly 'on business' as Georgia buttered up a big client, and Hannah knew they had never managed to bag any clients up that way, and if they had, surely she would've been aware of the trip. There was another bill filed for luxury hampers given as Christmas gifts to their clients when Hannah had already sent each of them boxed bottles of champagne. And when Hannah confronted Georgia about that one, she'd eventually admitted the hampers were in fact her Christmas shopping, but only after Hannah began to phone each and every client – existing and previous – on their lists to ask whether they'd received the additional gifts. The confrontation came to a head with Georgia claiming she'd paid enough damn taxes in her time in London, and questioning what was the point of owning your own business if you couldn't enjoy a few little perks along the way? Hannah and Georgia had argued about their varying moral standards, the rumours that had circulated, Georgia's inappropriate behaviours with clients, and Georgia had ended up quitting the business leaving Hannah to pick up the pieces.

Hannah had taken a week off after everything blew up and she'd gone home to see an old school friend in

Wales, well away from Georgia, away from the business. She'd switched off her phone, not checked her email, all she wanted was to go back with a clear head and talk to her friend, find a way forward out of the mess. She'd decided perhaps they both needed to man-up and establish boundaries, ground rules, if this was ever going to work. But when she'd returned and asked Georgia to come over and talk things through, Georgia had shown up guns blazing, yelling at Hannah. Luke had walked in on the row. He knew what she'd done to Hannah and he'd told Georgia to get the hell out because she wasn't welcome any longer. G.H. Bookkeeping had reached its conclusion under a veil of spite and betrayal, with Hannah and Georgia wrapping the business up for good. And Hannah hadn't seen or heard from Georgia again, until today.

Standing in the narrow hallway of Lantern Cottage, Hannah asked, 'Why come here now, after all this time?'

'I left it too long, I should've come sooner.'

'You refused to talk rationally to me.'

'I know I did. I was awful to you and you didn't deserve it. I hate the way we left things.' Georgia hooked a stray wisp of blonde hair that had escaped her ponytail, behind her ear. 'I swear to you, I'm so very sorry. I was pathetic.'

'How did you know where I was?'

'I saw an advert for Tied Up with String and there was your name, bold as anything.' She smiled. 'I followed the links on the Facebook ad, found the website and had a look. You've done so well.'

'Thank you.'

'It suits you far more than accounts, you look good too, less stressed.' The irony of Georgia being the one who'd caused a lot of that stress wasn't lost on Hannah but apparently it was on her friend as she carried on. 'I'm happy for you. I just thought it was high time I came and apologised for everything I did. Maybe it was something about turning thirty. I mean, we're old.' She ventured a grin.

Hannah almost grinned back but settled with a conciliatory nod. When she'd turned thirty she'd got so drunk, not because of the turn of a decade but because she'd received a letter similar to the ones wedged on top of the shelf in her hallway now and it reminded her of the ways her life hadn't exactly stayed on the track she'd intended.

'I appreciate you taking the time to come and apologise,' said Hannah.

'But . . .'

'No buts, Georgia. Life's too short to hold a grudge.' Even after everything that had happened, she could at least manage a little civility. She thought about how she'd scolded Mr G for assuming Flo was a misery and didn't want company, how she'd told him to keep trying. Everyone made mistakes, but not everyone tried to make amends like Georgia was doing now.

'I found work at an accountancy firm in Edgware after you left,' Georgia explained. 'I think part of my problem was immaturity. I didn't think it'd be so hard starting out on our own.'

Hannah softened. She'd found it hard too, a shock to the system at how many little extras being a business owner entailed, at how exposed they'd both felt with no safety net of a firm sitting beneath them to back them up. Maybe her personality had simply been better able to cope with the transition. 'Perhaps we were too young to do it,' Hannah speculated. Georgia had never been one to take orders even as kids, she'd always been the bossier one, the girl who made the decisions. No wonder their business had never worked. 'And I'm happy you found work. Are you still there?'

She shook her head. 'It was a contract position, so I've been moving around for a while, mostly within the City, a few places on the outskirts. I'm not as lazy as I once was.'

Hannah could tell the attempt at flippancy was rattling Georgia more than she was letting on, and she didn't ask for more details. She wanted to make sure she didn't condone a single thing that had gone on.

'Tell me about your business. It sounds different, creative, you always were really good at that sort of thing.'

Uneasy with the supposed compliment, Hannah said, 'You've seen the website, it's pretty much laid out on there.'

'Hannah, I mean it. I'm so, so, sorry for what I did. There's no excuse. I was a cow, I was wrong. But I'm really trying here.'

She was and Hannah couldn't find it in her heart to be horrible any more. They'd been so close as children and losing their friendship had felt like another part of her world had ended along with the business. 'How about we wipe the slate clean, move on.'

'Really?' Aghast, Georgia froze on the spot.

'Tea?'

Georgia finally allowed herself a smile. 'If you're offering.'

'I'm offering.'

Hannah led her into the kitchen, made some tea and did her best to make light conversation when Georgia asked more about Tied Up with String.

'I'm loving it,' Hannah admitted.

'I can tell. And this cottage is adorable, quaint.'

'I can't believe my luck in finding it, I've always wanted to live out this way.'

'It suits you.' Georgia hesitated, curling a strand of blonde hair round her finger. 'So you're not with Luke any more, what happened?'

Hannah shrugged. 'It just wasn't right.' And when Georgia didn't push it she asked, 'What's new with you, still contracting?'

'I'm having a change of tack actually,' Georgia admitted.

'Away from accounting?'

'You could say that. Jason lined something up for me. Do you remember him?'

'Is it the same Jason who invited us to Luke's party when Luke told him the more the merrier?'

'The very same,' Georgia laughed. 'And Jason did take the request literally, didn't he? I still remember Luke's face when a minibus full of people he didn't know showed up at the manor house. At least we were well behaved. You hear horror stories about social media igniting interest in house parties with enough guests to fill the O2 arena.'

'Linda and Rupert were very matter of fact about it.'

'They sure were.' Georgia managed a smile across at her friend that Hannah returned. 'See, we had some good times.'

She glossed over the remark by asking, 'What's Jason lined up for you?'

'He's running a sports centre just outside of Tetbury so needs someone to take the spin class.'

Hannah almost spat out her tea because Georgia's laziness hadn't just been around the workplace, it had extended in all facets of her life. It had been next to impossible to get her off the couch some evenings to go for a walk and she'd joked that the only exercise she got was lifting her finger to press the lift button in her building or to move a glass of wine towards her lips. 'I didn't know you were into anything fitness.'

'I've grown up a bit over the last year or two, and not just in a work sense. I took up spinning, Pilates, I run and lift weights. Healthy body, healthy mind and all that.'

'Blimey. I mean, it's great, just that I'm shocked.' She looked good for it too. She was toned, her clothes showed off her svelte figure in skinny jeans and a top that would be unforgiving if she wasn't so slim.

They talked more about Georgia's foray into personal training and Jason's job offer. 'Give him my best when you next see him,' said Hannah. And then a thought dawned on her. 'Where will you be living?'

'I've rented a flat about four or five miles from here, past the farms as you drive out of Butterbury. You pass the big supermarket and onto the main road and just keep going until you reach the new development. It's quiet which is taking some getting used to, and there's no village feel, but it's practical. Nowhere near as lovely as here though. Butterbury is gorgeous. Apart from the farm smells that is.'

'You do get the odd dodgy waft from cattle or fertilizer or whatever it is they're doing out on the land. But it's a stunning part of the country.' They were making peace, but Hannah wasn't sure how she felt knowing Georgia was only a few miles away. And now she was uncomfortable, she wanted to move this on. 'I really should be working, I still have a ton of things to do today.'

'Of course, of course. One of the perils of working at home eh? Everyone assuming you can drop everything the second they knock on the door. But you were always very self-disciplined.'

'I'll take that as a compliment.'

'You should.' The air settled between them as Georgia stood up and went through to the hall to pick up her bag and coat. 'I'm glad you were willing to hear me out. Thank you, Hannah.'

'I agree, it was good to clear the air.'

Georgia pulled a leaflet from her bag. 'It's for the new gym. If you're ever on the lookout for somewhere to exercise, it's reasonably priced, no joining fee. It'd be good to see you. No pressure. And I'll be able to get you a discount.'

'Thanks, Georgia.' The power of an apology had given Hannah a sense of equilibrium she hadn't felt in a long time. 'I'll think about it.'

Georgia adjusted the handbag on her arm before stooping down near the front door to pick something up. She handed Hannah an envelope. 'I think this must be yours.'

One of the letters must've floated down to the floor again when Hannah shut the front door. It was taunting her to open the damn thing. And she already knew the postmark hadn't escaped Georgia's notice.

'Came recently,' was all Hannah said. For all that they weren't best friends any more, Georgia knew her past well enough to know what a postmark from Cambridge meant. She'd received enough of these similar letters over the last few years and Georgia had been her only confidant.

'I'm surprised you're still in touch.'

'Understandably his parents never got over what

happened.' What Georgia didn't realise was that Hannah never really had either.

'But they're writing to you to ease their pain and causing you suffering in the process. You told me once before remember?'

Hannah couldn't hide the tremble in her lip and when Georgia reached out to hug her she didn't resist.

'I'll be fine,' she said when Georgia let her go.

'Are you sure?'

'I'm sure. And thank you for stopping by to talk.'

'Thank you for listening.'

Leaning against the front door after her friend had gone, Hannah knew that Georgia must've picked up on the emotional baggage that she'd never managed to shed a long time ago. And despite their friendship coming to an end, it felt good to have someone here who actually understood the things she rarely liked to share.

Maybe their friendship wasn't beyond repair after all. Didn't everyone deserve a second chance?

10

'Flo looks happy enough.' Hannah slyly observed the woman sitting in the usual chair she favoured at Butterbury Lodge, with the view over the garden and the trellis at the foot of the longest flower bed, ivy woven around its poles and refusing to let go no matter the season. Hannah had come up for afternoon tea and a reading session with Mr G, Grace and Ernest, and looking over at Flo now she hadn't missed the CD case clutched on the woman's lap.

'I was watching her yesterday,' said Mr. G. 'Whatever she's listening to, it's working. She got a parcel a few days ago and I assume the listening device was inside.'

It warmed Hannah to know somebody out there was thinking of the elderly resident. Flo, headphones pushed into her ears, her head tilting left and then right in time to something or perhaps in thought, certainly looked content.

'It's *Sounds Over the Bridge*,' Hannah whispered, peering at the CD case to read the name of a local choir who got together at the church further up the hill.

'Sounds over the what?'

'Sshhhh . . .' Hannah couldn't help but laugh at their

mischief and repeated the name. 'They're a local choir, very impressive, and I think she must be listening to the second CD they've put together because the first had a bright blue cover rather than the darker version.'

'Well, your eyesight is far better than mine,' Mr G remarked. 'It's good to see her looking happy though, isn't it?'

'It is, but I want to see her get involved with the rest of you.'

Mr G patted her hand. 'Maybe we just need to let that come. And you know, if you keep frowning like that, the lines will set in and you'll look older than you really are.'

'Got a few things on my mind, that's all.' Hannah used her fork to break off a piece of fig and plum cake.

'I thought you'd finished the big order for the card shop.'

'Five days earlier than expected,' she beamed, hand in front of her mouth.

'Well then, what've you got to worry about? Man trouble?' He tried so hard to say it casually as though he talked about relationships every day.

'Something like that.' She sipped her camomile tea. 'This cake is wonderful,' she told Maggie when she breezed past with another two portions for Grace and her visitor.

'An old family recipe,' Maggie winked.

Mr G tapped his teaspoon against his china cup before setting it down on the saucer. He always waited for his tea to be lukewarm before he picked it up, worried he might wobble too much and slop it.

'Is it Doctor Joe, the man trouble?' he prompted.

She smiled. He was right about one thing. It was man trouble. 'It's not Joe, no. It's someone I used to know.'

'Ah, the one who broke your heart.'

'What makes you think someone broke my heart?'

'It's written all over your face.' He finished the last of his slice of cake.

'What, in between the lines that are forming when I frown you mean? Actually I ended things with someone before I came to Butterbury.'

'You were the heartbreaker?'

'Yes, I suppose I was.'

Mr G nodded, chewed some more.

'What's with the face?' she asked.

'I don't think we're talking about the same man.'

'OK, now I'm lost. I only broke one person's heart.'

'Then the person who broke yours must've come before him.'

Hannah piled the plates on top of each other, finished the rest of her tea. 'Let me take these out.' And she scuttled over to where Maggie had left a trolley, already piled with empty plates and slotted hers and Mr G's into a space.

'I don't want to talk about it,' she told him when she went back over, because she could tell more questions were fighting to get out. When he wanted to say something he got this impatient look as though he'd burst if you didn't let him share. But with the unopened letters still lurking in her cottage and Georgia turning up, not to mention locking lips with Luke and dancing with Joe at the fair, her head was all over the place. 'Would you like me to read to you first, or shall I go round-up one of the others?'

'Whatever suits you, Hannah.'

She'd rather he was being bossy. Empathy always seemed intent to undo her if it was delivered too generously. 'I'll go see Ernest.' And off she went to find the jolly resident who was ready to hear another chapter of Ian Rankin's latest. Not really Hannah's sort of book, but this wasn't about her, and they even managed to discuss characters and plot when Ernest dissected the story as it went along.

After two chapters with Ernest it was on to Grace and another instalment of *Pride and Prejudice* and on her way back to Mr G, Hannah stopped at Flo's side.

Flo removed her earphones. She must've thought Hannah worked at Butterbury Lodge but it didn't take long to register she was a visitor. 'I don't want to play their games or sit and talk about how old we all are,' she said sternly, pre-empting Hannah's thoughts. 'I'm happy as I am, thank you.' There was a non-vocal full-stop after her sentence and she pushed her headphones back in.

Hannah stood her ground until Flo reluctantly pulled the buds from her ears once again. 'What are you listening to?' She feigned ignorance and perched on the windowsill rather than looking down on the woman who had made it clear she didn't want to be coaxed into talking or taking part in any activities. Yesterday Ernest had tried to get her to come and do Tai Chi in the gardens, and as well as telling him to bugger off – her exact words – he said she'd been unable to hold back a wobble in her voice which gave away her amusement. Hannah had heard the tale earlier and it had given her the confidence to approach Flo now, wondering whether she'd get a good reception or an ear full.

'It's a choir,' said Flo.

'A famous choir?' She'd pretend she had no idea who they were.

'No, amateur, but a favourite. Sounds Over the Bridge, they're local, very talented.'

'May I?' Hannah held a hand out for an ear bud. 'I won't push it in, I'll just let it hover so I can hear them.'

'Very well then.' Flo handed her an ear bud and let Hannah have a listen.

'They're really good.' She looked at the CD case. 'A Christmas collection too. Was it a gift?'

'From my daughter. She lives in Aberdeen so doesn't visit much, but we write all the time. And talk on the telephone.'

Hannah had been about to ask more but she suspected Flo didn't want to be pushed too far so she'd have to settle for little and often. It was a start. 'I'll leave you to it.' And with a smile she returned to Mr G and picked up the copy of their latest read, a story about a group of men and women in a care home who liked to break the rules. Quirky and a little naughty, it was Mr G's sort of novel and Hannah was enjoying it too.

He sat back in his chair as he always did, eyes shut, smiling every now and then, laughing sometimes, frowning as they progressed through the text. Hannah loved to watch his facial expressions over the top of the book as she read, little snippets of this man that she took in briefly so she didn't lose her place. She learned just as much through his facial expressions as she did his conversations. She'd watched him frown with contempt when she'd once read about a spoilt child acting up for his parents, she'd seen him belly laugh at any books containing rebellious behaviour in the workplace – she'd have to ask him more about that another time – and she'd seen him wipe his eye when they read a love story that had a heartbreaker of a finish.

When she shut this book for the time being, they had a quick chat about their favourite characters and the antics they were getting up to and when Ernest walked by she called over to him. 'You'd love this book.' She gave him a brief rundown of the storyline and the characters. 'If you lot all got together and read or listened to the same story, you could have some great discussions afterwards.'

Mr G grumbled an agreement. 'We could never agree on a book.'

'Then you take turns to choose one, meaning everyone gets a turn, everyone is happy. You could get some really passionate debates going and I could even dream up some questions to raise talking points.'

'And throw them into the ring when you leave?' Ernest laughed.

'Well . . .' An impish look crossed her face.

'Thought as much.' Ernest went over to chat with Maggie, probably asking when the fireplace was going to be lit. The man was fixated on it.

Mr G almost looked sold on her idea until he said, 'I'm too old for a book club. My daughter has one, so does her husband, although my son-in-law seems to use the words book club loosely, I think it's all about beer and time away from the wives. Can't blame him really, my daughter takes after my late wife . . .'

'I've met her, she's lovely.'

'Oh, she is, just likes a bit of control that's all.'

'So come on, what do you think? Should we start a book club, get people involved?'

He pondered the idea. 'I doubt it would ever work to be honest. Grace would have me reading some ridiculous romance, Ernest would choose a thriller.'

'It's only a suggestion.' She tried to hide the smirk. Older people were refreshingly honest, they didn't humour you in case they hurt your feelings – although her mother had only waited until middle-age to become hypercritical, and sometimes Hannah wondered how much worse it would get. 'I tell you what, I'll ask some of the others and perhaps get a suggestion box going for the first read. I can leave it at the front desk and everyone gets to post their ideas anonymously. I know all of your tastes, so I can have the final say in what book we go for and then I'll read to you as a group.'

He relented. 'You're never going to take no for an answer; you're too bossy.'

'I can be if I think something is worth pushing. And if it doesn't work, we stop. Simple as that.'

'I'll do it on one condition.'

'What's that?'

He patted the chair beside him in the alcove at the side of the room. From here they could see the big oak tree dominating the rear lawn, its branches swaying in the wind, gold leaves leaving their post and drifting towards the ground, others clinging on as long as they possibly could. 'That you sit down and talk to me.'

'We've been talking for ages already.' But she did as she was told.

'Are your grandparents still around?'

Not sure where this was going, she shook her head. 'No unfortunately, my mum's parents passed away before I was born, my dad's when I was very little.'

'Then you don't know the grandparenting secret. My grandsons have told me things they'd never tell their parents.' He tapped the side of his nose with his fingertip.

'Some of it would make your hair curl. But I get to offer my advice without the stress if you like. Because they're not my kids, they'll get into scrapes, they'll find their way through in the end just like their parents did.'

'I wish my mum had that approach.'

'She worries about you?'

'She worries about my untidiness, my less than conservative career choice.'

'Don't be too hard on her. Parenting is a tough job, not always easy to get it right. Do you confide in her?'

'We're not what you might call on the same wavelength. She worries about dust, dirt brought in from the outside and whether her soft furnishings are perfectly looked after and respected. I couldn't imagine troubling her with my problems.'

'You never know, she might give you some advice.'

Hannah wished she'd been able to talk more to her parents about Liam when he'd left her calm and cosy world that had once been heading in a steady direction. Later she'd wanted to talk more about the mess with the business and what Georgia had done, but she didn't want her mum to run on and on about getting a proper job with a reputable firm, and she didn't want her dad fretting over whether she was managing.

'Grandparents get to be the confidante, the fun member of the family who can guide kids in the right direction without them realising. Take my youngest grandson, Billy. He thinks I've been in my eighties all my life and when he confessed to being behind a practical joke at school, I told him I'd done similar. We had a laugh about it, both of us as naughty as each other, but when I told him I got caught the next time I played up and my punishment involved a cane, you should've seen his face. It dawned on him that he should behave a bit better in class. Or at least that's what I hope.'

'They're energetic boys,' said Hannah. 'I think they must've run twenty laps of the garden last time they were here.'

'They go crazy inside these walls when they visit so we always let them outside. Bit like having a couple of puppies really, they need to run off their energy before they'll listen to any instruction.' They watched as Maggie loaded up the birdfeeder hanging from the bird table in the garden. 'Daft woman. The squirrels will only get it all, just like last time.'

He turned to Hannah and got back to the subject in hand, just when she thought he'd forgotten. 'If you can't talk to your parents, then who do you talk to?'

She shrugged. 'My friends have dispersed across the UK but I have a few around here, Rhys, Lily, for starters, I'm slowly getting to know people.' But she couldn't hide the tears that prickled the corners of her eyes. She hadn't wanted to rake up her sorry story to the new people she met, threaten the new friendships she was building, because then she'd just be that misery arse from Lantern Cottage.

'Get it off your chest, think of me as a grandparent.'

And over a second cup of tea – peppermint this time – Hannah did just that. She started from the beginning, back when she met Liam, and when she clammed up Mr G prompted, 'What happened between the two of you? He sounds like a wonderful lad.'

She looked right at him. 'Liam died.' She heard the gasp of air through his lips, she saw the tiny head-tilt of sympathy. 'He was killed on an army training exercise.'

Mr G set down his half-drunk tea. 'You know, just because someone has gone it doesn't mean we can't love them any more.'

'But that's the problem,' she confessed, 'I was so in love with him, I never said goodbye, and I don't think I ever really moved on. I got together with Luke, our relationship wasn't all bad, but I think I met him at the wrong time.'

'Do you think meeting him later would've made it work between you both?'

She waited until Ernest had passed by chatting to Maggie now she'd come back inside, talking about kindling supplies, logs for the fire. 'Part of me thinks it might have. He showed up in the summer. I hadn't seen him since we broke up.'

Conversation gave way to the business she'd once had with Georgia. 'She turned up more recently. It seems my past doesn't want to let me move on without it.' And then there were the letters, still waiting to be opened.

'So everything is catching up with you,' was Mr G's summation. 'How do you feel about that?'

'There's more . . . Liam's mother has written to me several times and I keep putting off reading her letters.'

'Why?'

'Because whenever I do, it brings back all the pain. Every time. I found her writing to me a comfort at first, but these days it's harder to deal with. I'm ashamed to say I haven't answered the last three letters.'

'Did Liam have siblings?'

Hannah shook her head. 'I think it would have been easier if he did. It wouldn't take away the pain from losing him, but I feel I'm the only link left to our generation, perhaps that's why she likes to stay in touch.'

'What does she usually write about?'

'The usual. What she's been up to, Liam's dad, asking after me and about my life.'

'So much like a letter from a mother to a daughter then.'

Hannah put her head in her hands. 'I feel terrible. It shouldn't be that big a deal for me, should it? It's the least I can do when she'll be grieving for the rest of her life.'

'Have you met with her?'

'Not since Liam's funeral.'

'It might help.'

'Or it'll set her up for disappointment if I don't meet up with her again after that. I seem to have this way with other people's parents. Luke's too,' she clarified. 'I bumped into his mum here actually . . . his gran was Bettie.'

'Bettie, the lady who checked in and checked out so quickly?'

'The very same.'

'Well I never . . . small world. And how did it go, seeing her?'

'I ended up having afternoon tea at the family home, Maplebrooke Manor, not long afterwards.'

He whistled his surprise. 'Well I never, that's a beautiful and impressive home. I always admired that place, the grounds. I'd walk past and wonder who lived somewhere so grand. I guess now I know.'

She smiled.

'Hannah, I think what you have is a gift.'

'I'm not sure I follow.'

'A gift for making people smile, for lifting their day. I

still can't quite fathom how you could've ever been an accountant, but Tied Up with String has your stamp on it. You have compassion, you show it in the way you come here and mingle with us, all old as the hills, some of us almost blind, others pretty much deaf. You diligently share your time between us, reading or playing games. You bring us cookies, you arrange movie nights with popcorn, although I did hear murmurings about that being a bit tough on dentures, and you light up our days with your presence and smile.'

'Mr G,' she blushed, coming over a bit emotional, 'you'll make me cry in a minute.'

'I think it's why Liam's mother writes to you. She's holding on to a part of him, it's the only part she has left, and you're so selfless you've let her do it.'

Hannah thought about it. 'It's not that I don't like hearing from her, in a way I do. When couples split up in whatever way it happens, extended family often drifts off, joint friendships flounder. But she's stayed in touch.'

'Then you have to ask yourself why you find the letters so hard to receive.'

Hannah had never admitted this to anyone. She didn't even think her parents knew the connection between Liam and the business she now ran from her home at Lantern Cottage. She took a deep breath. 'Liam was the first person I ever sent a care package to.' Mr G maintained a respectable silence while the story tumbled out. 'I'd make up a special box with his favourite toiletries, plain chocolate Hobnob biscuits, warm socks, Yorkshire tea. He loved getting them so I made it a regular thing.'

'Didn't know he was from Yorkshire.'

It raised a smile in a melancholy moment for Hannah.

'He wasn't, just loved the stuff, never drank anything else. I'd never thought about a care package service as a business until the accounts venture fell flat on its face. I'd been at home, making a card for my dad's birthday, loving the creativity, and it reminded me of making up the packages for Liam. I started searching online for troops who received care packages, getting teary at all the stories about them and their loved ones, and the idea evolved from there.'

Maggie came and collected their empty teacups and asked if they'd like another slice of cake but both declined. And by the time Hannah finished talking to Mr G she was glad she'd finally confided in someone.

She hadn't realised how much she'd needed it until today.

II

Mrs Ledbetter was polishing her front windows when Hannah came out of her front door to take two more care packages to the post office a few days later, although Hannah wasn't sure why the woman was bothering, because the bright, sunny autumn days were due to come to an end with weather forecasting nothing but rain for the next week.

Hannah shut the gate at the end of her path and hadn't heard her neighbour creep up on her. 'Oh, you gave me a fright, Mrs Ledbetter.' One hand still on her trolley, she put the other across her chest.

'I apologise.' Mrs Ledbetter looked down at her feet. 'I shouldn't come outside in my slippers, the soles are too soft for these pavements.'

'Well at least it's dry today.'

'I wanted to thank you for the care package.'

Hannah had put together a small package with Lemsip, tissues, throat lozenges, two tins of chicken soup and some lemon and ginger Teapigs teabags, and left it on Mrs Ledbetter's front doorstep in a brown box all tied up with string. 'You're most welcome. Are you feeling better?'

'Much better thank you. A bit of rest and your magical ingredients, and I think I scared the cold away.'

'Good for you.'

'I have a little something to say thank you, if you'll let me.'

Hannah didn't really have time to stop, but this was so unprecedented, she could give her neighbour a few minutes. She followed Mrs Ledbetter back to her home, left her trolley on the doorstep, and they went inside through the compact hallway and into the lounge. Her mum would be impressed. There wasn't a thing out of place, in this room at least, no dust to be seen, a smell of furniture polish lingering on the air.

'Here.' Mrs Ledbetter handed her a small pink gift bag. 'Just a little something. I figure it's usually you doing the sending.'

Hannah did her best to hide her surprise at the thoughtful gesture. 'Well it's nice to be on the receiving end.' She peeled back the Sellotape fastening the top and reached in to take out the gift. 'Ouch!' Something stabbed her palms and she didn't miss a swift look of amusement from Mrs Ledbetter. 'What is it?' She peered in first this time.

'A cactus, cacti, whatever you call them. It's low maintenance so I thought it was perfect. You could put it on your kitchen windowsill. I got it from the florist. I said I wanted a gift for someone who didn't do well with plants.'

Hannah resisted the barb. And anyway, it was true. That was why she had Rhys. 'Well, thank you, Mrs Ledbetter.' She carefully took it out. 'Actually, it's very pretty, and I like the idea that I might not kill this one.'

'You can check with Rhys, but I asked him yesterday and he said to tell you to water it when the soil is dry and to let the water run through the holes in the bottom of the pot when you do. Or words to that effect.'

'Thank you, it's wonderful.' She prepared to go on her way but not before she noticed the same CD cover she'd seen Flo holding up at Butterbury Lodge. 'Do you like the choir?' She picked up the CD from its position on the side table.

'They're wonderful. Not like some of the row that comes from radio stations nowadays. This is proper music.'

'I'll have to have a listen sometime.' She replaced the CD. 'I'd better get on.'

'More packages?'

'Just another couple to take to the post office.'

'Who for this time?'

Momentarily flummoxed by the interest she told Mrs Ledbetter, 'One for a university student, another for someone who isn't very well.' That was an understatement. The second person had been diagnosed with a terminal illness and Hannah's heart had all but broken when she read the email from her son who wanted to send his mum a surprise package filled with her favourite chocolates – Hannah had gone all the way to Cheltenham to source them – as well as a range of teas, a beautiful set of aromatherapy oils plus an owl design oil burner and a set of tealights.

'I'll bet your package will put a smile on their face like it did for me.'

Gratitude, compliments and a prickly cactus, all in one day? Maybe Mrs Ledbetter was warming to her neighbour at last. The woman rarely said much unless it was a criticism or an exchange of gossip and it was easy to forget that behind her stern demeanour perhaps hid a vulnerable old lady who was misunderstood rather than had a hidden agenda to make others miserable.

'I'm glad to see you settling in to the village,' said Mrs Ledbetter as Hannah stepped outside again and manoeuvred her trolley to go on her way. 'You've had plenty of visitors too, lucky you kept the cottage garden looking so nice.'

She ignored the subtle attempt to delve into her private affairs, but rather astutely, her neighbour was spot on. Hannah's brother Brendan had come to visit with his girlfriend and they'd stayed a couple of nights to catch up and tell her all their tales of hiking in Scotland. Her parents had been down for a day trip too, and add those visitors to Joe stopping by, then Luke, then Georgia, Mrs Ledbetter's curtains and her mind must've been twitching away nineteen to the dozen. 'The garden is all part of the cottage's character,' she said. 'I want to keep it looking nice. Thanks again for the gift, I'll look after it.' As hard as she was trying to leave, maybe Mrs Ledbetter was just like anyone else. She needed someone to talk to, a bit of companionship.

'I'd better get on myself, my windows are looking terribly dirty.'

'I think Mrs Addington has a window cleaner once a week and he's pretty good. You could ask for his number.'

She blew a fast puff of air from between her lips. 'I'm still young enough to do it myself.'

'Of course, I wasn't . . . I didn't mean . . .'

'Don't fret, dear, it'll take more than a comment to upset me.' Hannah felt sure she wasn't wrong there. 'But idle fingers won't do me any good. I like to be busy.' And with a wave of the cloth she still had in her hand she was off, cleaning fluid on the cloth, her wrist moving in circular motions across the glass.

Hannah took the packages to the post office and then trundled her trolley back home, but not before she caught a waft coming from Lantern Square that was decidedly better than any smells emitted from neighbouring farmland. Curious at the sweet aroma snaking through the air she dumped her trolley at her cottage and then made her way over to the square.

'Annie?' She followed the smell and could by now see where it was coming from. 'Whatever's cooking smells wonderful.'

'Churros!' Ellen popped up from the other side of the cart.

'We're testing the market,' Annie explained. 'Call it market research for when we open up our own place.'

'Wow, very entrepreneurial.' Hannah's stomach rumbled beneath her chunky burgundy cardigan.

'Takes one to know one,' Ellen beamed. 'What do you think?' She held up two different types of churros, one long and straight, the other curled into a circle, their edges brown and ridged and already dusted with sugar. 'Which shape works best?'

'Either . . . I think it's the smell and the taste that'll sell them,' said Hannah.

'Taste test?' Ellen held out the straight churros.

'Only if you let me pay you?'

Ellen tried to bat her away but she insisted, knowing how hard it was to get a business off the ground. Hannah had helped herself to the cinnamon sprinkle dust in a shaker behind the chocolate sauce and added it to her churros.

A family of four were already hovering nearby and Hannah knew they were about to come and buy something. The bottle of chocolate sauce on display with the plastic container filled with multi-coloured sprinkles would've drawn their eyes this way if the smell hadn't got to them first. Eager not to miss out on business, Annie began to make more. She took some dough from the bowl she'd made it in, pushed it into a plastic tube-like container and used the end of a wooden spoon to shove the mixture all the way in. Then she fixed it onto a machine that looked a bit like a home coffee machine, turned a handle and hey presto, out came long, ridged, dough pieces ready to pop into the pan of oil. The young kids were in awe of the entire method.

'Verdict?' Ellen asked as Hannah popped the last piece into her mouth.

'My word, they're delicious.'

'That's what I wanted to hear,' Ellen beamed.

She waved her goodbyes and set off for home again. And as she crossed the street Joe was just about to climb into his fancy car before he saw her and caught up with her.

'How are you?' Without a jacket on, he rubbed hands against the skin on his forearms to warm up.

'I'm well, thank you. And yourself?' The stilted conversation was a contrast to how openly they'd talked that night at the summer fair, dancing in each other's arms, the tantalising smell of a crisp aftershave drifting out of his open-necked shirt much like it was doing now.

'Busy, but good.'

Busy with all those women? He certainly had his fair share of female interest, but she guessed it was none of her business.

'Was your . . . friend . . . happy with the care package?'

His lips twitched with what may have been a smile. 'Vanessa loved it, she was very happy, so thank you.'

'All part of the service, I'm glad she liked it.'

'I actually wanted to organise another.'

Wow, Vanessa was a lucky woman. 'No problems, just email me.'

He raked a hand through his hair. 'It's definitely easier to do that than show up at the cottage. Sorry about doing that by the way. Did you get another customer coming to ask the same?'

'Sorry, I'm not sure I follow.' She pushed her hands deep into her pockets.

'The man who turned up after me. Sorry, it was a while ago, you probably don't remember.'

He showed a lot of interest for someone who'd been romancing pretty much every woman he could lay his eyes on, or maybe it was just her. Maybe her lack of activity in that department made her all the more sensitive to anyone who had a bit of luck. 'He's an old friend, nothing to do with work.'

His eyes settled on her. 'I'll email you then.'

'Good idea. And I still have your last email so I have Vanessa's details already.'

'This isn't for Vanessa.' He seemed amused. She'd been sprung, perhaps a hint of jealousy had seeped through during their conversation, but she wouldn't give him the satisfaction of asking who it *was* for.

'Then send me everything.' She took her keys from her pocket, ready to escape. 'Happy to help.' And she walked off wondering if she sounded as stupid as she felt.

Hannah spent the rest of the morning updating her

blog, ordering in some more packaging supplies, and working on a couple of prototypes of Valentine's day cards to pitch to Castle Cards.

With her new designs set aside and ready to post, she turned her attention to her accounts. She had to stay on top of those, but with her background it wasn't too difficult, just a chore compared to her other work. She updated her expenses spreadsheet, filed the receipts and updated income that filtered through from her website orders.

Over cups of tea and a rushed meal of reheated lasagne she caught up on all her paperwork, popped the proto-types in an envelope for Castle Cards and double-checked their address from their email footer, when another email popped into her inbox. And she could never resist any-thing titled as a new customer enquiry.

She read through the request, spurred on by the header in the email, using the word Urgent. This package was for a little girl, younger than most of her clientele, who was returning to Canada the day after tomorrow and the customer, her dad, Mark, wanted the package tonight or if not, tomorrow first thing. Hannah wondered what the story was here, why his daughter was leaving and he wasn't, how did he feel about that? Would he try to stop it happening? Had he spent much time with her over the years? She often got wrapped up in the stories sitting behind these requests but having to put together a pack-age so quickly left her no time to dwell.

She skimmed through more details. The girl, Amelia, was eleven, hated anything pink, worshipped her iPhone, was mad about horses and crazy about London, and she loved Harry Potter. Hannah did a quick check of the sender's home address to see he lived in Notting Hill. He'd also shared that it was his permanent abode and she had visions of a man grappling with the last moments of his little girl's childhood, trying to think up the perfect gift that would send her on her way and leave a lasting impression.

Hannah grabbed a scrap piece of paper and began to jot down ideas. She emailed the client to ask whether Amelia had any food allergies and whether she preferred white, milk or dark chocolate. Then she added in the other suggestions she'd thought of – she'd take her phone when she went shopping and if he wasn't happy to go ahead with some of them, Hannah was pretty good at thinking on her feet and could find alternatives. She also wanted to find some trendy writing paper – it was old-fashioned and most kids were allergic to anything handwritten but if Amelia could write to her dad it could create some really special memories for him to treasure. Texts were deleted all too quickly, not the same thing at all.

Hannah knew she'd have to leave now if she had a hope of fulfilling this order and catching the last post. She drove out to a big shopping centre and began her quest in a stationery shop where she was spoilt for choice when it came to writing paper – but from the brief in the email she could tell Amelia wasn't a girly girl, and so when she saw the Harry Potter writing set with its olde worlde paper and the stickers that looked like old-fashioned sealing wax, she dropped it into her basket before choosing a stylish set of pens. She paid for those, checked her emails and sure enough Mark had replied saying they were go-go-go with her suggestions, but don't whatever you do buy white chocolate. Apparently he'd tried to do that last week and she'd told him it wasn't real chocolate! Hannah had gone straight to a nearby newsagents deciding to fulfil the chocolate quota with quintessentially English items: a Curly Wurly, a generous slab of Dairy Milk, a packet of Munchies and a Lion Bar.

She finished her shop finding a delightfully multi-coloured pair of fluffy socks – trendy and practical for a cold country – an iPhone case with the silhouette of a horse, and a keyring with a glittery initial A. But a souvenir to represent the city of London remained elusive and she had no luck finding anything. She stopped, grabbed a large americano and emailed Mark about her predicament. She was just beginning to think she'd have to drive closer to London when he emailed back with a photo attachment of the items he'd picked up from the shops that were on every other street in the more touristy areas of the city. He'd found a London telephone box on a keyring, a set of playing cards with the Union Jack on the packet, a mouse mat featuring a display of the underground system, and even a red double-decker pencil sharpener. Hannah quickly emailed him back to say that she'd head home now, the package came tied up with string anyway and so she'd ease off the fixing up of that part and he could easily slip the items inside.

Bags hooked on her arms, she managed to finish the americano without spilling it, threw the cup in the nearest bin as she went through the automatic doors out to the car park and fed the parking machine with her credit card. She put her bags onto the back seat, jumped in, ready for the off.

But nothing.

'Oh come on, don't do this to me now.' She willed her

little car that had so far been a reliable runabout, to start. 'Just start for me today, you can break down tomorrow, have a day off,' she pleaded, but no amount of turning over the engine worked and she whacked her hands on the steering wheel and let out a wail as well as a few blasphemous words she wouldn't want the toddler in the buggy being pushed past to hear. Just as well it was autumn and the windows were up.

She'd have to call the AA, but as she was looking for her membership card in her purse there was a knock on her car window. 'Georgia?' She pressed the button to open the glass panel separating them.

'Car trouble?'

'Yes, and at the worst possible time.'

'Have you called the AA?'

'Just about to do that.'

Georgia pulled a phone from her pocket. 'No need, they could be ages. I'll call my friend who works in the garage right near here, he'll come.'

'Honestly, it's fine.'

'Let him come.' She'd already found his contact and phone to her ear was waiting for an answer. 'If he can't sort it, then we'll call the AA.'

Hannah went with it. But all she kept thinking was that Mark wasn't going to get this care package on time. His daughter was going to be disappointed and she was in the business of making people feel better, not worse. She wondered whether he had a car, could drive here and get her with the bits and pieces, go to her house, and make up the package.

Thankfully her insane train of thought was interrupted by Georgia telling her, 'He'll be here in five.'

It wasn't entirely comfortable between them as they waited but thankfully Georgia's mate Chris, who looked as though he'd literally been beneath a car at the time of the desperate call given the amount of oil and grease on him, turned up in the time he'd promised. And even better, he found the problem quick enough.

Wiping his hands on an already filthy cloth, the mechanic told her, 'It was your spark plugs, all sorted now.'

'I don't know how to thank you. Apart from paying you of course.' She leaned into the car and pulled out her purse.

'On the house, no worries.'

'I can't possibly . . .'

'A favour for Georgia,' he winked and Hannah suspected the two of them had been a little more than just friends at one time. Georgia had always been flirty, a flutter-the-eyelashes-type girl to get what she wanted. 'Nice to meet you, Hannah.'

'Thanks again,' she called after him, but before he reached his tow truck he stopped again.

'I think you've got a bigger problem.' He was looking at the front of the car and when Hannah and Georgia joined him it was obvious what problem he was referring to. The front tyre was noticeably deflated.

The same could be said of Hannah's spirits. Disappointment flooded her body, because she'd never get that care package finished and sent now.

12

The rain had begun to hammer down on the multi-storey car park where her little Fiat 500 sat helplessly waiting to be rescued.

'This is all I need,' Hannah frowned.

Bending down, Chris confirmed her fears. 'You must've gone over a nail at some point and it eventually took its toll. Doesn't always do it straight away, could've been jammed in there for days or weeks. You'll need a whole new tyre.'

'Really? Can't we do a puncture repair?' she begged, visions of repairing her bicycle puncture at age nine and totally impressing her friend's teenage brother whom she had a crush on at the time.

'No can do, I'm afraid. I could do a puncture repair if the damage was in the minor repair area, but this one is too close to the sidewall.'

'In English,' Georgia urged.

He pointed to the tyre. 'This area, the sidewall, is where the tyre gets the most load when you're out on the roads. Repairing the puncture would weaken it. It's safer to get a whole new tyre.'

'Then let's do that.'

He nodded. 'Pop the boot open and I'll change it in no time, get you on your way and you can bring it to the garage tomorrow and we'll sort out what to do.'

Hannah moved to open the boot but froze.

'You do have a spare, don't you?' Georgia had finished the cup of coffee she'd been nursing ever since she knocked on the car window.

'I do, of course.' She looked at each of them, reality dawning. 'But it's the old tyre that's been there since the summer when I last got a flat. Dad changed it for me and I never got around to replacing it.'

'Should always have a spare,' Chris reiterated.

'I know that now.' She berated herself for dropping the ball on this one.

'Why are you fretting so much?' Georgia asked. 'I'm sure Chris can go to the garage, get a new tyre, come back, change it.'

Chris held up a hand. 'Sorry, no can do. I just left for the day and I've got to pick up Lottie from the childminder by four o'clock or my other half will kill me. Best I can do is sort this tomorrow. We'll clear it with the car park to leave the vehicle – I know enough people who work here, been doing their cars cheap for long enough – and I'll do it first thing. I'll bring you a spare too.'

'Thanks,' Hannah just about managed.

'I've got to go. Hannah, get my details from Georgia, text me tonight and we'll sort arrangements.' He raised a hand to both girls before running over to the man in the booth who was ready to jump out and help anyone who had an issue with the automatic barriers. This sort of excitement probably made his day.

'Thanks, Chris!' Georgia called after him with Hannah

doing her best to enthusiastically join in. 'Don't look so down, he'll sort it tomorrow.'

'Well I'm not going to make last post now.' She shook her head and pulled her phone from her pocket.

'Emergency care package?'

'You joke, but it kind of is.' Hannah reiterated the order and the sense of desperation she'd picked up from Mark's emails.

'Then let me give you a lift home; you can work fast, get the package out on time.'

Hannah hesitated. It did make sense. Getting the bus would take forever as it stopped a good distance from Lantern Square and that was only after it had been all round the houses first, leaving no corner of the neighbouring villages and towns ignored. 'Are you sure?'

'Of course I am. Come on, this way, I'm over there.'

Hannah hauled her shopping from the back seat of her own car, locked up, double checked with the parking attendant that she wouldn't come back to her car tomorrow to find it clamped or with a ticket demanding a horrendous fine, and followed after Georgia.

'Why aren't you leaping out?' Georgia asked when she pulled up outside Lantern Cottage. 'Thought you had to make last post.'

'It's almost five o'clock. I've got no hope. I'll have to get in touch with a courier, hope they can slot me in.'

'Call them now, I'm sure it's not too late.'

Hannah found the number in her contacts but a few minutes later her hopes were dashed. 'They're fully booked, can't slot me in until tomorrow.' She set her head against the headrest not making any effort to get out of the car.

The rain hadn't relented at all during the drive back and it matched her mood. She felt deflated. And more than that, she knew it was this man's bond with his daughter and the thought of that breaking across the miles in two days' time, because all it did was remind her of Liam's parents' heartbreak and how every day she didn't open those letters, let alone reply, she could be giving them an extra dose of undeserved sadness.

'Don't give up.' Georgia was busy tapping at her phone at the same time as asking Hannah for details of where the parcel needed to go. She called one courier, no luck, another, same story. But then with the third, she punched the air before the call had even finished. 'Sorted, they'll be here at seven o'clock tonight for delivery over in Notting Hill.'

'Are you serious?' She squealed and threw her arms around Georgia. 'You'd better come in for a cuppa as a thank you for saving the day more than once.'

'I'd love to. Can I help you with anything?'

Hannah reached into the back seat for the shopping bags. 'Shove this one under your coat, I'll take the others.' And between them they managed to dash from the car to the cottage and kept all the items dry.

'Don't you add an extra charge for cases like these?' Georgia asked as they sipped on tea and regained a sense of calm.

'No, I never add on to the cost. Delivery is usually covered and in cases like these, I don't do it often so it's not too much of an issue. And the courier you found wasn't charging an extortionate rate either.'

'Shame you can't get some kind of agreement from a courier company, a cheap deal.'

'I thought about it, but the post office serves me well

given the number of packages I send. And besides, I want to keep it local, too many post offices are shutting their doors and people in Lantern Square rely on it.' She thought of the many people she saw in passing coming in and out of there and knew it'd be missed if it was ever taken away.

'It could make good business sense though.'

Hannah smiled. 'Maybe.' She wouldn't change from using the post office, but she didn't want to appear rude. Georgia had been a lifeline tonight and she couldn't be more grateful.

Hannah quickly fed Smokey and Bandit while Georgia made a fuss of them both and when Hannah announced she had to get on to have the package ready, Georgia asked, 'Can I watch? See what you do?'

She didn't feel she could say no to any of Georgia's requests right now, so in the dining room with the lights on now that the skies outside darkened so much earlier, Hannah and Georgia between them – because Georgia insisted she help rather than stand around idle – wrapped each item individually and Hannah found a suitable brown box that would allow room for the other items Mark wanted to pop in.

'You seem busy.' Georgia nodded over to another package sitting on the side waiting to have confetti added, then tied up with string, packaged and labelled. 'How do people contact you, is it via email?'

'Mostly, or by phone.'

Georgia picked up the piece of paper near the other box. 'Ah, so they list what they want.'

'They generally have an idea, but not always. Some come to me and just say help, what shall I put inside? I'm thinking of doing set boxes perhaps to make it easier for me to buy items in bulk, but I'll still keep the option for bespoke packages should customers prefer it.'

'What's this package waiting for?'

'It's all ready, just needs confetti.'

'Could I do it?'

Hannah grinned. 'Sure. I just hadn't got around to it. I kind of dropped everything for this. Use the pink and champagne one.' She nodded over to the shelf where she kept it.

Georgia opened the bag and grabbed a handful. 'How much?'

'Enough so it looks pretty. Excuse me,' she said when there was a knock at the door. It was someone collecting for the local scouts and she dug around in her bag, found her purse, and gave them a few quid before returning to Georgia.

'Who was it?' Georgia had added confetti, sealed the box and had a ball of string in hand ready for the next step, although Hannah was oddly protective about that part.

She explained, but couldn't help being a little put out that Georgia had sealed the entire thing up already.

'Something wrong?'

'I was going to have one more check over the contents.'

'Done,' Georgia concluded. 'Everything on the email was in there.'

'Well, thank you.' The parcel was almost done so Hannah took charge, did the honours with the string and put it into the outer packaging, adding the label last.

'You need a label maker.'

She'd already moved back to the urgent box. 'Maybe, although I think the writing looks more personal.'

'I suppose it does.'

She added confetti, ensured she hadn't used anything remotely pink, wrapped it in brown paper fastening it very lightly with minimal sticky tape, and cut the right length of string that she tied loosely around so her customer would be able to pop in the remaining items he wanted to include.

'Your business is all about the personal touch,' Georgia observed. 'I like it.'

'I'm not sure about leaving this to a man.'

'What, tying the bow?'

'I don't mean to be sexist, but no man I've ever known has had any particular skill at making gifts look that extra bit special.'

'It's just a bow. I know you're fussy, but . . .'

'Take my dad for example. He's a whizz at changing a tyre, he's very practical, but as for delicate gift-wrapping, absolutely not. Liam was always all fingers and thumbs too. Every Christmas when it came to wrapping the presents, I pretty much did all of them for him. And then with Luke, I suspect the only bow he ever tied was the one in his shoelaces.'

Georgia grinned. 'I guess you have a point.'

Hannah tied the bow very loosely around the package. 'Hopefully this client will see what it looks like, maybe slot the items in so carefully it'll easily do back up again.'

'You'll just have to hope so.' Georgia shooed Bandit away when he looked like he was about to jump up on her lap and possibly the table. She checked her watch. 'Twenty minutes until the courier, nice timing.'

'Thanks.' She finally let out a breath. 'I need a glass of wine.' She hadn't meant to voice those thoughts aloud, planning a glass of wine the second she shut the door to Georgia.

'There's a local pub, right?'

'The Butterbury Arms.'

'Then how about we go for a drink, relax. The parcel will soon be on its way.'

'As long as I can buy.'

'Hey, you'll get no arguments from me.'

The parcel was on its way as scheduled, but Hannah clutched her phone tight as they sat in the pub, which was busier than usual for a weekday evening. She knew she wouldn't completely let go until she knew the package had been delivered safe and sound and she might even ask for a photograph of it tied up as it should be.

'Are you serious?' Georgia took Hannah's phone and set it on the table. 'Did you really ask him to take photographs of it? Is that so you know he can tie a bow?'

She was right. 'I know, I just like to keep my customers satisfied, word of mouth is so important.'

'I think the fact you put together the package at such short notice will have impressed the customer and no matter how he tied the package up with string, he'll have good things to say. The gifts were perfect from what you've told me about his daughter, you did it all on time and on budget, mission accomplished.' She raised her glass of wine to meet Hannah's.

Hannah chinked her glass into Georgia's and smiled a hello at Colette, the landlady, collecting glasses at the next table, another to her husband Patrick who was manning the bar.

'What do you do with yourself when you're not working?' Georgia wondered.

'I put in a lot of hours, but I come here a couple of

times a week, there's usually people to talk to.' They'd already said hello to a few familiar faces although Hannah hadn't made any introductions yet. The village was small but not so tiny that people wondered who the strange new face was. 'And there are seasonal events that I get involved in. The summer fair was the latest one, with the dance too, and then there'll be the fireworks coming up at the weekend. Oh, and the New Year's dance which I'm already looking forward to.'

'You sound really community minded. I'm being genuine,' she added, when Hannah caught her eye. 'And did you meet anyone at the dance?' Georgia sipped her wine and wiped the corner of her mouth for any left-behind signs of red wine, her bright-red lipstick still perfectly in place and most likely layered given how it managed to resist the liquid going past it.

'What makes you ask me that?'

'I heard someone at the gym raving about it when I was there talking work with Jason one day,' she explained.

'I didn't *meet* anyone but I did dance with a few men.'

'Oh really?'

'It's the done thing at the summer fair. And it's not as exciting as you think. Charles Bray, a local elderly gentleman, used to dance in his younger days, before his wife passed away, and he showed me some moves.'

'Right, and who else showed you some moves?'

She hesitated. 'The local doctor.'

'And how old is this local doctor?'

'Not sure.'

'Come on . . . grandparent age, our parents' age, or our age?'

'Our age.'

Georgia began to smile. 'Interesting.'

'There's nothing in it . . . he's a bit of a ladies' man, to tell you the truth.'

'One of those, eh.'

'One of those.'

'And what else do you do when you're not dancing with eligible – or not so eligible – bachelors?'

Hannah told her all about Butterbury Lodge, how often she went there, the people she'd got to know. 'I started volunteering when I was new to the village, I thought it'd give me something to do for a while, but I really enjoyed it so kept it up.'

'Life's too short to do anything you don't want to, I'll raise a glass to that.' Her wine almost gone, she found her purse and insisted on getting another round lined up.

When she was left alone Hannah waved over at Rhys who was talking to Malcolm and Miriam Styles. They were a friendly, approachable couple and Malcolm especially liked a good chat. Lily was behind the bar having fun while she worked, and Dawn and Troy were settled across the other side at a table for two with a pint each.

'There you go.' Georgia handed Hannah her second glass. 'Get that down you, let's show these locals how it's done.'

'What makes you think they don't know already?' Then she whispered, 'See Mr Styles over there?'

'The one with the thick-rimmed spectacles who looks a lot like Mr Wallis who taught us in our last year of primary school?'

Hannah laughed. 'He does a bit. Anyway, word has it he got so legless last New Year's Eve that he fell into the pond in his back garden when he got home.'

'I'm impressed, way to go Mr Styles!' She held her glass aloft and Hannah quickly shushed her.

'Quiet, he'll hear you.' She smiled over at Malcolm hoping the noise in the pub would've drowned out Georgia's remark. 'And see Dawn and Troy over there at the table with the painting on the wall beside them . . . well they go to Ibiza every year, and not the quiet part. Between you and me, I wouldn't mind seeing their holiday snaps.'

Georgia collapsed into a fit of giggles, recalling a trip she'd been on to the same island that involved a lot of tequila, dancing and a brief dalliance with a wildly unsuitable older gentleman whom she refused to discuss.

'That tash!' Hannah guffawed. 'He looked like an eighties porn star.'

'Shut up, he did not.' Georgia took one look at Hannah and admitted, 'OK, so he did. But what a kisser.'

'Did it go any further?'

'No, thank goodness. He'd lived on the island for ten years, I'm thinking he'd dipped his wick a few times if you know what I mean.'

'Hey, ladies.' Rhys, drawn over to their table by the roars of laughter, introduced himself with a grin. 'Nice to meet a friend of Hannah's who's under the age of seventy.'

Georgia found that pretty funny. 'I keep telling her she needs to get out more. With people her own age. I'm here to rescue her.'

It was only in the odd moment that Hannah remembered their big falling out. She was glad they'd made peace, she'd done it with Luke too, and what was the harm in sharing a drink and a few laughs anyway? She needed to at her age.

Rhys did his best to chat up Georgia, and Hannah made herself scarce by going to the ladies. When she looked in the mirror and saw her mascara had run from all the laughing, she knew she'd probably had enough to drink, but when she returned, Georgia had brought over a round of tequila slammers.

'Oh no . . . no chance.'

'Come on, Hannah. Live a little!'

'I've got to sort my car out in the morning.'

'Get Rhys here to go pick it up.'

'He's got a job to do,' Hannah laughed, pushing away the tequila slammer.

'She's right, I have. But I don't work all the time. My evenings are pretty free.' He was trying, bless him, but Georgia needed a sledgehammer to come down and get her attention that he might be asking her out. Either that or he needed a bit of bravery.

'Georgia, would you go on a date with Rhys here?' Hannah's suggestion met with daggers from him. 'What? She'll never go out with you unless you strap on a pair.'

Georgia's laughter was boiling over but she turned to Rhys and clasped his hands in hers. 'You're gorgeous, you know that? But I have a boyfriend.'

'First I've heard,' said Hannah. But she left it at that as Rhys and Georgia downed three tequila shots each. They laughed at Hannah's lack of common gardening skills, they talked about Rhys's sad excuse for a love life and how the village was too small to meet anyone. Georgia did her best to persuade Rhys and Hannah to take a gamble and go on a date, but it only met with amusement. They were solidly in the friend zone and liked it that way, and finally Georgia gave up. Hannah had forgotten that once her friend got an idea in her head, it was pretty hard to get her to let it go.

When Rhys returned to his own friends Hannah suspected he'd be out of his depth with Georgia anyway. She'd always been a ballsy, wild one, too much for a lot of men, especially one as kind and gentle as Rhys.

'I really appreciate you getting the mechanic out for me today,' said Hannah after asking Lily to bring over a couple of glasses of water for them.

'Not a problem. He's reliable, he lived near us in London but I didn't have a car then. We did date for a while.'

'Thought as much.'

'It didn't last long, and now he's turned responsible, has a partner and a child and is well and truly settled with his life and his business.'

'Well it's a good job we didn't have to flag down a stranger. Remember last time I had car issues with my old banger?'

Georgia gasped. 'I'd totally forgotten about that! I'll never forget the bloke we asked to help. Had an arse crack the size of Mount Vesuvius.'

Hannah almost choked on her water earning herself a big pat on the back from Georgia which just made them both collapse into more giggles. 'Roger Dicky, what a guy!'

'It's our own fault,' Georgia concluded when they both recovered, 'if we'd had any clue how to use jump leads ourselves we could've saved him bending over at all. My eyes will never recover.' The stranger had been all too happy to help and had been a dab hand at getting her car started when he pulled his up alongside, but his jeans had a habit of coming down and he didn't seem too put off that the cold winds of December had been blowing right up his backside. 'You were very polite to take his business card.'

'I thought it would say Roger Dicky, mechanic, or garage manager. Not Roger Dicky, Cat Behaviourist.'

'Do you think he sat on them if they didn't behave?'

'I dread to think.' With all the laughing Hannah's cheeks were beginning to ache. 'Anyway, let's wind back to the topic of boyfriends.'

'When were we ever on that?'

'When you turned Rhys down.'

'Oh that.' She hid behind her drink with a coy look, unwilling to share.

'Come on, are you seeing someone or did you only say that so you didn't break his heart by saying no?'

'I'm seeing someone . . . but it's early days.'

Since Hannah had been with Luke, Georgia hadn't had a serious boyfriend, content at larking around with whoever came her way. 'And what's he like?'

'Nice, good looking.'

'I need details.' It was as painful as the time she'd tried to wheedle out care package details from Joe.

'I don't want to tempt fate.'

'In case it doesn't last?'

'Exactly. When have you ever known me to last five minutes with anyone?'

'Good point.'

'You were always better at relationships than me.'

'It's not a profession you know. And I don't think I ended things with Luke very well at all. I hurt him.'

'He's a big boy, he'll get over it.'

'I feel bad though. He came to see me recently.'

'Really?' Georgia didn't bother to try to hide her shock.

'I didn't know what to say to him.' She almost admitted

about the kiss, the afternoon tea, but she had enough trouble working things through in her own mind.

When Lily rang last orders Hannah didn't offer to go another round, it was time to leave or she'd never be able to get out of bed in the morning and meet the mechanic to sort her car.

They pulled on their extra layers and bustled their way between punters who weren't so eager to leave, euphoric from the good time they'd had tonight. But as they stepped down the single step at the front door and into the cool evening that held the scent of the earlier downpour, Hannah stopped smiling. She'd held the door open for whoever was behind her and caught a glimpse as she did.

'What's up?' Georgia slurred, linking her arm. But Hannah said nothing and her friend eventually registered the problem when she turned around.

Luke was standing behind them with his dad.

When she said nothing Georgia hissed, 'What the hell does he want? Is he stalking you? I thought he hated the countryside.' It was a lot of emotion to come out at once and Hannah was reminded how Georgia had never got on with Luke, how Georgia had told her more than once that she was too good for him.

Hannah tried to say a polite hello, but Rupert hugged her like a long-lost friend, and Georgia looked as though she was sucking on sour grapes the daggers she was giving both of them.

As far as awkward moments went, this was one of the worst and when she dragged Georgia on their way her friend was still glaring at Luke as though warning him to back off.

13

Hannah hadn't gone to Butterbury Lodge yesterday because it had taken all her energy to go to meet Chris and sort out her car – thankfully the new tyre fit didn't take long – and get back to the village before doing the minimal in the way of work she could get away with. She didn't have any care packages to fulfil which meant she was spared a trip to the post office, and so she focused on updating her accounts. When Mark emailed a photograph of his daughter's care package complete with a bow tied well enough to satisfy Hannah, plus another picture with the box open and styled so that all the contents could be seen easily yet the attractive confetti and even the lid and the undone string could still be seen, she added it to her website and social media. He'd titled his email For Promo Purposes and Hannah had wondered then whether he was in marketing or advertising to have done such a sympathetic job.

Georgia had texted after her spin class in the morning to ask if she could meet with Hannah for lunch and seeing nothing wrong with the rekindled friendship, Hannah agreed. She'd even appreciated the united front Georgia had tried to put up last night outside the pub;

it reminded her of how they'd stick up for each other at school if ever anyone tried to pick on the other or tease them in any way.

Now Hannah was at Butterbury Lodge with Georgia in tow. They'd walked up the hill in the nippy autumn temperatures that blanketed the Cotswolds and sent leaves spiralling from all directions. They'd passed Rhys in Lantern Square raking leaves into enormous piles before letting local kids leap into them, and now there was a low-lying mist that hinted winter wasn't far off. Hannah only hoped it cleared later when the fireworks began. Crowds would gather in Lantern Square tonight, but Hannah had heard a few residents bemoaning the fact that they didn't get to enjoy fireworks any more these days, and she, Maggie and Frankie had made arrangements for an event to be held at the lodge. They'd have residents gather out at the front to see fireworks launching in the distance in the fields beyond Lantern Square and her cottage. And in its elevated position, Butterbury Lodge might just end up being the best place to view after all, weather permitting. She couldn't wait to see the familiar faces light up with surprise at how special the night could be even though they weren't kids any more. Fireworks were for any age, Hannah and Frankie had readily agreed.

'What are we doing here anyway?' Georgia asked as she shut the gate behind them and they followed the path towards the front entrance.

'You didn't have to come,' Hannah said.

'I wanted to see what you get up to. What's the box for?' She eyed what Hannah was carrying.

'It's for the book club I'm organising. This will be at the front desk to take suggestions.'

'Can't they organise it themselves?' Georgia had already unbuttoned her coat and was flapping her collar as they went through the front doors and met with the toasty inside of Butterbury Lodge. 'I mean . . .' she whispered, '. . . it's not like they have much else to do is it?'

'I need to be in charge or there'll be arguments.'

'You make it sound like you're managing a kids' club.'

'Keep your voice down.' Although Georgia was giggling Hannah wondered whether she'd made a big mistake letting her none-too-subtle friend come with her. Older people told it like it was, maybe they'd earned that right at their age, but Georgia sometimes needed a filter. It was fine in the pub when noise tended to drown everything else out anyway, but not here.

Hannah introduced Georgia to some of the residents and then to Maggie, before saying hello to Frankie, who wanted to know everything about Hannah's new friend. And when Georgia said she worked for a new gym, Frankie wanted to know all about pricing, the timetable, classes on offer.

They passed through the lounge and residents were keen to know who the new face was too, although Georgia took some persuasion to talk. 'What's wrong with you? Usually I can't shut you up, you're a live wire,' said Hannah.

'Not really my kind of place, that's all. Gives me the creeps if I'm honest.' But she stopped talking when Mr G called over.

'Come on,' said Hannah, 'I want you to meet someone special.'

They'd only done the introductions when Mr G said, 'So this is the one leading you astray, Hannah?' For a moment she thought he meant regarding the mess with

G.H. Bookkeeping that she'd told him about but then he said, 'The gossip mill has already told me why you didn't make it here yesterday to see me.'

'And what gossip mill would that be?' Hannah lay her coat over the back of a chair and indicated for Georgia to do the same before she sat down.

'I heard it from Ernest, who heard it from Maggie, who heard it from Rhys. Word has it you were a little inebriated.'

'We were letting our hair down, I'd had a dreadful day.' She recounted the tale of rushing around to fulfil the order, her car refusing to start and then having a flat tyre, Georgia stepping in, the courier saving the day. 'And Georgia's friend did the new tyres for me at a good rate, so I'm a lot calmer now.'

They talked about the book club: Mr G's favourite reads, what he detested, and Ernest came over and joined in enthusiastically, although the two men couldn't agree on anything. And for the most part Georgia looked like she'd rather be anywhere else but here. 'We'll see what the suggestion box reveals after a week. Actually, before I forget, I'm going to do the rounds and remind people, then I'll read to you, Mr G.'

'You don't need to read to me today, you must be busy, have a life, or at least one that isn't already fifty per cent done.'

Georgia stifled a laugh and Hannah left them to talk while she encouraged everyone she spoke with to pop a suggestion in the box no matter how crazy they thought it, even if they assumed nobody else would be interested. 'I can't work with nothing,' she told them, 'but a whole heap of suggestions is a starting point.' She managed to get Flo firstly to remove her ear buds and secondly to agree to take part and she finished up talking with Grace who'd just emerged following her afternoon nap.

When she made her way back to Mr G she was a little disappointed to see he and Georgia weren't even speaking. Georgia was fiddling with her nails – a habit she'd needed to quit for years, it had driven Hannah crazy when they were working – and Mr G had the newspaper on his lap. And if Hannah wasn't mistaken, he wasn't even reading it.

'Right, Mr G, where's that book?'

He dismissed the suggestion without looking up. 'I'm reading the newspaper instead. You two go and have a lovely afternoon.'

'If you're sure.'

'Go on, off you go. I'll see you back here tonight for fireworks I hope?'

'Wouldn't miss it for the world.' She couldn't wait. Frankie said she'd stood at the front gate on the path to the lodge last year and seen so much, but they hadn't suggested it to any residents because of the cold and the worry that some might wander off. After Hannah floated the idea this year, Frankie and Maggie had called in other workers to do extra shifts so it was perfectly manageable. Mr G and everyone else were in for a real treat.

Right now though, Hannah wanted to whisk Georgia away. She should've known coming here wasn't everyone's cup of tea. She told Mr. G, 'Make sure to pop a suggestion for a book-club read into the box at the front desk. You're my ally, we're in it together.'

'We are.' He shot Georgia a peculiar look.

As she shrugged on her coat and said her goodbyes,

Hannah could hear Ernest rambling on to Maggie. 'It's high time the fireplace was lit,' he said.

'Not yet, be patient. It's still fairly mild.'

'Not in the evenings it isn't.' Hannah loved how he stood his ground. Hands in pockets he was following Maggie around whenever she moved. 'I might not live until Christmas,' he went on. 'How can you deprive an old man of a simple pleasure?'

Hannah grinned and returned Mr G's wink. Ernest was one of the most robust residents here and Hannah had a sneaky feeling he'd have a whole host of Christmases left in him yet.

'He's doolally,' Georgia claimed as they passed through reception ready to leave.

'Who, Ernest?'

'No, not him. He seems to have all his marbles. I mean the one you made me sit with.'

'Mr G?'

'That's the one.'

'He's lovely,' Hannah insisted as Georgia opened the main door to Butterbury Lodge.

'I didn't like the way he was looking at me, that's all. He could've been a bit nicer.'

Hannah supposed he had been a bit hostile, but still, it felt nice to have someone looking out for her. 'He's being a grandparent for me, worrying about me.' She shut the main doors behind her and they made their way down the path. The willow tree had shed plenty of its leaves, the greens, yellows and golds littering the ground as the mist continued to blanket Butterbury in the distance.

'Don't you think that's kind of weird? Doesn't he have his own family?'

'He does, but I don't know, I guess we've always got on and he's become a good friend.'

'He's ancient!' She shuddered as she shut the gate behind them and scraped a divot of soil against the step to get rid of it from the heel of her trainers. 'I don't ever want to be old.'

'Careful what you wish for,' Hannah grinned. 'Better to be over the hill than under it.'

Georgia linked Hannah's arm, something she hadn't done in a long time. 'You're right as always. Now, where to for lunch? I worked off a billion calories at spin, I'm starving.'

After a slap-up ploughman's lunch at the Butterbury Arms, with crumbly farmhouse cheddar, freshly baked bread, creamy coleslaw and thickly sliced ham with pickles on the side, Hannah and Georgia made their way back to Lantern Cottage. They'd been talking about the letters still lurking, still unopened.

Georgia took out her car keys. 'Go inside and get it over with.'

'You never were very patient,' Hannah shivered.

'Come on.' Georgia put her keys away and instead, ushered Hannah towards the door. 'I won't go yet, I'll wait for you to open them and then pick up the pieces if you get upset.'

Hannah didn't bother arguing. As bossy as Georgia was being, she was right. And the second they were inside they went through to the kitchen and Hannah tore open the envelope of the first one as quickly as you'd rip off a plaster. She skimmed the words, took them all in, and did the same with all of them.

'They're just words, Hannah. Just reminders of the past. What do they say?'

'The usual . . . their annual summer holiday up in the Lake District, Liam's dad's furniture business, the tree Liam planted in their garden that's still going strong . . . she asks what's going on with me, how the business is going.'

'All pretty harmless stuff then.'

With a sigh, Hannah said, 'I feel it's hard to let go when they're still contacting me.'

'But you don't want to forget Liam, surely.' Georgia took charge of making a brew.

'Of course not.'

'Then what's the harm in a letter now and then?'

She pulled a tissue from the box in the corner next to the microwave and dried her eyes. 'You know, I never mentioned Luke much whenever I wrote to them.'

'But you and he were together a long time.'

'I know, but it feels like I'd be rubbing it in that I've been able to move on when Liam . . . well, Liam is frozen at age twenty-seven, he'll never meet anyone else, never grow old.'

'Thank the Lord for that, after seeing some of those shrivelled old people at Butterbury Lodge.' Hannah was about to reprimand her when she said, 'I'm just trying to get you to laugh.' Georgia passed Hannah one mug of tea and cradled the other between her palms, blowing on the liquid. 'Who was that man who came out of the house with the red door as we were coming past?'

'That'll most likely be Joe, the doctor. Dark brown hair, about our age?'

'Sounds like him, although you forgot to mention the most appropriate adjective . . . hot!'

Hannah set her mug down. She'd eaten such a lot that even warm liquid was a bit much and was really only doing the job of a handwarmer. 'He's not bad to look at.'

'Not bad? You need your head read! He's the local hottie by far from what I've seen.'

'He's a bit arrogant.'

That got her attention. 'Ah, he's the one you danced with.'

Hannah recapped what had happened when he used his contacts to steal a scheduled radio slot she'd organised to promote her business, and she told Georgia all about the women coming and going from his home. 'Bit of a player if you ask me, good looking and knows it.'

'But you admit he's nice looking. You do! You're blushing!'

'I am not.'

'You so are! Come on, spill . . . there's more, isn't there?'

'I may have enjoyed our dance more than I should.'

'It sounds like you're interested in him to me.' Georgia smiled. 'And the more you deny it, the more I'm convinced.'

'I admit he's nice, but he's not for me. He also upset me right before the dance. I had nothing to wear and ended up putting on my polka-dot dress.'

'The gorgeous one, the one in the box, the dress you freaked out about when I wanted to try it on at your parents' place?'

'That's the one.' Georgia and Hannah had stayed in her old bedroom one night when they'd gone up for Hannah's parents' wedding anniversary, tagging it on to a girls' weekend away, and Georgia being nosey had found the dress in the box under Hannah's bed. While Hannah was still bleary eyed from the effects of the partying the night before she'd taken it out of the box and was stepping into it to try it on, demanding to know why Hannah hadn't worn this, ever, and especially why she hadn't put it on the night before. Hannah had gone ballistic.

'You never did fill me in on the full story.'

'Yes I did, I told you Liam bought it for me.'

'But that's not all, is it?'

She shook her head. 'Liam bought the dress and had it sent to me. I got it delivered in the mail just like Carrie from *Sex and the City* when the Vivienne Westwood dress arrives in the box to her apartment.'

'Love that bit . . . what a dress. But back to you,' she urged. 'Carry on.'

'I put it on straight away, it was a beautiful fit and I could tell it was expensive. I felt a right loser because I kept it on for hours and hours. It was a weekend, I was sitting around reading books, I watched a movie and all the while I had a soppy smile on my face. Liam and I used FaceTime before he went on a training exercise – he rarely got to make contact so it was extra special. He told me I looked beautiful and he couldn't wait to see me in the dress for real. I didn't want to take it off, I was missing him so badly. I left it on and watched another movie, ended up falling asleep and woke to a knock at the front door.' Georgia waited for her to go on. 'It was Liam's dad, and just from the look on his face I knew . . . I knew that the FaceTime call would be the last time I ever saw him alive.'

Georgia had her arms around Hannah before Hannah even realised she was crying. 'Why did he have to die? It's so unfair. Such a waste of life.' Her tears were flowing now but Georgia held her until she was ready to talk again.

Georgia handed her a fresh tissue. 'Life can be cruel sometimes.'

'I get so angry that everything was going the way it should be and in one moment, it was over.'

'I know how much you loved him.' She hugged Hannah to her again and when Hannah had dried her eyes and the tears faded, she asked, 'Better?'

Hannah managed a smile. 'Nothing like a good cry.'

'Bawl like a baby, I'm here for you.'

'Thank you. I do feel a bit better now.'

'Hang on a minute . . . you said you put on the dress for the summer fair and this Joe, aka Mr Hottie, upset you. What exactly happened?'

'I was on my way to the fair after stopping at the post office to send a package, and I bumped into Joe. Literally bumped into him. Slap bang, his iced coffee went all over my dress.'

'And I'm guessing you went mental.'

'No, not this time. I ran off like a little girl. Eugh . . .' She covered her face with her hands. 'I was such a baby, I'm still embarrassed about it now. But it had taken a lot to put on the dress in the first place.' She explained how long the dress had stayed at her parents' house, how she'd run out of clothes on the day of the fair, how she'd done her best to overcome the silly notion that bad things happened when she was wearing the dress. Miriam from the haberdashery had been the first person to hear her tale of woe but having another friend to tell allowed her time to process the story through her mind as she recounted it.

Hannah picked up the letters again. 'I'm going to write back, send them a Christmas card as usual.'

'That sounds like a good idea. No point dithering about it. Can I ask you something personal?'

'Go on.'

'Did you ever feel about Luke, the way you felt about Liam?'

'What do you mean?'

'Did you ever love him as much as you loved Liam?'

'I suppose Luke came along at the right, or possibly wrong, time. I was vulnerable, he was there, he picked me up and yes, I loved him.' She wasn't sure she'd ever loved him enough, but she wasn't ready to lay all her feelings out there in the open to Georgia. As much as her friend had gone a long way to making amends, a tiny part of Hannah was holding back, in case Georgia fell into her old ways. Trust took a long time to build in the first place, even longer to earn back once it had been broken.

'Do you still love him?'

'Luke? I'm not really sure how I feel . . . about anyone. Seeing him again has left me confused.'

Georgia set her empty mug in the sink. 'I really should go, but I meant what I said a while ago. It would be lovely to see you up at the gym.' She grinned. 'If you can fit in a session in between your visits to the old people's home that is.'

Hannah smiled, appreciating the attempt to make her laugh even though it hadn't quite worked. 'It's Butterbury Lodge, which sounds so much better than your description.'

'It's a place where people go to die, Hannah. You need to be with people your own age.' She always had been blunt. Probably what their clients had taken exception to along the way.

Hannah showed her friend to the door. 'I'll bear it in mind. And, Georgia . . . Thank you for making me open the letters.'

'My pleasure.'

It felt good to have someone back in her corner again, no matter the doubts that crept into her mind occasionally. And after she'd waved goodbye to Georgia, she re-read the letters, this time experiencing a strange and unexpected kind of contentment.

Bundled up in her coat Hannah joined in with the excitement at Butterbury Lodge. Residents were talking so loudly in their eagerness to get organised. Frankie, Maggie, Hannah and two other staff had ushered everyone outside, at the same time double checking appropriate clothing was in place, issuing blankets, helping some residents into the chairs that had been positioned around the edges of the front garden so that the view wouldn't be obscured by those standing in the middle of the lawn.

'You're an absolute darling to suggest this,' said Josephine after Hannah had taken her a blanket. Her legs were too tired to stand, she'd said. 'I thought my firework days were over.'

A childlike excitement glistened in Ernest's eyes. 'I saw a few fireworks last year from my window.' He pointed to the top of the lodge. 'But there's nothing like the cold air against your face to feel a real part of it.' And then he surprised Hannah by giving her a hug. 'Thank you for bringing the most life to the lodge in a long time.'

Almost overwhelmed, Hannah huddled with Butterbury Lodge's residents in the gardens out front, ready to see the first firework launch from the display in the distance.

'Maybe next year we could give them all sparklers,' Rhys whispered when he came over to join her.

'That might be a little dangerous,' Hannah replied.

'Fun though,' he grinned. 'How's the cactus? Still surviving?'

'Of course it is. I might get a few more if things work out with this one.'

When Rhys moved to chat with a few of the women from Butterbury Lodge, Mr G joined Hannah. 'How's your neighbour?'

'Which one?'

'Mrs Ledbetter. Is she still a misery and moaning about you? I wouldn't mind betting she's hoping you'll prick your finger on that cactus.' Hannah had filled him in on her neighbour's gift and he'd been as surprised as she was.

'She's not that bad. And you, Mr G, usually give people the benefit of the doubt.'

'I haven't seen her in a long while, but I don't ever recall her as being particularly cheerful.'

'Me neither, but I think she may be very lonely.'

'Now that's not nice for anyone.'

He had a heart, one of the reasons she adored him. 'When my wife died, loneliness was my biggest worry. I didn't care about getting old, not being able to do as much as I used to. I cared that I wouldn't get to laugh and talk the way I once had. I miss her more than I can tell you, but having friends and companions, well it's the only way to be, isn't it?'

She gave him a hug and they watched Rhys charm his

audience, the ladies of Butterbury Lodge all ears with everything he had to say.

When Mr G joined Ernest, Rhys came over again. 'I had a delivery earlier.' He rubbed his hands together and blew on them for warmth. 'Someone left a generous donation with the local WI to cover more Christmas lights for Butterbury this year. A couple of the ladies came to tell me, they won't reveal who it is, but let's just say Lantern Square and the rest of the village will be lit up like a Christmas miracle this year.'

'That's amazing,' said Hannah, especially when Rhys told her how much money had been donated. 'Do you think it's a cover and the money really is from the WI?'

'I don't know. Perhaps.'

'Do you think it could be Mrs Addington?'

'What makes you ask that?'

'She's the only one with a bit of dosh to splash around.'

'I don't think she'd hide it if it was. I think she'd be proud to be involved. Anyway, whoever it is, it's fantastic news. So when will you choose the new lights?'

'Me and the lighting committee will discuss that this week.'

'You big kid.' Hannah giggled as he put on an air of importance.

'Hey, it's once a year, and I love it. Hate winter, my extremities suffer badly, but Christmas injects a lot of cheer.'

'You need to move to the square.'

'I would if I could. Nothing for sale and if there was it'd be snapped up. I'd love to live here in Butterbury – it kind of fits, do you know what I mean?'

'I know exactly what you mean.'

Rhys knew so many people here, he went off to chat to

Ernest next, making him laugh about something. He was right, finding a home was about more than bricks and mortar, it was about the fit.

But when her phone pinged her thoughts flew elsewhere as she read a text from Luke. It was friendly, asked how she was, said it was good to see her at the pub. He didn't mention the kiss, but he did ask if she'd consider meeting up with him again. And for a moment, she remembered the tender moment by the treehouse when their lips met and she'd tumbled into the comfort and easiness of their relationship, and she wasn't entirely sure whether she'd say no to him.

Was she setting herself up for a big fall by letting her occasional feelings of loneliness push her back in his direction?

'You look like you're up to mischief,' said Frankie, joining Hannah as she pushed the phone back into her pocket.

'Hey, Frankie. I said hello when I arrived but I don't think you heard me, you were so busy.'

'The cleaner just handed in her notice.' She sighed, tugging on a pair of gloves while still keeping a watchful eye over the residents as Maggie and another worker were doing too. 'It's left us in a bit of a hole to say the least. I don't suppose you know anyone do you?'

'You're asking the wrong person. I just let the dust gather, I clean when I have to.'

'Well if you hear of anyone, let me know. I'd better go do the rounds.'

Hannah let her get on with her job, seeing to all the residents, ensuring nobody got too cold. And when she saw Joe coming through the crowds she said, 'I thought you'd be down in Lantern Square.'

'I would've been but when Miriam saw me she let me know what was going on up here tonight and recommended it as having a better vantage point.'

'Right.' Hannah saw Miriam glance her way briefly and she waved over to her. 'Well she's probably got a point. It's going to be amazing.'

'I'm sure it will be.' His attentions turned to someone coming towards them and with a smile he said, 'Hello, Flo.'

Hannah turned to see that Joe's charm had worked magic on Butterbury Lodge's newest resident when Flo beamed back at him.

'Good evening, Joe.' Flo wasted no time standing at his side. 'I'm glad you're here, now I want to hear more about those wonderful European vacations you take.' It was the longest sentence Hannah had ever heard Flo come out with. It was as though ten or twenty years had fallen away from her in an instant by coming out here into the fresh air.

Hannah left them talking about Zürich where he'd been for a conference earlier in the year and Flo seemed smitten. Hannah rubbed her gloved hands together to keep warm and went to find Mr G again who by now had a flask of something hot, lucky thing.

She sneaked a look back at Joe. As much as he hadn't been her favourite person once upon a time, the dancing in the summer and small moments like this one now where he had all the time in the world for an elderly woman he barely knew, almost made up for his lothario ways.

'She's been charmed,' Mr G observed as he watched Flo and when Flo's laughter carried on the night air he concluded, 'Maybe there's more to the old girl than we thought.'

Hannah was about to agree when she caught a waft of something other than the wayward scent from the bonfire lingering in the sky as the crowd awaited the fireworks to start in the distance. 'What's in that flask?'

'Sshhhh . . . Maggie and Frankie will have me court-martialled if they find out.' He lowered his voice some more. 'They think it's coffee, but Ernest added a drop of whisky to warm the cockles.'

'Where did he get it from?'

'No idea, but I'm all for a bit of contraband.'

Hannah and Mr G stood back for a better view as they chatted about the likely sources of the whisky. The foliage surrounding the lodge and its grounds had died down now summer had passed by for another year but the mist from earlier had cleared leaving a night sky punctuated with stars and a bonfire in the distance showed them in which direction they would all need to look for the firework display. Hannah found herself wondering whether she should've asked Mrs Ledbetter what she was up to this evening. She hadn't been brave enough to knock on her door, but now she wished she had. Was she at Lantern Square with many of Butterbury's residents, or was she hiding away in her home avoiding the celebrations?

'Do you remember the CD Flo was listening to?' Hannah asked Mr G, an idea whirling around in her mind. 'Mrs Ledbetter had the very same one in her cottage,' she added when he nodded.

Mr G took another satisfying swig of his hot toddy. 'It's a local choir, very talented. Why do you ask?'

'It's a shared interest, between Flo and Mrs Ledbetter.'

'You're planning something.'

'I might be,' Hannah grinned, turning away when she caught Joe looking at her again.

'You just don't want Flo to get hold of Doctor Joe,' Mr G concluded. 'You want him all for yourself.'

And this time Hannah really did laugh loudly. Because that hot toddy must have gone to Mr G's head if he thought she would ever entertain the idea of dating a man like Joe.

Rhys came over as people grew impatient waiting for the fireworks to start. Any second now, it would be bang on the hour.

'I forgot to mention,' he said. 'I saw your friend earlier. She must prefer doctors to gardeners, I can't possibly imagine why,' he added with a flurry of sarcasm.

But Hannah didn't get a chance to ask what he was talking about because the first firework launched into the air with a pop, bang and a whizz, announcing the start of a spectacular show. Swallowed up in the sea of people trying to get the best view, Hannah and Rhys turned their attention to the sky, smiles of delight on their faces, surrounded by whoops of joy. And all Hannah could think was how pleased she was to have helped organise this. She was a part of life in Butterbury, with every day she felt happier, but was she going to regret letting part of her past back in?

Opening the letters from Liam's parents had unlocked something inside of her. It had made her feel open to possibilities – even reconsidering if she'd rushed to end things with Luke last year. And Georgia had been there for her with the car fiasco. It had felt good having her support. But could she ever really trust her again?

Hannah shied away from Joe's gaze when he looked her way, her insides fizzing at the thought of how close they'd danced in the summer. But she soon had a new focus with Rhys waving over at her. He was mouthing something she couldn't make out, but he had his phone in his hand and tapped it in a way that suggested he might have messaged her and wanted her to check.

She took out her phone and smiled because she was right, there was a message waiting.

But what she didn't expect to see was a photograph of Joe with yet another woman. And this time it was someone she already knew.

Despite the spectacular fireworks launching into the sky above her, Hannah's spirits sank. She'd thought she could reconcile her past with her new life in Butterbury, but it seemed like trouble might be brewing once again.

She hoped it wasn't, because she'd had enough complications to last her a lifetime.

14

The Christmas tree which stood tall and proud in Lantern Square had everyone talking. Early that morning, after the fog had cleared, Rhys had rounded up enough helpers to somehow manoeuvre the tree from lying flat on the trailer of a tractor to standing sixteen-foot-tall in the corner of the square. Hannah smiled as she passed it on her way home to get changed before heading up to Butterbury Lodge. She'd be back here with all the locals for the big switch-on of the Christmas lights tonight and she couldn't wait.

Hannah waved at Dawn and Troy, who were holding hands like teenagers as they walked down the street. They may have been married for decades, but when they shared a kiss she could tell it was just as special as the day they met. Reminded of what it felt like to be close to someone, Hannah tried not to think about the way she'd danced in Joe's arms at the summer fair, and the look they'd shared on Bonfire Night, as they'd been waiting to watch the firework display from high up on the hill in front of Butterbury Lodge. After a rocky start, Hannah had begun to change her mind about the local doctor, and to think of him as someone she'd like to know better.

But as the beautiful fireworks fizzled to a close, Rhys had texted her a photo of the latest woman leaving Joe's house on the square after dark: her so-called friend, Georgia. Hannah had seen plenty of other women coming and going through the same red door, and everything pointed at the pair of them having some kind of fling.

She sighed, a feeling of loneliness coursing through her. Luke was back on the scene, at least as a friend, and moments like this made her wonder whether she should give their relationship another chance. She'd finally agreed to meet up with him last week in an attempt to keep things light and civil, rather than creating drama by awkwardly avoiding him. She'd had enough of animosity and she was sure she could at least manage friendship, especially after the way she'd ended their relationship so abruptly. But his parents had joined them for lunch which had made her uncomfortable, as though she were still part of the family. And as lovely as Rupert and Linda were, they were clearly hopeful of a reconciliation for their son and his ex-girlfriend, and Hannah didn't want to feel any additional pressure when she had no idea how she felt. Part of her wanted to move on, leave the past where it should be, but the other part of her responded to Luke's charm, his interest, his kindness, making her wonder if she'd made a mistake by ending things.

Inside Lantern Cottage Hannah changed and made a cup of tea to warm herself up. The temperatures lately had reminded them all that Christmas was right around the corner. And with the season that highlighted the importance of family and loved ones on her mind, Hannah took out the collection of letters Liam's parents had sent from where she kept them in the kitchen drawer, hidden from view but ready to look at every now and again. Last night she'd decided to make Liam's parents a special Christmas card which she'd left to dry until now. She picked up a calligraphy pen to add a personal message, good wishes for a wonderful Christmas and New Year, and she smiled, knowing they'd love the hand-drawn fireplace design on the front and a stocking bulging with presents.

She added her love and left the ink on the card and envelope to dry while she went up to Butterbury Lodge, and on the walk there she reminded herself it was time to turn her thinking around. Rather than wishing to push away reminders of the life she'd had with Liam before he was killed, she needed to embrace them and remember the Liam who'd made her so happy.

When she reached Butterbury Lodge, Hannah pulled off her winter layers and went through to join the residents. It was weird to imagine ever having been without these familiar faces who passed the time of day in the hallway, laughed and joked with her, shared details of their ailments even when it was way too much.

It was late November and the first book club meeting was about to commence.

'I see the fire's going at last,' Hannah told Maggie, before she joined the group settling into the chairs arranged in a semi-circle.

With a roll of her eyes Maggie confessed, 'Ernest went on about it so much I had to. Anything for a peaceful life. And it has turned much colder.'

Hannah settled down in front of the group and reiterated that this was only the first book of many, and they'd all get a turn to choose a novel as they went along. She felt rather like a primary school teacher, but the suggestion box had been almost full just a week after Hannah had positioned it on the lodge's walnut reception desk at Butterbury Lodge – it seemed much as residents had originally dismissed her idea of a book club, nobody wanted to miss out. It had taken Hannah a good couple of hours to collate the responses, group them into genre, and then choose a starting point. She'd made a list of ten books and the order they'd be read in and today they were starting with *The Little Old Lady Who Broke All the Rules*. Mr G had already read it so Hannah had cleared it with him. She felt it was a good starting point and a few other residents had nominated one or two books from the series, so Hannah felt comfortable that at least more than one person would enjoy it. She felt sure she'd get a few converts too.

Residents were surprisingly enthralled, even those she'd known were sceptical at the choice of text, particularly Ernest, the dedicated thriller reader. Perhaps the fire had lulled him into a more receptive state, but whatever it was, Hannah thoroughly enjoyed reading the prologue and the first few chapters and when she declared an end to the session, she didn't even have to encourage chatter: residents were talking amongst themselves, even Flo looked happy, and Mr G gave Hannah a conspiratorial wink.

'I'm gasping,' said Hannah as residents continued on and Maggie came over. She'd not paused much during the reading; once she'd got their attention she'd wanted to keep a hold of it, and now she gulped down the glass of water on the side table.

'What do you have in there?' Hannah peered more closely at the box Maggie had been holding in her arms but had set down quickly due to its weight. 'Are those copies of this book?' She crouched down to see that it was in fact a further dozen copies of the same novel, the spines all lined up neatly in a row.

'I found them at the back door. And get this – whoever delivered these must've seen the list you left of the books and the order you'll be reading them in, because there are a dozen copies of each and every text.' She and Maggie had talked about getting the books for everyone, plus a few extras, but Maggie had confided to Hannah that the budget at Butterbury Lodge was stretched even tighter this year and it was impossible. And so Hannah had settled for reading to the group and she'd leave her copy of each book for anyone else to peruse until the next time.

'I can't believe someone would be so generous. That's a dozen copies of ten books, not cheap.'

'That's not all of it . . . there are audio copies too, so an option for those who struggle to read or prefer listening to the stories.'

'I'm lost for words, pardon the pun.'

'Me too, it's incredibly kind. Do you want to hand come copies round?'

'I'd love to.'

Hannah had wondered whether anyone would shake their head and say they didn't want a copy, but those who didn't snatch up the physical book took an audio version, others said they'd enjoy sharing the book with relatives who sometimes read to them.

'What did you think, Ernest?'

He tried to be all nonchalant about the genre way off his usual taste, but admitted, 'It was a refreshing change – I found myself quite hooked.'

Hannah touched his shoulder lightly, noticing he'd bagged an audio copy. 'I assume we'll see you again tomorrow night for more of the story?'

'Heck, I can't wait that long, I'll be listening to it before I go to sleep.'

'No spoilers,' she winked.

Grace came trotting over and thanked Hannah yet again, while Frankie brought round cake and cups of tea for everyone, but it was time for Hannah to go. Her work here was done and she bundled up in her coat, scarf and hat, and called out her goodbyes to the room.

Outside, Hannah said hello to Charles Bray, who introduced his son, Nigel.

'I recognise you from photographs,' Hannah told Nigel. 'Lovely to meet you. What brings you both here?'

'I've come to look around,' Charles claimed.

'For yourself?' Even though she'd noticed him slowing down these last few months, she couldn't imagine him leaving his little cottage.

'It might be time.' He didn't offer more detail but seemed happy with the possibility at least. 'And the girl I spoke to – very chatty, could hardly get a word in edgeways – suggested I come and look at the place whenever I liked, so I took the opportunity when Nigel stopped by.'

Frankie appeared in the doorway to welcome them and before Nigel followed his father inside, Hannah put her hand on his sleeve. 'Is he doing OK?'

'It's hard to see him getting older and slower, but he suggested this,' Nigel admitted. 'Tonight is my chance to check it out as much as him. I don't want him to go anywhere that makes him unhappy. He's lived in the cottage so long it's almost a part of him. I grew up there and have so many memories, but sometimes . . . Well, you can't live in the past, can you?'

'No, you can't.' His words struck a timely chord. 'Rest assured, this place is wonderful and on a clear day you can see the square from up here, so he won't feel too far away.'

They said goodnight and Hannah pondered the thought of Charles moving in to Butterbury Lodge. He'd fit in well, and perhaps everyone reached a point in their life where change was inevitable. She thought again of Mrs Ledbetter and her discussion with Mr G about how they could involve her neighbour with more people of her own age. Hannah truly believed it was exactly what Mrs Ledbetter needed, and now that she had the phone number to Mrs Ledbetter's favourite choir group, Sounds Over the Bridge, she could soon put her plan into action.

She pulled her hat down over her ears as the wind whipped around. She walked down the hill and when she arrived at Lantern Square ready for the tree lighting, Annie was the first to call out to her. She swore Annie and Ellen were trying to fatten her up with offerings from their food cart. She waved over but then stopped to talk to Pamela from Number Six who was happy her sons would be coming home for Christmas, and then Kimberley who worked behind the post office counter, both of whom had already had their first mulled wine. She listened to Rhys explain to two little boys why trampling in the flower beds wasn't a good idea, and then Joe was beside her all of a sudden.

She hadn't been able to get Joe's sparkling green eyes and broad chest out of her mind since the summer fair dance.

He looked at her hands. 'Thought I'd better make sure

you haven't got a mulled wine yet. I wouldn't want to get a soaking.'

'Very funny. And always remember, you soaked me first.' The memory of that day back in the summer when he'd spilled coffee on the dress Liam bought her, and then the revenge of sloshing dirty water all over him after the summer fair, flashed through her mind.

He smiled, hands shoved in the pockets of his dark waxed donkey jacket under which he had on a dark-navy funnel-neck jumper. He had the slightest area of skin exposed at his throat and Hannah imagined that was where the aroma of a crisp aftershave came from. She remembered it well from being so close to him in the summer.

'The tree's a stunner isn't it?' His eyes followed the wide branches at the bottom of the Christmas tree in Lantern Square all the way to the top.

Hannah turned her gaze the same way. 'It sure is. I would've loved to watch it being put up this year, all part of the fun, but I've been a bit busy. Maybe next year.' The thought warmed her right through. She belonged in Butterbury, of that she was certain.

'You'll decorate your own cottage, surely?'

'I'm a little disorganised, but I'll have to sort out a tree soon.'

'The big switch on isn't for another fifteen minutes or so,' said Joe, 'and already I can't feel my toes.' He blew into his palms to warm his hands and then pushed them back into his pockets. 'How are you keeping? I haven't seen you around much. The care package business must be busy.'

So was the shagging business if the number of women coming out of his house on a regular basis were anything to go by. Or perhaps they were house calls, a new kind of doctoring in the village. The thought of Joe being involved with Georgia made Hannah uneasy, especially as her friend had suggested that she had a boyfriend – though she'd never told Hannah any details about him. Not that Georgia had confessed. Even when she stood in her dining room chatting away a few days ago, she said nothing about coming out of Joe's house on the square in early November. Hannah hadn't asked for more details either, because she wanted Georgia to come to her first, tell the truth. She really wanted to be able to trust her again. It didn't sit well that Georgia said nothing, but Hannah had left it, and she wondered whether the reason why she hadn't confronted her was because she didn't want to know the answer, because her feelings for Joe seemed to wax and wane. One minute he drove her mad, roaring around Butterbury in his flashy car; the next he was this attractive man whom she wanted to talk to and get to know better. Hannah only hoped there was an innocent explanation and Georgia wasn't stringing along her mysterious boyfriend.

'It's a busy time of the year, for sure,' Hannah replied. She'd been inundated with Christmas care package orders as well as fulfilling a follow-up order for more Christmas cards from Castle Cards. Great for business, not so good for her mental wellbeing when she already had so much to do.

'I have another couple of orders to place. But I've learned my lesson, they'll come to you via email. Promise.' Did he have to be so devastatingly handsome when he looked at her? Of course he did, that was his superpower when it came to his popularity with the opposite sex.

'You're keeping me in business,' she told Joe. His care packages were always for a different woman: first it had been Vanessa, then someone called Tilly, then came Evie. Hannah wondered who was next, or whether anyone would get a second chance.

'I'm happy to hear that.'

'How's life at the surgery?' she asked, uncomfortable at the way the conversation was heading. They moved closer to one another when more people packed into the square, the excitement mounting.

'Busy. Flu vaccines coming out of my ears almost, winter bugs starting to rear their ugly heads.'

'I'm surprised you're not sick all the time, all those germs.'

'I think my immune system is quite hardy.' He took one of those big hands of his out of his pocket and crossed his fingers. 'Let's hope so anyway.'

'Hannah, Joe!' It was Ellen this time, beckoning from their cart, although the smell was pretty hard to ignore.

'They're not doing much for my waistline,' Joe confided and Hannah did her best not to think about the body hidden beneath his clothes.

'Mine neither, but I am hungry, I came straight from Butterbury Lodge.'

'You're up there often. I see you in passing occasionally, yesterday I was up to see to someone's bunions – can't specify who, patient confidentiality and all that – and . . . well I won't ruin your appetite by giving you more details.'

At the cart Ellen was already holding out churros caked in sugar. Hannah had a feeling that 'No' wouldn't be an option today, and sure enough they both walked away with giant churros curled into a circular shape, held in a napkin to protect their fingers against the heat.

They didn't talk for much longer before Rhys took up position in front of the Christmas tree and, over a loud-speaker, was revving up the bystanders for the switching on of the tree lights, followed by the lights that would il-luminate the length of the small high street in Butterbury and the rest of Lantern Square. Hannah had already seen Rhys and a team of other helpers putting them up yester-day and finishing it off today, but you never got the true effect until they were turned on.

Rhys had everyone counting down from ten and Hannah and Joe, wiping away the last crumbs from their churros, joined in until they got to one and the tree lit up with the flip of a switch. The Norwegian spruce created a winter wonderland in the square with hundreds of golden lights looping in between branches, small gift decorations with loopy red bows, so many blue and gold baubles going all the way from the bottom to the top that she'd never be able to count them all.

'It's beautiful.' Hannah was mesmerised as crowds clapped and nobody wasted any time filing out of the square to the street ready for the next countdown. The entire village was bathed in Christmas spirit.

Hannah moved to bundle out of the square with Joe but before they left through the gate, Joe grabbed her sleeve and ducked so they could see something lower down in one of the flower beds.

'What is it?' Hannah couldn't see anything but dark-ness, well aware of the intoxicating smell of this man.

'Keep watching.'

'We'll miss the lights along the high street.'

'They'll be there for weeks.'

'All I can see is darkness.'

'Patience.'

They could hear Rhys doing another countdown and when it got all the way to one, there was another beat, and the illuminations took over the sky. And right in front of Hannah and Joe, in the flower beds curving and winding through the square, were woodland creatures illuminated with soft white lighting.

'They're amazing.' Hannah grinned. 'A squirrel,' she said, eyes darting to the next, 'And a hedgehog!'

'I see a rabbit over there.' Joe was investigating another flower bed. 'And a reindeer.'

'Wow, the kids of the village won't even realise until they come back.'

'And we saw it first,' he said in a whisper.

Hannah was glad he'd shared his discovery with her. But the intimacy of the moment had her head in a muddle and she shivered.

'You're cold.'

'A bit.'

'Only one thing for it.' He led the way, calling over his shoulder. 'Time for a mulled wine.'

The spiced aroma reached Hannah the second he said it. With people only just filing back from the high street they were first in the queue at the cart, and she was soon warming the palms of her hands through the polystyrene cup.

They stood sipping the orange- and clove-laced beverage, surrounded by the soft glow of the lights all around the square, and shimmering in the street beyond.

'First mulled wine of the season,' Hannah grinned,

enjoying his company. Moments like this made her forget his flaws. 'This always marks the start of winter for me.'

'Your first in Lantern Square.'

She wasn't sure whether to be flattered or embarrassed he'd noticed. So instead of answering, she put her cup to her lips and took another sip.

'I'm glad I came back here.' He looked around and nodded hellos, raised a hand to a couple of other people who passed them by. 'It's not so small that it's too quiet, but it's not so big that people don't know each other. I like the community feel.'

'I think more places should be like it.'

'Hear, hcar.'

'You know, most of the residents up at Butterbury Lodge were from the village originally. That's kind of nice, don't you think?'

'It is. I might reserve myself a spot.'

'I don't think it's quite time to worry about that yet.' Her laughter mingled with the sweet-smelling wine on the air and the scent of churros and cinnamon doughnuts from the other cart. 'I saw Charles up there tonight.'

'Charles, the dancer?'

'He'd love to know that's what you call him.'

'You can't deny he was good. I didn't dance with him myself but he looked like he was showing you all the moves.'

And so had Joe, after Charles had foxtrotted her round the square. 'He was a champion in his day.' But she didn't get a chance to elaborate because a redhead came bustling over to Joe's side and threw her arms around him.

'I've been looking for you everywhere.' She took his mulled wine and gulped it for herself.

'Julie, this is Hannah.' He took his wine back but didn't reprimand her, which only proved one thing: that Joe's moves were equally as good as Charles Bray's, just in a different way.

'Nice to meet you.' Hannah gulped back the rest of the mulled wine, glad to see Rhys coming over. 'I'll catch you later. I'm going to check out the lights on the high street. Rhys!' She called out and left Joe with his lady friend, determined not to be a gooseberry, and feeling ridiculous because yet again she'd been drawn in by his charm rather than seeing him for the smooth-talker he was.

'He sure gets around.' Rhys looked over at Joe and Julie, but Hannah linked his arm and turned him the opposite way to walk out of the square.

'I think I've lost count of how many women he has on the go,' she said, a little crossly – but all thoughts of Joe fell away as they emerged on to the street. 'Oh, Rhys, these are beautiful.' Up above them, strung across from shop fronts to the square, from lamp post to lamp post, were village lights worthy of winning a competition. There was a toy train, lit up in gold, chugging from up above the bakery all the way over to the corner post of Lantern Square; shooting stars on the sides of posts; Father Christmas and a sack full of presents, transforming the village in a riot of colours.

Rhys recalled the installation of the lights and the efforts to haul the Christmas tree into place, reducing Hannah to fits of laughter at his tales of Terry Granger from the sweetshop yelling at Stella from the dry cleaning place when she dropped a heavy box on his foot, local teacher Malcolm trying to wind lights round the enormous tree and getting his legs in a tangle, and the secret installation of the woodland creatures in Lantern Square that nobody had really noticed until the lights went on.

'I saw the woodland creatures,' Hannah admitted.

'Well, no need for you to go to Specsavers then.' He nudged her arm. She didn't mention it wasn't her who'd spotted them but ladies' man, Joe.

She stopped a moment. 'I totally forgot to say congratulations to you.'

'For the lights?'

'Well that, but also the long-term gardening contract at Butterbury Lodge.'

'I was surprised I got it. I wasn't as cheap as some of the other gardeners who quoted, but it came down to reputation.'

'Ah, the all-important reputation. I told you.' She hugged him tight. 'I'm so pleased for you.'

Unusually for him, Rhys pulled back, and lowered his voice. 'Steady on, don't want people to think we're a couple.'

'Is there someone you're trying to impress?'

But he didn't answer, instead he cleared his throat and Hannah realised someone was behind her. When she turned she saw Georgia bustling her way through the crowds, waving at them both. 'What brings you here?'

Georgia hugged Hannah enthusiastically. 'I've been doing leaflet drops in the neighbouring towns, and ended in Butterbury – I dropped a leaflet at your place, by the way, and with twenty-five per cent off any class from now until Christmas there are no excuses not to come to the gym – then couldn't resist coming to investigate what was going on with all these crowds. I just ate the most heavenly sugar-laden doughnut by the way.' She was operating at full speed, high energy, as usual.

'That'll be Ellen and Annie's cart, doing the rounds. Heaven help us when they open their bistro, although it might be good for *your* business. Sorry,' Hannah said when Rhys cleared his throat again. 'You remember Rhys, don't you?'

'Yes, from the pub. Nice to see you again.' She looked around her. 'What's going on here, why's everyone out and about?'

'It was the big Christmas lights switch-on tonight.'

Georgia didn't seem overly impressed, but then again, this wasn't her home, she was more herself in the big city. Small village displays were probably the last thing on her mind.

Hannah caught sight of Joe briefly before he was obscured by the crowds, and wished she could go back and finish her conversation with him. But maybe it was better that they'd been interrupted before she could fall for any more of his well-practised flirtation. She noticed Georgia looking over in his direction too, prompting Rhys to blurt that he'd seen her coming out of the doctor's house.

'Oh, that was ages ago,' Georgia tried to dismiss the remark. 'I'd cut my finger at the gym and the plaster had fallen off and the damn thing wouldn't stop bleeding.'

'You needed a doctor for that?' Rhys asked sarcastically. Already he seemed rather less enamoured with Georgia than he'd once been.

'Of course I didn't, but he offered to help, went and got his first aid kit. Arrogant tosser. The next thing I knew, he made a pass at me. You were so right about him, Hannah. He loves himself a little bit too much, in my opinion. He's lucky I didn't kick him where it hurts. Which reminds me, you should come to a Krav Maga class, learn some moves for men like that.'

Hannah knocked back the rest of her mulled wine. She couldn't decide whether she was happy to hear Georgia had been the innocent party with Joe or not. But that was enough talk about the local doctor and his many women. 'Georgia? Can I interest you in one of these?' She held out the cup, the smell lingering on the air. 'Rhys?'

'Won't say no,' said Georgia. 'But make it small, I'm driving.'

'I'll be back in a bit.'

She counted through her coins to get rid of loose change and joined the queue that had by now formed and as she stood in line she noticed Joe was no longer with Julie, but with the brunette she'd seen him with in the summer.

She shook her head. How could anyone keep up with a man like that?

'Hannah . . .' A voice came from beside her and a hand landed on her arm.

'Luke?' First Georgia and now him. She wasn't sure which one had surprised her the most. She wondered whether this encounter was inevitable when Luke's family lived so close by, or if he was deliberately trying to show up unexpectedly and rekindle what they'd once had.

He leaned in and kissed her on the cheek. 'It's good to see you.'

She was saved from saying much else as it was her turn and she stepped forwards, ordered three mulled wines and offered to buy one for Luke.

'Can't stand the stuff.'

She laughed. 'That's right, too poncey for you, eh?'

When they moved out of the way of other people in line to get drinks, Luke carrying one of the polystyrene cups for her, Hannah explained Ellen and Annie's cart of temptation. 'I almost think their new business should have the word Temptation in the title, you know. Whatever they make goes down a storm. Even Georgia, Miss Fitness and Healthy Eater, has been scoffing doughnuts.'

'Wait . . .' He moved in front of her so he was looking at her rather than standing by her side. 'You have three drinks here. Who are they for?'

'My friend Rhys, and Georgia.' She didn't wait for his reply, but led the way over to them and hoped neither Luke nor Georgia would make a scene. Back when the crisis with the bookkeeping business she'd started with Georgia had come to a head, Luke had fiercely defended Hannah, and been furious with her friend's behaviour. That was one thing to be said for her relationship with him – he'd always fought her corner. And when Luke and Georgia had met outside the Butterbury Arms in the autumn they'd simply ignored one another, the best thing to do under the circumstances.

She handed the first wine to Georgia, another to Rhys.

'Where's yours?' Georgia asked, the darkness not having revealed the mystery wine carrier just yet. Then she caught sight of him, and her expression changed. 'Oh.'

'Hello, Georgia.' Luke at least was magnanimous enough to say something polite.

The grimace from the usually vocal Georgia had Rhys looking from her to Luke, then Hannah, bewildered as to what was going on.

Hannah steered the topic of conversation to safe ground by asking Rhys all about the work he did for Lantern

Square and the awkward atmosphere subsided a little, but Hannah was still glad when her phone rang and she was rescued.

'I'm sorry, I can't hear you properly,' she explained to the caller, moving away from the hordes in the square, to the railings at the side. 'Who am I speaking to?'

It was one of her customers and they weren't particularly happy. She listened to them rant and tried to calm them down, apologising profusely although she had no idea how the mix-up had happened. When the customer finally rang off she slumped against the railings, defeated, and slid down so she was sitting on the very edge of the kerb below. An illuminated rabbit was looking at her from the flower bed nearby as if to ask what the matter was.

'Hannah?' It was 'Doctor Joe' – she always thought of him by that name when he irritated her – minus his plus-one this time.

Luke was next to come to her side. 'I've got this, mate,' he told Joe. 'Hannah, are you OK?'

'No, I'm not.' She let herself be steered away from the sea of faces, out on to the street, and Joe followed. 'That was an irate customer.'

'Really?' Luke's boyish face looked at her with concern.

'The last order I sent out yesterday went to a five-year-old girl, as a thank you from her auntie for being a bridesmaid at her wedding.'

'And she didn't like what you sent? Not enough glitter?'

'Stop joking around.' It was Georgia at her side now, pushing Luke out of the way and ignoring Joe apart from a cursory admiring glance. He was an attractive male after all and it took a lot to extinguish Georgia's natural tendency to flirt, no matter whether they'd had a run-in before. 'What happened, Hannah?'

'I must've mixed up the chocolate that I sent and put in a bar containing nuts rather than the milk chocolate they'd specified.'

'So the person got the wrong chocolate,' said Georgia. 'It's not the end of the world.'

'I'm so careful usually. I lay everything out and triple check before I package it all up nicely.' She let out a long sigh. Joe, Luke and Georgia were all waiting for her to go on. 'I've been so busy, orders have been flying in, I must've lost concentration. I was supposed to include the chocolate with biscuit pieces rather than nuts.'

'Like I said,' Georgia, arm around her shoulders, encouraged, 'it's just a flavour. No big deal. Maybe send something to the client to apologise.'

Hannah hadn't realised she was crying until she looked at Joe, Luke and Georgia, and also Rhys by now. 'It's worse than just a flavour. The girl I sent it to had a peanut allergy and ate some. She started wheezing, had trouble breathing.'

'Is she OK?' Joe stepped closer and ignored Luke's warning look.

'Her mum used an EpiPen. She went to hospital. She's fine now.' Her words came out staccato, the shock overpowering.

'Why didn't her mum double-check? Or the girl herself?' Georgia was angry on her behalf.

'She did but in the short time between her double-checking and the girl taking a bite, it was too late. I feel sick.' Hannah could sense the wine and the churros churning around in her stomach. 'She could have been seriously ill. Or worse.'

Everyone stayed silent apart from Joe who had his bedside-manner-wits about him and put a hand to her shoulder. 'The little girl is fine, the mum is obviously very upset, but it was an honest mistake.'

'But one I made. I feel terrible.'

Rhys deflected attention away from Hannah when a few people looked their way. Hannah's mind went into overdrive thinking of a kid in hospital, being taken to court and sued, maybe being put in prison, starring in an episode of *Watchdog*, hauled up to explain herself by one of those heavies who confronted unsuspecting dodgy dealers. Oh God, was that what she was?

She had to think of a way out of this, and fast.

15

When Hannah told her friend what she had planned to sort out the mess with Tied Up with String, Georgia insisted on driving Hannah to the client's address in Stratford-upon-Avon, telling Hannah she'd be in no fit state to drive. And she was right, Hannah was too much of a mess to be finding her way along winding country lanes in response to the satnav's confusing commands, while imagining confronting the mother of the child who'd ended up in hospital because of her carelessness.

'Whoa, this is some place. Are you sure this is the address?' They'd pulled up in front of a set of electric gates bordered by gorse bushes on one side and a prickly holly bush on the other.

'It's the right address.' Hannah phoned the number again, not sure what kind of reception she'd get, but the gates slowly opened up when she announced who she was. 'I'll be fine, you stay here,' she told Georgia.

'Are you kidding?'

'I mean it, this is something I need to do on my own. If I'm not back in half an hour, alert the murder squad.'

'Don't joke.'

'You're right, this is so not funny, but if I don't joke I'll cry.'

After the phone call last night, once Hannah had got over the shock, she'd gone home and put together a big and generous care package by way of apology. Rhys thought she was doing the right thing by delivering it in person, Luke and Georgia had finally agreed on something – that she was crazy to do this – and Joe's attentions had been diverted elsewhere with the woman who'd turned up to join him in the square.

Hannah rang the doorbell, clutching the care package in its brown box, all tied up with string. With the run-up to Christmas well underway, Hannah still had orders she hadn't yet fulfilled, so she'd raided the shopping she'd already done and stored away and would replace at a later date, and put together a package that would be a five-year-old girl's dream. There was a unicorn activity set with magical stickers, colouring books and pens, she'd added a hardback book of Goodnight Stories, she'd even included a make-your-own kaleidoscope set. She also ensured no food was included this time round.

The door opened and when Hannah introduced herself she gave Georgia one last panicky glance and went inside.

A few hours later, in the warmth of the Butterbury Arms, Hannah held up her glass. 'To Tied Up with String.' Immediately after leaving the address, a very happy little girl and a mum who, while not entirely placated, at least wasn't going to make an example of Hannah and ruin her reputation, Hannah and Georgia had gone straight back to Butterbury and into the pub to order a bottle of Merlot.

Georgia repeated the sentiment and clinked Hannah's

glass. 'I can't believe the woman was smiling by the time she showed you out. At least now you can stop beating yourself up.'

'I'm just glad everyone is happy . . . and well. I got off lightly.'

'Enough of that talk, time to move on.'

When Georgia gulped back some more wine Hannah did the same because up until this point, her nerves had been in shreds. 'Thanks for posting the card to Liam's parents, too. I wanted it to get to them way before Christmas so they know I'm thinking of them.'

'No worries at all,' Georgia dismissed. 'Happy to help.'

Their chatter went on until Hannah spotted Nigel Bray making his way over to them.

'I'm sorry to interrupt,' he began after Hannah had made polite introductions. 'I just wanted to say you were right, Butterbury Lodge is a wonderful place. Dad is moving in tomorrow.'

'Wow, that's great news. You've got yourselves organised very quickly.'

'Dad didn't want to wait. He's more excited than anything, ready for a change.'

'He'll love it there, I'm sure. And I visit all the time – I expect I'll see him more than I do now!'

'End of an era for us though. I'm here to help clear out his house.'

'Is he terribly sad?'

'Less so than I thought he'd be, given all the memories wrapped up in those walls. But I think the view of Lantern Square helps and he was very impressed with the book club you've got going, even took a copy of the most recent novel so he could get up to speed.'

It was the best news she'd heard in the twenty-four hours since that dreadful phone call. 'Send him my regards and do shout if you need a hand moving.'

'Thank you, but I should be able to manage. I'll be around for the next week or so getting it ready for sale.'

'You're not keeping it?'

He shook his head. 'Our lives have moved on. Dad understands that.'

'Who's Charles Bray?' Georgia wanted to know the second Nigel left them to it.

Hannah filled her in. 'He lives in The Little House, same side of the street as this, down . . .' She looked out the window to make sure she had her bearings as the pub sat on a corner. '. . . that way,' she pointed right. 'It's the tiniest house on the square, hence its name, and probably the cutest. He's lived there a long time.'

'I can't picture which house it is.'

'It's the one with the buttercup-yellow front door. Next door to the cottage with the huge lemon tree out front, almost obscuring its green door.'

Her remark immediately set off a rendition of Shakin' Stevens' Green Door song. Years ago Georgia and Hannah had been to an 80s night with Georgia's older sister and hadn't stopped singing the tune for weeks. That one had even inspired Georgia to paint her bedroom door in her rented flat a vivid green, to the fury of her landlord. She'd had to strip it and put it back to rights or lose her deposit, but thankfully she hadn't been evicted.

Hannah laughed at the memory. Georgia might not be the most tactful of friends, but she was undeniably fun to be around, and she'd really needed that after a disaster that could very easily have cost her her business.

A few days later, while making her way home to Lantern Cottage after taking three more parcels to the post office, Hannah ran into Rhys. He'd stopped off at the bakery to buy a couple of cheeky mince pies to feast on during his work up at Butterbury Lodge.

'Manual labour gives me quite an appetite,' he justified. 'How's everything going at Tied Up with String?'

'Well, thank goodness. No more hiccups. And no more tears.'

'You promise?' He pulled a face. 'I don't do well with emotional crises, they're a little scary.'

'I promise.'

'What's all this anyway?' He'd noticed she wasn't in the usual attire of denim dungarees or jeans and a scruffy oversized jumper, but instead had on black lycra leggings and a hoodie that kept her warm when she only had a T-shirt underneath.

'I'm off to the gym later.'

'You're not serious?'

She batted his arm. 'I'm perfectly serious.'

'Your mate persuaded you, did she?'

'That and the discount voucher.'

'Well it could be good for you to de-stress, you do seem a bit overworked.'

'I'm not that bad.'

He coughed, hard. 'I beg to differ. I'm a business owner, I know the deal, but you're running around everywhere.'

'It's the season, Christmas is fast approaching.'

'Don't remind me! I haven't done any shopping yet. I always leave it until the last minute.'

'I might be able to help. I have some wonderful care packages I'm sure your family would love.'

'My family already laugh that my gifts seem to be of the same variety. Last year everyone got slippers, the year before it was photo frames – all different, but the same concept. Maybe I'll make brown paper packages this year's theme.'

Hannah encouraged him to do just that and off he went, while she walked home. She had a spin class booked and Georgia was picking her up at six o'clock sharp which was why she was already in her gear, so she could work right up until the knock at the door.

Back at the cottage she let both cats keep her company in the dining room as she made up a package that was to be sent to Scotland, to a retired gentleman with a penchant for cheeses and fancy chutneys. She'd found the most delightful cheeseboard with a wooden carved mouse at one end for his gift as well as a selection of chutneys and a fancy cheese knife to go with it.

Rhys was right to notice she'd been busy. Castle Cards had approved her Valentine's design, they'd requested more Christmas cards after selling her selection faster than any other in store, and she'd had no end of orders via her website. She was working longer hours, doing her best to stay on top of her accounts and blog and website updates, not to mention keeping supplies of standard items topped up and reordering more packaging. Since the mistake with the nutty chocolate, Hannah had also taken to triple, sometimes quadruple, checking every order which included edible gifts and if the customer didn't state they had a food allergy, she made a point of confirming this before the order left Lantern Cottage. She never wanted to make such a stupid, not to mention dangerous, mistake again.

When there was a knock at the door announcing Georgia's early arrival, Hannah beckoned her inside while she finished making up an order.

Georgia was impressed to find her in her gym gear. 'Are you looking forward to it?'

'I'm looking forward to finishing, if that counts?' She took a glass of orange juice through to the dining room, a little sugar hit before the gym class she suspected she'd struggle with, and set it on the shelf behind the table. 'Bear with me, I just need to concentrate on this.'

'Let me help.' Georgia spotted the email on the table next to all the items and read each out in turn so Hannah could ensure they were all packed.

'Now I just need to package it all up.' Hannah sipped her orange juice. 'And I know you only came here early to make sure I didn't try to back out.'

'As if,' she grinned.

When the package was all ready and looking glorious, she put it into the outside packaging and left it beside another round of a hundred cards ready to send off to Castle Cards in the morning. While Georgia hung back to use the bathroom, Hannah took her trainers outside the front door to give them a bang and get the mud off. Goodness only knows when she'd last worn them for anything more energetic than traipsing around Butterbury.

Georgia came out of the front door after her. 'Ready?'

'I guess so.' Hannah grimaced, locked up behind them and prepared to go to her first gym class in years.

'My entire body feels battered,' Hannah moaned as Georgia pulled up outside Lantern Cottage an hour and a half later.

'Did your undercarriage survive?'

Anyone else might have thought it an odd question, but after that spin class Hannah knew exactly what her friend meant. 'I do feel a bit delicate around my lady parts. Good job I don't have a boyfriend.' When Georgia laughed she added, 'Speaking of which, I was on the look-out for yours tonight. Was he around?'

'Not tonight, thank goodness or you'd have been quizzing him.'

'I would not.' Hannah took off her seat belt. 'Thanks for making me go. As tough as it was, I needed it. I didn't think about my business the whole time. Only about the pain in my legs . . . and more vulnerable areas.'

'Same time tomorrow?'

Hannah climbed out of the car and leaned in to talk to her friend through the window. 'Not a hope in hell. Maybe in a week or so when, or if, I recover.'

'I'll hold you to it.' Georgia waved as Hannah let herself into Lantern Cottage, giving the front door a decent shove.

Apparently exercise gave you endorphins or something like that, and although she was exhausted, Hannah kind of understood the appeal. 'Smokey, you've got the right idea.' She eyed the cat curled up on the bottom stair. 'After a shower I'm going to do exactly what you're doing, on the couch, with a big fat portion of lasagne.' She made a quick fuss of him before heading up to wash away the aches and pains already making themselves felt. She sang her way through a long shower as the heat took away the battering her body had taken in the class, and hummed her way downstairs rubbing her hair with the towel draped around her shoulders. But when she saw the dining room door open, she shook her head at her stupidity. She must've left in such a rush earlier that she hadn't shut it. She hoped the cats hadn't done anything untoward to her supplies or the package waiting to be sent.

But it wasn't the supplies or the parcel she needed to worry about. 'No!' She charged into the dining room when she saw the glass of orange juice lying on its side on the table, its contents rudely seeping into the bundle of cards ready to be sent to Castle Cards. 'No, no, no! Bandit, what did you do!' she yelled when her other cat trotted over from the windowsill where he'd been stretched out above the radiator. He weaved between her ankles as though he hadn't a care in the world.

'They're ruined.' She snatched up the first batch of cards, desperately hoping not all of them had been affected, but it seemed as though the orange juice had deliberately soaked through each and every one.

She slumped down on the chair. A hundred cards. All ruined. Just like that. And with each one taking between five and ten minutes to make, excluding drying time for glue and ink and anything else she wanted to add on, that meant a good six to eight hours absolute minimum to rectify the mistake. She was usually meticulous about shutting the dining room door. How could she have been so stupid?

Idiot, idiot, idiot! She scolded herself before scooping up the soggy pile of cards, taking them through to the kitchen and slinging them into the recycling bin below the sink. She took out a glass and poured a large red wine.

She'd only just come back from the colossal mistake she'd made with the care package and now this.

Sometimes running your own business really did suck.

16

The next day Hannah woke early with a foggy head. The insides of the windows of Lantern Cottage were steamed up, a sure sign it was getting colder and the depths of winter would soon be upon them.

She climbed out of bed, tugged on her dressing gown and stumbled downstairs and into the kitchen. She crouched down the second Smokey and Bandit trotted towards her, Bandit's tail tickling her chin as he competed with his brother for prime stroking position. 'It's not your fault, it was all me,' she told them. Last night she'd been so angry she'd barely fussed over either cat. All she'd been able to think of was those hundred pristine white cards she'd decorated so meticulously. The cards that were now sitting in the bottom of the recycling bin. She'd tossed and turned all night thinking how stupid she'd been. The cats would've thought it was party central in her work-room and she was surprised – and thankful – they hadn't destroyed anything else.

Hannah took out her phone when it pinged, but ignored Georgia's text asking how her 'undercarriage' was. *Bloody sore actually*, would be her response, but right now she could only think about getting on with her day. She made a cup of tea to warm up, fed the cats and then made a couple of hot buttered crumpets. But there was no time to sulk; she needed to get down to the business of rectifying what had happened.

As the tell-tale clicking of the old radiators woke the house up from its slumber and the temperature in the cottage slowly rose, Hannah took her dressing gown off, rolled up her pyjama sleeves and got on with her day, fired up by a much-needed sense of urgency. The post office wasn't open until nine o'clock so she'd do a batch of cards now, take a break and walk to the post office to clear her head, then come home and do more. If she tried to do a hundred at once she'd only make mistakes and if she went wrong again she swore she'd lose the plot completely.

Georgia didn't give up with the texts and eventually Hannah messaged back saying she was having a shit day, they could talk later.

But her quick trip to the post office soon turned into a much longer outing. Marianne was behind the counter today, rather than Kimberley, who at least wasn't such a chatterbox, and insisted on talking on and on about the delectable cinnamon rolls in the bakery this year. As soon as Hannah stepped outside clutching the receipt for the care package she'd sent on its merry way, she bumped straight into Mrs Ledbetter, who cornered Hannah to discuss the Lantern Walk that she'd taken charge of.

As much as Hannah wanted to move along, her desire to involve herself in as many events as possible as she put down roots in Butterbury took over. 'It's not until Boxing Day,' Hannah smiled.

'We need to plan or it'll be chaos. Mrs Addington is

usually in charge but I've volunteered my services this year.'

'Good for you.' A fine drizzle had set in and was doing its best to dampen Hannah's jeans and slick her hair into a hideous 'wet look'.

'I've got all the lanterns and given them a good clean,' Mrs Ledbetter continued, undeterred. 'They're all waiting in my dining room, lined up on the table that I never use. I have plenty of tealights, thank goodness. Five hundred flameless LEDs were left in a box on my doorstep this morning. I'd only just speculated that we may not have quite enough for everyone, but someone has been very kind. It's a very popular event I'll be responsible for, you know.'

Hannah rubbed her arms impatiently. Even the Butterbury Christmas lights couldn't brighten this cold, damp day, and she suspected she'd have to dry her hair when she got home at this rate. Then she remembered the call she'd made yesterday as she waited for Georgia to collect her things from the staff area in the gym. A call that was part of her plan to get Mrs Ledbetter integrated into the community even more.

She snapped out of her melancholy. 'Mrs Ledbetter, I seem to remember you liking the choir, Sounds Over the Bridge.'

'That's right. They're one of the best groups around.'

'They're doing a carol concert, up at Butterbury Lodge.' Her phone call had confirmed arrangements.

'Really?' She saw the old woman's spirits lift – and then sink again. 'Lucky for anyone living there I suppose.'

'It's not until Christmas Day itself.'

'Christmas Day? What a strange choice.'

'Not for them, there are a couple of choir members with relatives at the lodge so they were delighted to do it.'

'Well then, they're very good people. It'll be wonderful.'

'I've been allocated two tickets.' Total lie. There were no tickets, but Hannah had already cleared her appearance and Mrs Ledbetter's and seeing as other relatives of residents might be there, Mrs Ledbetter wouldn't suspect a thing. 'Would you like to come with me? I enjoy listening to them but I'd love the company.'

'You're inviting me?'

'If you're not too busy.' Ever since she'd first met Mrs Ledbetter Hannah realised this was a woman who liked to know her place in the world. She was independent and kept her own house and garden spick and span. And she always made a point of keeping abreast of everything going on in the square.

'Well . . . I don't know what to say . . .' It was probably one of the few times the woman had been lost for words.

'Say you'll come.'

After Mrs Ledbetter agreed she asked, 'Will you be around in Lantern Square over Christmas then? Not heading off after the concert?'

'I'll be here actually.' Her mum had suggested she come home but Hannah wanted to stay in the village this year, to be a real part of it.

'Will your new friends be joining you?'

'Which friends?'

'The young man who came here, and that girl too?'

She certainly spent a lot of her time hovering behind her net curtains. 'No, not this year. But there are plenty of people in the square to keep me company.'

'Then would you consider giving up some time to help

us get ready for the Lantern Walk on Boxing Day? It's all for charity remember. I do the Lantern Walk every year. I take it nice and slow, not like you youngsters, you'll be power-walking no doubt.'

'I'd love to, Mrs Ledbetter.'

Hannah eventually extricated herself from her neighbour's chit-chat and let herself into Lantern Cottage, but not before she spotted the big removal van outside The Little House and Mr Bray's belongings being carted out. According to Nigel, Charles was taking the move in his stride and she doubted it would be long before someone showed an interest in The Little House. Hannah had known a lot of change in her life, but sometimes it was for the best. Moving out of the townhouse she'd shared with Luke had been hard – she hadn't wanted to hurt him – and moving in with her parents after having independence for so long was even tougher, but moving here to Lantern Square . . . well, it was the right thing to do.

Inside, she took off her wet clothes, whizzed a hairdryer over her hair, made a cup of cocoa which she drank in the kitchen rather than take it anywhere near her dining room table, and when she had the feeling back in her fingers, it was straight to work. She ploughed through more cards, took a quick break for lunch, and then responded to her emails. There was another message from Joe, who wanted not one, but two care packages sent this time. Hannah tried not to think too much about who Natalie and Katrina might be, or the fact that he'd come on to Georgia. How many women did one man want? But all she needed to know right now was that these women both lived in Tetbury, and were getting the same package filled with items ranging from stationery and candles to bath products and chocolate. He clearly couldn't be bothered to think of anything more personal, she thought.

Hannah returned to her cards, carefully inking in the snowmen's hats in varying styles and shades. Each snowman had a checked scarf in red and white, a carrot nose and coloured buttons on his chest.

As the sun began to descend bringing the afternoon to a close, she put the latest batch of cards to one side to dry and not taking any chances when there was a knock at the front door, she checked that Smokey and Bandit weren't hiding in the dining room, shut the door firmly behind her, and padded through the hall, wincing as her feet touched the freezing floor. As toasty as Lantern Cottage could get, the flagstone floor never seemed to warm up, and Hannah's toes felt like little ice cubes.

She opened the door to the grey, misty outside, and Luke's frame filling the doorway.

'I was in the area, thought I'd say hello.' The drizzle was still coming down and when he spoke his breath met with the cold air and came out in little white puffs.

Despite the confusion she always felt when it came to this man, she couldn't leave him out in the cold – and she didn't want to run up her heating bill either by letting the warmth escape. 'Come in. I'm busy working but I can take a quick breather. Cup of tea?'

He beamed. 'Please.'

She took his coat and hung it on the bannister before leading him through to the kitchen.

'You're walking funny. Bit like John Wayne,' his voice trailed after her.

'Blame Georgia.' She briefly explained her dalliance with the spin class.

'You're insane.' He thanked her when she handed him a cup of tea. 'And are you sure you know what you're doing, getting involved with Georgia again?'

'I can look after myself. But I appreciate the concern. And anyway, her persuasion got me out, got me exercising and working out some stress.'

'After the nut debacle you mean.'

'My part in sending someone to hospital, yes.'

'Oh come on, not that again. You can't blame yourself.'

'It could've been a whole lot worse.'

'But it wasn't. And you still seem a little stressed, if you don't mind me saying.'

She didn't, because he was right and she appreciated the intuition. She told him all about the cats destroying the card order. 'I'm in the middle of remaking them now.' She looked at her watch. 'So I can't be too long before I go back to work. I'm due up at Butterbury Lodge soon. It's on with the current book for the book club I've formed and residents are eager for the next instalment. They're all trying not to read ahead – apparently they prefer listening as a group. I never thought they'd love it this much.'

'You sound settled here, at least.'

'I really am.' She felt like she'd finally found a place where she could really belong.

'Very different from London.'

'Well we always said that when we came this way, didn't we?' She looked away at the sudden recount that they'd once been together.

'Mum and Dad would never go anywhere else.'

'Why would they? Their house is gorgeous.'

'Mum said to remind you about another afternoon tea, soon.'

'She knows you're here?'

He shrugged. 'Not a lot gets past her. She worked it out for herself.' He took a couple of gulps of scalding hot tea. 'I came up from London again because I wanted to see you, Hannah. I wasn't just in the area; I came to talk to you.' He set his mug down on the benchtop. 'I wondered if you'd like to go out for dinner some time?'

She hadn't been expecting him to get to the point just like that. 'Oh, Luke. I'm not sure that's a good idea.'

He moved a step closer. 'We got together a long time ago, when I was hungry for success.'

She couldn't help but let a laugh escape. 'You're claiming you're not doing that any more.'

'Fair point. I suppose I still am, but that fast-paced London vibe doesn't have such a grip on me now. I've been spending more time this way with Mum and Dad and it's grown on me a lot.'

'You . . . leave the big city? I don't see it somehow.' She couldn't back away, it would be too obvious, but he was closing the gap between them and his gaze had dropped to her mouth more than once. Had she pushed him away, thinking he was wrong for her when really both of them needed time to evolve, to grow into a better version of themselves?

'I'm not leaving just yet, I'd have to put plans into place. But one day,' he said.

Hannah turned and deliberately picked up both their mugs, moving to the sink well out of his way.

'What do you say to dinner?' His voice came from behind her, but he stayed back this time.

'Maybe. I don't know.' She looked outside at the veil of darkness the sky brought with it now that daylight had faded. 'Don't you think we're done, Luke?'

'I'm not so sure we are.' He took a step towards her again when she turned around.

'Luke, I really need to get on, get this order completed and sent off.'

'Right.' He wasn't moving.

She looked at her watch. 'Actually, the cards will have to wait for now, I have to get up to Butterbury Lodge as promised.'

'Just think about dinner,' he urged as out in the hallway she tugged on her boots, picked up her coat and shrugged it on before stepping outside in a big rush to get away from the situation she didn't know how to judge.

Luke was still pulling on his own coat as she locked the front door.

To placate him she said, 'I'll think about it, I promise,' and turned on her heel to set off down the high street.

'At least let me take you up to the lodge. Come on,' he added when she hesitated. 'It's cold and dark and it's starting to rain again.'

She relented. She didn't much relish the thought of getting wet a second time. 'I appreciate it.'

The smell of the butter-soft leather upholstery enveloped her as Luke drove her from Lantern Square up to Butterbury Lodge, and despite everything she began to relax. It felt good to have someone looking after her for a change. She'd got used to doing everything herself these days.

'Thanks, Luke.' She undid her seat belt as he pulled up outside the front entrance.

'I'll hang around and drive you home again,' he offered.

'There's no need. I can walk down the hill.'

'It's dark. Can you imagine what Mum would say to me if she knew I'd let you walk home alone?'

She grinned, stepping out into the cold night air and then turning back once more. 'Never mind your mum, Mr G would have you hung, drawn and quartered for that.'

'I'll park up just here, I can reply to the emails I didn't get to at the office, I've got plenty to keep me busy.'

'I'll be about an hour.'

'Go on, off you go, don't keep them waiting.' When he winked she smiled back at him.

Frankie hadn't missed a trick. The second Hannah stepped inside she grabbed her arm, whispering 'Who *is* that? He's gorgeous.' Frankie craned her neck to get another look – from the reception you could see Luke's profile illuminated by the interior light of the car.

'Just a friend.'

'Seriously? What a waste.'

Hannah hung up her coat and turned back to find that Frankie had vanished behind the desk. 'What are you doing?'

'Christmas decorating,' came a voice from down low.

Hannah looked over the walnut reception desk, careful not to knock any of the leaflets flying. Frankie had the artificial tree out of its box and was trying to fathom which part went where. 'Biggest part at the bottom,' Hannah hinted.

'Obvious really,' Frankie laughed. She inserted the bottom section of the tree into the base, tightened up the eyebolt and went to slot in the next section, but it wouldn't stay in place and the pole kept on sliding too far into the one below it. No matter how many times she tried, she couldn't fix it.

'Could be time for a new one.' Hannah left her to it and went through to the lounge. The chairs had already been arranged in the semi-circle, her chair was already there, the fire was lit and expectant faces gradually turned her way. Most of them clutched a copy of the book in their laps, a few of them hinted they may have taken a sneaky peek at some more of the story and Hannah was glad to see Flo had joined them again. It was good to see the once-quiet newcomer joining in more and more.

Mr G quietened everyone down and they caught up with the next instalment of these naughty elderly people who were having the best adventures. Hannah only hoped it didn't give those at Butterbury Lodge any ideas.

After the reading it was tea and cake time, a ritual that had been adopted pretty swiftly after Grace suggested they had to repay Hannah somehow. Maggie and Frankie had readily agreed and served scones with jam and cream as well as tea – herbal or regular – as they talked about the book.

'Why don't you invite your friend in,' Mr G suggested.

'Sorry?'

'The man in the car.'

'He's happy enough outside.' She knew that if she invited him in Mr G would interrogate him, demanding to know if he was her boyfriend.

Mr G smiled knowingly, but picked up on her reluctance and let it go for now, while they lost themselves in the cake and chatter.

When it was time to leave and Hannah had said her

goodbyes, she told Mr G, 'I'll see you again soon. No robbing any banks like the characters in the books.'

'Damn, we'd made a proper plan and everything,' he smiled, repositioning the glasses that were skew-whiff from her hug.

'I'll see you soon.'

She went out to the car and climbed in, the interior still just as warm. 'Thanks for waiting.'

'No worries at all.' The smile Luke gave her left her in no doubt as to where he wanted this to go and as he pulled away from the lodge, down the hill and towards her cottage, Hannah wondered whether she should agree to go out for dinner with him. Or should she leave her past exactly where it was – behind her?

17

Hannah's work-life balance had been out of kilter since the night Luke had taken her to Butterbury Lodge. As he drove her back to Lantern Cottage the conversation had flowed easily; they'd chatted about his family, London, his new-found love of the Cotswolds. But she hadn't told anyone else that she'd met up with him, especially not Georgia who would most likely think she was making a mistake, and definitely not her dad who would almost certainly say the same. And if she let it slip to her mum, who'd always adored Luke, she'd probably be encouraged to leap back into a relationship she wasn't sure about. The only thing Hannah had been able to do since seeing Luke was to immerse herself in Tied Up with String.

'That's a lot of packages.' Kimberley was behind the counter today when Hannah wheeled her latest few into the post office.

'With Christmas fast approaching, it's a busy time of the year for the business.'

Kimberley and Hannah did the merry dance of weighing each parcel, then putting it through the flap at the end of the counter for Kimberley to stick the postage on it.

Hannah shivered when she met the cold outside once again, the December winds battering Butterbury village and Lantern Square. Rhys was busy clearing paths through the slippery leaves and clomps of mud that had blown onto the square, turning the pavement debris to mulch. But the woodland creatures that lit up in the beds kept it festive and Hannah loved seeing them in their hiding places. She'd miss them when they were gone in the New Year.

Hannah crossed the street, trundling her empty shopping trolley behind her, and Rhys stopped what he was doing so he could chat. 'All set for me to bring the Christmas tree to your door at the weekend?'

A grin spread across her face. 'I can't wait to put it up. It'll really feel like Christmas is coming then.'

'What, the village decorations aren't enough for you?'

'Of course they are, they're amazing, but so is waking up and padding downstairs with the smell of pine lingering in the air.'

'Couldn't have said it better myself.'

Every year Rhys took charge of the locals and their Christmas trees, a little side business or service that made him a real part of this community even though he didn't live in Butterbury itself. 'I saw that friend of yours the other day. She was coming out of The Little House with an estate agent.'

'What friend?'

'The one who isn't interested in me.'

'Now, that might be a long list,' she teased, although she knew exactly who he meant. Since Rhys had seen Georgia at Joe's place he'd stopped using her name so much and often referred to her as The Friend. 'What was Georgia doing looking at the house?'

'Exactly what I wanted to ask you.'

'I've no idea. She hasn't mentioned it to me.' Georgia had only ever been disparaging about Lantern Square to Hannah, complaining about the farmyard smells that often drifted this way and how some of Hannah's neighbours looked at her funny. Curtain Twitchers, she'd called them.

'Well she looked pretty taken with the place, took photos of it with her phone, spent a good fifteen minutes chatting with the estate agent out front.'

For once Hannah was distracted from how busy she was – and her feelings about Luke. She couldn't help worrying about what Georgia was up to. They may have made peace, but did she really want her friend moving in to Lantern Square, right on her doorstep?

When evening came, Hannah bundled up and made her way over to Mrs Addington's grand house in readiness for the Christmas wreath-making session, Christmas decorations lighting up the night sky and leading the way. From Mrs Addington's home she had a full view of the square and the tall Christmas tree that Hannah lingered outside to look at again. Its hundreds of white lights were like twinkling stars against the darkness.

'Come in, come in!' Mrs Addington had either been on the mulled wine or was caught up in the festive spirit because when Hannah knocked on her front door the woman was the most relaxed she'd ever been. She ushered Hannah inside the wooden-floored hallway with the Persian rug runner lining the centre of the boards and even without the home's owner leading the way, Hannah could've found which room to go to because classical

Christmas music was belting out and competing with chatter coming from the second door to the left of the corridor.

'Look at all this! Wow, it's amazing!' Hannah took her coat off and handed it to Mrs Addington as she took in the supplies spread out on the main table. It was at least twice as big as Hannah's dining table at home and Hannah could imagine the retired judge hosting many a formal gathering here. There were separate piles of everything you could possibly think of to design an individual wreath: variegated evergreens; winterberries in both reds and golds; ribbon lengths in tartan, green, gold and silver; pine cones; holly and ivy; lengths of dogwood and birch; even red chillies had made an appearance although Hannah wasn't sure about those.

'You've done us proud, Mrs Addington.' Annie had come in after Hannah. Ellen was already ladling out some lethal-looking winter punch with thick slices of apple and orange in it.

'Be warned,' Frankie whispered to Hannah, 'it's got a high content of Pimm's and a stratospheric addition of brandy. You'll be wasted on more than a glass.'

'Thanks for the tip.'

'You could soak up the punch with truffles.' She indicated the two enormous platters waiting by the side of the punch bowl beyond the glasses. 'Gingerbread truffles, some in white chocolate, and I think there are rum balls too. Mind you, they might have just as much booze in them as this.' She took another generous sip from her own glass, not heeding her own warning.

Hannah went over to fetch a glass of the punch. The beauty of not having to drive was that she didn't have to worry too much about the alcohol content, and a nip of brandy might dampen her concerns about Georgia's plan to move to the square – and the fact that she'd neglected to mention it to her friend who already lived here.

She plucked a few truffles from the plate, going for one covered in gold leaf and another dusted in cocoa powder. Yep, Frankie was right, they were laced as much as the punch. She reached out to touch the branch of the tree standing tall and proud in the corner, even more excited to put hers up at the weekend. Along with the wreath she would make tonight, Lantern Cottage would soon be dressed for Christmas. All that would be missing was a little snow on the ground outside.

Hannah took the chair next to Pamela who was chatting to Lily, who'd been able to join them on one of her nights off from the pub. Then came Cate, eight-months pregnant and waddling a little, but still determined to join in the fun. She must've found a babysitter for the evening, with her husband often working away. Next, it was Dawn and Troy who quickly claimed responsibility for the truffles, and Marianne Temple from the post office had squeezed in at the end of the table and was holding court with some story about Rhys being very bossy during the organisation of the Christmas tree in the square. Hannah had to laugh. If he hadn't been, they probably wouldn't ever have been able to get the thing up and lit.

The evening was a total blast. Hannah was called on more than once, deemed to be one of the most artistic members of the group, but she claimed she was better at parcels than anything involving greenery. 'Rhys reckons I kill most things just by looking at them in my tiny little garden.' Maybe she'd better lay off the punch, she was far too vocal.

'I do wish he'd move to the square,' came Ellen's voice.

'I forget he doesn't already live here,' Hannah remarked. 'Last month he had to sleep on the sofa at my cottage after a few too many at the pub and he was saying how much he felt a part of life in the square.'

'Bet that had Mrs Ledbetter's curtains twitching.'

'It probably did, but she knows by now that we're just friends.' Hannah saw Rhys around so much that she felt he was part of the figurative furniture in Lantern Square, but actually he had to drive to Butterbury most days from the flat he shared ten miles away, in a village that was literally one street with no facilities, not many houses and no character at all.

'He's interested in The Little House,' said Lily. 'He told me last night in the pub, but he's still in talks with the bank.'

Hannah suspected he hadn't shared that information with her because of Georgia's interest and she felt a pang of disloyalty that she was friends with the enemy. No matter how much Georgia apologised, Hannah resolved to always put Rhys first from now on. He'd never wronged her and she couldn't imagine him doing so either.

'Wonder if there've been any other offers on the place,' Cate pondered.

'Has Charles left it in his son's hands?' Hannah wondered. If Charles Bray knew Rhys was interested, surely he'd want the house to go to him. He certainly wouldn't want an outsider.

'No idea, but Rhys had better get in quick,' said Mrs Addington who was twisting up a piece of florists' wire to push into the wreath and fix on a cluster of red berries. 'Lantern Square is popular, that's for sure.'

When the truffles were almost demolished, the punch bowl down to its final dribbles and wreaths were at last finished off with a bow – and in one case, a few chillies – it was time to end the evening and Hannah, wreath carefully placed in a carrier bag, bid everyone goodnight and wandered back to her place.

She'd even had enough punch not to mind seeing Luke's car outside Lantern Cottage and tapped gently on the window.

'What's in the bag?' he asked when he climbed out of the driver's side.

She opened it enough for him to peer inside. 'What do you think?'

'You're a woman of many talents.'

'It's going on the front door.'

'Ah, so that's what the nail is for. I did wonder.'

'Rhys popped one there for me. I figured I'd use it every year so why not.'

'Right.' His breath met with the cold air. 'You haven't given me an answer about dinner yet.'

On the spot, she suggested, 'Maybe we could just go for a drink?'

He began to grin. 'Smells like you've had enough of that already.'

'Mrs Addington's punch claimed to have apple and orange juice as key ingredients, but it sure didn't feel like it. And the only thing to soak it up were truffles which also had unknown quantities of alcohol.'

'You still haven't given me an answer.' He wasn't going to be distracted.

Right now, she just wanted to slouch on the sofa. But she didn't want to offend him when he was trying so hard. 'How about you come in for a cup of tea and we can talk some more?'

'Sounds like a start.'

'But first . . .' She took the wreath from the carrier bag and standing on tiptoes, hung it on the nail on her front door. She stood back to admire it. 'Perfect.'

While Hannah made the tea, Luke got the log burner going and by the time Hannah came through to the lounge it was crackling away and he closed the little door at the front.

She handed him a mug and curled up with her own. 'It's probably good you stopped by. I might've collapsed into bed if you hadn't and this tea will sort me out a bit better, stop the hangover brewing.'

'Glad to be of service.'

They talked about his parents' plans for a huge Christmas dinner at Maplebrooke Manor. 'You're welcome to join us,' he told her when she revealed she was staying in the square.

'It's really kind of you to offer and I must be nuts to say no to your mum's cooking, but there's a full Christmas dinner happening over at the pub so it'll be good to eat with everyone else. And then I have a carol concert to go to up at Butterbury Lodge.'

'Is there anyone who lives in these parts that you don't know?'

'I do know a lot of people now,' she concluded. 'And we might get another addition. There's a house up for sale.'

'Yeah?' He took a ginger biscuit from the plate Hannah

had set down on the coffee table in between their chairs.

'Apparently Georgia has been looking at The Little House. It's only just gone on the market.'

He spluttered and patted his chest when his tea went down the wrong way. 'What the hell is she playing at?'

'I wondered the same. I know I changed and wanted a slice of the quieter life after London, but she doesn't seem to have done the same. When she's here it's like the village is too small for her, or not good enough, so I can't understand why she's even interested.'

'Have you asked her?'

'I haven't, not yet. Maybe I should.' It felt good to have him on her side, to see he was as shocked as she was. 'More biscuits?' She didn't wait for an answer because she was ravenous. They were at least going some way to soak up the alcohol.

When Hannah could barely keep her eyes open, it was time to say goodbye to her guest. She hovered at the front door, shivering as she met the outside late evening temperatures. There'd be a frost on the ground tomorrow for sure.

'Get back inside, stay warm.' Luke had car keys looped over his fingers. 'And think about dinner, OK?' He leaned in and kissed her on the cheek, his lips just grazing her skin. For a moment it looked like he was contemplating kissing her properly – and then Hannah's gaze locked with Mrs Ledbetter's as she bustled down the street in the direction of her own house.

'I'll see you again soon,' Hannah smiled. 'You'd better go or the neighbours will be gossiping.'

'Who cares?' He wasn't moving.

'Goodnight, Luke.' She shut the front door anyway,

leaving him to make his own way to the car parked on the street. It wasn't Mrs Ledbetter's presence that bothered her at all, but her feelings for Luke and the temptation of falling into a relationship she wasn't sure needed to be re-opened at all.

'That was brutal.' Hannah wiped her neck with her towel after they finished the spin class Georgia had set up at the gym. 'I only came because you made me.'

Georgia grinned. 'You owed me for taking those parcels to the post office for you earlier.'

'Ha! You only did that so I'd have time to change and you could drag me here.' Georgia had turned up at her cottage lamenting the need to pre-empt the calorific intake over the festive period by ramping up the exercise beforehand. Apparently it was the only way to stay fitting into your jeans through the silly season.

Georgia didn't deny it and they made their way to the cafeteria as they came down from their endorphin-packed spin class. Georgia's bossiness and enthusiasm suited this new job of hers and she'd rallied every participant today to give it their all. Hannah had been counting the minutes until the end, unable to believe she'd been cajoled into coming again, but she was calling it preparation for the Christmas period, when she planned to adopt a moratorium on all things exercise apart from the Lantern Square walk.

Georgia was clearly thinking the same way and talked about the feast she had planned for Christmas Day back with her folks. 'Come January, I'll ramp up the energy levels and back to it.' She patted a taut stomach beneath her vest top. 'Don't want to get the middle-aged spread ten years too early.' She swigged her water. 'Or make that ever. What are you doing?'

'Just checking my emails.'

'Work or pleasure.'

'Work of course.'

'Hannah, take time for yourself. The class and now the downtime. Enjoy it.'

'You're right. Actually, do you mind watching my bag while I nip to the ladies?'

'Of course. Can I get you anything?'

'Just a banana please.' She set her phone down on the nearest table and left her bag under Georgia's watchful gaze while she zipped off to the bathrooms.

Back in the cafeteria with a bottle of water and a banana to reward her stomach after a gruelling session, Hannah asked, 'Will this mystery boyfriend be going home with you for Christmas?'

'He has his own plans this time, but we've talked about it for next year.' She crossed the fingers on both hands.

'I really want to meet him.'

She looked sheepish. 'I'm worried it's early days. I don't want to introduce someone who ends up being a dud.'

'I understand.'

'So how about you? It's been quiet on the man front for a long time, maybe it should be your New Year's resolution to put yourself out there.'

'Yeah, maybe.'

'Is work busy?'

'Manic. I feel like I'm chasing my own tail most days.'

'I guess it's the season. Do locals use your services?'

'Some of them do. Rhys just ordered twelve care packages.'

'Twelve?'

'He buys Christmas gifts in themes – this year Tied Up with String wins and I've done packages for his mum, his dad, siblings, aunts, uncles.' She wouldn't mention Joe's orders or Georgia would seize the opportunity to go on about him again. And anyway, there was another order of business she needed to attend to. 'I spoke to Rhys today.'

'How is he? Now he's definitely not my type I'm afraid . . . I prefer office men rather than muddy types. Men in good suits.'

'He's lovely.'

'Then why don't you go out with him?'

'He's just a friend. Which reminds me. He said he'd seen you, coming out of The Little House.'

Lips pursed around a straw going into the uber healthy, post-work-out shake she'd ordered, Georgia paused after taking a satisfying gulp. Hannah felt pretty sure she'd vomit if she had to eat something quite so green. 'It's such a cute place,' she added.

'It is.'

She waited to see if Georgia would add anything else but when her eyes remained on the green goo she asked, 'Why were you looking? For someone else?'

'It was for me, silly.' She said it as though Hannah had asked why she'd been picking out a particular brand of trainer rather than making a life-altering decision, uprooting her life and probably Hannah's by coming so close.

'But you hate small-town life.'

'Things change.'

Not that much they didn't. 'Is it because of your new job?'

She gulped down more goo. 'It makes sense to get on

the property ladder. Long term I want to be back in the city, back in London with the bright lights and vibe. My dream is to run my own gym business, huge, massive.' She made the actions with her hands. 'I want to attract the richest of clients, celebrities, have other people working for me, me calling the shots.'

'That sounds great, but buying in Butterbury is a bit backwards if that's your goal.'

'It's strategic, not backwards.'

In the past, Georgia's only strategy had been getting the wine out of a bottle fast enough to get in another round before last orders. It didn't make sense to Hannah. 'I don't see it.'

'What, me running a business?'

'No, no I didn't mean that. I promise. I think with the right business you'd make a good go of it.'

Georgia leaned forwards. 'We could do it together, take the fitness industry by storm. Didn't Liam always talk about starting his own fitness franchise one day? He didn't want to be in the army forever, surely.'

'Possibly . . .' She wasn't sure how she felt about discussing the man who'd been the love of her life once upon a time. 'But that was his career plan, not mine.'

'Look, I know it didn't exactly work before with the accountancy business, but I think my problem was that my heart wasn't in it.'

Exactly, and hers wouldn't be in the fitness industry. 'I have a business already, one that I love.'

A look of frustration flashed across Georgia's face until she slurped up the rest of the green drink and pushed the cup aside. 'Fair enough. Look, my reason for wanting to buy in Butterbury is that property is more affordable here. I hadn't thought of buying outside of London until I began coming here so much. It's not far from the gym so I could live in the place for a while as I get my plans sorted for something big. Then, I think renting it out would be another investment, another string to add to my bow. It's so cute, it's small and perfect for one or maybe two, and seeing Lantern Square and hearing about its community and events, well that's got to attract holidaymakers hasn't it?'

Hannah almost shuddered. Holidaymakers? In Lantern Square? They loved out-of-towners who joined in with the dances and the fairs and gave local businesses a nudge, and residents were always keen to show off how stunning their village was. But as for people dipping in and out on a regular basis, staying in the most beautiful properties but not being a part of the community? It didn't bear thinking about.

'I'm pretty sure that wouldn't be popular with people who live in the square,' Hannah said diplomatically, hoping her friend had an ounce of compassion.

'Then they need to get their heads out of their arses and move with the times.' OK, so maybe not. 'They need to realise it's not all 1960s streets with ice-cream vans, penny sweets and neighbours chatting in the street. Not anymore.' She grinned. 'Hey, I sound like a hard-nosed businesswoman. Who'd have thought?'

The fact Hannah's disapproval was blatantly written across her face had escaped Georgia's notice as she ran on and on about the gym empire she wanted, the little village escape in the cottage when she chose, how lucrative the home could be if she went ahead and rented it out.

Something had to be done about this and fast. Hannah

didn't want Lantern Square turning into a series of rental properties, but she also wasn't sure she wanted her friend living so close by, especially when it meant that Rhys would miss out if he was hoping to buy The Little House.

In fact, Hannah was beginning to have doubts about whether she ever should have resurrected this friendship in the first place.

18

Hannah almost had to take the phone away from her ear the woman was yelling so much.

'Once again, I'm so sorry,' Hannah pleaded when she got a word in. 'I don't know how this happened.' Well she did, she'd probably been in such a tizzy about Georgia that she'd muddled up a parcel intended for an eighty-year-old with Crabtree & Evelyn hand cream, gorgeous fawn alpaca socks, birthday cake truffles and a blackberry jam artisan candle, with the highly inappropriate parcel for a twenty-nine-year-old woman preparing for a hen night. Needless to say, the sight of the chocolate body paint and the strawberry flavoured condoms, not to mention the phallic lollypops she'd felt so naughty and clever adding in, hadn't gone down well with this customer.

'Can you imagine my mother opening that this morning? For her birthday!' the woman went on.

'I'm so sorry. If you'll let me, I'll deliver a parcel personally today. You can bin the contents you received.'

The woman seemed at least placated, blabbering something about rushing off on the school run, but not before she put her mother, Elsie, on the phone.

Hannah was in for it now.

It took a while for Elsie to speak. 'Sorry, dear, just waiting for my daughter to bundle the kids out the door.' More waiting, crashing about in the background, and then she was back, but if Hannah had braced herself for more yelling she'd read the situation all wrong. 'Oh, thank you, thank you, thank you, for, quite frankly, the best giggle I've had in almost a year!'

'Excuse me?'

'I was anticipating the same old dull gifts for my birthday, you know, the rose-petal soaps, embroidered handkerchiefs, all the usual. Strawberry condoms and lollypops in unmentionable shapes made my day.' She was laughing hard, and Hannah started to chuckle with relief.

'I'm so glad you're not upset. But your daughter is and she's my customer so I'll be bringing your replacement parcel.'

'That's fine, I'll see you whenever you get here. Will you take this parcel back?'

'Oh no, you can bin it, that's fine.'

'You're joking! I'll be taking this to my "knit and natter" group this evening. We'll enjoy sucking on those lollypops.'

Hannah put the phone down quite uplifted although she did wish it was the evening and she could fix a stiff drink, rather than nine o'clock on a cold, grey, damp day in Butterbury, where her only sensible option with her workload was tea. But not yet. Now she had to call the other recipient and sort this mess out.

Five minutes later and she was nursing a mug of tea while using Google maps to check the locations of both houses so she could do the parcel swap. The old lady lived in Bath and the hen lived in Bristol, and as soon as she'd made up two more parcels she'd go and rectify her embarrassing mistake. She wondered how she'd let her mind wander so badly that she'd mixed up those delivery labels.

Parcels done and loaded into her little car, Hannah drove at a crawl down the street past Lantern Square. Her de-misters were going at full blast and the windscreen was clearing gradually, just enough so she saw Joe coming out of his house with not one woman this time, but two. She certainly didn't want to start thinking about him in terms of threesomes – those phallic lollypops and strawberry condoms must have gone right to her head.

Whatever it was, she needed focus. She was a business-woman, she couldn't afford to be making these kinds of mistakes.

'You look shattered.' It was Frankie, hauling a box into the store cupboard near reception when Hannah arrived at Butterbury Lodge that evening.

'You know I'd be offended if that wasn't so true.' Hannah managed a smile as she unwound her scarf and hung it with her coat on the old-fashioned stand. She filled Frankie in on what had happened at Tied Up with String.

'It's all getting on top of you. You need a rest.'

'Not the best time of the year for one of those.' She'd driven to each recipient's house with their amended parcels and she was dog tired, but she'd committed to coming here and hated letting anyone down.

Frankie brushed dust from her top and picked off a few pieces of lint. 'You'll have to excuse me, I've been hauling that blinking tree around again.'

'I thought you fixed it and put it up.'

'I did, but then it was superseded by a surprise delivery from an unknown organisation. Or person I suppose.' She tilted her head towards the double doors that led through to the communal lounge.

Hannah took a few steps closer and as well as the golden glow from an impressive crackling fire that must've pleased Ernest no end, there was the most spectacular tree stretching from floor almost to the ceiling. It had to be at least an eight-footer.

'The residents love it.' Frankie stood beside her, evidently fed up of moving boxes and packaging up a spikey Christmas tree that was a poor second to this one. 'It was like the biggest Christmas present for them all. And you'll see they've set up the reading circle so that they're facing the fireplace and the tree.'

'I'll have my back to it, but I don't care, it's gorgeous.' She waved to Mr G who had already spotted her.

Frankie sniffed the air. 'What's the perfume you're wearing, it's gorgeous?'

'Marc Jacobs Daisy.' She sniffed her wrist to remind herself of the floral scent. She didn't wear perfume much these days but it always gave her a lift when she did.

'Is that the one with the fancy bottle and the flower on top?'

'That's the one, and I'm nearly out more's the pity.'

Frankie smiled. 'Go on through. I'm bringing mince pies in as soon as the reading is finished, and there's mulled wine if you're interested.'

'Actually I'm very interested. I walked in the dark tonight, don't tell Mr G.' She'd been stuck in the car all day and needed the air so driving tonight wasn't an option.

They read the final chapter of the current book club

choice and afterwards they talked about the plot, the characters and the good and bad points of the story. Everyone seemed to have a totally different opinion but it made for a lively discussion. Even Flo spoke up this time which was wonderful to hear as she told the group that the main character reminded her of her late husband.

After the mince pies had circulated courtesy of Frankie, Hannah stayed on for a chat with Mr G in the chairs he'd had Maggie position close to the window with the tree in front of them and the fireplace to the side. She filled him in on what she'd been up to.

'They're serving mulled wine tonight,' he said.

'I know, Frankie told me.'

'Takes a good recipe to get it right you know.'

'You're a fan of mulled wine?'

'I enjoy a tipple. But never buy it at a pub where they've told you it's fresh but it's been sitting there all night. They just turn the warmer on and it's not the same.' He pulled a face.

'Thanks for the tip.'

'Frankie used a good recipe tonight I can assure you.'

'I love the stuff,' she admitted. 'Marks the start of winter, makes me feel all warm inside.'

'Good to know. You enjoy a glass before you leave. You do look tired, Hannah, if you don't mind me saying.'

'Frankie said the same, don't worry. And I am. I'm really busy and these mistakes aren't helping.'

'You need a break, please tell me you're taking time off over Christmas. And no more of those brutal exercise classes.'

'I think you're right.' She wasn't intending to let Georgia persuade her to attend any more classes. Her throat was already scratchy and she figured an early night could nip any ailments in the bud if she was lucky. One of Georgia's classes would send her body in the opposite direction. Not to mention the stress of thinking about her friend and The Little House in Lantern Square.

'Did you hear, Rhys has made an offer on Charles Bray's Little House?'

'That's great!'

'And it was accepted.'

Hannah let out a long, relieved sigh. 'Well, that's the best news I've heard all day.' Buzzing that the house wouldn't be a tourist residence or indeed a place where her friend could be too close for comfort, she turned their conversation to Elsie in Bath. 'She was such a lovely woman and thank goodness her daughter was out when I stopped by. She told her daughter she'd thrown out the contents of the first care package in the outside bin, deep in a black sack it was so ghastly. She hadn't. She'd hidden it under her bed.'

'Good for her, mischievous thing.' Mr G accepted a mince pie from Frankie who was doing the rounds again. 'That's why I like living here. I'm surrounded by people who get that we haven't always been this age. We weren't born "old". We have a sense of adventure just like every-one else.'

'I know that, Mr G.' She patted his hand and the scent of the real tree pulled her gaze towards it and its gorgeous wooden soldier ornaments with their red hats, white breeches and navy jackets. 'Do you know who sent it?'

'The tree?' He shrugged. 'No idea. Word has it, it was at the back door to the lodge when Frankie arrived this morning. She had to call her boyfriend to come and help haul it inside. There was one of those fancy stands that holds water alongside it already as well as a box of ornaments, those toy soldiers included. Whoever gave it must have inside knowledge because they clearly realised how few ornaments we had, given the other tree was a dwarf in comparison.'

'Well I'm glad someone was so kind, it looks amazing.'

'I'm going to suggest Frankie put the artificial one in the dining room instead. Then we'll have it to decorate the room when we eat our Christmas lunch.' Hannah began to laugh. 'What is it?'

'She's going to love you, she's hauled it out, finally managed to stuff it back in the box, and now you want it put up again.'

'She loves me, she won't mind.'

Hannah wasn't so sure and when she went to find Frankie for mulled wine, she floated the idea.

'Keeps me busy,' Frankie concluded surprisingly. 'And I haven't taped the box up again yet. Otherwise I might have a few choice words to say to Mr G.' She bit into a mince pie, scooping her palm beneath her chin to catch any crumbs and before another bite said, 'I went to one of your friend's spin classes a couple of days ago.'

'They're not easy, are they?' Hannah was way happier chowing down on mince pies and the mulled wine she had between her palms right now rather than putting herself through anything so brutal ever again. 'I went a few days ago and it near killed me.'

'Bit dramatic.'

'You're younger than me. Wait until you're the wrong side of thirty.'

'Or forty,' Maggie chipped in as she passed by with

some fresh sprigs of holly she was going to use to adorn the gilded mirror above the fireplace and some of the paintings dotted around the grand room. 'Then everything starts to hurt.'

Talking of pain and discomfort, Hannah's bones had suddenly begun to ache something rotten and all she wanted to do was curl up and go to sleep. Even the mulled wine wasn't working its usual magic.

'I think I'd better take off home and have an early night,' she told them eventually, before bundling up in all her layers again.

By now her head was pounding – she couldn't decide whether from the small sip of mulled wine or the cold she was getting – and even as classic tunes from the carollers standing in Lantern Square in front of the big tree hummed on the wintry air, she couldn't bear to stop and listen. She wanted her pyjamas and her bed. She'd rest up and whatever had been going wrong, whatever stresses had come her way, as of tomorrow she'd have a great and relaxing Christmas.

But the next morning, her body had other plans. She'd woken half an hour ago, her mouth drier than a desert, and she swore her soft down pillow had been squeezing her temples all night.

Down in the kitchen she found the paracetamol and a big glass of water. It was still dark outside and even the Christmas lights she'd strung across the pelmet board in the kitchen and the piece of holly with its rich berries tucked at the top of the kitchen clock weren't enough to lift her spirits. There was no doubt about it: she was sick. With only nine days to go until Christmas, she had come down with the worst cold in history. Her bones ached, it was painful every time her body came in contact with anything and she crawled back to her bed by going upstairs on her hands and knees.

By mid-morning after she'd tried to get up and work twice but reluctantly concluded it was impossible, she called the doctor's surgery and made an appointment. Maybe they could give her some rocket-like pills, a potion that could at least allow her to stay upright and sitting in her dining room to get things done. She had an international order that had come through last night and she absolutely had to send it today because it was going all the way to Canada to celebrate a family's first year of emigrating out there from the UK. Quite why the sender had left it so late Hannah couldn't understand, but that wasn't her concern, her priority was maintaining her reputation that had come under such strain lately. Her mind swirled with the memories of her recent disasters. First had been the nut incident, which could've been so much worse than it was, then the cards that had been ruined when she stupidly left the dining room door open and the cats knocked liquid onto the order, and then the bachelorette parcel mix up with poor Elsie. As least she'd found more joy and amusement in the wrong parcel and so Hannah had ended up feeling quite uplifted.

But the strain of everything going wrong combined with this busy time of year was taking its toll. And so mid-afternoon Hannah attempted to get dressed and make her way down the street towards the surgery tucked behind the main post office. But her body wasn't playing ball. She called the surgery and said she'd have to cancel her appointment and as she lay at the foot of the stairs – she hadn't had the energy to haul herself anywhere else since she'd found her phone on the ledge in the hallway – it was only a knock at the door that made her move.

She shivered and pulled herself upright using the wall as support. Opening the door she knew she looked fright-ful and Joe's reaction confirmed it. 'Didn't know you made house calls,' she croaked.

'I do for our most needy patients.'

'I'm not . . .' She couldn't even be bothered to finish the sentence and leaving the front door, moved back to the bottom stair and sat down.

Joe came in and closed the door to the cottage. He crouched down on his haunches. And when his cool hand touched the skin of her forehead she opened her eyes, not really realising she'd shut them in the first place and more than likely fallen asleep in a milli-second.

'You're burning up,' he said. 'You need to be in bed.'

'I'm too hot.'

'You have a temperature, but you're shivering. You have the flu.'

'I do not.' She thought she might have fallen asleep again for a second before she managed to add, 'It's a bad cold. I have work.'

'Not today you don't.' He opened up a bag. 'Judging by your symptoms given over the phone I thought you might've succumbed to the dreaded flu so I've brought you along some painkillers.' He whipped out a thermom-eter and after pushing on a plastic cover, put it in her ear.

'Ow.' Even that hurt.

'Baby,' he teased.

She was pretty sure she frowned and fell asleep simul-taneously and only woke upon hearing the beep from the thermometer when it found what it was looking for. Her head lolled against the bannister and she roused when he confirmed her temperature.

'Let me help you upstairs to bed.' He wanted to take control. And she quite liked it. Oh, she really must be sick. She was going to be one of his floozies, taken advantage of in her hour of need.

'I'll get you plenty of water and you can take some of these.' He gestured to a packet of flu-strength pills that she saw when she wrenched open one eye. 'If you rest now, chances are you'll be good by Christmas.'

'Christmas!' She tried to yell but it brought tears to her eyes and she held her hands on either side of her head to dull the pain.

'Doctor's orders,' he said softly.

'I have a parcel that must go out today.' She pointed to the dining room.

He sighed and led her upstairs anyway. She must've fallen asleep when he went downstairs and returned with a tall glass of water, set down his phone on her bedside table and popped a couple of pills from a foil packet. 'Here, sit up, take these, but no more for four hours. And I think you need someone here with you.'

Was he volunteering to stay? 'I'll be fine.' She popped one pill on her tongue, swigged the liquid and repeated for the next, set the glass of water down but not before his phone began to chime and she saw the name Heather pop up on the screen. Another one of his harem then.

He picked up his phone. 'Look, I need to go, but I'm going to ask Rhys to check on you in a few hours. Would that be OK?'

'There's no need, honestly.'

'I'm the doctor, you're the patient.'

And actually, she didn't have the strength to argue. She simply told him to give Rhys the spare key from the kitchen drawer beside the sink and then she fell asleep yet again.

But it wasn't Rhys who woke her. The next time she opened her eyes was when Luke felt her forehead with the back of his hand.

'I saw Joe leaving and volunteered to keep an eye on you after he told me you had the flu.'

It wasn't what Hannah wanted but right now she didn't have the energy to put up a fight.

'Work can wait.' He was brushing her hair away from her face as she rambled on about care packages and Must Go Out Today guarantees. 'You're boiling.'

'I need to send the package.'

'You need to sleep.'

She forced her eyes open and was ashamed at the tear that snaked its way out. 'Too many things are going wrong.'

'Everyone gets sick.'

'Too many things are going wrong with my business,' she sniffed. 'The parcel has to go.'

'Hannah, I'm not one to take orders from another man when it comes to a girl I know a hell of a lot better than him. But Joe's right, you need rest, water and regular doses of paracetamol.'

She managed to garble on about the package for someone in Canada, the order she desperately wanted to fulfil and meet the final guaranteed posting date. And before she knew it Luke was running around her little cottage, feet padding up and down the stairs bringing in cardboard boxes, string, items she'd thought of to include. She dreaded to think of the state of those storage boxes in her dining room given the clattering around, but eventually each item had been individually wrapped in tissue paper, and somehow he'd managed to parcel it all up with a respectable string bow.

'I'll pop this into the post office,' he told her.

'Thank you, Luke. I . . .'

'Ssshhh . . . you sleep.' She felt his cool hand against her cheek and then she must have fallen asleep, because the next thing she knew she'd woken to a smell drifting up the stairs.

Lantern Cottage was wrapped in darkness and when she sat up she could just about make out the remnants of brown paper, scissors, tape, packaging and wrap from some of the items and extras they hadn't needed for the parcel as well as one of the see-through bags of ice-blue confetti.

The parcel. Had it gone in time to make the last post? She opened her mouth but nothing came out and she lay back and drifted off again.

She woke this time to Luke with a bowl of soup on a tray and some toast. 'It's only tinned soup. Chicken,' he said.

'I'm not hungry.'

'Maybe not, but you'll waste away, you need something. Have a few mouthfuls, then go back to sleep.' He pre-empted her question. 'The parcel went off just fine.'

'Thank you,' she said sleepily, sitting as upright as she could against the bedhead and obediently opening and closing her mouth as he fed her the soup. It was surprisingly welcome, and she ate almost half the bowl and managed one piece of toast before he got her to drink more water and take more paracetamol.

And that was the routine for the next forty-eight hours. She stayed in bed, Luke waited on her hand and foot, and by the time she came round a couple of days later she managed to go downstairs.

'Good morning, sleepyhead.' He was in the lounge where a blanket and a bundle of cushions showed her where he'd been sleeping himself.

'I don't know how to thank you.'

'You needed someone.'

He'd always been there just at the right time. 'Well you're off the hook today, I feel so much better.'

He came towards her, put a hand against her forehead and declared, 'You know, I think you might be right.'

She went to the window and leaned her hands on the sill feeling the coldness of winter seep through the glass. She smiled. 'It's good to see the outside again. I haven't been out in days.'

'Hannah, I need to get going, I've got to be back at work.'

'Of course, thank you. How did you swing it anyway?'

'You have been out of it,' he mused. 'It was a weekend so I was around, but now it's back to the routine until Christmas. And Rhys delivered your tree, it's out back in a bucket of water. I wasn't sure where you wanted it so he said to text him and he'll give you a hand to get it inside.'

'I'd forgotten all about the tree. And thanks again for doing the parcel, I didn't want anything else to go wrong.' She frowned as a thought occurred to her. 'Did you take any other deliveries here in the last couple of days?'

'Not apart from boring brown envelopes that usually

indicate bills. I left them in the kitchen for you.' He collected up his things ready for the off. 'Why? You expecting a big Christmas gift?'

'Just some supplies, that's all.' She followed him towards the door.

They opened the door to Rhys who had some spare time and was hoping Hannah was ready to get the tree inside. 'Is it safe to come in?' he asked.

'Of course.' Hannah said goodbye to Luke, thanking him again, and stood back for Rhys to follow her. She grabbed a coat and some boots and between them they manoeuvred the tree in through the kitchen, along the tiny hallway and into the lounge where she'd cleared a space last week, in the corner, beside the window, so that if she sat on her favourite spot on the sofa she'd be able to enjoy the log burner and the tree all lit up at the same time. Her boxes of decorations were already waiting patiently and she couldn't wait to get the tree decorated for Christmas.

But first, as soon as Rhys left, she downed another glass of water and then headed upstairs to shower. It felt so good to have clean skin again, the lather on the puff covering her body and the smell invigorating her enough to feel almost back to normal when she emerged.

She got straight on to chasing up the supplier who should have made a delivery by now. She was almost out of brown paper, almost out of labels, and supplies of the string were low not to mention the outer packages she used. The supplier was usually so reliable too.

'I emailed the order through,' she reiterated on the telephone to the woman who was telling her there was no such record in the system. On hold again, Hannah felt sure the person on the other end of the line was probably coming down with the flu she'd got herself and wasn't thinking straight. But no. When the woman came back on the line she said there was an order but it was cancelled by Hannah herself via email.

'I didn't cancel it.'

'It says here that you did. And I can only tell you what's on the system,' came the jobsworth on the other end.

Hannah knew it wasn't worth arguing – they were clearly making excuses – and placed the order again. She had just about enough supplies to keep her going but had she not realised and reordered today, she would've had to run around and find alternatives to keep her customers happy and her business branding top notch as it should be.

She slumped down into the sofa and stroked Bandit as he leaped onto her lap. 'Did you miss me?' Thank goodness cats didn't get the flu. Or did they? 'Luke must've looked after you, too.' He and Smokey seemed perfectly happy and given Luke's dislike of felines they seemed to have coexisted together perfectly happily for the last couple of days. Luke was changing in the most unexpected ways and it left her more confused than ever.

Smokey had already stretched languorously on the sofa now Luke had vacated it and seemed determined not to budge, even to investigate the Christmas tree – although it might be a different story once the ornaments were in place. Hannah looked out of the frost-framed windows of her cottage as Bandit staked his claim on the rug in front of the log burner. She smiled and waved to Mrs Ledbetter who returned the gesture with a wave as she scuttled, head down against the wind, to her own cottage.

The fresh scent of Hannah's tree filled the lounge, making her realise that she must be getting so much better. She finally had a proper sense of smell again, when before she hadn't been interested or very much aware of anything apart from a pounding head and the desire for sleep.

She wondered why Georgia hadn't been in touch while she'd been unwell. Since Georgia had reappeared on the scene it seemed she wanted to be with Hannah most of the time, whether it was at gym classes, going to the pub or just gossiping. But maybe like so many others she was cosied up with her boyfriend for the winter. Or perhaps she was perturbed at Hannah's clear reluctance at the thought of Georgia buying a house in Lantern Square. Hannah might not have come right out and said it, but her lack of enthusiasm surely must've given the game away.

Hannah put any worries out of her mind and instead pulled the Christmas lights from their box and after she'd checked they were in good working order, she wound them round the tree ensuring all branches got the benefit as her jumper collected plenty of needles along the way. She added baubles, delicate glittery ornaments, silver bells she'd had since her first Christmas away from home, and the angel on top that she'd found at a charity shop and decided to give a good home.

And when she was done she felt well enough to make a hot cocoa on the stove, milk in the pan like her dad used to do when she was small, and treated herself by curling up on the sofa to enjoy it.

With every sip her worries dissipated. Christmas in Lantern Square. Her first, she hoped, of many. And she couldn't wait.

19

A flurry of snow began in the early hours of Christmas Eve and carried on well into the afternoon, and as Hannah trudged up the hill towards Butterbury Lodge, she was in good spirits. She'd finished work for the season, her supplier had delivered everything she needed yesterday and she was well and truly over the flu.

As always on special occasions, and particularly at Christmas, her thoughts turned to Liam. It marked another year he'd been gone, taken too young. It was hard to keep smiling when you knew how damn unfair life could be. But she could picture him grinning away in that ridiculous Christmas hat with Santa's legs waving in the air as though stuck in a chimney, telling her to get on with it, to pull herself together. He never had been one to dwell on emotions, on the negative parts of life. It was what had drawn her to him: his positivity and energy, and his outlook on life that you never knew what was around the corner so what was the point worrying about it. It sounded so simple when you summed it up that way.

She grinned as she pushed open the gate to the path that wound like a ribbon all the way to the Butterbury Lodge entrance. Liam had never been one to care what people thought – he'd worn that hat to a family Christmas dinner and then to the pub for a pint with his dad, he'd worn odd socks because he knew how much it wound Hannah up, and he'd found it hysterical that she winced every time he called his dog, Pansy – named by his nan, not him – across the park and people sniggered. Sometimes Hannah supposed the discipline in the forces meant that when he came home he needed to let loose a little bit.

'You're in your own world there.' It was Frankie, mopping the entrance floor. 'Sorry, don't mind me, just clearing up the wet. The snow has been trodden inside with so many visitors. How are you feeling?' She rested her hands on top of the mop as she chatted.

'Much better, thank you.'

'Are you sure you weren't faking it so you could avoid the spin class yesterday? Last one before I scoff my face with mince pies, turkey and all the trimmings. I'll feel less guilty then.'

'I'm impressed. Maybe I'll try again in the New Year.' Maybe. Georgia had texted this morning and apologised for being incommunicado, but she'd been working hard and playing hard, family commitments had run riot, and she had some huge news for Hannah. Hannah wondered whether it could be a Christmas engagement on the cards, perhaps it could help her friend settle down a bit.

She tucked the gift she'd brought with her beneath one arm so she could slip off her gloves and push them in her pockets as she stepped over the wet area. The reception lights glittered above the desk. Hannah suspected they'd be on for the rest of the winter if it was anything like today. The sun wasn't daring to come out at all.

She left Frankie to it and went through to see Mr G.

She put the gift under the coffee table before he spotted her and smiled over at Flo who was sitting in the chair she usually favoured. Funny how quickly you could stake your claim to something. Flo called over to Hannah to remind her about Sounds Over the Bridge coming to the lodge tomorrow and Hannah smiled, told her she wouldn't forget, and shared a conspiratorial wink with Mr G as Ernest asked Flo for a game of cards and she actually agreed.

'He's keen on her,' said Mr G. 'Oh,' he added as Hannah raised an eyebrow, 'I don't mean any funny business, just that it's been a project of sorts for Ernest to get Flo to come out her shell. She even talked a bit about her family. Ernest tells me things,' he explained. 'No children, no spouse, but one sister with whom she hasn't been on speaking terms for three decades.'

'That's sad. I can't imagine it going so long without speaking to my brother.'

'It's a pity, yes.'

'How about you, Mr G? Are your family coming to see you this Christmas?'

'They'll all be popping in over the next week. I've told them if it snows they're not to come, but fingers crossed. I want to see those grandchildren of mine before they're too grown up to appreciate an old person.'

'I doubt they'll ever be too old to appreciate you, Mr G.'

'You're very kind.' He took out a small package from the floor beside the leg of his chair. 'Merry Christmas, Hannah.'

'Mr G, you shouldn't have!'

'I should, and I did. Go on, open it.'

With a warm smile she pulled off the silver wrap and its delicate ice-white bow to reveal a black box, inside which was a bracelet with just one charm, a lantern. 'I don't know what to say.' She couldn't take her eyes from it. 'It's absolutely gorgeous, really. I love it.'

'I wasn't sure whether charms were modern enough or if it's an old-fashioned idea, but I figured I'd give it a go. A friend helped me to choose it from a catalogue last month.'

She wrapped her arms around him and hugged him tight. 'It's perfect. And I already know what I'll add to it next.'

'Do tell,' he beamed.

'A book.' She didn't even hesitate. 'It will remind me of this place, of all of you and the evenings we share with the book club.'

Hannah got to the floor and stretched over to the coffee table to retrieve the gift she'd stashed beneath. Wrapped in tartan paper with a thick green ribbon, she handed it to Mr G. 'You didn't think I'd forget you, did you? It's just a little something,' she added before he could protest too much.

'Looks big to me.'

'I meant it's a small thought from me to you.'

He peeled the paper off slowly to reveal the burgundy, padded-velvet book rest. At the book evenings she'd noticed he usually had a book in his lap rather than holding it and she knew he struggled to hold things sometimes. His plate for a mince pie would more often than not be set on a side table, his cup of tea would be housed on a saucer close to him rather than in his hand to savour the warmth. But she didn't want him to know she'd noticed these small things that gave away his age. 'What do you think?'

'What is it?' And his face had them both laughing. 'Is it a cushion?' He propped it behind him but couldn't position it comfortably.

'It's a book rest.' She grabbed a paperback sitting on the shelf nearby and demonstrated by putting the cushion on his lap, the book upright on one of the ledges of the pyramid cushion. 'You don't have to hold it, you can enjoy your tea or a snack and keep reading.' She pulled down the in-built bookmark to hold it open on a particular page. 'See?'

'It's wonderful! And it'll come in useful on book night.'

Hannah and Mr G had a game of Scrabble, she chatted with Grace for a while, Ernest made her laugh when he almost did a miniature jig at winning his game of cards and she was pleased to see Flo looked amused more than anything.

'Merry Christmas, Flo.' Hannah ventured when Ernest excused himself to go to the bathroom.

'Merry Christmas, dear,' Flo smiled.

'I'll see you tomorrow, wouldn't miss seeing the choir for anything.'

'You're in for a treat.' Her eyes sparkled. 'They're wonderful.'

'Will you have any visitors this year?' Maybe she shouldn't have asked but perhaps Mr G's direct approach to life was rubbing off on her.

'No.' She shook her head, not sad, not content, but somewhere in between. 'You get to my age and there aren't many people left. And those that are often live too far away to come. Are you having your family with you this year?'

It was the longest conversation they'd managed in all the times Hannah had seen her. 'My family are having Christmas back home but I wanted to stay in Lantern Square this year. And it means my brother and his girl-friend will have to do all the washing up, which kind of tickles me as I know he hates it.' She was feeling brave. 'I hear you have a sister.'

She wasn't sure whether Flo was going to completely clam up when her lips stayed resolutely shut, but then, 'Leona. We don't speak.'

'That's a shame.'

'We fell out. Petty stuff, all blown out of proportion.'

'You must miss her.'

'Yes and no.' She smiled now. 'She was very bossy, very nosey and always thought she knew best.' The wobble in her voice belied her claims that her sister was more of a pain than not.

Hannah shrugged on her coat and wondered how their plan would go tomorrow. She and Mr G were convinced Mrs Ledbetter and Flo would be a good match, they both needed the company, were around the same age, and Hannah was sure Flo could be a lot chattier than she was. She just needed one person she clicked with to unlock her reservations.

And when she stopped to talk to Frankie who was moaning about her workload now the cleaner had handed in her notice, Hannah added another part to her plan. One that could come in very handy indeed.

Hannah loved Christmas Eve. It had all the promise of things to come, all the magic, and when she bumped into Rhys on her way home to Lantern Cottage they grabbed a mince pie each from the bakery and stood on the street corner chatting. The snow had stopped for now but pavements were dusted with frost and with nightfall close the temperature had struggled to get above negative figures today.

Amongst other things they talked about his offer on The Little House. 'I think we need to drink a toast to you joining us in the square,' said Hannah. 'We'll do it at Christmas lunch tomorrow.'

'I look forward to it.' With a grin he said, 'I've wanted to get into the square for a long while, even wanted to buy your little place but wasn't in a position to then.'

'Please don't hold it against me.'

'I would if I didn't like you.' He shoved the rest of his mince pie in his mouth. 'Right, I need to get on, but not before I grab another mince pie. Interested?'

'No thanks, one was enough.'

Rhys pushed open the door to the bakery just as Joe emerged from inside.

He held a bag aloft. 'Cinnamon rolls.'

'You have good taste, they're delicious.'

'Good to see you up and about – you look much better.'

'I am. And thank you again for coming over.'

He looked about to say something in return but settled on telling her, 'Dawn and Troy said they're starting the parkrun in the New Year.'

Hannah couldn't help laughing. 'And you believe them?' She lowered her voice given the bakery doors were opening regularly with customers going in and out. 'They've been saying that as long as I've lived here and according to Lily, for quite some time before that.'

'Ah, well. Bang goes my community-minded activity

to get rid of that extra Christmas food layer we'll all be putting on this year. What about you? Would you be interested? I thought if a few people went it could encourage those who are doubtful.'

Actually, to give him credit, it was a pretty nice thought. And, the parkrun, as much as she'd turned her nose up in the past, could be preferable to the sweaty environment of a gym. 'We'll see.'

'I'll ask you again, don't worry.'

His voice was teasing and her tummy did a funny flip as he looked at her. Those kind eyes that had told her she needed to rest up and get better, that body she'd pressed so close against as they danced in the summer. He had no worries whatsoever when it came to anything closely resembling a Christmas food layer. Maybe all those women kept him agile and fit.

'Enjoy the cinnamon rolls.' It was all she could think of to say. Where was an interruption from Mrs Ledbetter or anyone else for that matter, when you needed one?

'I'm going to eat one by my tree, with the fire roaring, and I'll save one for my dessert tomorrow too.'

'Not going anywhere for Christmas?' Or having company, she wondered.

'Just me, myself and I this year. I was due to be skiing but plans fell through when my friend broke his leg. He's with his cousin in Scotland instead.'

Should she invite him to the pub tomorrow? Did he already know they were all congregating there? But she needn't have worried because Rhys picked that moment to come out of the bakery a second time, together with a waft of the enticing scent of warm pastries. 'Come to the pub, Joe! We'll all be there, and they do the best pigs in blankets.' He began chowing down on another mince pie and Hannah wondered quite where he put them all.

'Yes . . . of course,' Hannah chimed. 'The more the merrier.' Just don't bring any women or I'll be jealous, she thought, but thankfully her filter was in full operation and she kept her mouth shut.

'The Butterbury Arms is way better than being a lonely old man looking at your Christmas tree,' added Rhys. 'Even though it's a good tree. I should know – I supplied it,' he clarified to Hannah.

'Yours looks pretty impressive,' Joe told her.

'Hannah likes her Christmas lights,' Rhys chuckled. 'You can pretty much see that tree from the moon. It competes with the one in the square.'

She gave him a nudge and he stumbled down from the kerb laughing. 'My tree looks amazing.'

'Again, all credit to me,' said Rhys.

She shook her head and left the men to it. 'See you both tomorrow.'

At home Hannah stoked up the log burner and it wasn't long before it was roaring away, filling the tiny lounge with its heat. Darkness had descended, the tree lights kissed the corners of the room, Christmas music filtered softly from the speaker on the mantelpiece. Already she couldn't wait to enjoy a mulled wine with Lily and Cate this evening, right here at Lantern Cottage. An evening with friends.

A knock at the door had her venturing into the cooler hallway and pulling the front door firmly to welcome her visitors.

But the couple on her doorstep weren't the two people she'd expected to see at all.

She wasn't even aware she was letting the cold air in and all the warm air outside as she stood staring at Verity and Michael, Liam's parents.

'Hello, Hannah.' Verity didn't look entirely comfortable. 'May we come in?'

She shook some sense into herself. 'Of course, come in out of the cold.' They'd taken her by surprise, but what was really unexpected was how happy she was to see them. Not long ago she would have found this very painful, but she'd finally managed to make peace in her own mind.

She took their coats and managed to fit them on the modest set of hooks that usually only had to fit a couple of winter items and now struggled to do it all. She draped scarves over the bottom bannister to make it a little easier.

'What a wonderful cottage,' Michael complimented.

'Thank you. It's a bit untidy, but I love it here. Tea?' she smiled but they seemed hesitant. She guessed this was a little weird for them all.

They accepted and before long Hannah had them seated in the warmth of the lounge on the sofa with the tree next to it as she took the separate armchair. She'd set out a plate of novelty Christmas cookies too. 'They're from the local bakery,' she explained. 'Troy is trying something new. Look.' She picked up one of the miniature gingerbread houses complete with white piped icing and garlands above the doors and slotted it onto the side of her cup. 'Total gimmick.'

'I like it.' Michael picked one up and slotted it onto his cup, then slurped a few quick mouthfuls. 'Don't want it to go soggy.'

'Troy was worried about that. I guess it depends how long you have the gingerbread house on there before you devour it.'

Verity hadn't picked up a cookie yet. Hannah supposed this small talk was delaying whatever had brought them here. 'Is everything OK?' She suspected this was more than a quick visit to wish her 'Merry Christmas'. When she'd been with Liam his parents had popped in quite often, something Hannah had never minded. They saw precious little of their son when he was working away from home so frequently and sometimes she'd felt guilty about hogging all his time.

'We came to apologise.' Verity was first to speak.

'Apologise? For what?'

Verity looked to Michael but carried on herself. 'For upsetting you, for not letting you move on, you know, after . . .' her voice trailed off.

Michael put a hand over his wife's. 'You were such a big part of Liam's life, and when he was taken from us, I guess we were clinging on to any fragment that was left. We sent you letters and while it was cathartic for us, we realise it might not have been for you.'

'Not sure I want to be known as a fragment.' Her smile managed to get one in return from Michael at least. 'And it wasn't you two who stopped me moving on, it was your son. He was the love of my life and losing him was the worst thing that ever happened to me.' She set her mug down and took a deep breath pre-empting the honest conversation they were at last about to have. 'I'm glad you both wanted me in your life and didn't cut me out altogether.'

Verity's brow creased. 'We just thought . . . well we

thought, when you didn't send your usual Christmas card, we thought it was time to let you get on with your own life.'

It was Hannah's turn to frown. 'I sent you a card. A special, handmade card.'

Michael shook his head.

'I promise you, I sent you a card. Over a week ago.' Their card had come just after she'd sent hers and now sat proudly on her mantelpiece with the jolly reindeer on the front smiling out at them all.

'We wondered,' Verity stumbled, 'well, if our correspondence over time had become a bit much and that was your way of telling us.'

'At first you wrote back quickly to every letter we sent,' Michael added, before apologising if this felt like an interrogation. Hannah assured him it wasn't and urged him to continue. 'Then your replies took longer and longer, then they didn't come at all. We knew we were clinging to the shreds. We knew we should let you go, just like we let Liam go. And when the Christmas card didn't arrive as usual, we thought we'd come, give you our blessing to move forwards. Not that you need it, just that . . . oh, I'm making a real hash of this.'

It was time for her to be even more frank and explain her feelings after all this time. 'You're not wrong to think I found the letters difficult. I found contact with you challenging. I don't think I handled my grief all that well.' She looked at each of them in turn and both were crestfallen. 'I tried not to think about Liam, to not think about either of you. I avoided reminders. I didn't go to some of the places he'd taken me to, because there were so many memories wrapped up in them. I found it painful to reply to your letters and told myself to do it for your sakes. But over time, I've begun to realise that instead of fighting your letters and my feelings, I needed to process them.

'I was holding myself back,' she said, on a breath that released a lot of pent-up tension from her body. Tension she'd thought had already gone. 'Nobody else was doing it, it was me.'

'You don't want us to stop writing?' Verity had taken the gingerbread novelty cookie but her fingers toyed with it on the side of her mug. If she wasn't careful the steam from the liquid and the fiddling would turn it to mush.

'I want to stay in touch. If it helps you that is? If it doesn't, I understand.'

'You're like a daughter to us,' Michael admitted. 'If you can put up with our wittering on then we'd very much like to keep doing it.'

'Deal,' Hannah grinned right as Verity gasped, 'Oh no!' The foundations of her gingerbread house had slipped into the murky liquid below and she peered into her tea. 'I guess it wasn't supposed to do that.' She sipped the drink. 'But actually, it adds a sweetness, a hint of Christmas spice that isn't altogether off-putting. Maybe it's a feature of the cookie rather than a flaw.'

'You know, you could be right.'

Before they left Hannah grabbed a Christmas card and wrote in it before handing it to Verity. 'I've no idea what happened to the first one, and I'm sorry this isn't as special.'

Verity hugged her. 'It's perfect.'

And when they left, Hannah knew they'd all found a new sense of normality. A way to move on but still cherish the memories that were so precious to all of them.

20

Christmas morning arrived dry and bright, one of those perfect crisp wintry days when the frost sparkled and clung to the branches of trees as though they'd been decorated. Hannah made her way towards the pub, dressed in her polka dot dress with opaque tights, knee-high boots, a sparkly black cardigan and of course a big snuggly coat, scarf and gloves.

Hannah had already called her family and via FaceTime her mum had shown how she was as organised as ever. She'd had an entire rundown of what they were having for lunch, including plenty of close-ups of the turkey crisping away in the oven, the pigs in blankets lined up and ready to go, and the Prosecco supplies in the fridge. Her dad and her brother were in the middle of a Monopoly battle and her brother had bemoaned the fact he was in charge of the washing up. She'd left them all satisfied that she wouldn't be microwaving a sad old meal for one but enjoying fresh food and vegetables with plenty of other people.

On the doormat that morning had been a gift from Luke, one that Hannah felt she had to call him in person to thank him for. It was a voucher for a stay at a spa in

Northumberland, a spa that looked so luxurious it wouldn't have come cheap. It promised accommodation for three nights, elegant dining and luxurious linen, a facial, massage, thalassotherapy pool sessions and body wraps. It was the perfect winter rejuvenation package, and she couldn't help worrying that he intended to come with her. But she didn't broach the subject when they spoke. She tried to say it was too generous, he insisted it wasn't, they batted the debate back and forth a few times and in the end she relented. He invited her, again, to Maplebrooke Manor today but she stood firm about her plans. He said to pop in later if she got a chance, but with the lunch and the carol concert, she knew she'd be too busy.

Since he'd kissed her that day by his treehouse, Hannah had been left in no doubt as to Luke's intentions. It was only hers she needed to question. She knew she could have him back just like that and she had to confess that sometimes she was tempted. She'd dreamed about him last night shortly after turning off her bedroom light, and in the early hours she'd been so restless she went downstairs for a glass of water and nursed it sitting in the lounge, the log burner long since gone out, the cold making her shiver and feel quite alone. But feeling lonely was no reason to go running into someone's arms, she'd done that to him once before. There had to be more to it than that. She was in a good place, despite being on her own, and she knew that Liam's parents coming to see her had given her another nudge towards happiness.

Hannah had always thought village pubs were on their way out. But not the Butterbury Arms, and when she arrived it was buzzing even more than usual. Music spilled out on to the street, a handful of people bustled from the doorway on the way to family gatherings, back to their houses to begin the celebratory lunch. Garlands looped along the walnut bar, fairy lights lined the ceiling and set off the shine in ornaments hanging on the Christmas tree in the corner. The scent of pine mingled with the comforting aroma of alcoholic beverages that always lingered in a pub and a long table had been set in the middle of the room.

'You're looking gorgeous!' Dawn from the bakery was first to admire Hannah's dress when she took off her coat.

'And so are you,' Hannah told her in return. 'Red is definitely your colour.' She had on a glamorous red dress down to her knees, one Troy seemed enraptured with by the way he was looking at his wife.

'Hannah!' Lily bustled over and hugged Hannah before giving her the instructions for today. 'When it's time, sit anywhere, there's no table settings, it's pile in and take your pick. And thanks again for the mulled wine and cookies last night.'

'It was my pleasure. How many have you got coming today?' She wondered had Joe told them he was joining in? Maybe he'd changed his mind, or got a better offer.

'Twenty, it's going to be manic. But we've got two turkeys in the oven, both huge, enough roasties to feed the whole of Butterbury and plenty of sprouts.'

Kimberley put her fingers down her throat in protest. 'You can have my share,' she told Hannah.

Hannah said hello to others as they arrived and chatted with Annie and Ellen about their business plans for a bistro. They were both so sensible, they'd done oodles of market research – it was bound to be a success, Hannah just knew it.

'Mrs Ledbetter, how lovely to see you.' Hannah smiled at her neighbour who came through the door right before they were due to take their seats and she did her best to hide her surprise at the latest arrival. The pub wasn't big enough to have the whole of Butterbury along for Christmas lunch, but everyone who lived in the houses surrounding Lantern Square had had an invite through their door including Mrs Ledbetter.

'Can't stop, I'm off to the lodge,' she said, a smile on her face.

'Butterbury Lodge? But carols aren't till later.'

'I'm joining them for lunch.'

How had that happened?

'Ernest invited me.'

'I didn't realise you knew him.'

'Of course I do, I know a few faces up there.'

Hannah suspected Mr G had concocted this plan with Ernest and had him invite Mrs Ledbetter, but she'd never let on.

'I'm sorry to let you all down here, but between you and me, I think Ernest might be lonely.'

He was anything but, although Hannah didn't say so. 'Well you have a wonderful time and I'll see you later for carols.'

'Is your young man coming to lunch?'

Hannah blushed; she must mean Luke. 'Just me today.' She grabbed a glass of champagne from the passing tray carried by Ellen, who'd joined in readily.

'And is your friend joining you?'

Maybe this time she meant Georgia. 'No, she has plans.' And Hannah wouldn't have invited her either. That was the thing about Georgia. Sometimes she could just be too

301

much. And today, she wanted to be a part of this without her.

'I must say she was quite rude to me a couple of weeks ago,' Mrs Ledbetter went on.

'Oh?' Hannah would usually skim over such an accusation but since she'd begun to feel increasingly uneasy around Georgia, she wanted others' opinions to weigh them up against her own.

'I was in the post office and I went over to the table, I needed to lay out all my cards, stick stamps on, add the air mail stickers, double-check they were all ready.' Hannah had experienced Mrs Ledbetter's pernickety ways when it came to her post; she'd been caught in the queue behind her too many times. 'Well she was already at the table and taking her own sweet time might I add. She was very rude to me as I waited behind her while she added labels to her parcels.'

'She can be a little offhand, I do apologise.' Now the champagne was flowing Hannah wanted to just chill out, to forget all her stresses, and thankfully Mrs Ledbetter let it go and was on her way up to the care home.

Festivities continued and the atmosphere swelled with everyone here for celebrations. There were kisses on cheeks, hugs shared, smiles all round, and when Joe walked through the door Hannah was already grinning his way and didn't mind the kiss he planted on her cheek in acknowledgment. She didn't miss the fact that he'd come alone either, nor the fact that she was glad.

Frankie was last to join them along with her boyfriend, someone else taking over her shift at Butterbury Lodge to give her the rest of today off. 'For good behaviour,' she declared, getting into the champagne. 'Although

I might go up later for carols, if I can stumble up the hill.'

Hannah ended up sitting next to Joe and by the time they'd finished their smoked salmon starter she'd thanked him again for coming to her cottage when she had the flu.

'You already thanked me.'

'I don't think I thanked you properly.'

'Yeah?' His voice was steady but his eyes sent her heart racing. That one word seemed to be laced with meaning, as though she was suggesting a proper thank you involved more than just words.

'When duty calls,' he added either uncomfortable himself or sensing her feeling that way. He picked up the red wine he'd chosen instead of the fizz. A Chilean Merlot; smooth, sophisticated, full-bodied. Not too dissimilar to him. 'And your boyfriend took over for a while so I was off the hook.'

She didn't want to talk about Luke. Not today. 'Well I appreciate it. I couldn't stagger to the surgery. I couldn't do much at all.'

'Flu can hit you like that, out of the blue. But you're completely over it now, no tiredness lingering?'

'Yes, Doctor Joe.' Oh no, she sounded like she was flirting, badly. 'Don't worry, no germs here.' She stammered over her words as he looked at her a little too closely.

'I see you wore that dress again. I'd better keep the red wine away from you today.'

'I'm sure if anything gets spilled it'll be my fault,' she assured him, 'gravy is the worst culprit at a Christmas lunch, I'm always getting something on my clothes.' She watched his fingers splayed around the stem of his glass. Even though she'd heard as a young man he wasn't too confident, he seemed to be over that now. He seemed so in control, unflappable, no wonder he could handle more than one woman at a time. 'Can I ask why you didn't bring anyone along today?' The champagne really had loosened her tongue.

'I could ask you the same.'

'I'm not with anyone. Luke isn't my boyfriend. Not any more.'

'Well, I'm not with anyone either.' She must've made a peculiar sound because he added, 'You seem surprised.'

'I've seen you with women, a woman, someone . . .' Oh dear, she was making a hash of this. 'I assumed . . .'

'Nobody significant, just acquaintances.'

Hannah wondered if the women knew that, and she tried to ignore the spark that shot through her when his knee brushed hers beneath the table. Jeans probably would've been a safer item of clothing to go for today, the denim offering a layer of protection. Miriam, who had been Hannah's confidant in the summer, cast her a knowing look across the table, which didn't help settle her nerves much. Perhaps people just assumed she and Joe would hook up eventually. But Joe was lucky, the gossip mill didn't seem to churn much surrounding his personal life. Even Mrs Ledbetter tended to hold her tongue. Maybe everyone held an unspoken respect for the local doctor.

Hannah managed to make it through the entire main course and not spill anything and after she'd helped to clear the plates, she let her head clear a bit and made sure she drank a couple of glasses of water. She didn't want to arrive at Butterbury Lodge too plastered to enjoy the carols or keep a watchful eye over Flo and Mrs Ledbetter to see whether her plan worked.

She caught up with Rhys who'd been down the other end of the table during the meal. 'Whoa, you're getting into it. I know it's Christmas Day.' She watched him sink the rest of his beer.

'Merry Christmas, Hannah.'

'Merry Christmas to my favourite gardener.' She hugged him and kissed him on the cheek, but she could tell something was up. 'Everything OK?'

'Fine, yes.'

'Bullshit.'

'Excuse me, that's no way for a lady to talk.' But at least his smile was genuine this time. 'Just had a bit of bad news last night that's all.'

'I'm sorry, if there's anything you need to talk about, I'm a good listener.'

He didn't hesitate for long. 'I was determined to forget it for today, to have a good time, you know.'

She did know. 'Why don't you share, get it out of your system, then we'll get drunk together.' Sod the carols if her friend needed her.

'I missed out on The Little House. I was gazumped. Don't you hate that word? It's just a euphemism for shafted.'

'Gazumped! I don't believe it.' Charles Bray wouldn't have allowed it, it must have been his son, who didn't have quite the understanding or attachment to Lantern Square that his father had. And an uneasy feeling was slowly creeping into her mind. Surely the other buyer couldn't be Georgia, could it?

'You win some you lose some. I'm getting another beer. Champagne?'

'Water, please.' The fizz was already going to her head. And while he was at the bar she took out her phone and fired off a text to say Merry Christmas to Georgia. A casual, well-wishing text without asking whether she was behind the gazumping.

As they waited for dessert Hannah chatted with Frankie, but she couldn't help noticing Joe looking her way. She almost wished he had a woman there to divert his attention because the more he looked at her the more she knew she couldn't put her attraction down to just the champagne. There was a connection between them, but could it ever really go anywhere? The answer was yes, if she wanted a bit of fun, but a definite no if she wanted to avoid being hurt.

When Frankie's boyfriend insisted Frankie dance with him by the Christmas tree despite how much they'd just eaten, Hannah's phone pinged and she returned to her seat at the table. But it didn't take long for her lovely Christmas dinner to churn around inside of her when she read the text from Georgia.

'Now it's my turn to ask you if everything is OK.' Rhys leaned in as he joined her and people began taking their seats at the table for the serving of the Christmas pudding.

'Everything's fine.' Of course it wasn't. She'd just found out her so-called friend had shafted this lovely, kind man sitting next to her now, a man she hadn't known all that long but whose friendship she valued highly. Georgia's text had of course wished her a Merry Christmas but it was the present Georgia had given to herself that gave Hannah cause for concern. *I'm moving to Lantern Square!* she'd written. *We'll be neighbours!* And Hannah's heart sank as she thought of every single word in that message.

'Sure it is.' Rhys wasn't fooled, but Hannah didn't want to discuss this now.

Georgia had once made a quip, during the ending of their friendship the first time round, when their business fell apart and Georgia walked away, about how Hannah always got everything she ever wanted, how her life was so easy and perfect. Hannah hadn't thought much of it at the time, but now, she couldn't help but wonder if Georgia wanted a hell of a lot more than friendship from her.

She tried to keep a smile on her face while Lily brought out the most enormous three Christmas puddings on a platter and set them on the table, Joe did the honours and poured on the brandy, and the landlord Patrick, leaned over to light each of them.

Was Georgia out for revenge? Was she trying to move in on Hannah's territory and destroy the life she'd built up for herself, a life that didn't involve her former friend? Was anyone really that insecure that they'd set out to do all of this? Work nearby, resurrect a long-buried friendship, buy a house in the same square, a house Hannah would have to see every day.

Surely she wouldn't be so vindictive. The problems with their business had largely been down to immaturity on Georgia's part. She'd made some mistakes, but Hannah really thought she'd learned from them. She seemed so much more together since the day she showed up in Lantern Square to apologise, but now, finding out what she'd done, gazumping Rhys, made Hannah's heart thump inside her chest that she may have misjudged Georgia completely.

A hot sensation cascaded through her body as realisation dawned. Was it possible that Georgia was behind some of the problems for Tied Up with String too? Surely she wouldn't be so nasty, so conniving.

Joe mouthed the word 'OK?' as a question. He was sitting opposite her and hadn't missed Hannah's inability to get back into the Christmas spirit.

She nodded, but it was a lie.

As Rhys topped up her champagne, Hannah refused to let Georgia take this day from her, and tried to summon up the magic of Christmas, surrounded by friends, a sense of belonging she'd spent so long trying to find.

But one thing was for sure. If Georgia was behind the problems with Tied Up with String, Hannah needed to cut this toxic friendship from her life before she did any more damage.

21

Boxing Day dawned fresh and bright. The sun woke Hannah from a deep slumber through the gap in the curtains where they didn't quite meet in the middle, and when she looked out of the window a smile spread across her face because the whole of Butterbury had a frosty glow that only served to make the village all the more special. She'd been hoping for snow – it was forecast for today – but with the annual Lantern Walk that raised money for different charities each year, perhaps it was a good thing, this time, that the forecasters had been wrong.

The carol concert last night had been the perfect ending to Christmas Day in Butterbury, and a welcome distraction for Hannah and everything that had been going on lately. Up at the lodge yesterday, Hannah had arrived to find Mrs Ledbetter getting into the thick of things with the other residents, and she was enthralled when her favourite choir, Sounds Over the Bridge, launched into action. Flo's reaction was similar and it hadn't been long before both women were extolling the virtues of the choir and engaging in a lengthy chat about their favourite Christmas carols and traditions. And after Hannah had exchanged a conspiratorial look with Mr G, she made sure that Mrs Ledbetter heard her comment on the amount of dust on the mantelpiece and the windowsill. It was all part of their plan to get Mrs Ledbetter involved with the community rather than simply gossiping about it – and, Hannah suspected, feeling very lonely – but Mr G had almost given the game away. Hannah had held in her amusement but he'd looked fit to burst with laughter at their ingenuity.

Now, at Lantern Cottage, Hannah padded downstairs and scooped Bandit up into her arms. 'I'll bet you're hungry.' She ruffled the fur between his eyes and was rewarded with a deep purring as she set him down and gave Smokey a fuss. After she had fed them and changed their water she touched her hand to the radiators as she made her way through to the lounge. Sure enough, the heating had kicked in, although with outside temperatures so low it was taking a while to warm up inside the cottage, so after she'd switched on the Christmas tree lights Hannah loaded some more pieces of wood into the log burner, closed the doors and knelt down beside it. She'd slept well last night considering the thoughts tumbling around in her mind, and today she was determined to think only about the Lantern Walk, keep her Christmas spirit among friends, and deal with everything else later.

But all it took was the time to boil the kettle for her thoughts to tap away and tell her brain that she didn't really want to leave it at all. She wanted to know what her so-called friend was playing at. She still held on to the mild hope that Georgia hadn't been involved in trying to sabotage her business, but there didn't appear to be any other explanation. She wasn't sure what made her angrier: the fact that her ex-best friend had messed with her reputation as a businesswoman, or that she'd messed with her head, leaving Hannah to think she was making silly mistakes, doing things wrong, doubting herself. If Georgia's aim had been to give her confidence a knock then she'd succeeded.

Before she had the chance to go into the dining room and do some delving, a knock at the door revealed Rhys standing on her doorstep.

'Good morning to you,' he said. 'How's the head?'

'After the antics at the Christmas lunch and the carols?' she smiled. 'Not bad actually. It was good, wasn't it?' She ushered him inside. The freezing temperatures in Butterbury carried on a wind that zipped right up her pyjamas through any gap they could find.

'Just came to check you're ready for the walk later, and on hand to dish out the lanterns.'

'Come through.' She led him into the kitchen and held up a mug to indicate tea was on the agenda and when he nodded she did the honours. 'I'm ready to help out. Mrs Ledbetter reminded me several times last night.'

'She's not a bad old sort.'

'I've warmed to her.' Hannah handed him the mug of tea and he helped himself to a heaped teaspoon of sugar from the pot nearby. 'I thought she was a bit of a busybody at first but she's just after some company.'

'She was thrilled to get the job of coordinating the lanterns this year when Mrs Addington asked her to take over.' The owner of the grandest thatched cottage in the village never missed a thing. Perhaps she was doing her bit to get Mrs Ledbetter more involved with the community too.

'Ah, but what was she happier about? The lanterns or the fact Mrs Addington has moved on from the time Mrs

Ledbetter gossiped about her son when he came out as gay?'

'Good point.' He slurped his tea. 'And well done for getting her up to the care home. What made you do that?'

Hannah filled him in on the plan that had formed in her mind for both Mrs Ledbetter and Flo, two women who needed companionship. 'I didn't even think to suggest she go there for Christmas lunch rather than the pub, that was all her doing, or rather Ernest's and Mr G's.' She'd asked Mr G if he'd had anything to do with it and the look he gave her in return said of course he had.

'It was probably far nicer for her to be there than the pub.'

'I agree – and by the look of her when I got up to the lodge for carols, she'll probably try to wangle an invite for next year too.'

'I'm glad you and she have started to see eye to eye.'

Hannah laughed. 'I wouldn't go that far. But I'm glad she's a bit more approachable. And both women really hit it off with their shared love of the choir.'

'And how exactly do you intend to have them carry on a friendship? Can't see our Mrs Ledbetter trudging up to see Flo each day. And she'll never move. She's already let it be known the only way she'll ever leave her cottage is in a box.'

'Oh dear. In a way it's nice she's happy in her home, but she really is very lonely. I have another part of my plan though. Phase two.'

'And what is phase two?'

This time Hannah told him about the cleaner at Butterbury Lodge handing in her notice and leaving Frankie with far too much to do as they hadn't found a replacement. 'I made sure I pointed out some dusty surfaces to Mrs Ledbetter, I also hovered near the coat stand at the lodge, next to which is a big advert for a cleaner. I'd already suggested Frankie put it up because there'll be loads of visitors to the lodge over Christmas and someone may have a relative who's a cleaner, or at least know of one.'

'And what does that have to do with Mrs Ledbetter?'

'You've seen her home, right?'

'I have.'

'It's spick and span; even my mum would be impressed. She's forever got a duster in her hand when I pass by, or she's cleaning windows when the rest of us don't bother. I thought, if Frankie and I can make it known that the lodge is desperate, that her cleaning skills are exemplary and that she'd be doing them not only a huge favour, but working, then everyone would win. There'd be no dent in her pride because she thinks she's being coerced to make friends, it'll give her a lift to be asked to work at her age because she's not one to sit still.'

'True point. But I can't help thinking maybe she is a little old. We don't want to do her in by working her too hard.'

'I've already thought about that and discussed it with Frankie. They'll put the feelers out for at least four more cleaners and she's agreed to ask Mrs Ledbetter to manage the team, coordinate their tasks if you like.'

'She'll love that.'

'Exactly. She'll get to boss people around, it's perfect for her. And I won't let it slip that you suggested her age might be a barrier.'

'No, please don't.' He grinned.

'The cleaning will give her a focus other than local gossip. Flo needs a friend too. And if Mrs Ledbetter works up there the chances are she and Flo will enjoy one another's company. Mr G said he'll make it his mission to ensure Flo is around at cleaning time so our plan doesn't fall flat on its face.'

'Ah, so you're in this together.'

'We sure are.'

'See, this is why I love Lantern Square. You all look out for each other.' His voice held a hint of sadness at missing out on The Little House and Hannah felt all her frustration begin to surface again.

He looked out of the kitchen window at her garden sparkling with frost. 'It looks beautiful today, and your plants should last nicely now I've wrapped the terracotta pots in hessian sacking.'

'I never would've thought of doing that.'

'Think of it as a fleece for your poor, neglected plants.'

'I'm a rubbish gardener, but I do love having a nice outdoor space, especially come summer.'

'Good job you've got me then, isn't it?'

'You're a professional, you know what you're doing.' Her tea had warmed her right through. 'I'm looking forward to the Lantern Walk.'

'You'll enjoy it.'

She couldn't wait to bundle up in layers, do the walk, then congregate in Lantern Square with everyone else to enjoy hot chocolates or mulled wines and whatever treats Ellen and Annie had at their cart today. She'd heard rumours about cinnamon churros, pancakes, doughnuts and hot mince pies.

Rhys finished his tea and turned from admiring the

garden. 'Speaking of professional, are you taking a well-earned holiday from Tied Up with String?'

'I am.'

'Truthfully?'

'Honestly, I am.'

'But . . .'

'There's no "but".'

He set his empty cup on the benchtop. 'I let it go at the pub yesterday because it was Christmas. But there's something bugging you. And you didn't let up until I shared what was going on in my head. So now it's your turn.'

'I'm fine.'

'Come on . . . we've been friends a while, you can confide in me. Anyone you want me to go beat up?'

'That won't be necessary.'

'Hannah, I might be able to help.'

She took a deep breath. 'You know how all those things kept going wrong with my business?'

'I do, which is why you need to take a break.'

'Maybe, but what if they weren't mistakes?'

'I'm not sure I follow.'

'What if they were done deliberately, out of spite, to harm me and Tied Up with String?'

'You mean sabotage?'

'Exactly.'

'From a competitor?'

This time she shrugged. 'It's just a feeling I have. Do you want to help me think it through?'

'Happy to help in any way I can.'

She fetched her diary, a notepad and pen and they settled in the lounge, both kneeling in front of the coffee table, but not before Rhys discovered the mince pies lurking beside the fridge on a plate all wrapped up. She'd eaten far too much over the last couple of days to curl up and enjoy them here.

'Help yourself,' she told him and he wasted no time tucking in. 'So first came the girl with the nut allergy.' She scribbled the word 'Nuts' on the paper and circled it and reprimanded Rhys for his childish laughter at the word. Although she let out a giggle herself when she imagined him in the way Miriam had described, as an unruly child acting up in class. She flipped through her paper diary where she made notes of packages and when they were sent, crossing them out when they were received. 'That happened back in early November.'

'I remember. You were devastated that you'd made a mistake and hadn't checked the contents of the package. You put it down to being busy.' He shrugged. 'Plausible.'

'Then do you remember me telling you about leaving the door to the dining room open and the cats ruining the card order I'd made for the retailer?'

'An easy mistake again.' He ferreted on the floor for the crumb of mince pie he'd just dropped while she wrote 'Drink Spill' on the paper. 'Bit like me and my eating habits.'

'I'm sure I double-checked the door, I always do. But again, I put it down to me being tired.'

'May I?' He indicated the other mince pie that she'd left there, not hungry yet.

She nodded her assent and flipped through her diary some more. 'The next mix-up was the hen-night pack-age going to the eighty-year-old.' She wrote the word 'Hen' on the page and circled it too. Writing things down helped her map everything out in her mind and would hopefully lead her to finding answers.

He began to laugh before he took another bite of mince pie. 'You never told me that one.'

She recounted what had happened. 'Luckily for me, the old lady saw the funny side, in fact it kind of made her day. But it was a lucky escape.'

'So do you think it's a competitor?' he speculated. 'Someone in the same line of business who wants you out of the picture?' When she told him how her urgent supplies order had been mysteriously cancelled too, and scribbled down 'Supplies' before encircling it in another bubble, he concluded, 'It has to be. Get on Google, think about who your rivals are. Happened to me once, a gardener undercutting my prices and he found out who my clients were, targeted each and every one.'

'What happened?'

'I caught him at it. He'd followed me to one house, then the next, I saw his van parked where he thought it was out of sight. I marched right up to him and gave him a piece of my mind. I knew the lad. I'd gone to school with him. But that worked to my advantage because I also knew his brother and all about his work as a taxi driver that he did for cash in hand and never declared on his tax return. Anyway, he was wimpy enough that he didn't stand up to me, and next thing I knew he'd moved on to selling used cars.'

Hannah plucked a chocolate from the Christmas tree and handed it to Rhys. 'Did you even have breakfast?' He'd devoured those mince pies in minutes.

'What can I say? I have a healthy appetite.'

'You're hungover, aren't you?'

Rhys gave a sheepish grin. 'Well, I might have had a bit too much last night. You should be glad you left the pub when you did. I drowned my sorrows so much that they're only just beginning to swim to the surface now.'

'The Little House?' His face said it all and she plucked another chocolate treat and handed it to him.

'Gutted, that's the only word for it. I really wanted to move into the square and you know how long it takes for properties to come up.' Should she tell him what she knew? But she didn't get a chance before he said, 'Anyway, this is about your problems not mine. Now where were we on project sabotage?'

'So dramatic.' She looked at all the incidences she'd scribbled down. He pulled his phone from his pocket. 'What are you doing?'

'Googling some competitors.'

'Right.' But Hannah's mind went somewhere else while he was doing that. Next to the 'Nuts' bubble she'd drawn she scribbled the word 'door' and the letter 'G'. Then she pondered the next bubble.

'What does "G" stand for?' Rhys ignored his phone in favour of her detective work.

'Bear with me.' Next to 'Drink Spill' she wrote a 'G', then next to 'Hen' she wasn't sure and so she left that word unannotated. She had to think hard when she got to the last bubble with the word 'Supplies' in it.

'Come on, out with it.' He'd turned the paper to face him. 'Who's "G"?'

'Georgia.' Her insides did a loop-the-loop. It was all making sense.

'Oh, The Friend.' He frowned. 'With my hangover, you're going to have to talk me through it.'

She pointed to the Nuts bubble. 'I had to answer the door the day I finalised the package for the little girl, and

I'd left Georgia alone with the parcels. When I came back she'd added the finishing touches, told me she'd checked everything and had done the package up.'

'Right . . .'

It sounded far-fetched, she knew it did. But she had to keep going with this train of thought. She pointed to the bubble which said 'Drink Spill'. 'When the juice was spilled everywhere, I'd been out to the gym. But before I left the house, with Georgia, I'd been cleaning off my trainers and she'd run back inside to use the toilet. She could've either left the door open for the cats to get in or she could've just poured the liquid over the cards.'

'Oh, come on, she's a bit full on, but why come back into your life just to ruin it?'

That's what Hannah couldn't understand. 'I've no idea.'

'So how could she have been involved with the penis lollies going to the old lady? What? That's what happened.'

Hannah grinned. 'I'm just relieved the lady was so nice about it and got so much enjoyment.' Her mind got back into gear. 'Georgia offered to take those parcels to the post office for me. Come to think of it, Mrs Ledbetter was saying how rude she'd been to her when she was at the little table in the post office. It struck me as odd because Georgia had no need to stop inside other than go up to the counter, post them, pay and collect the receipt.'

'You think she swapped the labels?'

Her heart sank. 'I really do.'

'So what about the email you supposedly sent cancelling your order of supplies?'

'Now that, I really can't work out. I can't remember having my computer on and leaving it unattended.'

'Would she know your password?'

'Never. I don't share them, don't write them down.'

'So she's not just a gym bunny then, she really does have a brain if she's been clever enough to hide her tracks until now.'

She plucked another chocolate from the tree when she saw him gaze over at them yet again. 'I've only had a couple, they're for guests,' she said when he refused to take it.

'Go on then, you've persuaded me.' He took off the purple wrapper and popped the brown square into his mouth. 'I don't understand why a friend would push their way back into your life and then go to all this effort to make trouble for you. She's not in the same line of business. So what gives?'

'Her business is totally different. And given her persuasive skills I'd be surprised if she wasn't busy at every class and gets exactly what she wants.'

'And what's that?'

'She eventually wants a big gym established in London. Between you and me I think she'd like to have celebrities using her, work her way towards fame and fortune.' How had she not realised how shallow her so-called friend was before now? 'She doesn't give up easily either. She turned up at the cottage more than once and told me to change, we were going to an exercise session. At the time I thought she was really being a true friend, getting me out there and clearing my work head.'

'And now?'

Hannah's tummy rumbled. 'And now I'm hungry.'

'Have a chocolate, they're good.'

'I will but I'm lining my stomach with good things first. I'll grab some fruit.' She went out to the kitchen and by the time she came back through to the lounge peeling a banana, the answer had dawned on her.

'What is it?'

She slumped down in front of the coffee table, shaking her head. 'I know how she did it.'

'Did what?'

She pointed at the Supplier bubble on the paper. 'It was when we were at the gym, I had my phone and double-checked the supplier email was definitely sent, and it was. But then I went to the bathroom and left my phone on the table. It's unlocked for three minutes, plenty of time for her to pick the device up and do some damage.' She put the banana down. 'How could I be so stupid? So gullible?'

Rhys plucked a chocolate from the tree, unwrapped it and handed it to her. 'For the shock.' And as she chewed, he added, 'Bitch.'

Hannah's eyes drifted over to the Christmas card from Verity and Michael as another thought popped into her head. Georgia had offered to post the card she'd made for them. And now, Hannah knew Georgia must have tossed it in the nearest bin and the reason it never got to them was because it had never seen the inside of the red traditional post box positioned on the pavement across from Lantern Square.

'Total bitch,' she said this time and looked right at Rhys. 'And you know what else?'

His eyes lit up at the prospect of more juicy gossip. 'What?'

'She's the bitch who gazumped you over The Little House.'

His mouth fell open and this time the expletives Rhys uttered were enough to make the angel at the top of the Christmas tree blush.

22

Hannah showered and got ready for the day. Her head was still all over the place as she pulled on the soft grey cable-knit cashmere jumper her parents had bought her for Christmas. It felt like a hug after the conclusions she and Rhys had drawn this morning, her world shaken up like a snow globe, her toxic friendship now out there for her to see in glorious technicolour.

Hannah had kept the problems with her business from her family until Rhys left and she called her dad for some much-needed support. He'd always been her voice of reason, the calm in a storm, always listening and never telling her what she had to do. They'd talked it through, she told him what Georgia had been up to, and he'd listened. Her mum was out and about at the time and she asked him not to say anything because she couldn't bear to hear the inevitable I-told-you-so. Her mum never thought this business idea was a good one, she didn't offer the same unconditional support as her dad did, and right now Hannah had enough to deal with and didn't need to hear more negativity.

She put some make-up on, lengthened her eyelashes with a bit of mascara, and added a slick of berry lip gloss.

She felt better after talking things through with her dad, it relieved some of the burden, and now she was determined that with Georgia well away from Butterbury during the holidays, she'd enjoy the village she'd come to love so much, the community she felt a very big part of. She had friends, she had purpose, and she couldn't imagine being anywhere else.

Hannah was due at Mrs Ledbetter's in an hour, along with other volunteers, to take the lanterns over to Lantern Square and help to hand them out, as well as ensuring everyone had the LED lights to go inside. But before she joined in with the organisation and the fun, she had something else to do. She grabbed her coat and pulled on her comfiest Timberland boots.

Up at Butterbury Lodge, Mr G clasped both her hands in his and squeezed them so tight she thought her heart might melt. 'To what do we owe the pleasure? We didn't expect to see you again today.'

'I'm really here to see Charles.'

'Me?' Charles had spotted her arriving and was already at her side. 'Then I'm a lucky man.'

Hannah smiled. This pair were so at home here, almost as much a part of the furniture as the heavily padded chairs majestically positioned near the enormous bay window. 'Could we talk? Wait, is that Mrs Ledbetter over there talking with Flo?'

Mr G grinned. 'It certainly is. She popped in before the Lantern Walk to bring Flo another album by Sounds Over the Bridge.'

Hannah smiled. Now that really was good news. She caught Mrs Ledbetter's eye and waved.

'Am I in trouble?' Charles asked as he sat down next to Mr G.

She turned her focus to the matter in hand. 'Absolutely not.' She still had her coat on, she couldn't stay this time, but this had to be said. 'It's about The Little House and the offers you've had.'

'My son's been dealing with it, keeping me in the loop, but taking away any hassle.'

'Then I think there's something you should know.'

Hannah recounted the entire story about Georgia, she left nothing out. For now she asked both men to keep it to themselves and Mr G didn't even utter one I-told-you-so about not trusting Georgia. All he did was assure Hannah that she was a good person and had done the right thing coming to the lodge to see them.

Charles wasted no time getting on the phone to his son. Hannah only hoped things hadn't moved so far along that they couldn't be stopped. Wrapping up the house deal before New Year might have seemed like a good idea, but she prayed they still had a chance.

'I knew there was something off about that girl.' It was Mrs Ledbetter standing behind them and Hannah realised she must have heard every word. But this time she didn't care. 'I get a feeling about some people and when she was rude to me that day, I started to watch her. She didn't like it. I could tell she was getting hot under the collar every time I glanced over.' She let out a laugh. 'She'd mutter, thinking I had no idea what she was saying, but I'm pretty good at lip reading.' She put a hand against her chest. 'The words she said were enough to make your hair curl.'

It felt unbelievably good to have these people in her corner. No questions asked, no need to wonder if she could trust them. Age had no barrier when it came to friendship and so many people had proven that since Hannah settled in Butterbury.

'We're going to have to go,' Hannah said to Mrs Ledbetter now. 'We have lanterns to organise, a walk to do.'

'And we'll be here with the roaring fire,' said Mr G, 'but we look forward to seeing you all. Keep an eye out for me and I'll wave.'

'For sure.' Tradition dictated that on the walk crowds would begin at the high street, continue up the hill and stop at Butterbury Lodge where they would congregate in the gardens out the back, hold their lanterns aloft and sing a Christmas carol. This year Flo's choice of carol had been pulled out of the hat and they'd be singing 'God Rest Ye Merry Gentlemen'.

Hannah breathed in the cold, brisk air as she set off down the hill towards the square with Mrs Ledbetter. And to her surprise Mrs Ledbetter didn't harp on about Georgia or The Little House. Instead she talked about the walk they were set to do, how much she'd enjoyed last night's concert and just as Hannah had wanted, she reiterated her concern at how much dust gathered on surfaces up at the lodge.

'Maybe I should send my mum up there, she's really house-proud,' said Hannah.

'But she couldn't possibly come and clean, doesn't she live far away?'

'She does.' Hannah tutted as though that was the problem. No way would her mum ever entertain the idea of a cleaning job even if she lived around the corner, but Mrs Ledbetter didn't need to know that.

'I saw the advert. Do you think they have someone already?'

'No luck so far.'

'It's not right, having all those people living somewhere so dirty.'

Hannah played up to the conversation. 'It's not; they might get sick, or worse.' It wasn't that bad, not at all, and she knew Frankie or Maggie would see to it themselves but she'd let them in on the plan and expressly asked them to leave a patch of dust for her to show Mrs Ledbetter. 'Frankie doesn't know what she'll do if she doesn't find a solution soon. Butterbury Lodge needs a team of cleaners, the place is quite big. And on top of that, Frankie says they'll need someone in charge who can organise and oversee the others to do the job properly.'

She let it go at that, but the seed had been well and truly planted.

The walk home cleared Hannah's head although she may as well not have bothered when she saw Luke's car outside her cottage. She couldn't face him, not yet. Part of her wanted to blab about what she'd found out about Georgia, but the rest of her didn't want him to see that he'd always been right about the girl ever since they'd butted heads when Hannah and Georgia started GH Bookkeeping.

'Merry Christmas.' He was leaning against the bonnet of his car, smart, well-fitted jeans on, his Burberry coat, hair styled, as though he was visiting a conglomerate in the big city not a tiny unassuming cottage in a village.

Mrs Ledbetter managed a brief nod hello but didn't stop, eager to get on with preparations for later.

'Merry Christmas, Luke.' Hannah let him kiss her on the cheek when Mrs Ledbetter continued on her way. 'I can't stop today, I've got the Lantern Walk.'

'Mum told me about that. She was going to join in this year but both she and dad have gone up to the Lake District today. They've got a big New Year's party with friends and they wanted to go before it snowed.' They both looked up to the sky to see if there was any sign, but not yet.

'The Lakes will be wonderful, it'll do them good to have a break. And thank you again for the gift.'

'You'll love the spa, it's an impressive place.'

'It looks like you spent far too much.' Her eyes met his but drifted away again as she saw Joe approach. He lifted a hand in greeting before going on to Mrs Ledbetter's place, most likely volunteering too. And it made Hannah real-ise how much she wanted to be with all these new people in her life rather than standing talking to someone she'd left behind.

Luke shifted so Hannah's view of Joe was blocked. 'You deserve something special.'

'I really need to go.' When Luke looked in the direction Joe had headed she added, 'A whole load of us are organ-ising handing out the lanterns.'

'Can we talk later?'

'I won't be home for a while.'

'The walk isn't that long, is it?'

'Four miles in total, but it's a major event. We stop at Butterbury Lodge and sing, we come down to the square and then it's time for food and mulled wine and celebra-tions.' She almost suggested he come, out of politeness, but this was a little slice of time for herself. No Luke, no

Georgia; just her. A new beginning in a village that already felt like home.

'How about we say eight o'clock, your place?'

She didn't particularly want to meet, but so she could get away, agreed, 'I'll see you then.'

At Mrs Ledbetter's cottage volunteers were beginning to come and go with boxes full of lanterns. Mrs Ledbetter could be heard dishing out handfuls of spare tealights to people as they left – Mrs Addington, Miriam and her husband, Lily and Cate – telling them to watch out for anyone's light that ran out of power or malfunctioned during the walk.

'Hey, Ellen. Looking forward to the food later,' Hannah called as Ellen passed her on the front doorstep, coming outside. The sky was a deep grey by now, almost velvet, and stars had begun to peek out.

'Annie has it all in hand, don't you worry.' She hugged a box against her chest, the tops of the lanterns poking out. 'She'll join the walk and then we'll both scarper straight to the food cart.'

'Who's in charge of the mulled wine?'

'Very important question,' added Lily as she too set off for the square with a container of lanterns.

'Declan, I think,' Ellen mused, 'and I'm sure Freya and Mason are home from University for the Christmas break and have volunteered to help out on the stall too.'

Hannah put her thumbs up to her friend and ventured further inside Mrs Ledbetter's place to grab a box. Mrs Ledbetter cast a look her way but if she'd taken a disliking to Luke as well as Georgia, she didn't mention it.

'You OK with that one?' Joe asked as Hannah went for the largest container on the lounge floor. She'd seen him the second she came inside, his presence hard to ignore.

She was sure none of his women friends would risk breaking a nail by lifting a dirty old box full of lanterns, but she wasn't one of them. 'I'm fine.'

'It doesn't look too sturdy, that's all.' He leaned over to look at the bottom of the box. 'Hold it there.' He picked up a roll of thick brown tape, tugged at the end and cut off a piece that he stuck on the join of the bottom of the box, which wasn't getting any lighter. 'Hang on, one more, or you'll be dropping those lanterns.'

Was he doing it to prove a point? She lasted another thirty seconds for him to tape the box and then handed it to him. 'You take this, I'll grab another.'

He managed not to smile and say 'told you so', and Hannah followed him out of the cottage, doing her best not to let her eyes fall to his bottom, which was tucked neatly into jeans, one pocket with a tiny tear. Good-looking he might be, but he was a player, and she'd had enough games to last a lifetime.

Lanterns were handed out, a couple of spares were called for, and the entire space in Lantern Square was filled with people anxious for the off, holding their lanterns, chattering into the cold, dark air. The woodland creatures were still lit up in the curved flower beds, the tree stood tall and proud and would be there until twelfth night. People chattered on about the after-party when stomachs would be groaning for food and the village would come together once more.

Cate had a giggling Heidi in the buggy ready to push on the walk. 'You're brave,' Hannah told her, crouching down to let Heidi look at her lantern. The little girl held a miniature one of her own and looked happy, at least for now.

'She's always good in the buggy. Wouldn't you enjoy it, being pushed around?' She tightened her scarf around her neck. 'At least it's not icy. Last year we couldn't do it, she was too tiny and the pavements were treacherous unless you had a good grip on your shoes.'

'Well, I hope she loves it and enjoys it for years to come.' Hannah waved them off as they went to join Cate's parents, and she just knew this was going to be her first Lantern Walk of many.

Mrs Addington was next to come and have a chat. 'I had my doubts Mrs Ledbetter could pull it off,' she said, 'but she's got everyone organised.'

'I think she really enjoyed doing it.' Hannah accepted a piece of fudge Mrs Addington offered her from the white paper bag in her pocket.

'That was my plan.'

'Wait, you included her on purpose?'

'I did consider asking if she'd like to work together but I thought she could own the responsibility if only to get her talking to people rather than about them.'

'Well, I'm glad you did it.' Their minds had obviously been thinking along the same lines. 'And is she forgiven yet? I know she spread gossip about your son.'

'Now it would have been worse if it wasn't true. I doubt I could've seen past a vicious rumour, but I saw a lot of wrong in my line of work as a judge, people who'd done some terrible things. Mimi Ledbetter is harmless in comparison.'

Hannah grinned. 'Mimi . . . so that's her name.'

'I wish she'd use it more, it's pretty, far better than Mrs

Ledbetter.' She said the name in a dreary voice. 'And I'm Judith. I do wish you'd call me by my first name. Everyone else does.'

'Judith it is.' Hannah popped the piece of fudge into her mouth and savoured the energy burst although she was so hungry that already she was hankering after what Annie and Ellen were going to conjure up later. She hoped it was enough to feed her and give her the energy to talk to Luke when he came back. She appreciated how much he was trying, she really did, but being alongside Joe she knew it was time to admit that she'd never been truly happy with her ex-boyfriend. Content, yes, but there'd always been the dream that there was more out there, whether it be with a special significant other, or simply finding her own place in the world.

Mrs Addington used her authoritative voice to announce to everyone that they were ready for the off and whoops of joy went up as crowds tried to squeeze out of the bottleneck of the square and trudge their way around the route. The same route that had been followed for over a decade by the people of Butterbury.

Tiny lights dotted the way as the air grew colder around them, little flecks of soft light from the lanterns bounced up and down all the way up the hill towards Butterbury Lodge, like a string of springy fairy lights on a tree leading all the way to the angel at the top. Everyone talked as they walked. Hannah laughed along with Troy from the bakery who was thinking up some naughty-ish cookies for Valentine's Day although his wife Dawn was quick to point out that they didn't want to offend anyone.

The front gate at Butterbury Lodge was so narrow it seemed to take forever for them all to funnel through and file around to the back garden, but by the time Hannah got through herself she was amazed at how beautiful the scene looked. Every tree in the garden had been bedecked with white lights winding up the trunks and the residents were gathered at the windows looking out, a couple of cheekier members blowing kisses. Flo was on her feet waving to Mrs Ledbetter who was doing her best to appear nonchalant to those around her although Hannah could tell the woman had found a true friend. And Joe was only a few feet away from her, she'd been aware of his presence behind all the way up the hill, and every now and then he looked over her way and the jitters she felt whenever he was near were impossible to settle.

Against the inky sky dotted with a thousand stars, sounds of 'God Rest Ye Merry Gentlemen' rang out as they all sang together, and as Hannah came to the last verse she waved to Mr G and Charles, their mouths making the shapes of the words as they sang along. The windows had been opened slightly to let the sound in, some residents had blankets covering their laps, the fire roared in the background with its heat escaping just for a while, and Frankie was taking photographs of pretty much everything she could from the residents' faces to the crowd of people holding lanterns against the dark, their faces lit up just enough.

After they'd waved goodbye to residents it was time to file out of the grounds again, around to the front of the lodge, and continue on with the rest of the walk. They still had to make their way through part-forest, down through the neighbouring village and past Maplebrooke Manor, which always drew admiring glances. Hannah felt strangely comfortable with the idea of passing by tonight, now she'd been there for afternoon tea. Then it would be round the bend that would lead the other way to Butterbury, past Hannah's little cottage, finally coming to a rest in Lantern Square itself.

'Hannah!' It was Frankie at the door to Butterbury Lodge as Hannah got halfway down the front path.

She turned back. 'What's up?'

'Charles Bray wants a word.'

Hannah checked that Rhys had already walked on. He'd not wanted her to say anything yet, he didn't want to upset Charles, but Hannah hadn't been able to let it go. If she had, Rhys might have risked losing out altogether. 'I'll catch you all up,' she called after Cate when she cast her a quizzical look. She'd have plenty of time, it would take a while for crowds to filter through the tiny gate once more.

Inside the hallway Charles was already waiting for her. 'What's up, Charles?'

'I got rid of the problem.' He tapped the side of his nose.

'I'm not sure I'm with you.' She pulled off her bobble hat. The heat was too much for it in here, even only for a minute or two.

'I called my son, he called his estate agent—'

'During the Christmas break?'

'Every day is a business day when it comes to Butterbury. I won't let that girl cause trouble.' He sat down on the chaise longue on the other side of the hallway.

Hannah joined him, apologising to Frankie that she'd brought a clomp of earth in on her boots. 'What did the estate agent say?'

'He's rejecting the offer. He's going with Rhys's original.'

'Does he need to up his offer to match what Georgia was willing to pay?'

'I told my son that under no circumstances should we do that. I thought he'd tell me I'd lost my marbles, but he said it was my choice. And it's only five grand more anyway, and I can swallow that if it keeps the integrity of this village.'

Hannah couldn't help it. She threw her arms around the man and hugged him tight. 'You are one of the nicest people I've ever met.'

He had tears in his eyes. 'Well I never, you could kill an old man with shock throwing yourself at him like that.'

She nudged him. 'Rubbish. But I should go and catch the others up.'

'You go!'

'Can I tell Rhys?' she called out.

But right then Rhys came pacing in through the entry doors himself, Frankie tutting as he brought even bigger clomps of earth in on his manly boots, and he came right up to Hannah, picked her up and twirled her around. 'Thank you. I know it was you.' He set her down and turned to Charles, held out a hand. 'And I owe an even bigger thanks to you. The estate agent just called. But, I'm happy to match the offer, it's only fair.'

'No, I won't have it. It's the price we originally agreed. Bloody country should change its rules anyway so this gazumping doesn't happen.'

Hannah couldn't agree more. 'We need to go, Rhys.'

'I'm going to stay and chat with Charles here for a moment.'

'No, you won't,' said Charles. 'I'm coming with you.'

Maggie was passing by and her ears pricked up. 'It's cold out there, Charles.'

'Then I'll wrap up. And I have my warm socks Hannah once sent me in a care package. I won't be cold. And remember, there's no such thing as the wrong weather . . .' he nudged Rhys. 'Only the wrong clothes.'

Rhys stayed with Charles and assured Hannah he'd bring him back to the lodge as soon as festivities were over. And before Hannah left, she saw Maggie discreetly go over to the telephone while Charles went to wrap up warm. She'd bet Maggie was calling his son to check whether this was going to happen or not. But Hannah doubted much could stand in Charles's way.

Hannah emerged from Butterbury Lodge triumphant for Rhys that this part of his story had worked out. She set her lantern down while she pulled her bobble hat on, picked it up again when she was ready and as she walked down the path with a vision of lanterns bobbing up and down and heading towards the forest she thought she might have felt the first flakes of snow, but looking up there was nothing.

'That was brilliant.' Joe made Hannah jump as she walked briskly towards the gate. 'Sorry, didn't mean to scare you.'

'Why are you lagging behind?'

'Some of those women can really talk. One grabbed me through the window.'

Hannah's giggles rang out against the night air. 'Which one was that? Don't tell me, Josephine.'

'Got it in one. I saw her last week and changed her medication and now, apparently, she feels like a new woman.'

'Watch out, Doctor Joe,' she teased.

'She thanked me tonight, over and over and over. I thought she was going to plant a smacker on my lips.'

Hannah laughed. 'Now I'd like to see that.'

'Don't joke.' He held his lantern aloft so he could see to do the latch on the gate behind them. He looked on to the crowds. 'Come on, if we walk quickly we'll catch the back of the line.'

Hannah led the way, conscious he was behind her on the narrow pavement that led towards the start of the forest. But she was glad he was there, she wouldn't have wanted to go through on her own, through the copse of trees that rather than majestically letting in shafts of sunlight during the day, now made shadows everywhere she looked. 'I can't see a thing,' she laughed, feeling her feet meet the changed surface from tarmac to solid mud, hardened from the winter.

'Let me lead the way, might be easier. Stick close, I won't let us get lost.'

She could still see the bobbing lanterns in the distance although they were closing in on the rest of the participants. She followed Joe along the winding track – she knew it wasn't very long, but it seemed miles in the dark.

Cate was ahead with her parents and they turned to wave to Hannah and Joe as they emerged onto the easier part of the walk that would lead onto the adjacent village to Butterbury, past the manor and all the way back to Lantern Square.

'Knew we'd catch them up,' said Joe. 'So tell me, are you taking a bit of a break from work now?'

'Definitely.' She didn't need to talk about the finer

points, the discovery she'd made, the confrontation she still needed to have. 'And I'm glad I got rid of my flu before Christmas.'

'It sucks being unwell at Christmas. I had flu last year, a bad cold the year before. I was beginning to think I was cursed.' When they came to a thinner part of the pavement their bodies brushed against each other until it widened out again. And as they chatted on, his lantern highlighted his jaw, the faint layer of stubble outlining his lips as they moved.

Oh, she couldn't fall for Joe. Wildly inappropriate Doctor Joe who had at least as many notches on his bedpost as Hugh Hefner.

She batted away the thought as they walked on, approaching the manor which you could just about make out down the long driveway, the home itself all lit up as Hannah remembered it in years gone by. And there was no sign of Luke, which was a relief. After he'd been so insistent they talk tonight she'd wondered whether he'd wait for her to pass and join in the end of the walk, which would've ruined it. Especially now Joe was at her side, a man she was wary of but a man whose company she couldn't resist basking in.

Floating on the air were people's compliments and remarks about the magnificence of the manor. Some talked about the Cotswold stone, others the surrounding grounds which were flecked with frost, some walkers mentioned the charity events held there and Hannah remembered Luke mentioning how much the visiting children loved the treehouse.

They continued their way along the pavement on the opposite side of the road, their lantern lights mingling with the glow from those dotted in windows of nearby houses.

'Word has it we've raised over a thousand pounds in donations,' said Joe. 'Tonight,' he clarified when he realised Hannah had disappeared into a world all of her own.

'That's incredible. I hear some of it will go to Butterbury Lodge for the upkeep, perhaps renovating a few of the rooms.'

'Most are modern, just a couple escaped the last remodelling plan so they need to bring those into this century.' He lowered his voice. 'I think locals like fundraisers that go towards Butterbury Lodge. Plenty of them see their home as the square for now but in later years, the lodge.'

'Like you, you mean.'

'Cheeky.' And this time, the flirtatious edge was in his voice, not hers. 'In all seriousness, I've seen some terrible care homes in my time, but not that one. They make the last days for their residents some of the finest in my opinion.'

She gulped at the realisation that many of those residents wouldn't be with them as time went on. They would pass away, their rooms would be cleaned out, someone else would take their place.

'You all right?' He'd stopped and held his lantern closer to her face.

'I'm fine.' She looked down so he couldn't see her eyes which inevitably gave her away. She just hoped her mascara was as waterproof as it said.

'You're close to Mr G aren't you?'

'I've loved spending time with him.'

'The book club is all he talks about, you know. How you persuaded them all and how it's helped form friendships and give them something else to chat about other than their ailments. You've been a ray of sunshine in that place.'

She gulped at the compliment. 'They've given me as much joy as I've given them.'

'You know, Mr G suggested I ask you out on a date.'

She didn't mean to but she laughed. 'Sorry, I wasn't expecting you to say that.'

He stopped, a hint of vulnerability in his expression and she remembered what Miriam had said about him and how he had found some social situations difficult in his school days. 'You're in love with the guy I've seen hanging around, is that it?'

She bristled. 'So the only reason I'm hesitating is because there's someone else? Kind of big-headed, don't you think?'

He sighed against the breeze that had turned into a full winter chill and had Hannah lifting her scarf a little higher to meet her chin. 'I don't seem to do very well with you, do I?'

'Come on, we're lagging behind again.' She'd have to have a word with Mr G next time she saw him, tell him all about the comings and goings at Joe's house. Maybe then he'd realise that the local doctor didn't necessarily live up to his pristine reputation and stop trying to fix her up.

'Hannah!' From behind them came a voice. It was Rhys, just in time to help her escape an awkward conversation. Charles was with him, using his arm as support.

'How you doing, Charles?' Joe wanted to know.

'All the better for knowing a doctor is on this walk.' He breathed heavily. 'I didn't realise it was so far and so cold.'

'I gave you a clean bill of health last week,' Joe declared. 'You'll do just fine. And word has it the food cart will be dishing out treats the second we reach Lantern Square.'

'And I'll run you home in my truck, Charles, before I get into the mulled wine,' Rhys winked.

All four of them followed the bend past the manor house on their left with its encasing wall curving round, up the little hill that allowed a view over the Cotswold-stone enclosure into the gardens. Most of the other walkers were well in the distance now and Rhys was already fretting that the food would run out by the time they got there.

Hannah walked quietly on at the back of the foursome and when she reached the peak of the little hill she turned to glance over at the manor. The guy Joe was accusing her of still loving would be inside, but one thing was for sure, she didn't love him any more. She'd moved on, she couldn't go back. And later tonight, she intended to end it once and for all.

Her eyes settled on the grounds and the treehouse that was high enough to make out from here amongst the bare branches of the tree it stood in. But before Hannah could turn to follow the others, she stopped, realising there was someone standing on the veranda of the treehouse that was illuminated against the inky sky tonight.

It was Luke.

And he wasn't alone.

23

Hannah felt her lantern fall from her hand in shock. She heard a voice saying her name, and then Joe was at her side. She yanked his coat to pull him behind the trunk of the tree. With only inches between them he looked down at her, their gazes locked, but before he could speak she put a finger to her lips, her other hand across his mouth.

He rolled his eyes at her overdramatic actions and she took her hand away. 'Let me get your lantern,' he whispered. Rhys and Charles must have rounded the corner by now and headed on assuming they were lagging behind for whatever reason.

Joe rescued the lantern, came back behind the tree and they leaned against the thick trunk, sturdy and sure of itself. He handed her the lantern and popped the tealight back inside. 'It was in the gutter, but it still works.'

'Thank you.'

'I know I asked you out on a date, but you didn't need to jump me on a winter's night on a charity walk.' Even she saw the funny side, despite the reason she'd hauled him behind the tree in the first place. 'Now do you want to tell me what's going on?'

'I just found out the whole truth, that's all.' She was reeling from shock, trying to process what she'd seen.

On the veranda of the treehouse, the place where she and Luke had shared their first kiss and more recently another moment of intimacy, Georgia and Luke had been locked in an embrace.

She felt nauseous. Her ex-boyfriend and ex-best friend, together. Not sworn enemies as she'd thought. Georgia not with her family as she'd originally claimed, but here, way too close for comfort and playing all kinds of sick games.

'We should keep walking,' said Joe. 'It's freezing.'

'You can go, it's OK.'

'And leave you on your own? No chance. It's dark apart from the lanterns, there's still a way to go to reach the square, and it's only going to get colder.'

'Fine. But I need to do something first.'

She peeked out from where they were hiding but all the lights on the treehouse had gone out now. Luke and Georgia must have gone inside the main house.

She expected to start crying, to mourn in some way at the discovery, but instead she felt numb. Why had Luke even come back into her life? Was it to ruin whatever shred of dignity she had left?

'Earth to Hannah.' Joe was still whispering. 'I don't mean to be rude, but I'm starting to lose all feeling in my fingers.'

'Should've brought gloves. Sorry,' she apologised.

'You like to berate me. Feisty, not a bad quality.'

'Now's not the time to flirt, or whatever it is you're trying to do.' Her stomach growled.

He glanced at her with a grin. 'Was that you?'

'I haven't eaten for a while.'

'Then I'd suggest we get whatever it is over and done with so you can get to Annie and Ellen's cart before their supplies are diminished. There are a lot of hungry walkers tonight. There's Rhys for a start.'

'He does like his food.' The banter between them had gone a little way to softening the blow of what she'd seen and when Joe blew on his fingers and swapped the lantern so he could blow on the digits of his other hand it brought her to her senses. 'Follow me.'

He did as he was told and they crossed over, followed the Cotswold-stone wall all the way back around the bend, and this time went through the gate to Maplebrooke Manor. They followed the path between the trees, the same road she'd taken in her car. Thank goodness Luke's parents were away, she wouldn't want to upset them with this. She would lay money on the fact that they didn't know a thing about Georgia either.

When they were almost at the front door Hannah said, 'I'll take it from here.'

'I'll wait.' Joe sat down on a low wall but got up pretty quickly. 'I'll have a wet butt if I sit there.'

She tried not to think of any part of his anatomy right now although his remark had lessened the fury she felt, at least for a second. 'Fine, but could you move somewhere more out of sight?'

He opened his mouth to answer but instead nodded and headed over to the tree closest to the house but so large he could stand behind it undetected.

'I won't be long.'

When she rang the doorbell it didn't have the same appeal as it usually did. The melody grated on her as it crescendoed to its finish.

'Hannah.' Luke's face drained of colour when he pulled open the door. He abruptly pulled it almost closed behind him. 'I was about to come over.'

'I thought it was easier for me to pop in on my walk.' She held the lantern up.

'Let me get my coat, I'll walk with you.'

'I'll come in and wait. To tell you the truth I could use a rest.' She didn't wait for him to answer, just bustled into the hallway, not allowing a pang of sadness that this really was a goodbye to get in the way and make her lose her nerve.

He grabbed his coat from the row of hooks and was about to shrug it on when a noise came from the kitchen.

'I thought your parents were away.' Actually, watching him squirm was quite a lot of fun. 'Do you think it's someone breaking in, should we call the police?'

He spluttered a non-committal response claiming it to be nothing but a draught probably catching something and knocking it over.

'Oh, come on, Luke. I'm not stupid. The game's up.'

'What game?'

'Whatever game you and Georgia are playing, I know.' He looked as though an icy hand had reached out and grabbed him by the throat. 'How long's it been going on?'

'I've no idea what you're talking about, Hannah.'

'No? Then let me enlighten you—'

It was that moment her so-called friend chose to step out and join them. In a tight-fitting burgundy dress with plenty of cleavage on display, a Swarovski crystal necklace glistening in place – no doubt a gift from Luke, given his expensive tastes – Georgia joined the party. 'Wondered how long it would take for you to realise.' She grinned and sidled up to Luke who took a step back.

'How could you?' She meant the question for both of them but this time she was looking at Georgia.

'Hannah, we're in love.' Georgia stepped closer to Luke again and hooked her arm through his, waiting for him to affirm her claims. 'We have been for years.' Her phone started to ring, but she ignored it.

Luke fiddled with the collar of his shirt, a familiar move Hannah knew signified discomfort. He could pretend it was from the warmth of the house but she knew otherwise. And then he pulled away from Georgia again. 'We are not in love, it was only ever a bit of fun.'

Georgia turned a venomous look on him. 'Fun? Is that all I was to you?'

'You know it was, Georgia.' He was toying with his collar again, but judging by the look Georgia gave him, Hannah wondered whether he'd thought it was a fling and Georgia was far more committed than she'd ever let on. A tiny part of her felt happy that Georgia had been wronged in all of this, that she'd been hurt at the hands of Luke too.

'Hannah . . .' Luke approached her but when she stepped back against the wall he held up his hands to say he wouldn't push it. 'I mean it, I am not in love with Georgia, we fooled around, that's all. I had no idea she was coming here today, she turned up and caught me off guard.'

'Why didn't you tell her to leave?'

'She made it pretty hard to do that.' He was sweating, she could see, but also Hannah knew his claim was plausible. Georgia had never liked the word no. He reached out to touch her and for a moment she let him until she snatched her hand away and moved to the side so she could put further distance between them.

Georgia watched on with a look that told Hannah she'd no idea Luke thought so little of their involvement with one another. She'd probably been thinking marriage, permanency, and he'd obliterated all of her dreams in a second tonight. But Hannah refused to feel any sympathy. Her betrayal and attitude had landed her in this mess and Hannah couldn't believe she'd been so taken in by her again.

Georgia's mobile was still buzzing insistently as Luke told Hannah, 'I'm really sorry. I swear to you that it was only ever sex with Georgia, a bit of fun when I felt lonely.'

Arms folded across her chest, Hannah demanded, 'How long has it been going on?'

'What?'

'Simple question. A few weeks, months?' He looked at the floor and she had her answer. 'You were doing it when we were together, weren't you?'

Georgia began to laugh as she overheard them. 'I shagged him a week before you ended it with him. I won that one, you lost.'

Is that the way she saw it? As some sort of battle?

Georgia finally gave in and answered her phone, retreating into the kitchen with a finger in one ear.

Luke stepped towards Hannah with a beseeching look. 'I felt I was losing you.'

'So you thought you'd get a backup?'

'No! She threw herself at me, she really did. I knew you were ending things. It took you a while to tell me that's all. And I know it's not an excuse, and I'm sorry. Believe me. I was hurting and she caught me in a weak moment. I should've said no.'

'Yes, you should.' She bit down on her lower lip to stop

it trembling with anger. 'Have you been together ever since I left?'

'Hardly. It's been on and off.'

So just sex, no feelings involved. Hannah wasn't sure whether that made her happier or not, but there was no time to think about it when Georgia came storming back into the hallway having finished her phone call.

'You bitch!' Georgia went right for Hannah.

Luke yanked Georgia back before she could claw at Hannah's face. 'Calm down, for crying out loud!'

'She ruined my purchase of The Little House!' Eyes narrowed, she zoned in on Hannah but thankfully Luke had her arms locked with his own from behind. 'You made the old man pull out of our deal to give it to that friend of yours, who you're probably shagging, the way he looks at you when you talk about your pathetic box-like garden. It's sad, that's what it is. You're all a bunch of village idiots. Get off me, I won't touch her.' She shrugged Luke off and true to her word she didn't advance on Hannah again.

'It was the right thing to do, the owner saw that.' Hannah's heart thumped at Georgia's reaction. Even when they'd parted ways a long time ago, she'd never seen Georgia this angry, this vicious. She turned to Luke, focusing on him alone, properly hurt and rightly so. 'I don't understand you. Why do this to me? I ended things with us because I didn't want to hurt you any more than I had to. I didn't want to carry on with you because you were reliable, because you were the man everyone expected me to be with. It wouldn't have been fair on either of us. But I didn't deserve you coming back into my life claiming you want me back and then having you hurt me by carrying on with my so-called best friend who I'd given another chance.'

'I never wanted to hurt you either.'

'And as for trying to ruin my business.' Her voice rose but soon fell at the shock of it all. 'God knows I've worked hard to get where I am.'

'You always thought you were better than me,' Georgia spat, intent on being part of the conversation again.

'I never did!' She couldn't believe this girl had so much animosity. How could she have read a person so wrong?

'I really tried to make our business work. I got a few things wrong, but it was as though you were the boss and I was just the lackey,' Georgia accused.

'It wasn't like that at all. We were equal partners, but it was you who messed it up.' She took a deep breath. 'It's all in the past, I moved on and started something else.'

'When we started GH Bookkeeping, we were a team, just like we'd been at school. I came to Butterbury to try to prove to you that I wasn't completely useless. I thought we could go into business together again, run a chain of gyms, make the big time.'

'You thought I'd give up my business to join in with yours?'

Georgia shrugged and Hannah realised that was exactly what she'd assumed. 'I've never been able to keep up with you. You were the one who had everything. You were the brains in the business in the end, you had the boyfriend with the top job and the money, you never wanted for anything.'

This was all down to jealousy, a ridiculous notion Georgia had built up where she saw Hannah's life as being perfect.

'You threw away everything you had,' said Georgia. 'I felt sorry for Luke when you ended things, you didn't deserve him.'

'And he deserved you more,' Hannah concluded with a sadness washing over her. 'I don't understand why you would apologise to me, all the while sleeping with Luke. Did you expect to come here, persuade me to go into business with you again, and then announce you were together? Or were you going to neglect to tell me that part?'

Georgia had the grace to look lost. 'I don't know.'

'I feel sorry for you,' Hannah began, and the words came tumbling out before she could stop herself. 'You're twisted. You've got something wrong with you.'

Her spiel was short-lived when Georgia, with the air of a raging bull, made to charge at Hannah again until Luke grabbed her and held her back.

With Georgia safely bolted to the spot Hannah told them both, 'I hope I never see either of you ever again, after what you did to my business, and I'll be calling the police if you try anything else like that ever again, you mark my words.'

Confusion crossed Luke's brow. 'Wait a minute. What are you talking about? I haven't done anything to hurt your business. Why would I do that?'

'You tell me, Luke.' Tears pricked her eyes but she wouldn't let them fall. 'I don't understand why either. You said you wanted me back, so doing something else to ruin me still doesn't make sense. And the Christmas present for the spa in Northumberland was a huge gesture, why plan on a break away with me when you were shagging someone else? Was it some kind of sick game?'

'I ended it with Georgia before I got in touch with

you,' he admitted. 'When she found I'd come here to see you she told me that if I didn't keep seeing her, she'd tell you everything.'

'And you thought you'd get me on side first, make me fall for you all over again, then admit the truth?'

'It was cowardly, I know that now.'

'Now hold on one minute.' Georgia held up a finger. 'What spa are you talking about?'

Hannah recalled the name, the location, and as she did Georgia lunged at Luke who grabbed her before her fists made contact with his chest. 'That was our place, where we did all that research and you talked the talk, saying it was the perfect example of what you wanted to do here eventually.'

Hannah let out a harrumph. She couldn't believe she'd been so naive to think Luke had changed so much that his dream of opening a spa here at his parents' grounds when they handed it over to him had altered and he'd started to respect village and community values, not to mention the wishes of his own family. 'I can't believe I began to think you'd changed.' She actually felt sorry for Georgia. It was clear Georgia thought she'd be able to keep hold of Luke in some way, or had he let her believe that? Whatever the reasoning behind it, she wanted nothing to do with either of them.

'Hannah, I can explain.' Luke had let go of Georgia by now and she looked in a state of shock at the realisation that the game was up.

Hannah held up a hand to stop him. 'There's no need, really. You've always been a businessman, always been after the next best thing.' So different to Liam, she hadn't realised that part of her attraction to him was that he was the total opposite of the boyfriend who'd been taken from her so early. Luke had taken her under his wing, enjoyed the vulnerability she came with at the time. But that wing had soon become a straightjacket. That's why she'd left and that's why she should never have entertained getting back with him. He was far more suited to someone like Georgia, someone who wanted and needed the constant spoiling and attention and to be part of a big future.

Hannah wondered whether seeing these two together tonight and having this confrontation now had been the best thing that could've happened.

'Wait a minute.' Further realisation dawned on Hannah. 'That spa you're sending me to. The one Georgia seems so intimately acquainted with. You both went there a long time before you and I ended things, Luke. Didn't you?' Luke's open-mouthed reaction confirmed it. Hannah had seen it as a claim under expenses for the business she and Georgia had once run together and it was one of the things she'd confronted her former partner about. It was all clicking into place now.

'That time was a one-off, a big mistake. I didn't intend for it to happen again.'

Hannah hated the way they'd both made a fool out of her. 'Cheating on me is one thing, Luke, but why did you both feel the need to ruin me?'

'Hannah, I honestly don't know what you're talking about,' Luke claimed, and when she realised that this time he was telling the truth, they both looked to Georgia.

'She deserved it.' Georgia had turned to face them as they stood side by side. 'She had everything, I ended up with nothing. She had Liam and his family, then found you. Oh, it wouldn't do for poor Hannah to be sad and single, would it? Oh no, she had to find the only man I wanted.'

'You were interested in Luke at the party where we first met?' Hannah asked. 'Why didn't you ever say?'

'Would it have made a difference?' She didn't wait for Hannah to answer. 'You know it wouldn't. You go after what you want and get it, Hannah. At first I wanted to make peace with you, I felt terrible after what I'd done with the business and with Luke behind your back, but when I realised he wanted to get back with you again I was angry. Luke and I were building a relationship, I was beginning to work towards a business of my own, but nobody wanted to do anything my way.'

'We were only ever a bit of fun, Georgia,' said Luke. 'I could never have been serious about you, you're wild, all over the place.'

'But a good shag, I take it. So there you go, Saint Hannah wins again.'

'Enough with assuming my whole life was perfect!' Hannah yelled. 'Why don't you take responsibility for your own happiness for once?'

Luke's anger mounted and Hannah could tell it took Georgia by complete surprise when he looked at her and asked, 'Was this really all down to petty jealousy?'

Georgia wouldn't answer him.

He faced Hannah, reached out for her but she wouldn't let him touch her. 'Hannah, I have changed. I realise now that I should've supported your career choices, I should never have got involved with Georgia. I'm still a business-man, that hasn't changed, and you're right, the spa idea is still in my head, and yes, my parents still hate it. But I have great plans. I would keep the integrity of this place.'

He looked around the walls that had cocooned him in childhood but he was trying to alter as an adult. 'My parents are older and I think they might even grow to like what I have in mind. You might too. I've talked to architects, other businessmen who've done similar. We could do weddings here, formal events, keep the coach house as accommodation.'

'Why are you still trying to sell yourself to me? Don't you get it? If you have to sell yourself to me like a business concept, doesn't that tell you something? Your parents only want to keep the home they've owned for decades, the home they raised you in, the home they probably hoped you'd raise your own family in one day. Instead you're intent on using it to make money.

'You have a very different perspective on the world than I do,' she said more softly. Despite the cheating, the lying and the determination to do something so against his parents' wishes, she felt sorry for him. She'd hurt him and it had taken coming back into her life once again for him to really get the closure he needed. 'It doesn't mean either of us are wrong, it doesn't mean your business plans aren't right. And it doesn't mean your parents' ideas are old-fashioned either.' She reached out for his hand and squeezed it. 'Do me a favour?'

'Anything.'

'Don't fall out with them over this. You'll never forgive yourself.' It was one of the reasons she hadn't told her own mother how she really felt when she criticised Hannah's choices, homemaking skills or whatever else came to her attention. 'And when they're gone, you won't bask in the glory of the financial situation you've put yourself in, it'll be ruined by guilt. Try talking to them, be honest. You never know, you might be able to come up with something together. And if not, respect that.'

They looked at one another, all the time they'd spent together suddenly producing an understanding and respect that Georgia would never grasp. She hoped Luke would realise the importance of all this before it was too late. His family were wonderful and she hated to think one day he wouldn't be a part of it because of his own determination to be a bigger and better version of a man who was already enough just as he was.

Georgia let out a long, impatient sigh. 'I've had enough of listening to this crap. I'm getting a drink.'

'Stop right there.' Luke turned to her. 'I want to go back to what Hannah said before.'

'And what was that?' Georgia rolled her eyes as though she didn't really have time for any of this.

'Hannah keeps talking about us ruining her business, and I still don't understand.'

It was then Hannah realised Georgia had acted entirely alone in her games. He really had no idea as to the extent of what she'd done, and Hannah almost felt pleased. He'd been played by Georgia and taken in by her, just as she had.

And so Hannah filled him in. On everything.

Luke sank down on the bottom stair. 'You did all that, to Hannah.' He looked at Georgia in disbelief. 'I knew you were a little unhinged, but seriously?'

Georgia walked over to him, leaned over, all cleavage and glittering jewellery. 'I had to do something, nobody hurts me or you and gets away with it.'

He pushed her hand away when she tried to caress his cheek. 'Stop trying to make out that we're a couple.

The girl with the nut allergy could've died. The parents could've sued. You could've ruined so many lives.'

'The girl was fine! They have injections, funny pens for stuff like that now.'

'That's hardly the point.'

'Luke, listen to me!' Georgia yelled. 'I had to take action.'

But Hannah had heard enough. She opened the door and walked out of Maplebrooke Manor, this time for good.

She was surprised to find that Joe was still waiting for her behind the tree, concern etched into his face. He could see from her expression that she didn't want to talk, so they followed the driveway all the way to the main road in silence, walked alongside the Cotswold-stone wall until the manor grounds were behind them, and made their way back towards Lantern Square.

'There you are! I was beginning to think we'd lost you.' It was Rhys, who'd spotted them the moment they passed by Lantern Cottage and was steering them across the road to join the festivities.

'I think I'll call it a night.' Hannah needed to digest everything, let it all settle.

'No way.' Rhys looked to Hannah, then Joe, then back again. 'What happened?'

'Nothing. Just not feeling great.' Hannah didn't want to spoil his night with her misery. He was clearly elated at having secured a property right here and he deserved to be happy.

'I'll bet it's because you haven't eaten. Come on, Ellen and Annie are serving cinnamon churros with chocolate dip . . . and sprinkles.'

She couldn't help but smile. 'You child.'

'Don't let her out of your sight,' he told Joe. 'I'll get back to Charles, I'm watching him closely out in the cold, and he just sunk a second mulled wine.'

'I'll keep an eye on her, you tell Charles to go easy on the alcohol.'

'I doubt he'll listen,' said Hannah when Rhys left them to it.

'You're probably right.' Joe's smile had the ability to settle her. 'You're not really going are you? What happened back there at the manor? I heard raised voices, I almost came in to check on you, make sure I wasn't going to be involved in a murder.'

Actually, she didn't want to go home now he was looking right at her, making her feel secure. What she really wanted was to tell someone everything. And then perhaps she'd be able to enjoy herself and get on with tonight's festivities. On the positive side, the business problems hadn't been her fault and wouldn't happen again, Georgia and Luke were both out of her life for good. It'd been stressful, but it was done.

'I'll tell you everything on one condition.'

'What's that?'

'You go in there,' she nodded towards the jam-packed square, 'and get me double churros.'

'You wait here.' Joe pointed to the iron bench where branches of the trees behind overhung, where she wouldn't be seen by anyone inside the square, where she could gather herself.

He was there and back within minutes. 'I had a quiet word with Annie, said you'd had a shock, she asked no questions and bumped my order to the top of the queue.'

He handed her the churros in a polystyrene cup, inside which was the chocolate sauce and sprinkles. 'Sorry, bit of a mess to eat but it's the only way I could carry it all.'

'Don't care,' was all she said as she devoured the festive treats, her stomach thanking her with every mouthful.

They sat there quietly and when she'd finished and swigged from the bottle of water he'd bought her too, she told him the whole sorry story, right from meeting Luke and the business she'd set up with Georgia, through to seeing them tonight, together.

'I don't know what to say.' He shook his head. 'It's like a soap opera. You should submit that as a script to a TV channel.'

Hannah let out a laugh. 'It's quite something, isn't it?'

'And they're supposed to be your friends.' He pulled a face. 'Who needs enemies?'

'I was completely drawn into her friendship, I wanted to give her another chance. More fool me, eh.'

'You're a good person, Hannah. Don't ever apologise for that.'

She looked up into eyes that spoke of his kindness. 'Thank you for listening. I didn't want to tell Rhys, I can't very well go crying to Mr G, and I don't really know anyone well enough to burden them with all that crap.'

'I'm sure none of them would think that.' He paused and then asked, 'Can I ask about the other guy?'

'What other guy?'

'You said you were vulnerable when you met Luke. I'm assuming there was a nasty break-up before.'

'You're half right.' She took a deep breath. 'But it wasn't a break-up. Liam was in the army, he died on a training exercise.'

'I'm sorry. You've been through a lot, it's a wonder that lovely hair of yours isn't fully grey by now.'

'Give it time,' she laughed. 'I think I only got together with Luke because I was in a certain place in my life, I needed something, some stability, a belief in something new. And he was so different to Liam right from their jobs to the way they dressed and the goals they pursued. Luke is all about the business acumen, getting to the top, succeeding and building his reputation. Liam was down to earth, didn't think long-term, was all about living in the moment. I loved that about him.' She licked her fingers to rid them of the sugar from her last churros. 'He bought me that dress.'

'Which dress?'

'The one you spilt coffee on.'

'Ah, and I'm guessing you didn't wear it very often.'

'He sent me it the day he died and I was wearing it when I got the knock at the door to tell me.'

'Shit.'

'Yep. That's one word for it. I'd done a selfie to send him so he could keep it with him wherever he was. I'd been twirling around in the dress feeling like the luckiest girl in the world. And then bam . . . the bottom of my world fell out. I couldn't bear to look at the dress after that, let alone wear it. But the day of the fair in the summer I literally had nothing to wear and I wanted to feel nice at the dance, so I braved putting it on.'

'No wonder you hate me.'

She whacked him on the arm. 'I do not hate you. If I did, I wouldn't be sitting here now. And life's too short to hate anyone.'

'Even Luke and Georgia.'

'I could almost hate them but actually, I'm not going to waste my energy.'

'Good for you.'

'Hannah, there you are!' It was Charles, Rhys following close behind. 'I'm going now, but I wanted to say good-bye. What took you two so long walking here?' He gave Joe a knowing glance and Hannah knew she'd blushed. Thank goodness for the dark.

'I'm glad you got to do the walk,' Hannah told him, ignoring the inference. 'Tell Mr G I'll be in to see him tomorrow.'

'Of course I will. Merry Christmas again, I can't believe it's almost over. Might not see another one.'

'Stop looking for sympathy,' she teased, 'you'll be around for years yet. And we'll see you at the New Year's Eve dance, won't we?'

'I'll bet your dance card is already full.' He gripped on to Rhys's arm and Rhys tried to stifle a laugh, knowing the mulled wine had been a bit too much of a tipple tonight.

'Nonsense, there's always a space on there for you.' She bid him goodnight as Rhys took him home.

'You look happier,' said Joe. 'Now, how about a mulled wine?'

'You're on.'

'And maybe I'll get myself on that dance card too.'

She responded to his comment with a smile as they went into the foray to find the mulled wine stall and enjoy the last few hours of Boxing Day.

She figured he might not have much space left if the amount of women he entertained all decided to put their names on there.

24

The pavements were icy, and frost tipped the trees and roofs across Lantern Square as Hannah left the warmth of her log burner and Lantern Cottage to walk up to Butterbury Lodge. It was the day before New Year's Eve and she'd had a busy few days since the showdown with Luke and Georgia. She'd had the energy to make a quick dip into work commitments, putting together an international care package for a birthday in early January, another for a one hundredth birthday celebration at a farm in Wales, and a third for a couple getting married in Plymouth over the New Year. She'd also accepted Castle Cards offer to sell her Easter cards following the prototype she sent. As she set off to read to the book club now, despite the cold outside, on the inside she was buzzing with warmth and renewed vigour.

It had been a funny few days since her confrontation with Luke and Georgia. Luke had apologised yet again, except this time doing it by text, finally realising that this was the end of the road for them and there'd be no turning back. And his parting gesture had been telling her to take the spa break in Northumberland with his blessing. He told her Georgia had left shortly after her, blaspheming all the way out of the door, something which had made Hannah momentarily panic that she'd head her way. Another text message told Hannah that he too was furious Georgia had been so vindictive and he'd warned her off. Told her if she made an ounce of trouble for Hannah again, then he'd make it ten times as hard for her to ever get a gym venture off the ground. Hannah wasn't quite sure how he'd be able to do that, but given the radio silence from Georgia, perhaps she'd thought him quite capable.

Hannah had gone ahead and taken the Northumberland spa break already, lucky enough to get in following a last-minute cancellation. She'd driven up there to the height of tranquillity, the beauty of thermae spas, body wraps, massage and facials. And she'd left feeling rejuvenated as though the trip had marked her new start, the true closure of the doors of her past and her walking towards a new life.

As she made her way along the high street Hannah waved to Cate who was zipping past in the car with her family, calling out her goodbyes through the open window and yelling that they were off to Suffolk to see her grandparents. Hannah had no doubt Cate's other half would be telling her to do the window up already, it was freezing!

Lantern Square – in fact the whole of Butterbury – was seasonally quiet, everyone resting in that lull between Christmas and New Year, gearing up for the village coming together again with the band and a New Year's dance in Lantern Square no matter the weather. Five years ago it had been torrential rain according to Mrs Ledbetter who it turned out had danced with Charles Bray – he'd been telling people after a few mulled wines that she was the best dancer next to his late wife. It had been gale force winds the year before last, taking the dance to the pub where the band had squished beneath a pretty hardy gazebo in the beer garden to do their thing.

Hannah wondered what surprises this year would bring.

When she reached the top of the hill she pushed open the little wooden gate and trudged up the path to Butterbury Lodge, checking her boots this time before she went inside.

Mr G was first to give her a big hug. 'How are you?' His eyes searched hers but only found joy.

'It'll take more than that pair to bring me down,' she told him. Yesterday she'd filled him in on the entire story, its conclusion included.

Plenty of other residents greeted her as she took her seat at the front of the semi-circle with their latest book, a Matthew Reilly, Ernest's choice. It was a bit heavy going and she wasn't sure how many would stick with this one but she hoped they'd at least have some lively discussions. And when Mrs Ledbetter joined them, Hannah rid her face of any surprise as she took a seat alongside Flo and for the next hour she lost herself in reading.

After her audience had discussed the story so far she accepted the offer of a cup of tea from Maggie.

'I really enjoy this group.' Mrs Ledbetter was first to come over.

'I didn't expect to see you, but I'm glad you came. The more the merrier.'

'I'm not sure about this book though. Ernest passed me a copy of the first text you read, much more my style.'

'I have to give everyone a turn to choose you see.' Hannah sipped her tea and took a shortbread in the shape of a Santa from the plate Maggie was passing around the room with.

Mrs Ledbetter wrinkled her nose. 'I suppose it's only fair.'

'You seem to enjoy being here.'

'I do. It's nice to get out and about rather than be home on my own all the time,' she admitted.

'Would you ever think about coming here to live?'

Mrs Ledbetter's face dropped. 'I love my cottage, I'm not too old to be on my own.'

'Didn't say you were.' Hannah picked up a crumb from her woollen skirt and dropped it in the bin nearby. 'But this place isn't about being so old you have to come here, it's about being with people who could be your friends. Most of them already are.' Her smile grabbed her neighbour and she knew it. 'You're good for Flo, I can see that much.'

'We get on like the proverbial house on fire.'

'So – think about it.'

'I couldn't afford the fees.' She was tempted, Hannah could tell. 'Wait a minute, are you trying to out me so that friend of yours can get her grubby little paws on my cottage?' Her voice rose, her hands went to her hips. 'I won't be pushed out, especially after what she did.'

Hannah reached out to one of those hands and patted it. 'Mrs Ledbetter, that so-called friend of mine has since shown her true colours and I doubt I'll ever see her again after what she did.' The woman's interest was piqued but she'd leave it to Mr G to fill her in, they could all use the gossip she was sure, it'd fill the room as much as the lively

363

book discussions. 'This is about you, I have no desire to take your home from you.'

'I do like it here. Their Christmas lunch was one of the best I've ever had. The gravy, oh my lord, heavenly.'

'Well if they can do a roast . . .'

'Oh be off with you, I couldn't possibly.'

Hannah seized another opportunity. 'Did you see the reception desk out there before Maggie gave it a clean?'

'I didn't. What was wrong with it?'

'Filthy it was. They need to get new cleaners, and soon.'

'If I was the cleaner the first thing I'd do is move every single chair and give the place a good hoover.'

The plan was working like a charm. If she wouldn't entertain coming here to live, then this was the way to get her integrating even more. 'Why don't you offer to do it?'

'Do what?'

'Take the job.'

Mrs Ledbetter laughed until she realised Hannah was serious.

'You'd have this place shipshape in no time I bet. And the way you organised the Lantern Walk shows you'll be able to manage a team of people. You could even be in charge of the other cleaners.'

'Oh, I don't know . . .'

'Think about it, more money in your pocket, you get to spend time here. And they'd be lucky to have you, but make sure they pay a good rate.' She added in a bit of business speak, she wouldn't want Mrs Ledbetter to catch on that this had been her plan all along. But judging by her reaction, Hannah wouldn't mind betting that Mrs Ledbetter would be leaving today, via reception, to ask about the job.

Ernest grabbed Mrs Ledbetter's attention and asked for help with the knitting he'd started since she came up and helped him learn the basics of the craft, and she scurried off quite happily. Feeling useful was obviously something the woman needed and Hannah had been happy to give her a little push in the right direction.

Out in the hallway she saw Joe as she reached for her coat. 'What brings you here?'

He held his doctor's bag aloft. 'People need me, what can I say?'

'Ah, Mr Peters?'

'How did you know?' When she grinned he said, 'I'm afraid patient confidentiality prevents me from sharing anything more, but I'll tell you it isn't too serious.'

'Oh, I know.' She leaned in closer so nobody else would hear. 'He doesn't usually say much to me at all, maybe Christmas brought him out of his shell. He's been telling everyone he might have gout, even started a conversation about amputation which led to all manner of stories being shared about gruesome medical blunders.'

'Thanks for the warning.' He pulled a face. 'Hello there, Josephine.'

Josephine had been at the care home forever, never read a book in her time within these walls until today's session, never more than lifted a hand to wave to Hannah until today either. It seemed Ernest had a fellow thriller fan. 'Hello, Doctor Joe, and there's no need to shout.' The frail woman walked gingerly over to the doctor, a slight limp that had been there since childhood. 'I have my new hearing aids remember. I'm like a kid with a new toy, although I do have one complaint.'

'Is that so?' Hannah loved the way Joe made his patients

feel as though they were the centre of his world when they needed him. She'd been that way too the day he helped her up to bed when she had flu, in terrible denial that it was nothing more than a nasty cold.

'I can hear everything now. I can hear the woman next to me singing in the shower and the man the other side going for a wee late at night.'

Joe held back his laughter and Josephine went on her way.

Hannah couldn't stop her own giggles. 'I'm sorry, but the image that just conjured up is one I'll find hard to get out of my mind.'

He stood close to her so this was their secret. 'There tends to be a lot of oversharing in this place.'

'I'd better go.' She pulled on her gloves using the distraction to look away from him.

'Hannah . . .'

'Yes?'

He opened his mouth but nothing came out except for, 'Never mind. Stay warm.'

And when she stepped outside and hugged her coat closer around her body she wondered what he'd been about to say.

25

Yesterday Hannah had gone out and bought a new dress. On her way home from the shopping centre she'd also dropped her polka dot dress at the charity shop in the same area. She wasn't keen on passing it on too locally, but she wanted someone else to own and enjoy such a beautiful garment. The dress came with memories; memories she'd laid to rest, some happy, some sad, but it was time to move forwards.

Now, on New Year's Eve, dressed in a heavy satin, slate-coloured dress with a skater skirt that flared out from the hips, she wiggled the zip up and ensured the strapless garment wasn't revealing too much. The dress would remain unseen at the dance in the square with the live band performing, unless the crowds and out-door heaters allowed her to remove a layer, but still, it felt good to wear something so special. She'd bought a tailored jacket with three-quarter length sleeves to wear over the top, figure flattering and chic, and didn't ruin the look of the dress, but with the temperatures out-side Hannah knew she'd have to keep dancing unless she wanted to turn into an ice cube. If her dad could see her going out like this he'd be throwing her another layer, namely her big puffy jacket, and most likely a scarf too.

She spritzed herself with the final few squirts of Marc Jacobs perfume. Perhaps she'd treat herself in the sales and get some more, she thought as she pulled on the jacket. She took out her patent heels from the bottom of the wardrobe and checked her reflection once more in the full-length mirror before heading downstairs, shoes in hand. It was party time.

She could hear the noise of the crowds outside as she came downstairs and gave the cats a fuss, not daring to pick either of them up in case they clawed her outfit. She slipped on her heels, opened the front door, and would've missed the package had it not been waiting right in the middle of the doorway, beneath the tiny porch roof overhead.

She picked it up. It was heavy enough. Addressed to her, it was wrapped in brown paper and tied with string, the same way as she did her packages. She took it inside, tore off the wrapping and opened up the box to find a small card resting on top of tissue paper. All it said was 'Just For You', and beneath the paper was Marian Keyes's latest book – she'd snuggle up on the sofa during a bleak January and devour it – a flowery top gave away the bottle of Marc Jacobs perfume – no need to look for it in the January sales now – and she smiled when she saw the Icy Blue Spruce Yankee Candle which would sit perfectly in the lounge on the mantelpiece. Lastly there was a smaller package containing everything she'd need to make mulled wine, and nestled right at the bottom encased in bubble wrap, a bottle of red wine.

'Mr G' she said out loud, 'you shouldn't have.' She'd tell him off later for spending too much money. No doubt

Maggie was in on it too and had done some of the shopping for him. They'd talked about mulled wine and his dislike of rancid, pub concoctions that were left in a warmer far too long, she remembered Frankie once quizzing her about her perfume, and everyone knew she loved a good scented candle. She had one on the windowsill in the lounge, but it was almost gone.

She left the items on the side in the kitchen, propped the gift card up so she'd see it again later and realise how kind people could be. What with Luke and Georgia doing the things they'd done recently, Hannah's ability to stay positive had waned a little, and although she could see positivity for others it was sometimes hard to believe the same for herself.

She set off to join the revellers and when she reached the square she found Mrs Addington dancing with Mr G. The minibus from Butterbury Lodge had already been down and dropped half a dozen residents at Lantern Square to enjoy the festivities. Kimberley and two other helpers Hannah had seen at the lodge were milling around keeping an eye on each of them. The pub was bursting at the seams on the other side of the road, people spilling out onto the pavements with their pints and glasses of fizz to watch the Lantern Square antics and listen to the band. Hannah suspected as with most years, anyone who wasn't so keen on the dancing would come down here with family members and make a sharp exit to their local where they'd meet like-minded people who wanted to mark the celebrations in their own way.

'You're just in time. And looking beautiful tonight.' It was Charles, bundled up in a coat.

'Why, thank you kind sir. You don't look so bad yourself.'

'How I'm supposed to dance properly in this get-up I'll never know. Maggie made me wear so many layers I'll probably pass out from being too hot rather than too cold. I pointed out I'd coped with the Boxing Day walk just fine thank you very much. And those outdoor heaters dotted about are like furnaces. But it's OK, I've seen Doctor Joe so if I pass out because I'm boiling, he'll be able to rescue me.'

Hannah hoped the colour that flushed to her cheeks at the mention of Joe's name didn't give anything away. She looped her hand through Charles's arm. 'Come on, let's get dancing.'

'Santa Claus is Coming to Town' was playing and Charles led Hannah by the hand to the dance area in front of the makeshift stage. Grass areas had been covered with special boards so at least they weren't dancing in mud, and he twirled her beneath an arm as they moved in time with the music, the band singer's voice as lively as the season. Some towns and villages probably quietened right down come Boxing Day, but not Butterbury. They liked to carry Christmas on for much longer and stretch it right towards the New Year, culminating in this New Year's celebration. The band had been funded by an unknown source, rumoured to be the WI again, and whoever it was had a definite love affair with Butterbury and Lantern Square because they kept on giving and didn't seem to want a single accolade.

The tempo picked up with more Christmas favourites and Hannah couldn't feel the cold at all. Even her legs in opaque tights were warmed through as she moved this way and that. She danced with Charles some more until Maggie took over – probably keeping an eye on him – and she moved to Mr G who was a delight to keep company although he said he was very tired. Concerned, she tried to make him sit down, but he was having none of it. His eyes shone with delight, he had no intention of not seeing in midnight.

'You're very kind,' she told him when the music paused for breath and they had a chance to talk. 'You already gave me the gorgeous charm bracelet which I have on tonight, although you can't see it under my coat.'

'I'm glad you like it.'

'I love all the presents, so thank you, the care package was perfect.'

'I don't know what you mean, young lady.' But his smile gave him away.

Mrs Addington sashayed past with Miriam Styles' husband and Hannah and Miriam stood chatting, tucking into hot dogs from Ellen and Annie's cart. Colette and Patrick were dancing away, Lily minding the pub for the couple who would have to leave soon enough, their takings tonight probably bigger than any other night, and the scent of mulled wine and cinnamon snaked through the air.

Mr G gave Maggie a turn at dancing and Hannah took a much-needed break although she almost wished she hadn't when she saw Joe, his head towering above others in the crowds. And he was looking right at her. She almost returned the smile when she saw he was attached to someone else. Not only that, it was one of the women she'd seen before, talking to him at his front door.

Her heart sank.

Maybe instead of her New Year's resolution being to allow herself to be open to new possibilities she should shut down any involvement with men. They were complicated, relationships were messy. She should stick with being a cat lady for now. She knew exactly where she was with Smokey and Bandit.

Oh no, he was coming this way. His lady friend must have gone to get them drinks or food.

Hannah looked over to Troy but he'd found Cate this time and everyone else was paired up, mid Christmas tune. The band were swaying to and fro, 'Holly, Jolly Christmas' filling Lantern Square, and she had nowhere to hide.

'Hannah, you look beautiful.' Smooth.

'I'm in my coat.'

He seemed amused by her rebuke and simply held out a hand. 'May I have this dance?'

It was customary to accept every invitation to dance in Lantern Square on such occasions so she wasn't going to be the one to ignore the rules. She could do this. She could dance close to him, breathe in his manly scent, feel the shape of him up close to her. Easy.

The band chose that moment to decide everyone needed an easier tune to rekindle their energy. Maybe it was as much for them as it was for the crowds and they changed to playing a rendition of Cold Play's 'Christmas Lights'. People moved closer to one another, couples found their other half. Cate found her husband, Mr and Mrs Styles joined together, Dawn and Troy danced close enough to begin the song with a kiss.

Joe put a hand on her waist and drew her closer, and even through her coat she could feel the firmness of his hand against the top of her hip, guiding her around the dance floor. She couldn't see his girlfriend anywhere. Maybe the woman didn't mind all the others, perhaps their relationship was so open he was free to do as he liked.

She spotted Rhys dancing with the girl who'd been with Joe, but if Joe had seen them he didn't mention it. But when she smiled their way, Hannah had to say something. 'Who is that woman, Joe?'

He turned briefly, not letting Hannah go. 'Vanessa.'

'Yes, but who is Vanessa?' She was one of the recipients of the care packages he'd sent – Hannah remembered the name – but what was she to him?

'A friend.'

'With benefits?'

He held her that bit closer as he laughed. 'A friend who needed help and is very grateful I didn't turn my back.' She let him lead her across the boards, his hands gentle on her, he wasn't afraid she'd leave despite her character assassination. 'Any more questions?'

She pulled back a bit so she could see him, gauge his reaction. 'I thought she was a girlfriend and that's why you sent her a care package.'

'She's a very good friend of my younger sister Milly. Vanessa stuck by my sister when she was going through a pretty hard time.' They moved slowly to the music. 'Helping Vanessa out was my way of paying it forward. She needed somewhere to crash when she fell out with her parents, my place was as good as any, and she talked to me, you know. The care package was a gift to lift her spirits a bit, make her realise she had friends.'

'What happened to your sister? If that's not too personal.'

He took her hand and led her off the dance floor to a nearby heater so they wouldn't get too cold. 'When our mum died it hit Milly hard and she withdrew from everything, from her friendship groups, broke up with her boyfriend, stopped going out of the house, lost her job. She wouldn't let anyone in. She wasn't coping with her grief at all.'

Hannah could see the pain laced across his brow even now. 'It sounds rough.'

'She was behind my need to snatch the radio station slot.'

'How?'

'I wanted to help. She was lonely and it was hard to get through to her, but she'd always held me on a bit of a pedestal.' The corners of his mouth twitched. 'I'm not big-noting myself, but I was the only one she'd talk to, she was always interested in what was going on with me, as though it was a constant when everything else had fallen apart.

'When I was a locum a few towns away I had a patient come to me. He'd had thoughts of suicide, he was in a bad way. But he finally started to talk. It got a few of us discussing the importance of community, letting people know when they could reach out. That was what led to me wanting to do a radio slot. I needed to get my sister listening, make her realise life goes on, that she could find her place again with our mum gone. My sister had talked about moving away to escape it all, but I knew deep down she'd be running rather than dealing with anything the way she should. And so timing was everything. I knew my sister would listen to me on air and I was desperate, Hannah. So desperate I couldn't see that it wasn't fair to push you out and use my contacts to get what I wanted. I feel guilty for that.'

Hannah reddened, thinking of how furious she'd been. 'I get it now.'

'We had a phone-in and plenty of people thanking us for talking about loneliness, depression, isolation. It's not an easy subject to talk about, it's swept under the carpet in many ways. Some of those callers were in a worse state than Milly but there was hope with all the voices on air and those who contacted us afterwards.'

'I guess that was more important than airy fairy gift boxes.' Hannah was glad when her quip made him smile. She hadn't missed the shaky voice as he recounted how desperately he'd wanted the radio slot, the subject matter hitting close to home with what his sister had been through.

'Hey, I don't think what you do is airy fairy at all.'

'Well I'm sorry I got so angry at you. How's your sister now?'

'She found a job, that was a huge step forwards. She sees a counsellor regularly. I can only tell her so many times that she's loved, she's not alone. But with a counsellor she has no image to uphold, she can be open, know she won't be judged. She's getting out of the house more and more, seeing friends.' He sighed against the wintry air. 'You've no idea how good it is to see her functioning normally. She came to the Lantern Square dance actually, you might've seen me with her.'

She shook her head as though she couldn't remember, but she did.

'Come on.' Joe reached for her hand again and she revelled in the feeling of his warm skin encasing hers.

'Where are we going?' She'd assumed they'd be going back to join in the dancing but he led her into the crowd, scouting people, weaving in and out until they reached the person he wanted.

All of a sudden she was being introduced to Vanessa. 'Nice to meet you.' Hannah hadn't expected the introduction to one of his women and was about to ask more questions when Rhys whisked Vanessa back onto the dance floor and Joe waved across at someone else.

The next thing she knew she was being introduced to Katrina, another face she recognised from comings and goings at Joe's house. Next it was Lucy, Heather, then Bev, then Diana who raved about the care package she'd received before she ran off into the crowd with a man. Joe pointed out more faces as they scooted around the square and Hannah recognised them all as his conquests, the women who she'd seen him with. Some far too old, some way too young.

Joe stopped with Hannah by the flower bed with the illuminated rabbit and an outdoor heater so warm it had her undoing her coat. 'You're wondering why I'm pointing all these women out to you.' His breath came out cold, but Hannah couldn't feel anything but the heat snaking through her body.

'Kind of, yes . . .'

'Don't judge me if I tell you the truth.'

'I can't promise anything.'

'I'm involved with the Women's Institute.'

She began to laugh but then stopped. 'Oh, you're serious.'

'I'm serious.'

'Come on, pull the other one.'

'It's true I'm afraid.'

'Right . . .' Was he waiting for her to congratulate him on finding his feminine side?

'The women I introduced you to tonight, they're all a part of it but are sworn to secrecy when it comes to my involvement.' He looked around to make sure they weren't being overheard. 'I've got to protect my masculinity somehow.'

'What do you mean, you're involved in it? How?'

'I contribute.'

This was almost as difficult as the time he'd been asking her to make up a care package for Vanessa and she'd had to prise information out of him. 'In what way?'

'I'm what's known as financial backing I suppose. My mum was really involved and when she died, well it felt the right thing to do. Women I'd never met before stood by me and my sister, they helped organise the funeral and get Mum the send-off she deserved and would've wanted. They looked out for Milly and I as if we were part of their family. Every time I help them out with anything, it brings me close to Mum even though she's gone.' He looked to the ground. 'You must think it's silly.'

'I haven't lost either of my parents so I can't judge, but I can imagine any thread to keep me close to them would help me work through the loss.' This was the most he'd ever revealed about himself, and right here in Lantern Square she didn't want him to stop.

'I've got more and more involved as time has gone on. At first I gave money, then I got into discussing ideas. Sometimes it led to more.'

'With one of the women?'

He laughed and shook his head. 'It led to me doing more things.' He stepped so close she could feel the heat from him. He leaned down to whisper in her ear. 'I funded the wreath-making evening, it was me who sent the Christmas tree up to Butterbury Lodge, I arranged the Easter Egg hunt in Lantern Square earlier in the year, I arrange and finance the bands who appear at the summer and New Year fairs. I had the railings around the square fixed up when they were damaged, I sent the books to Butterbury Lodge ready for the book nights.'

It had all come out on a breath that made her melt inside. 'It was all you,' she said.

'All me.'

'But you never told anyone.'

'I didn't want to.' He grinned. 'But you should also know, I had an accomplice.'

'Let me guess – Mr G?'

'We got chatting one day when I was at Butterbury Lodge checking up on another resident and he happened to mention his late wife's involvement with the WI. We talked for more than an hour and by the end of it we'd both made a pact to carry on their support through us, the men, but it would have to be anonymous.'

'To protect your manly reputations.'

'Something like that,' he grinned. 'But I also wanted the WI to get the recognition. They're a great organisation and do plenty more than I could ever offer. Mr G saw it the same way. Between you and me, that man is full of mischief.'

'You don't need to tell me.' Her brow creased. 'So all those women you were with . . . they were . . . well, I suppose they were like work colleagues?'

'I guess they were.' He pulled a face, he saw right through her. 'Wait a minute. Did you think . . .?'

She covered her face with her hands. 'Uh-huh,' her voice came out muffled.

'You thought I was sleeping with them?'

She was cringing on the spot.

'Even Bev?' His voice wobbled with laughter at her assumption he'd been fooling around with a woman more than old enough to be his mother.

'Maybe not Bev, but the rest?' She shrugged. 'I really did.' She looked at him again. 'Wait, you don't seem too surprised that I'd made the assumption.'

'That's because I'm not,' he admitted, scraping a hand through his hair. He looked like he was thinking through what he wanted to say. 'I noticed the way you reacted after seeing me with other women, and I'm ashamed to say I enjoyed it.'

'Why?'

'Because I never thought I stood a chance with you and you were paying attention. It was kind of nice.' He took a while to add the rest and she saw the vulnerability he'd apparently had since he was younger. 'You were peeved I took the radio slot and I get that, but you never seemed to like me all that much. You gave me daggers whenever I drove past in the square, I felt I couldn't do anything right.'

'Now you're making me sound awful.'

'I'm sorry, I'm not putting this very well am I?'

'I never hated you.' He was right though. She'd sneered at him sometimes, in that flash car of his, the way he always dressed so smart like he was superior. She'd judged him when all this time she'd hated the way her own mother did the same and had vowed never to be that way herself. 'I'm sorry if I made you feel uncomfortable.'

'But you didn't like me and it was about more than the radio slot.'

'You're right.'

'Come on then, truth time. Hit me with it.'

The way he made a joke at least managed to make her feel as though she should just be honest. 'You drive too fast.'

'I do. I know I should slow down, I promise I will. But that can't be it.'

'I thought you were arrogant.'

'It was the suit, wasn't it?'

'And the car.' She pulled a face. 'Not just the speed, but how flashy it is.'

'No, not the car.' He put a hand against his chest as though he was really hurt. 'My beloved, cherished car. You do know that I once owned an old banger. I had it for years until it gave up on me on the way home from Wales in the middle of the night where I was stranded surrounded by nothing but rolling hills and sheep.'

'Sounds scary.'

'Don't joke, it was. Mum spent her last few months living in Wales in the middle of nowhere, it was where she was born. I got that. But I also knew I needed reliability. Sometimes I'd go there in the middle of the night to see her when we thought it was the end, that she wouldn't be with us by morning. Neither she nor I, nor anyone else in the family needed me to break down in the middle of nowhere and not make it in time. Or worse, for something to happen to me as well.'

'I'm so sorry. I get judged all the time for wearing scruffy clothes and there I was doing exactly the same – making assumptions on appearances.'

'I never quite knew myself when I was a kid, I didn't feel comfortable in my own skin. That came later. And then when I started work Dad told me that if you wore a suit like he always did, it made you confident and purveyed that to everyone else. I know it looks silly when I don't have to go into a posh office, but I found it did help at the start and I guess I never lost the habit. Ridiculous really.'

'It's not ridiculous. And I really should've known better than to judge.'

'You should. But consider yourself forgiven. If you can see past my big fancy car and well-cut suits that is.'

'I could try,' she teased. 'I still don't get why you played the game making me think you were involved with all those women. And wait, what about Georgia?'

'Your friend? What about her?'

'I saw her slinking out of your door. And she told me you'd made a move on her.'

His laughter had the attention of other people until he quietened. 'She wishes. I went to get my first-aid kit and a plaster after she cut her finger and after I'd cleaned the wound, put the dressing on, she tried to make a move on me. She didn't take no for an answer straight away either, and when I told her absolutely not, she got really huffy, called me a few choice names and stormed off.'

Hannah shook her head. 'I suppose I shouldn't be surprised with what she's been up to over the years.'

'I'm sorry, I didn't think anyone had seen and I was just glad when she left to be honest.' The way he was looking at her did little to calm the butterflies zipping around inside her tummy, the clammy feel of her palms despite the freezing cold. 'I was going to put you straight about all those women, but then I saw you with Luke enough times to assume you were a couple so no matter how much I wanted to put him out of the picture, he was well and truly in it. There didn't seem any point in me telling you I was categorically single so I decided to have a bit of fun with it.' He pulled a face. 'I should probably get out more.'

Nerves skittered around inside of her when he stepped even closer.

'Hannah, if I'd thought I stood a chance I would've told you from day one.'

'Right.'

'So do I?'

He was so close she could feel the heat from his body. She looked up at him, opened her mouth to respond.

But they didn't get a chance to continue the conversation because Rhys barrelled over, handed Vanessa to Joe and told Hannah, 'The local doc has been hogging you all night, it's my turn for a dance. And you can't say no, it's tradition!'

Hannah's eyes met Joe's over and over despite dancing with Rhys, laughing against the night air, twirling round and round. And every time she caught Joe looking her way she realised how wrong she'd been about him. All those women had been acquaintances, nothing more.

'Hannah, are you even listening?' It was Rhys, demanding her attention.

'Can't hear you, music is too loud,' she shouted and he steered her over to the trees and a flower bed beneath with a cute illuminated squirrel.

'What do you know about her?' he asked, discreetly eyeing Vanessa who was dancing with Joe. Joe was right, she was a lot younger than him, and now they didn't seem like much of a match at all. 'I love your company, but I only wanted to dance so I could find out more.'

'So you're using me?' Hannah joked. 'Well I'm afraid I don't know much. She's a friend of Joe's sister, Milly.' She watched Rhys eyeing up the newcomer. 'You're completely smitten.'

'So are you.'

'Hey this isn't about me. What's the hesitation? Why don't you go for it with Vanessa?'

'I don't seem to have much luck. Women see me as a friend and nothing more. Look what happened with Georgia, she didn't even consider hooking up. OK, so she was shagging your ex-boyfriend at the time, but even still.'

Hannah sighed. 'That's like me saying I'm not going to make any more friends because Georgia was so toxic. Ask Vanessa out, what's the worst that can happen?'

'Do you think I should kiss her at midnight?'

'Yes!'

'Really?' This time he looked at her.

Conspiratorially she added, 'If she doesn't respond well blame it on alcohol and New Year's Eve. On the other hand, if she likes it, keep on kissing her and the rest . . . well, I'm sure you'll update me tomorrow.'

Vanessa beckoned him over and Hannah was coerced into more dancing with Mr G who definitely wasn't ready to leave just yet. All she wanted was to get back to Joe and their conversation.

When she got her chance she weaved through the throng and stood on tiptoes trying to see Joe but she couldn't find him. Everyone was piling into the square with the time approaching midnight, and slowly the band started to quieten as the countdown began.

'Ten!' The band's singer called, holding out the microphone towards the crowd who yelled it with him.

'Nine!' Everyone hollered.

'Eight,' Hannah called out and grinned to Heidi who rested her head on her mum's shoulder.

'Seven.' She turned left then right but still no Joe.

'Six.' She waved at Annie and Ellen whose faces were alight with excitement.

'Five! Four!' Hannah called a little louder.

'Three!' Hannah yelled when a familiar deep voice next to her did the same.

Joe was so close as the crowds called out, 'Two!'

'One!' they all yelled. And in the next second everything happened.

The Post Office clock chimed midnight, the crowds yelled 'Happy New Year!', and Joe spun her towards him, his bare hands cupped her cheeks and his face moved even closer. 'Happy New Year, Hannah.'

'Happy New Year, Joe.'

Their lips met, just once, but the warmth, the softness, the promise of more lit up a million fireworks inside of her before the crowds grew louder and the band launched into 'Auld Lang Syne'. They were still looking into each other's eyes as the female saxophone player took the mic and her soft sultry voice fell across Lantern Square.

Hannah's head rested against Joe's chest as they swayed slowly together, drinking in the season, the festivities, the feel of winter all around this place that was home. She'd wondered for so long how it would feel to kiss him and now she knew.

The sounds of the keyboard tinkled along with the glittering stars above as Joe hooked her hair across her shoulder sending a shiver right through her as his hand grazed her bare skin inside her collar. 'You smell so good.'

'Why thank you,' she grinned.

'Marc Jacobs?'

'I'm impressed. Knowing your perfumes is definitely being in touch with your feminine side.'

'You're starting to shiver.' He held her closer.

'I'm not cold at all.'

'Are you sure? Maybe we need to warm up. I could use a mulled wine myself.'

'Hang on a minute . . .' She jabbed a finger to his chest. 'Don't tell me, you'd also like to light a candle, say an Icy Blue Spruce?'

'Well . . .'

'It was you!'

'Guilty as charged. I thought you deserved a treat of your own. So did the care package put a smile on your face?'

The fact she was grinning said it all and she had no need to ask who his sidekick had been in all this as she remembered talking with Frankie about her favourite perfume, discussing her favourite holiday tipple with Mr G.

The crowds called for another round of 'Auld Lang Syne' but Hannah and Joe had already come to a silent agreement that they'd leave the revellers for now and head over to Lantern Cottage.

They left Lantern Square, passed through the gate with its golden lanterns on each post lighting the way and as he bent to kiss her again they both stopped, because a snowflake had landed on her eyelashes, then another on her cheek, a few in his hair, a sprinkling all around them. Joe hooked an arm around Hannah's shoulders as Butterbury welcomed its first heavy snowfall of winter. 'Look at that.' He pointed over to the minibus where Maggie and Frankie were trying to cajole some of the elderly residents into the minibus to go home. Charles was protesting saying there was plenty of life in him yet; Flo hugged Mrs Ledbetter goodbye. Mr G looked over at them both as the snow continued to fall and when he winked Hannah knew the next time she saw him she'd thank him for being such a meddler.

As they reached the tiny gate of Lantern Cottage a voice behind them said, 'You two behave yourselves tonight.' Hannah turned to see Mrs Ledbetter returning from the festivities too. 'This is a respectable village you know.' And she passed on by.

'I hope she doesn't think we're terrible,' said Hannah as Joe closed her front gate behind them. 'Although I'm sure she was smiling when she gave us the warning.'

'Of course she was.'

'Do you think?' She found her key from her pocket and let them both into the cottage.

Joe shut the door behind them and took off his boots and coat. 'Who do you think helped with the Easter Egg hunt?'

'No! Really?' Hannah hung the coats on hooks.

Joe followed her into the lounge where she switched on the tree lights. 'She almost gave us away, she couldn't stop laughing as she went round stuffing eggs behind tree trunks, between railings, I had to tell her to pipe down so she didn't blow our cover.'

'Well I never would've guessed.'

He planted a sure kiss on her lips but she pulled him back when he tried to get away to go and light the log burner for them. 'I always wondered what it would be like to kiss you.'

'Well now you know.'

'I think I need reminding again.'

'If you insist.'

And as they kissed neither of them would've had any idea that instead of getting into the minibus, the old folk from Butterbury Lodge had seen them going off to the cottage together and had followed them along the pavement, waited for them to go inside, and were now all huddled in a little group outside, Mrs Ledbetter included. The snow on the windows of Lantern Cottage framed their faces of delight and joy at this match made between two of Butterbury's most-loved residents.

Hannah and Joe.

8 months later . . .

Epilogue

The last eight months had been a whirlwind for Hannah and Joe. They'd cuddled up on cosy winter nights sharing their time between his place and hers; they'd carried on the mischief of the mystery giver in Butterbury, Hannah a perfect accomplice as they, along with Mrs Ledbetter, rose at the crack of dawn on Easter Sunday to hide chocolate eggs all around Lantern Square. Joe was right, Mrs Ledbetter was so excited it had been next to impossible to keep her quiet. And after the fun of being in on the secret, they'd all sneaked home and only resurfaced when raucous kids zipped about beneath the sunshine finding little treasures.

When Hannah and Joe stepped out of Lantern Cottage and into the sunshine on the day of the summer fair, Mrs Ledbetter had just finished watering her window boxes at the front of her cottage, and watering can still in hand, came to remind Hannah to do the same. Rhys had installed two beautiful window boxes out front of Lantern Cottage, one with dark purple ruffled blooms and the other with bright pink flowers, and as usual, Hannah couldn't for the life of her remember what either were called. It had taken her a while to learn any of the names of the flowers in her back garden, maybe one day she'd get the hang of it.

'I'm glad it's not as hot as it was last year,' Mrs Ledbetter told them. 'I walk to Butterbury Lodge twice a week to clean and manage my team. Much warmer and I'm not sure I could do it.' Frankie joked that now Mrs Ledbetter was cleaning up at Butterbury Lodge, they'd have to dock her hourly rate she talked so much as she bossed the other cleaners around. Then again, she was there for twice as long as she charged for anyway, with a sense of pride that ensured she always left the place as spick and span as she could, checking the work of others and ensuring they'd missed nothing.

'Drink plenty of water,' Joe advised. 'The walking is doing you good. And don't stress, I'll make sure Hannah doesn't forget to look after her flowers,' Joe assured the woman who'd always had a soft spot for him like so many other women.

'I see you got a beautiful corsage this morning too,' Mrs Ledbetter said to Hannah with a wink. She was in on yet another secret of course. And she loved that they were the only ones who knew.

Hannah smiled and held up her wrist, the August sunshine and the summer breeze catching the petals of the layered pink daisy flower. 'I love it, excellent choice, whoever was responsible,' she grinned back. Between them and the women of the WI they'd left boxes at the doors of every resident in Lantern Square with a mixture of buttonholes and corsages to wear to the summer fair or the dance tonight, or both as most would probably choose.

They went on their way and Joe said, 'Bit difficult to put mine on without a collar.'

Hannah put a hand against his chest. 'You look so scruffy, don't know how I can be seen out with you really.' In a lemon-yellow dress with white flowers and a light-weight white cardigan she was the height of summer and Joe had foregone anything smart for a pair of shorts and a regular T-shirt.

'Careful or I'll send back the fancy car and get a clapped-out old thing to drive you around in.'

'As long as it has heating for the winter, I don't care.'

He hugged her to him but frowning said, 'Isn't that . . .?'

Hannah peered in the same direction. The sun was out today and despite the sunglasses she still had to cover her eyes to see properly. 'Mum?' She knew her dad had told her mum everything about Luke and Georgia and the problems with the business, but her mum had kept any opinions to herself in their phone calls, even on the couple of times Hannah had been up to see them at their home in Whitby.

'Hannah, we thought we'd surprise you!' Her dad pulled her into a hug and then shook hands with Joe.

Her mum hugged her and then Joe. 'It's a beautiful day.'

'It really is,' Joe agreed.

'We're staying in a cottage for the weekend,' her dad announced.

'We thought we'd turn up out of the blue.' This from the woman who hated it when people didn't give plenty of notice that they were coming.

Joe knew things weren't the easiest between Hannah and her mum. He'd seen the way she tensed up as they'd driven closer to the family home when she took him home to meet her parents, he'd heard the sigh of relief when they left.

Joe, aware that Hannah's summery mood had darkened somewhat, whisked her dad away for a swift pint at the pub and Hannah suggested to her mum that they go back to her place for a cup of tea. There'd be too many people at the fair to talk properly and it was so unlike her mum to show up like this that there had to be a reason.

In the kitchen of Lantern Cottage, Hannah took out a couple of mugs and made the tea. She handed her mum the bottle-green vessel with white spots, settled down on the little table out in the back garden with her own multi-coloured striped mug.

'How about I get you a matching set for Christmas?' her mum suggested, noticing the colour differences. 'That way when you entertain, everyone can have the same.'

'I don't mind, Mum. Honestly.'

'Sorry, I'm interfering, aren't I?'

Never bothered her before.

'Your dress is pretty, and the flower. It seems to be a theme. I saw other people wandering towards the fair with corsages. Does the whole village join in?'

'It's a new thing this year.' Hannah let her in on the secret mission early that morning. 'Joe's enjoying it more than anyone, should've seen him at Easter.' She'd told her mum about the Easter Egg surprise hunt last time they'd driven up to see her parents. At least Joe could do no wrong in her eyes. Although she'd made sure he hadn't worn his smart clothes the first time she introduced them. Hannah had wanted her mum to see Joe for who he really was. She'd almost been tempted to tell her a fib about his job, say he worked in a darts factory or something and watch for a reaction, but Joe had told her not to play games, the casual dress was enough.

'You've kept this garden looking lovely,' her mum noticed. 'And I saw the cactus . . . or is it cacti? . . . on the windowsill.'

'I can't believe it's survived this long.'

'You never were green-fingered.' She looked nervous as though her remark might cause upset and moved swiftly on to ask, 'How's work going?'

'It's going well, busy, but good.' She elaborated on the Return to School, College, University popularity with the care packages.

'I'm very proud of you for making a real go of your business.'

'Really?'

Her mum moved her chair around so the sun wasn't blazing on the bare skin at the back of her neck. 'I know I don't say it enough.'

'Well I appreciate hearing it, any time.'

'Your dad is always talking about you and your special parcels.'

Hannah wasn't sure she liked the description but she'd go with it. 'Thanks.'

'I know Liam always liked them.'

'He did.'

'It was why I didn't want you to start the business in the first place . . . I thought that if you did that as a business, then you'd never get over him. You were so very sad for a long time. Even with Luke, I knew you weren't happy, but I kept trying to jolly you along when really I should've tried talking to you. You didn't seem to want to let anybody in.'

Hannah bit down on her lip, surprised at the candid discussion, clearly the reason behind her parents' impromptu visit here. 'I know I didn't.'

'We're not that bad, are we?'

She ran a finger around the rim of her mug, looked at the pale brown liquid settled inside. 'It was just easier to deal with it myself.'

Her mum swished away a fly that returned to her mug for a second attempt at landing. 'Your dad and I talked. I know you and he are much closer than you and I ever were, and well, he was worried about you.'

'But I'm doing fine.'

'He told me all about the business with Luke and Georgia. I wish you'd told me too.'

'I didn't know how to, Mum. You always seem so keen on perfection, I'll never come close. My cottage is a mess, I'm usually a mess – today is the best version you'll see – but it's the way I am.'

'I can't help being the way I am either, Hannah.'

She didn't want to fight. 'I guess we're all different.'

'I'll do my best to keep my nagging under control, how does that sound?'

'You're really not that bad. Maybe if I talked to you once in a while . . .' She smiled at her mum who wasn't perfect, but then, none of them were, were they?

'If I ever get my hands on Luke or Georgia, I'll bloody well—'

'Mum! You never swear.'

'I do when something gets right up my nose. Did you tell Linda what went on? I know you and she were close.'

'I never mentioned it. I didn't think I needed to, I just hope he knows how good he's got it with parents like his, and I really hope he never ever turns the manor into a hotel spa.'

'Is that what he was planning? The sneaky toad.'

Hannah laughed. The man who could do no wrong in her mum's eyes had plummeted to an all-time low in her mind now. 'Linda stopped by a week ago and I'm just treating it all as water under the bridge.'

'It's nice you get on with her.'

Hannah didn't miss the low-spirited edge to her voice or the little bit of insecurity in her mum's remark. 'She left me a jar of her elderflower jam. It's nice, but to be honest, it's nowhere near as nice as the elderflower cake you bake.'

If her mum was a bird her chest would've puffed up with pride. 'As a matter of fact, I have one for you back at the cottage.'

'Why didn't you bring it?'

'I wasn't sure, with all the food over at the fair, whether you'd want it.'

'How about you come over for lunch tomorrow, both of you, Joe will be here too. I'll make something and we can have the cake for dessert.'

'Well that would be lovely.' She sipped her tea and then added, 'Have you had Linda for lunch, you know, since you went to the manor?'

'No, Mum. That won't happen.'

'Well, the cake is safely stored in a tin so it'll taste fresh for tomorrow.'

'Great. Come on, we should get going before Dad and Joe sink more than one pint and dad isn't fit for any dancing later on.'

'Good idea. And Hannah . . .'

'Yes?' She'd picked up the mugs to take inside.

'Liam was a fine man, Luke had his good points at the start. But Joe . . . well he's something else.'

'I'm glad you like him.' Hannah's lip trembled, on the verge of tears and she let herself be embraced by a hug from her mum, a warm, genuine sign of affection that marked a new understanding.

As they made their way over to the pub to meet the men, they talked about what Hannah would make for lunch the next day. She'd thought perhaps a lasagne from the supermarket served with a fresh salad. Her mum had suggested she come early and teach Hannah how to make it, but the way she'd asked hadn't been critical but rather a way of getting closer to her daughter who lived quite a distance and who'd kept her struggles quiet.

The men were already out of the pub and waiting on the bench outside the square.

'We never made it,' Joe told them.

'Here you go, love.' Her dad handed her a can of traditional lemonade. 'It was too nice a day to be inside the pub so we've been sitting here people-watching.'

'Sounds interesting.' Hannah cuddled up to Joe, glad she'd been able to talk to her mum.

'Everything all right?' he whispered.

'Everything's fine,' she answered, watching her parents. For all her mum's faults, the relationship between them just worked. She was the woman her dad had chosen to be with and he didn't seem to be under much strain as they laughed together, he undid her bottle of juice, and she handed him a napkin to mop some of the condensation on his drink before it dripped on his lap. Who knew what faults he drove her crazy with when it was just the two of them.

Mrs Ledbetter didn't miss a trick and came over to introduce herself the second the foursome made their way into the square. Her dad had sniffed out the churros and was keen to try one with plenty of chocolate sauce and she led the way, chattering on about who knew what. Hannah, Joe and her mum trailed behind, briefly saying hello to Rhys who had his money belt on and was chatting with punters at his flower stall.

'Wait.' Hannah tugged at Joe's arm when the girl bending down near Rhys stood up and whispered something to him to make him laugh. 'Isn't that . . .?'

'My sister, yes.'

'Wow, I know things didn't work out with Vanessa, but Rhys is normally a pretty slow mover.'

'I'm keeping an eye on him,' said Joe protectively.

They queued behind her dad and Mrs Ledbetter at Ellen and Annie's cart and as they were waiting Frankie came by, admired Hannah's dress and showed Hannah the cookies she had in a white paper bag. It seemed Troy and Dawn hadn't been content making corsets in brazen scarlet for Valentine's this year, they'd also done a naughty collection of skimpy bikinis and boxer shorts on cookies for their stall at the summer fair. Thankfully most of the kids hadn't noticed, they were too focused on the essentials: cookie, sugar, coloured decorations.

Hannah enjoyed the afternoon with her parents, introduced them to whoever she could, even Mr G who arrived in a minibus shortly before the main dance was due to kick off. He'd been in on the corsage plan and wore his own as he linked arms with Flo before he lost out to Mrs Ledbetter who wanted to talk to her friend.

When her parents said they'd go back to their cottage

and change for the evening dance, Joe saw his opportunity. 'Come on, let's head back to your place and put our feet up for half an hour.'

'Old man.'

He was about to protest. 'You're right, and I don't care. I want you to myself. Seeing you in this dress is playing with my mind, I need to get you out of it for my sanity.'

They discreetly escaped the mayhem and hand in hand ran over to Lantern Cottage.

'What's this?' The second they were inside her cottage Hannah picked up a brown paper package tied up with string that had been left on the stairs.

He shrugged, but the smile that often woke her in the mornings was still there.

She tugged at the string, pulled the Sellotape and opened up the box. She lifted the tissue paper inside and caught a waft of the delicious freshly baked treat. 'It's a cookie.' She turned it round so she could read the writing. 'Your place or mine?' she recited. 'Well, I think we're in my place.'

He took her hand before she could lift out the cookie and take a bite. 'I'm talking about moving in. Here, or at my house?'

'Are you serious?'

'Very. Although if it's going to be here, we might need to have Mrs Ledbetter give you some cleaning lessons, your dining room is a mess.'

'I prefer to think of it as organised chaos.'

He put his fingers beneath her chin and looked into her eyes. 'So what do you say?'

'I say, yes!' She threw her arms around him. 'You know this'll make Mrs Ledbetter's curtains twitch, don't you?'

'You leave her to me . . . it's her birthday next week, I'm planning on having a cookie made for her to soften the blow.'

'Good idea.'

'Now we need to seal the deal.'

'You mean . . .' Her heart raced at the thought of running upstairs with him now, having a lot of fun before they went back to the dance.

He lifted the cookie out of the box. 'We need to eat this.'

'Oh, I thought . . .'

'That'll be dessert,' he winked.

And they both bit into the cookie at the same time, devouring a few bites before they left it in the opened brown paper package that had been tied up with string and showed one another what it really felt like to be in love.

Here at Lantern Cottage, in Lantern Square, Butterbury. The place they both called home.

Acknowledgements

There's a row of cute cottages in a village not far from where I live and one day I noticed one had a gorgeous lantern and a plaque saying 'Lantern Cottage'. As I often do when I'm out and about I quickly made a note on my phone as I knew I wanted to include it in a book somewhere along the line. When the task to create another setting for my next book came along, I decided that a square would be the perfect place for a community to come together.

Sometimes it's hard to come up with career choices for my characters but one of those random notes in my phone a few years ago had been 'care packages' and so I plucked this idea for Hannah's occupation and thought it would fit perfectly with the story I wanted to write about community, neighbours who pull together, friendship, and of course, love.

Most of my books have intergenerational relationships and The Little Cottage in Lantern Square is no exception. I had so much fun writing the characters Mr. G, Mrs Ledbetter, Ernest, Charles and all the other residents of Lantern Square. I hope I have as many special friendships when I reach their age!

A very big thank you to Laura from Where Bluebirds Will Fly who answered my many questions about running a care package business from home. Laura helped me create a realistic work environment for Hannah and helped me see how wonderful it would be to receive such a package.

Thank you to my wonderful husband and children, my biggest supporters in this career I love, and to my parents who are my cheerleaders, even recommending my books to libraries and the mobile library that visits their local area. As always, Mum and Dad will read my book and spot anecdotes from my life and childhood and I hope these mentions bring fond memories back for them as much as they do for me.

I've been working with the wonderful Olivia Barber for a while. A talented editor, I have no doubt her hard work has helped this book to end up being the best it can be. Her energy and enthusiasm for my stories is something I am always grateful for. I look forward to working on plenty more books with her in the future!

An enormous thank you to everyone on the Orion Publishing team. From contract to publication, there are so many people involved in the process and I'd like to pass on my gratitude to each and every one of them. In particular Anne from contracts who is a pleasure to work with and answers my many legal questions, as well as Britt and Tanjiah who have both worked on graphics for me to promote my titles. Thank you to everyone else behind the scenes for all of your hard work.

Helen Rolfe x

Credits

Helen Rolfe and Orion Fiction would like to thank everyone at Orion who worked on the publication of *The Little Cottage in Lantern Square* in the UK.

Editorial
Olivia Barber
Clare Hey

Copy editor
Kati Nicholl
Kate Shearman

Proof reader
Linda Joyce

Audio
Paul Stark
Amber Bates

Contracts
Anne Goddard
Paul Bulos

Jake Alderson

Design
Rabab Adams
Tomas Almeida
Joanna Ridley

Editorial Management
Charlie Panayiotou
Jane Hughes
Alice Davis

Finance
Jasdip Nandra
Afeera Ahmed
Elizabeth Beaumont
Sue Baker

Marketing
Brittany Sankey
Tanjiah Islam

Production
Ruth Sharvell

Publicity
Kate Moreton

Sales
Laura Fletcher
Esther Waters

Victoria Laws
Rachael Hum
Ellie Kyrke-Smith
Frances Doyle
Georgina Cutler

Operations
Jo Jacobs
Sharon Willis
Lisa Pryde
Lucy Brem

If you enjoyed *The Little Cottage in Lantern Square*, you'll love Helen Rolfe's heartwarming story of romance and second chances

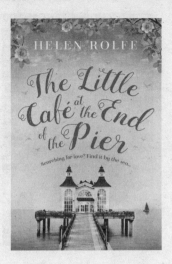

Searching for love? You'll find it at the little café at the end of the pier . . .

When Jo's beloved grandparents ask for her help in running their little café at the end of the pier in Salthaven-on-Sea, she jumps at the chance.

The café is a hub for many people: the single dad who brings his little boy in on a Saturday morning; the lady who sits alone and stares out to sea; the woman who pops in after her morning run.

Jo soon realises that each of her customers is looking for love – and she knows just the way to find it for them. She goes about setting each of them up on blind dates – each date is held in the café, with a special menu she has designed for the occasion.

But Jo has never found love herself. She always held her grandparents' marriage up as her ideal and she hasn't found anything close to that. But could it be that love is right under her nose . . .?

Welcome to Cloverdale, the home of kindness and new beginnings . . .

Sometimes it takes a village to mend a broken heart . . .

Cloverdale is known for its winding roads, undulating hills and colourful cottages, and now for its Library of Shared Things: a place where locals can borrow anything they might need, from badminton sets to waffle makers. A place where the community can come together.

Jennifer has devoted all her energy into launching the Library. When her sister Isla moves home, and single dad Adam agrees to run a mending workshop at the Library, new friendships start to blossom. But what is Isla hiding, and can Adam ever mend his broken past?

Then Adam's daughter makes a startling discovery, and the people at the Library of Shared Things must pull together to help one family overcome its biggest challenge of all . . .